Of Life and Love

Short Stories by Alan Martin

Kipper Night

The Teddy Bear

Searching for Mathilde

The Photograph

Red Socks

The Pump

Beyond Frank

Where the Walloo Blows

This book would never have been published except for the continual and selfless support of Gillian, my wife, and the efforts and editing of my nephew Richard. I owe a debt of gratitude to both.

From whence do such stories come? I can only speak for myself and for me they start with an experience or sometimes several experiences added together and not necessarily at the same time. The experience may be trivial or significant but always the experience has to have observations of human nature added to develop it into a story.

Thus 'The Pump' contains, at its heart, three experiences while 'Searching for Mathilde' only two but a great deal more in observation.

I am sure that those who know me well will derive much pleasure out of guessing the origins of all the stories

Alan, July, 2012

Kipper Night

Now there are only a few major decisions you take knowing they are absolutely right. Usually decisions are hedged with 'ifs' and 'buts' however this particular decision sprang from a certainty I cannot explain.

My marine replacement, a thin, small man, had a prematurely morose face and the mean, fault-picking manner of one permanently looking for trouble. However much you tried it was difficult to warm to such a character. He seemed as out of place as a banana in a toolbox when he finally took over and sat at my cabin desk. 'Where's your kit?' He grumbled, peering and sniffing about as if it might need fumigating.

'Already gone ahead.'

'Ahead?'

'That's right.' Being magnanimous was easy; all his questions – some of which I felt to be stupid or at best naive – had been totally answered. He looked frustrated with nothing left to complain about so I bent across, swept some space in all the documents we'd been agreeing, found a couple of glasses in my old drinks locker and pushed across a bottle. 'Job done, chum. You're in charge now, so get yourself resigned to it. Help yourself to a gin and tonic.'

He said nothing and for a time he looked at his glass as if he'd never seen one like it in his life before. Then he said 'No thanks,' and opened his mouth to smile meaninglessly. 'Sorry.

1

You know… we're not allowed to drink within 24 hours of sailing.'

Any conscience I might have felt about leaving him to it fled that instant. I splashed some gin and took a drink before explaining, very calmly I thought under the circumstances, 'If you read your work agreement again, you'll see it says in the explanations that: "All times referred to in this document are to be read as being in GMT".'

My replacement's smile faded as his brain began to work it out. 'As the ship is on local time…' I pointed my glass at him. 'You lucky devil, you're left with just under an hour to get drunk. I should get started if I were you – could be six months before you've another chance.'

'Uh…' He poured himself some tonic but no gin. It was obvious he was busy thinking up a new line of complaint. 'That trunkway,' he said. 'It seemed in a bad state to me…'

'Burst steam pipe to the donkey engine as we were about to moor up. You'll find it in the day log and it's been reported to the Super.'

He grunted again, unconvinced, but that was the end to any help he was getting. I zipped up my briefcase and just sat and finished my drink.

'I've read your docs,' he said eventually. 'You're only thirty and could make Chief Engineer after your next trip…'

'…So why throw it all in now?' I finished for him.

He nodded. 'That had occurred to me.'

'I've spent my last twelve years almost entirely at sea, and it has occurred to me that there might be something more to life.'

'But the pay… the pay is good.'

'Sure. And you can enjoy salting it away for you're in no position to spend it.' I was growing tired of this conversation. 'Anyhow, we're signed over, she's all yours and I'm off. You've got no problems unless, of course, some kind soul has left a bomb on a time fuse under the stern bearing.'

'You're joking, of course?'

'About terrorism? Never.' I shook my head solemnly. 'I should check it if I were you. There are strange people on board and if the shaft gland goes you'll be in immediate danger of going down like a stone.'

With that, I left him to worry his guts out. My last sight of him was sipping tonic water and looking blankly ahead.

The bo'sun happened to be in the afterwell as I passed along. He gave me a very warm farewell but after that last firm shake of the hands, freedom was at hand. I marched down the ship's gangway in search of a new life and felt not the slightest need to look back.

Our family home is in Surrey, near the beauty spot of Box Hill. The family had been warned of my coming but I happened to be early. Only my father, a just-retired civil service chief, was there to greet me.

3

'Oh, there you are, my boy, a bit before your time, eh? We expected you later.'

To me, my father's voice sounded as enthusiastic as that of a man who had just recovered his jacket from a premature disappearance in the Oxfam bin. To his credit, he did put down – I sensed with reluctance – a letter he'd been reading. And he did manage a smile.

'Well now you're here, welcome home. Your mother will be back shortly; she is still out shopping.'

You cannot hope for much more from the old man: his success and a lifetime in the civil service in charge of safeguarding monuments – Stonehenge, or something like that – had come at the expense of being a normal human being.

I dumped my two bags on the hall floor and we embraced, or just about. He's considerably shorter than me. 'You've changed the colour of the door,' I said, disentangling myself.

'So you've noticed? Ah, yes, it has been changed. I was forced into it, and the windows, all incredibly expensive and quite unnecessary. Women want to change things for no reason at all, your mother...' His trailing tone collapsed into a frown before he suddenly seemed aware again of my standing before him. 'But never mind, I don't wish to pass on my problems to you.' He looked me up and down rather more kindly. 'So, now then my boy: how's the sea nowadays?'

'The sea?' I could only repeat the word as a means of avoiding saying something rude. It is well recognised that my father understands nothing about the sea; it starts where the land ends, that's all he knows. However, the good thing about my father is that his reactions are always predictable. 'Dad,' I said, 'I've left the sea for good.'

'I say! Really old son? You mean you've left it for good? For good?'

I nodded. He tries hard. It takes time for news to sink in.

'Ah, yes, well then…' he murmured wisely before stroking his chin and trying to look understanding. Somebody might as well have told him the baker down the street had just closed. He added as a profound observation: 'Become bored with being a nautical engineer, eh?'

'Something like that. We can talk about it later. What are you up to, now that you're retired and don't have to go everyday to London?'

'Dear Boy, I'm terribly busy at the moment in the garden. Take one look! But you were never very interested in the garden, where you?'

'No, funnily enough. Not after twelve years at sea, Dad.'

'…I can't keep up with the weeding after all the rain last month. Don't have any new ideas for slugs and snails in your engineering bag?'

'I should imagine they hate fire. But if you've got some heavy digging to do, I can give you a hand.'

The slightest of frowns passed over my father's face. 'It's August, Robert,' he said gently as if this completely explained everything. 'It's mulch time, not digging time, but thank you for the thought.'

Already I wished my mother was there to greet me; she has an enthusiasm to sweep things along. My father has never been an easy conversationalist. In the awkwardness, my father's chess set with all the pieces arranged caught my eye. 'Still involved with the chess, I see.'

'I do my best. The championships have started in Blackpool and we have the possibilities of an English boy genius. Oh, but of course you will have followed all this on the BBC?'

The temptation to say, 'I've been glued to the radio,' almost overwhelmed me. First meetings with my father are always the same. 'It can be difficult to follow anything, Dad,' I explained, carefully. 'I've been at sea working six hours on, six off.'

Just for a moment we recognised the gulf between us had grown bigger, not smaller over the years. My father's eyes seemed to register puzzlement. A move had to be made. 'Perhaps I'd better go and unpack this lot,' I offered.

'Good idea, Son.' His relief was palpable and showed in a fresh smile. 'I'll put the kettle on; your mother will be here any moment.'

I took my time, even after I heard my Mother's voice downstairs. To meet my Mother, a powerful lady, after a year of absence, is to be physically attacked by a big, black-haired and excited dog. You need to be prepared.

6

It was as I had expected. 'Robert! Darling! It's you! Oh my dearest, dearest boy!' And instantly I – a fourteen stone man – was rocked back on my heels with her arms around my neck, drowning in endearments and almost overwhelmed by scent. 'Steady on, Ma! Leave something for tomorrow!'

She thrust me to arms length and, taking her time, studied me, her huge dark eyes sparkling with tears of emotion. I smiled back, thinking that those same huge eyes looking at you could be like staring down the barrels of a double-bore shot gun if she felt she had cause. 'Tom,' she called over her shoulder, 'isn't he exactly like his brother Harry at the same age?'

'Thought the same thing,' my father said, amiably; 'It's the hair and beard.'

'And his size...'

'More or less. What's your height, son?

'Six foot two, I think.'

'Solid, too,' said my mother, squeezing my shoulder hard enough to hurt.

'Yes, how is brother Harry?' I asked, trying to escape. 'I haven't had a word from him for years and years.'

My mother let me go as if the question vexed her. 'We don't know, and that's a fact.'

Knowing my mother, this seemed unlikely. 'He can't have disappeared so, where is he?'

'We don't know, do we Tom?'

'He's in Scotland,' said my father, as if it didn't concern him.

'Exactly! You see what I mean? In Scotland. Where's Scotland?' My mother raised her hands, palms upwards in despair.

I tried to make some sense of all this. 'Where in Scotland, do we know?'

'We haven't the slightest idea,' said my mother.

'A place called Loch Eliaze,' said my father.

'Find it', challenged my mother, turning on my father in indignation. 'I asked you to find it. It's not on the map. If it's not on the map it could be anywhere, couldn't it?' She turned on me for confirmation. 'If you can't find a place on the map, it doesn't exist; isn't that true?'

'Could be...'

'...to discover it, I had to look it up on the large-scale Ordinance Survey map in the library,' explained my father, ignoring my mother. 'It appears to be a minor hamlet on the West Coast.'

'You see, you see, you see, Robert!' shouted my mother. 'A hamlet. A hamlet in Scotland. I mean, why does he have to go to some foreign place like that? Why couldn't he have gone to somewhere nice like Paris? I keep saying he's far too young to disappear.'

'He's forty,' mused my father, 'Not so young...'

'Exactly! You see what I mean, Robert,' continued my mother, who by this time had taken to walking up and down and flapping her arms as if in the gym, 'Your father's always been so good at train times. Anyway, what was I saying? Harry has been there for so long in wherever-it-is that nobody can remember when he disappeared!'

'Eight years come November, 'corrected my father.

'And not a single word all that time!'

'We do get Christmas cards with a scribbled message.'

My mother stopped and turned on my father to snap, 'Oh do shut up, Tom, and be sensible: a Christmas card is not a word.'

'But it shows the lad is alive and well.'

'Then tell me this: why hasn't he any children by now? He was such a gentle, kindly man as well as being handsome, any woman would grab him. I want to hear some grandchildren in the garden, a boy's laughter as he kicks a football around...'

I saw my father's face express annoyance in a way familiar to me. 'Oh dear oh dear oh dear oh dear,' he snapped back at Mother, 'For God's sake stop imagining things for once. Just think of the damage a football would make to the delphiniums.'

'I was speaking metaphorically – an aeroplane if you like or a tortoise, or anything. And stop picking me up on everything I say, Robert.' My mother turned on me to give that stare, the stare she gives to boys caught with their pants down and making a mess; the stare that haunted my youth, the stare that puts trembling fear into any sales assistant and send dogs yelping down the road, 'Robert!' She hurled at me as if I was on the other side of the road, 'You must promise me at once that you won't go to Timbuktu like your brother.'

'No. Or even to Scotland,' said my father, sternly, looking over his glasses at me.

It crossed my mind that my father must have developed a special technique for dealing with my mother. I dare say he got it from the Chinese.

'Yes, or Scot – Oh my God!' My mother put her knuckle to her head as if in acute pain. 'Oooh!' she wailed as we both looked at her in wonderment. 'Can you believe it? Oh what fool I am. In my excitement at your coming home I forgot to buy any butter at the supermarket.'

The solution came immediately. 'Never mind, Robert will go for some, won't you Robert?' It was not a request: it was a brusque order from my father to a junior clerk.

The passage of time had changed nothing for any of us. At that moment I knew I had to escape. I decided to go and see what Harry was doing in Scotland as soon as possible.

Intention and action are two different things. It was over a month later before the long gentle descent starting from a massive shoulder of a mountain lay before me and my car could roll of its own accord down towards Loch Eliaze.

It was a desolate landscape as far as I was concerned, vast sweeps of grey and purple heather as far as the eye could see, only a few lichen covered rocky outcrops and a few bushes stunted and bent before the wind to break the monotony. Only much later did I discover it was recognised as the finest grouse habitat to be found anywhere in the Kingdom.

And there was no reason to expect much better when I got to my destination. Loch Eliaze, no more than a narrow inlet from the sea and without the slightest claim to recognition, lay at the end of a single narrow road which led to nowhere else, a dead end and not the place for a casual visit. Eight miles off the main road north and in such a desolate area, I began to speculate what had led to my brother being and staying in such an isolated spot.

Ten years my senior, Harry had been so far above me as to be beyond idolisation. I only knew of him as being a dominating but kindly personality, and one leaving a gasping trail of feminine admirers pestering our mother. Appropriate to his physical strength, he trained as a blacksmith and farrier for he loved horses and wild things. Money never dominated his life. Then, for some reason, a wandering urge took him away and, being at sea, I saw little of him. I could only speculate as to what I might find when we met after so many years.

By now it was past five and the light, while still very bright already had a soft, greyish tinge to it. I stopped my car on the last rise to look down at the hamlet, if it warranted such a title for I saw it consisted of no more than about twenty slate roofed stone cottages scattered along a stony shore. It had every indication of being lonely, even the telephone line by the side of the road drooped as if forgotten. However, standing beside my car, the breeze felt cool, and the choppy waters of the loch sparkled and speckled like the scales of herring. I listened hard but the only sound was the wind in the heather, sighing regretfully at the passing of summer.

A few more crofter's cottages were scattered, apparently casually, on the moor above the hamlet while below a short, stone quay jutted out into the water to provide a mooring for a beam trawler. She lay half on her side for the tide appeared to be out. On more careful inspection of the place I saw a tin-roofed hall of some kind and one or two cattle yards or pens. Adjacent to one cottage was a shack, several ancient cars and a pair of even more ancient petrol pumps; this must be where Harry worked for his address was 'Eliaze Garage.'

A mystery lay before me and I drove forward with the feeling of mild excitement that goes with anticipated discovery.

In the garage, a man lay beneath a car up on chocks. There wasn't much to be seen, however his feet told me it was not my brother for both my brother and I share the same problem of finding shoes big enough. The feet wriggled. 'Mr Harry?'

'His brother, Robert.'

There was an abrupt scrabble of overalls and eventually, from that grubby, oil stained mass, a head erupted. 'Christos!' it said.

Some faces are unforgettable. This one looked like the bottom of a tin kettle into which, in the centre, a pock marked potato had been jammed. Frightening, wasn't a sufficient description. It had very little hair and what little there was streaked back in yellow strips across a white skull. Pale blue eyes like rivet holes squinted at me in a way I judged to be calculating but not unfriendly.

It was the face of a man so ugly that, if he wasn't totally trustworthy he would have to be in jail. Since clearly he wasn't in jail, I took to him cautiously.

'We knew you were coming but not the day. I'm Stefan, Stefan Petolski.' He offered a wrist to shake. 'I'm the mister who does the work.'

We introduced ourselves. 'Where's my brother?'

'Up at the big house.'

'I didn't see any big house.'

'No?' The splattered face broke into a toothy smile that was about the only thing which could make the face uglier. 'You go back past the cross roads and down the mountain.' He spread his stubby but powerful arms. 'It's bigger than large. Owned by lots of oil men or perhaps they work for the bankers but the place is run for them by Lady Bishunt. Imagine! Twenty five bedrooms in the middle of nowhere and nobody owns the land here except them.'

'And my brother's there?'

'I think that is correct.' Stefan inclined his head politely. 'Of what is the time?'

'Almost six.'

'Mr Harry will be back within the hour – it's kipper night at the pub.' Perhaps my looks told him something for he added, 'Everyone comes to kipper night, but if it's tea you're wanting, my friend Mrs Ferguson at the shop will look after you.' Then he smiled turned into a chuckle. 'If you want to know anything about me – Stefan Petolski – or anybody else, she'll happily oblige.'

One last question bothered me. 'Who's the owner of that new Bentley I see behind here?'

He smiled again. 'Isn't she beautiful? She belongs to someone from the big house. Here for a service.'

I looked about the primitive garage. There was a hydraulic ramp but the rest was dated. I looked for electronics but couldn't see any. 'Can you service cars like that, here? It seems unlikely to me.'

A shrug of mid-European size almost dislocated Stefan's shoulder. 'Best you ask your brother: he brings in the business and sees the clients. Nobody has ever complained.'

It was an odd way of answering but I dismissed it from my mind as I went in search of some tea.

Mrs Ferguson's shop was betrayed by a soft drink advertisement, otherwise it looked the same as any other cottage.

A bell on a spring rattled a rusty warning as I thrust open the heavy door and in an instant the lady herself appeared, pushing her way through a curtain to the rear. Her appearance reminded one immediately of a robin – grey dress, rosy complexion, round of body and pugnaciously cheerful.

In less than ten minutes I was established with tea and biscuits in her back room and had gathered that there were twenty seven people in Loch Eliaze, six of those were off the trawler and one 'poor, dear soul,' was a loony. Also, that the centre, and indeed the only place of activity, was the pub, run by Maggie Brown, a recent widow. 'Och, she deserves a medal, does that one.'

My own details were clearly filed for reference and it was certain that all facts would be generally dispersed around the community within the next twenty four hours.

While all this was going on I learned that Stefan had a reputation for fixing everything that went wrong; that there were far too many cats and, in case it worried me, the mooing in the distance meant that a new calf, belonging to someone called Angus, was on its way.

At this point, after taking breath and pouring a second cup of tea, Mrs Ferguson tilted her head to say, perkily, 'Now, would you be taking it as a compliment if I said you looked exactly like your brother?' I replied that, as I hadn't seen my brother for many years, I could not answer the question. Not that it mattered a jot for Mrs Ferguson was in such a gallop that what the fox got up to was quite irrelevant.

'Our Mr Harry is a Saint,' she said firmly. 'We all love him dearly.'

'Yes?' I tried to look simultaneously impressed and unsurprised while, at the same time, coping with a damp Scottish shortcake and a hot cup of tea.

'We all say he's the Saviour of the village. So kind and thoughtful. Ye do ken, don't you, that there wouldn't be anyone left here at all if it weren't for him and his considerations?

'Frankly, I'm completely astonished,' I said, thinking of my brother's reputation with Mother. Recognising a flicker of concern, added hastily, 'I mean, amazing to think a village like this could simply disappear, why it's such a...feature of the countryside.'

Cackling her appreciation, Mrs Ferguson lifted the teapot in salute. 'Aye, you're right there, of that you can be sure – to one who has eyes to see and ears to listen.' She became confidential. 'Tell me now, Mr Robert, when you first came in to the shop, did you happen to notice my wonderful new fridge?'

There was no avoiding the intense and proud look on Mrs Ferguson's face. I replied immediately that of course I'd noticed it.

'Paid for by Mr Harry,' she said triumphantly. 'And not just me; Campbell got his deaf aid paid for by you-know-who and Maude – that's Mrs Slattery – had a complete new chimney built for her. All of us have similar stories to tell. Who got the gates painted, tell me that?'

A polite nod of encouragement was all that was demanded in order to gain a smile of approval and an almost sly, 'This is such a small world, you see, and the longer you're here the smaller it gets.'

I smiled back at her thinking that politeness costs nothing. 'Size isn't everything,' I suggested.

A keen glance was flicked in my direction. 'Too be sure! And you're so right! But in a small village, do be mindful of what you ask or say.'

'Good advice... but, having only just arrived, I don't even know what questions to ask.'

'In a place like Loch Eliaze, until you know everybody it's best to ask only what you need to know. People know people and small places can hold big secrets.' With that she nodded wisely and drank some tea. The silence was momentary and yet said something I could not fathom.

'Listen, Mr Robert,' she began once more, and with that warning put her cup down with much deliberation to lean forward so that her knee touched mine and she could stare up into my face. 'There's not a soul in Loch Eliaze, not a soul, who will hear a word against your brother y'hear, and that's a fact.'

Something in her watchful bright eyes made me think that this, if not a concealed threat, was a strong notice. If it was, she immediately dropped the subject for she sat back and smiled widely, as if at a child who'd just done something clever. 'Now...Northern Skies,' she said. And as I groped for a meaning she narrowed her eyes and nodded slowly and meaningfully, adding, 'the trawler that belongs to Willie McFarlane and his wife being sick, an' all.'

'Uh-huh?'

'She can't sail, can she? I'm told there's something wrong with a water pump. Aren't you a marine engineer? Couldn't you do something for him? He hasn't fished for a week and needs the money.'

I may be daft but I recognise a life-raft when I see one. 'Perhaps I'd better go now and have a look while there's some light left, 'I suggested.

'Aye. And we'll be seeing you for kippers,' she said.

Coming from her, it sounded like an order.

An hour later and I had seen McFarlane and arranged to look at the problem in the morning. By now it was growing dusk; one cottage had a light in a window as I started to walk the narrow street towards the garage. A car passed me to stop fifty yards ahead and a man began unwinding himself from the driver's side.

My first thought was to wonder at how such a large man could have packed himself inside such a relatively small car; the unwinding of body and arms seemed to go on forever. The second, recognising the man was in full Highland dress, was to think how incongruous it was to see such a sight; it was like seeing a man in full evening dress walking down Oxford Street in London. My third was the startling realisation that this man was my brother, Harry.

We hurried towards each other like two express trains meeting head on. 'Good to see you, Robert!' he shouted through his whiskers as we embraced.

'And you, Harry!' But some devil in me spoke my mind. 'What on earth are you doing in this rig?'

'The kilt, y'mean? Why, it's my working dress.'

'But you're English, you're not a Scot!'

He squeezed my arm and dropped his tone. 'Keep y'damned voice down...what do you mean?'

'I mean... You're not entitled to wear a kilt and dirk an' all that tartan stuff.'

Then followed what must have been the strange sight of two large men hissing words at each other from inches apart.

'I'm as entitled as anyone here, I'll have you know.'

'Harry! Our father came from the Isle of Wight, our mother came from Sussex and you grew up in London. You are as English as Big Ben.'

'The family name is Munroe, or have you forgotten?'

'It might be Napoleon but it doesn't mean we come from Corsica.'

'Is that so?'

'Yes.'

At this point his stare would have frightened almost anyone, but not me: when I know I'm in the right I'd fight anyone. 'You're English,' I said, 'and that's that.'

We had our horns locked together.

'See, now, Robert, I've had it researched,' he said in a voice just above absolute freezing, 'It's proven whatever you might like to think. Four generations back, our line came from Falkirk.'

'If you go back far enough we all came from the Rift Valley but it doesn't entitle you to dress as a Zulu.'

'We Monroes fought at Culloden, d'y not know that?'

'Really? On whose bloody side?'

Past being provoked, he sneered back, 'I see, you're as stupid now as you were as a brat: I'll have ye recognise that the kilt is an essential part of work.'

If there's one thing to annoy any brother, it is to remind him of his youth. I snapped at his face, 'Oh! I see! We're in the acting business, are we?'

We moved apart. In seconds, we were very close to trading punches. Suddenly the realisation came to me that, whatever the reason he wore the kilt, he did look quite magnificent. He could well have been used on a poster for Scottish National publicity. And he was my brother.

He, too, seemed to have second thoughts for he took a deep breath and looked around for anyone listening. 'Listen, Robert, let's not start with an argument so soon. Come with me back to the garage and we'll get ready for kipper night. We can talk better then. Tell us about Mum and Dad: everything just the same?

And we did just that, talk and make up as we walked arm in arm back through the one street of Loch Eliaze.

Stefan, my brother's lieutenant, joined us to go to the pub. He had discarded his oiled overalls and now wore trousers too big for him round the waist and held up by bright red braces. They didn't improve his face one bit. Neither did the white sailor's cap and neither did the medallion to some European Saint which hung over a purple silk shirt.

Harry had changed into a pair of jeans and a heavyweight check shirt. To much the same, I found it necessary to add a jerkin, still being sensitive to chill air. With Stefan being half our height and walking between us, we must have presented a strange sight.

As we progressed, it became apparent that, while Stefan raised his cap to everyone in politeness my brother greeted the people we passed with, to me, almost medieval courtesy. I came to feel that I was walking alongside royalty by the deferential way people responded to his: 'And a very good evening to you, Mr Douglas, or, 'Tis a fine night you'll agree for such an event, Mrs Donovan.' True, nobody bowed or curtsied but I felt they might well have done so.

All I could do was to smile at all and sundry until we reached the pub, originally two or three low, stone cottages knocked into one. It was busy with some standing by the door. 'Stay here,' said Harry, pointing to a bench outside 'and I'll try and sort something out.'

Left on our own, Stefan took over the task of explaining the situation. 'Maggie Brown and her husband were noted for smoking their own fish. When Maggie's husband died of a sudden heart attack three months ago, we all feared the fish smoking would stop but in fact Maggie does it even better now she's on her own.'

'But what's so special about kipper night?'

'Why, all the kippers you want to eat are free! People come from miles away.'

'She just gives them away?'

'When the herring are running.' Stefan began grinning at me proudly, like someone who has drawn the dustsheet off a newly designed engine and is now showing it off. 'You can eat as many kippers as you want. Later on she sends around a collecting box for a charity and you can put in whatever you feel like giving.'

Very good, I thought but something else puzzled me. 'What does everyone do round here apart from stuff themselves on kippers?'

'Visit each other, talk, I read a lot…' Encouraged, perhaps by my look, he went on; 'I come from Poland. My English to speak is good, eh? But my writing is bad so I try and read.'

'What are you reading now?'

'It's a book called War and Peace.'

'Really…Why?'

'It was the biggest book I could get for the money. But at first I found it very difficult with all those names to remember but now it is easy: I write each one down and cross them off as they get killed.'

'All of them?'

'I don't know, it's such a big book and I've only been reading it for a year.'

Harry reappeared. 'I've captured a table, come on.'

The pub was small, the ceiling low, the packed crowd noisily cheerful. We pushed our way through greetings and hand shaking and again I sensed the deferential attitude of everyone to my brother in the way they made way for him.

Seated at last, I found myself looking up into the blue eyes of a very, very fair-haired woman, startlingly attractive. 'An what'll you Gentlemen be having to drink tonight?' It was a question put softly and with a slight smile: she radiated signs of genuine kindness.

Before I recovered, 'He'll have a lager like me, Maggie, if you please,' said my brother leaning back and with authority, 'and the usual double Polish for Stefan.'

Such an assumption of drinks I found particularly irritating, but having started one row with my brother that day I held my tongue.

'You're wearing your lucky medal, I see, Stefan,' she said. 'It's very unusual.'

Stefan swelled with pride.

'A pair of Kippers all round?' she asked, looking at us.

'If that would not be putting you to too much trouble,' said my brother.

'Nothing's too much trouble for you, Harry Munroe,' she said, and she gave him a suggestive push with her hand as she left with the order.

'Quite a lady,' I said, my eyes following the one I now knew to be Maggie Brown.

'The best,' said my brother. 'And if you've got any ideas you'll have to get in the queue with the rest of Scotland.'

'There is old Viking blood in these parts,' said Stefan earnestly. 'I once got a book from the travelling library.'

I was watching her and her two helpers behind the bar. Maggie wore a cheeky, long-peaked cap in the modern style and a wooden bead necklace in matching blue. She was clearly the tallest of the girls: statuesque, I guessed: handsome, big boned but not fat. They all wore long white aprons and were attractive – particularly the one with big earrings – but only Maggie interested me.

'Viking blood can be traced genially,' Stefan added, frowning with effort at producing such knowledge.

At that moment, I think we were all studying Maggie. 'Swedish?' I wondered aloud.

'Nobody knows,' said Harry to me. 'She came here already married to a dour Scot called Alister – years older than her, and they took on the pub. That was before I arrived so it must have been as much as ten years or so ago. I once worked out that she must have married before she was eighteen.'

The helpers arrived with our drinks together with our kippers and bread and butter on cardboard plates.

Someone, breathing heavily, leaned over to say in a rough voice, 'You've got to be Mr Harry's brother.'

I looked at him. He had wild, uncombed hair and staring eyes but I thought him safe. 'Good guess,' I said.

'Come for the kippers? Everyone comes for the kippers. They're the best in Scotland. Best...' and with that he lurched and, by my bad luck, almost fell into a seat next to me, '...Best ... from anywhere. For sure if one of those London Chefs tasted one of our kippers they'd blow their brains out.'

'I'm about to try one for myself,' I said, picking up my fork.

'Nawooo, not like that!' He complained. Lifting his arm disclosed that a large kipper dangled in one hand. 'Like this', he said. With that he ran one thumb ran up the kipper, stripping all the meat off in one movement and letting it tumble into his mouth. 'Lovely stuff!'

How to respond to such a man? But my brother interrupted us: 'Very well demonstrated Mr Stewart. Never seen it better done in my life but he's a tired lad so perhaps this time you'll allow us to eat in peace.'

Had we been lucky, that might have been the end of it but just then one of the bar helpers sang out, 'Call for Mr Harry,' and with a grunt of annoyance my brother stood to take the phone by the coat rack, a couple of yards away. The space he'd vacated was immediately taken by a long-faced individual in a tweed hat, old gabardine coat and wellington boots with a distinct odour.

Stewart eyed the newcomer with hazy mistrust. 'Would that be six you've eaten tonight, Connie?'

'It might be, but then again, it might not be: who's counting?' The newcomer took to sitting bolt upright as if facing an inquisition.

'Maggie Brown smokes them in a special way,' said Stefan, 'Is that not right, I'm sorry, is that not so, Connie?' He turned to me, 'Connie buys and sells animal food.'

I now understood the smell and sensed he was trying to head off trouble.

'It's not a special way, it's the temperature in the chimney, Stef.' Connie did no look at him but eyed the ceiling. 'Never less than two-fifty, that's the secret.' He filled the silence that followed this piece of scientific knowledge with a slow and deliberate, 'Cent-i-grade.' The self-satisfied smack of his lips could have been those of a man laying down four aces on a baize covered table.

To my left, Stewart bowed his head as if he needed time to think about such a technical issue. To my right I could hear my brother on the telephone: 'Of course, Lady Bishunt. You believe the couple are from Detroit and you think their car is a Ford Mustang?'

Stefan winked at me. 'More work to come.'

'And where do you take the temperature, just tell me that!' Stewart became suddenly belligerent. 'At the bottom or at the top?'

Connie's eyebrows shot up in astonishment. To recover his poise he drank, elaborately, from a large engraved glass I assumed was his own. With a lofty expression, he lowered his glass, placed it on the table and pursed his lips, 'Now that, as everyone knows… depends on the chimney.'

I decided he wasn't as far into the evening as I had thought.

My brother was trying to speak above the noise of the pub. 'Are you certain it'll be a full service and not a small, ah, adjustment that's wanted? I'm not sure we can cope at this end with another major job so soon…'

Stewart was having problems trying to remember all the chimneys he'd seen. 'It's got a lot more to do with the wood smoke – a bit too much or too little and they'll all be ruined.' With that said, he groped in his jacket pocket and pulled out another kipper, this one somewhat bent. He eyed it with almost as much surprise as I did.

'I was told, or I think I was told, that Maggie uses some peat as well as wood,' suggested Stefan, cautiously.

He found himself being boisterously congratulated, 'Aye, y're ab-so-lutely right, Stef! Stewart slapped Stefan on the back, hanging on closely to this unexpected support. 'That's what gives them that extra bit o' sweetness.'

'I have mah doots that that is sooo,' whinnied newcomer Connie in horsey derision while looking down and sniffing at his glass as if it were a nose-bag 'Be sure I was told it was by adding a little malt whisky.'

Stewart seemed to have trouble seeing him. He cleared his throat, a sound resembling someone running a stick along a row of pewter tankards. 'If you believed that, you'd believe anything.'

'Well, you may be right and you may not be right but that's what I was told.'

Stefan had been looking from one to the other. 'Some say the sweetness is due to the nature of Maggie Brown herself,' he said.

This caused some silence and thought around the table. Feeling that it was best if I said nothing, I ate some fish and followed it with bread and butter. My brother could be heard clearly speaking on the phone: '...would you say this Mustang is an old model or fairly new? I know it's a delicate question but it effects the time necessary...'

The huge paper bag, clipped to each table for waste, received Stewart's two or three kipper remains; he delivered each carcass with exaggerated care. 'Agreed. Our Maggie's a fine lassie,' he accepted, as if conferring an honour on her. 'A very fine lassie.' He sucked his fingers one by one. 'Nobody would deny that. I'd fight any man who denied that she's finest woman in these parts. But I still think the sweetness comes from the peat.'

Stefan hurried to give support. 'A fine lady...' he began

'...And only the best peat to be found anywhere in Scotland,' pronounced Stewart, suddenly assuming massive authority. 'It comes from our island across the Loch.'

'No it doesn't,' said Connie in triumph. 'It comes from the old bog below Castle Stones.'

'From the Stones? Y'say the Stones?' Stewart couldn't believe his ears. 'Now that is something I simply cannot agree to.'

'You can be quite sure I'm right in that.' Connie eyed Stewart without affection.

'Maggie's husband, Kenneth,' said Stewart collecting himself, 'told me once that it came from the island and he should have known.'

'Well, he was wrong – or you were wrong: as always. You're a fool, Charlie Stewart.'

Silenced, Stewart could only gape at this disregard for the rules of pub argument.

Again I could hear my brother. 'What I suggest, Lady Bishunt, is that I come up tomorrow about eleven and we can discuss the details.' My brother seemed to strain to hear the reply and then said quickly. 'No, no, of course I'll leave all the talking to you.' He put down the phone.

'...So you may say,' said Stewart laboriously, returning to the subject like a dog only temporarily chased away by a stone and now returning to his favourite bone, 'that it comes from The Stones,' he stared hard at Connie, 'contrary to all common knowledge. But another thing I differ on is the temperature of the smoke. It all depends upon the fat in the herring.'

Not having a seat any longer, my brother stood and watched for a moment, then signalled to me to go. 'Robert and I have things to see to,' he announced for general benefit.

'Two-fifty degrees. No more and no less,' said Connie, flatly. Clearly it was his final offer and he stuffed his hands into his pockets.

I stood to leave: nobody took a blind bit of notice. Stewart leaned across the table to wag a finger of accusation. 'Two-fifty or not and chimney or not, a Scottish herring is a Scottish herring and best in the Wurld, just tell me that it isn't...'

'..Not when it's a kipper, it's not.'

Leaving them to get on with it, I went to the counter and put a twenty pound note in front of Maggie. From below the beer pumps she produced a bag full of kippers in return. She whispered, 'It often happens, as you see: Stewart and Connie live for an argument every kipper night.' She handed the bag across the counter. 'These are for Harry but I've added a couple of haddies for your breakfast. I smoked them only yesterday.'

In the street outside, my brother and I walked in a silence broken only by the crunch of our feet on the gravel and the distant rumble of the sea. I said, 'Word has it that you are the local philanthropist.'

'Don't believe everything you hear.'

My mind considered the day, the people and the reactions. 'I've heard enough,' I said.

'Enough? Believe me, y've heard nothin'. My brother stopped and pulled me by the shoulder to turn me round and look at the thin straggle of houses, their white doors standing up like ghosts in the broken moonlight.

'Y'see that lot?' He pointed. 'Poor devils, they're all on the knife edge of survival. Costs are high, everything gets affected by transport. Most are on pensions, some not even that. They've just about enough to live on and nothing for emergencies.' He snorted through his nose, not so much in derision as in concern. 'If I put five hundred into the house at the far end, you can watch the money ping from one house to another: ping, ping, ping – Paying off debts, giving loans, buying essentials and with luck a few luxuries thrown in. It's

31

like watching a pin table machine lighting up as the ball works its way down the table.'

'How much ends up in Maggie's pocket?'

'Not all that much, and remember, Robert, that pub is the centre of the village: no pub, no centre. No centre, no life.'

But there was something just about suggestive in the way Maggie Smith had brushed against my brother. 'You have any interest in that department? She looked most attractive to me.'

No answer came from the darkness for some time. 'She's a kind and gentle soul.' My brother's voice was almost indistinguishable against the noise of the sea. '....far too good for the likes of me – and perhaps for the likes of you an' all.'

There was no answering that. I began walking again and he fell into step beside me. 'You see yourself having any ambitions in that direction?' He held my shoulder in a brotherly way.

'Being at sea, I don't have much experience, you must know that. I don't want to make a fool of myself.' When he chuckled a second time, I growled, 'All right. So, where do you get your money from – surely not just from the poky little garage?'

'From the big house, servicing cars, taxi fees... a mixture, here and there... And, sorry, that phone call means that I will be occupied all tomorrow and probably the next day, a big job.'

'Don't worry about me, I will be moving on. I've a bit to do on that fishing boat; then I'm off.'

'So soon? You've hardly arrived. Damn, me, it's not that bad place to drop anchor.'

'There's two more trawlers due to arrive next week, or so I'm told. I've learned one thing already: if I stay here a few days, I might end up staying here forever – like you.'

My brother only grunted.

'I meant that.'

He grunted again.

There seemed no point in saying more and we walked in thoughtful silence until we reached the garage. One light scarcely illuminated the sign. Beyond the garage there lay only the blackness of the moor.

He pushed back the unlocked door and led the way. 'You'll be back,' he said. 'It's that sort of place.'

My brother was right. Three months later I did go back but only by coincidence – I was on my way south, dutifully intending to be with the parents for Christmas.

From a distance everything looked precisely as before except that the trawler was missing from the lonely picture: the little harbour was empty. I went straight to the garage. There was nobody in the workshop but in the backroom, to my surprise, both Stefan and Mrs Ferguson were sitting by the fire. Stefan got to his feet with an alacrity that was suspicious. Something had to be wrong. 'So where's my brother?' I asked, shutting the door carefully for the thing, made up of planks, was loose on its hinges.

'He's gone,' said Stefan.

There was an immediate explosion of activity by Mrs Ferguson as she rose then sat then rose and sat again. She tried to laugh but changed that into a panicky, 'Sit yourself down, Mr Robert, sit y'sell down. Here, sit y'sell down and and warm ye sell' up while Mr Petolski will recount as sorry a tale as you'll hear this entire year.'

There was no disguising that particular lady's fluttering discomfort as she touched and retouched her brooch gabbling on: '...In fact I was only here to discuss what we might all be doing next and me with my shop empty. I'll go and make some tea.' And she shot away to rattle every pot and kettle in the kitchen.

'What's all this about?' I demanded of Stefan, who looked rueful but unmoved by Mrs Ferguson's behaviour. He sat on a stool rubbing his knuckles and scuffing the floor with an idle foot.

'Mr Harry's walked out on us; not that I'm blaming him mind, not after what happened, but he's gone and that is that.'

It was easy to imagine that the tragic tone of his voice sprang from reading too much Tolstoy. I took a chair. 'Start at the beginning: what happened and when.'

'About a month after you left,' Stefan shrugged, not looking at me but at his boot. 'Well, something like that, it was a kippers night with nothing unusual...' He broke off to raise his head and shout, 'Nothing unusual that night, Molly, was there?'

So quickly that it was obvious that she was listening hard to every word came back – 'Not a word out of place and Dru and Malcolm on his flute entertaining an' all.'

'But you're brother wasn't there,' muttered Stefan, turning to cracking his knuckles, 'he'd been working or doing something up at the big house.'

'Not until the end of the evening,' came the voice from the kitchen.

'Yah,' said Stefan, 'that was when it happened. Mr Harry arrived just as the pub closed.'

'Stone sober,' qualified the hidden voice. 'And as courteous as ever.'

'So we all called out, "Pub's closed, Mr Harry."'

'You did, I didn't say a word,' came the voice with some indignation.

'May be you didn't,' said Stefan calmly, 'but the rest of us did. Anyway, Mr Harry said, "Maggie always keeps a pair of kippers for me in case I'm late." So with that he walks into the pub and disappears inside.'

Something told me that a climax was coming for Mrs Ferguson could no longer contain herself in the kitchen but arrived at the door with a kettle in her hand.

'So next thing...' began Stefan.

'...There was a scream and a bang.'

'Several bangs and crashes, they was chairs I believe...'

'And shouting...'

'And and some glasses breaking and the bar doors flew open...'

'And then, 'Our wonderful and dear Mr Harry...' Mrs Ferguson paused for maximum effect, '...comes flying backwards through the doors. Through the doors and, would you believe, totally out of control!'

Eyes wide and overcome by recounting such a tale, she abruptly turned and hurried back into the kitchen, clucking her agitation.

I watched her go, and thought. It seemed to me that Mrs Ferguson could make a drama out of a dead mouse, but Stefan added his confirmation. 'Oh, yah!' He declared, nodding a violent agreement towards the door hiding Mrs Ferguson. 'His legs and arms were flailing, sure, and without a word or yell he falls backwards on to Callaghan's bike and smashes it up completely. I had to help him home, your brother I mean.'

This seemed unbelievable: my brother was strong enough to toss a caber with ease. 'Maggie... My brother... Are you sure about all this? With him the size he is? I can't understand it.'

'Of course he's sure!' Came the hidden voice in the kitchen. 'We all saw it happen.'

'Ah! That was the start but worse was to come,' Stef continued, happy to sound miserable, 'For then she – that is, Maggie – appears at the door and throws kippers in all directions, yelling at everyone, "That's the last kippers any of you will ever get from me!" And with that she slammed the door and wouldn't open it to anyone.'

'And Maggie never raised her voice to anyone!'

'Never heard her before.'

'No and you wouldn't have.'

Such an apocalyptic event deserved the respectful silence it received between the three of us. Eventually, I felt I had to say, 'And is that the case: she's never smoked kippers again?'

'Not only that. She shut the pub, locked it and the next day went to Glasgow! Aye, that she did.'

Now, agreed that there was some self-satisfaction in his despondency but that wasn't important: all the questions concerned my brother. I looked from Stefan to the kitchen door and back. 'But what explanation did my brother give?'

'Wouldn't say a word, not a single word.'

Good grief! 'And nothing from Maggie?'

'You couldn't force a knife through her lips.'

It seemed so extraordinary that clarifying the situation became essential. 'Are you telling me that my brother has gone off without a word and that Maggie has gone off without a word and that the pub's closed down?'

Yes,' said Mrs Ferguson appearing with a tray of tea. 'And now we have no reason to stay in Loch Eliaze any longer.'

'No work,' said Stefan, gloomily.

'Aye, and no money either,' said Mrs Ferguson, primly counting out sugar lumps.

Nobody said any more than that, but you would need to be totally insensitive not to realise that they both looked to me for a solution.

It did not take me long to track down my brother. Stefan had a forwarding address for mail, a small hotel in Paisley, just outside Glasgow. Over the telephone, and after some prevarication, he agreed to meet me at a pub down by the river.

It was natural to expect some change in him but he seemed much the same, perhaps a little quieter but looking well.

The pub was empty – we were early, probably the night's first customers, and we took a place near the fire. After Harry had ordered a lager, me a gin and tonic, we fished about for what to say. 'Got a job?' I asked.

'In the distillery. I was able to offer my blacksmith skills. They ship old sherry casks over from Spain and I help knock them together again ready to take whisky for maturing.'

This seemed reasonable. 'Reckon you've got a long term future here?' I put the question over my shoulder as I paid the girl.

'Only while I think things out,' He took a drink. 'Listen, brother, if you've come looking for an explanation to what's happened, don't bother to ask, that's all.'

In situations like this it can be better not to try and rush things. I looked around the room. It was not very inspiring. 'Mum and Dad – I spoke to them yesterday – want to know how you're doing, and emphasised that I was to give you their love.'

'Their love, that's a joke! Their love, how about ours? Haven't you found out yet that you can give some people love and it's like pouring water into the desert?' Harry slowly developed a laugh that startled the barmaid. He finally had to stop to wipe his eyes, shaking his head at some hidden thought. All the while I said nothing, waited, sipped my drink. He stuffed away his handkerchief and the barmaid, who'd been listening, turned away and diplomatically recommenced polishing glasses.

He said, 'you cannot imagine the funny side to what you are saying, Robert. Love? Why, love is like time: you can't order it, can't buy it, can't keep it... Anyway, what's love got to do with the rotten state of Denmark?' And he ranted on about how the world was stuffed with romantic nonsense and he'd given it up.

Fair enough, he had his say but it wasn't getting us anywhere. All I could do was to wait for normality to return. However it began to look as though if we went on long enough, the real problem might get exposed so, in a meandering way I spoke about my leaving the sea and searching for a different life and something by way of companionship.

The more I talked the easier he became, until I judged that he wanted to explain or say something but did not know how or whether to do so.

We had another drink, then another. The bar was beginning to fill and private conversation was getting more difficult. I suggested we went back to my hotel room where there was a mini-bar and we could talk in peace. Two hours later and he was lying on my bed, I was slouched in the chair and various empty cans and bottles lay between us. We'd discussed almost everyone in Loch Eliaze except one.

I tossed him another can of lager. 'So Maggie threw you out then? What was she eating, raw spinach?'

'To tell you what happened, I'd have to tell you everything. Sorry but I can't do that.'

So we talked on and we drank on. To tell the truth, I was beginning to wonder how to call a halt to a wasted evening when my brother, lying there and looking up at the ceiling said, 'I've never lied in my life, Robert and yet telling the truth has ruined me.'

I finally lost my temper. 'Oh for God's sake, man, stop wasting my time by feeling sorry for yourself!' In a thoroughly bad mood, I swept aside debris with my arm. 'You'll never sleep easy until you say what all this lot is about!'

Equally, or even more drunk, he lay there unmoved by my tantrums. 'Tell... that was a school slogan: Tell all or tell nothing.'

'Then tell nothing,' I snapped, 'as if I bloody care.'

This finally silenced him. In a more contrite voice he said, 'All right, I'll explain – but only to you.' And after collecting his thoughts, he said, 'You remember I used to look after horses? That's how I came to work for Ann, that is, Lady Ann Bishunt. After a bit, from shoeing horses and sorting out her stables, she introduced me to, shall we say other sports of a more indoor nature. And that went on until she broke a leg badly in a riding accident.'

'This the Lady Bishunt who runs the huge shooting estate and with all the cars for servicing?'

'Of course. By this time I'd borrowed money from her to buy the crappy garage and had started using my car to run a taxi service, but that comes later. No, just at that moment Ann, with a badly damaged leg, had no special use for a man. However one day, a girlfriend she was with at university, arrived for the weekend and that girl certainly had a use for a man. Well, that time was just fun and it must have been very successful to the other party for it gave Ann an idea.'

Still listening hard, I picked up a dry biscuit to nibble. 'Let me get that right. You say, that time was for just for fun...?'

'It has turned out to be almost the only time. Ann is a businesswoman who ought to run the country. She immediately saw an opportunity. You see, all these very select shooting parties turn up and go out on the moor shooting grouse or deer. Fine for the men. But after being cold and soaked for two days, the women get fed up with all that: some go home, some return to Glasgow shopping, and one or two of them look around for something more interesting.'

'Oh, interesting. Now I'm beginning to understand,' I said, wondering if I did. 'The interesting bit meaning what, precisely?'

'Masculine. Rough. Something very Scottish. A bit primitive, wild, dramatic. Something unlike anything you could find anywhere else in the world.'

I thought of my brother, massive in his kilt and whiskers, striding through that ancient house full of hunting trophies and in rough contempt for all he saw. I could not imagine his equal.

'So that's why you've developed an accent.'

'Perhaps. I've also learned to play the bagpipes, more or less.'

The picture was getting clearer by the minute. 'And this Ann, Lady Bishunt,' I said, probing further, 'she arranged it all, very diplomatically, no doubt.'

'Precisely. And I provided the service, whatever the lady wanted – and some of things they wanted were weird: from a song to sex and back again. I admit it. Now you know.'

My glass was almost empty and my weariness had spread to Harry who tried to get up but failed. Yet something bothered me in his story. 'Their husbands... Surely they must have wondered?'

'Marital boredom, dear boy. As long as their wives kept out of the way and didn't disturb the shooting – which costs a fortune, by the way.' With a great effort he swung his feet to the floor. 'Wealthy men of that sort trade wives like you would trade a car.' He yawned. 'Must be going...'

'But all the talk of servicing...?'

'Ann's cunning again. We have a code between us. The cars are complained about or said to need a service and the woman drives them down to the garage. There, of course, while Stef works on the car, they need my taxi to drive them back to the big house – which I do, or appear to. The husbands, if they bother to think at all as they blaze away with their guns, assume the wife is waiting for the car to be finished. On the way back there's a gillie's hut set up by Ann for me to entertain the lady in private.'

'How much do you charge?' It was a blunt question but I needed to know.

'Good grief, Robert, what do you take me for? Nothing, of course. That would have been completely wrong. We're talking about women who drip money but don't discuss it. Some are in the process of robbing their husband blind. Often they're as sensitive and proud as peacocks. Ann sorts all that out, calling it a present for the sake of a wonderful memory.'

'Ah... The Lady, Ann,' I said, drawing a circle in the air with my glass and thinking aloud, 'She's the one who controls everything.'

'Only the arrangements. And don't think it always means one thing: one black African lady only wanted me to tease her about in private, dress her up in the Tartan with sword and shield and take her picture. She gave a rough diamond to Ann for that which Ann sold for nearly four thousan' poun'.'

'But over the telephone the words ''a full service'' is a code for...'

'Everything asked for. Now you know the whole damned business so good night.'

I wanted to know more, but he brushed aside all questions: 'Too drunk and too tired, see you tomorrow.'

And to tell the truth, I was too tired and drunk to ask or care for more.

Of one thing you can be certain in life: next day, nobody wants to be reminded of what they said when they were half drunk the night before.

I'd given some thought as to how to make further progress towards my main goal, that of finding out what happened with Maggie and seeing if things could be put right. Accordingly I suggested to Harry that we drove down the coast to a well recommended restaurant. It was possible that, if not rushed, the story would emerge. What I had not allowed for was the weather, which happened to be blowing a gale.

My idea of having a stroll along the beach and talking had to be scrapped. Instead, we reached a parking place on a cliff top where I stopped the car, expecting to sit there and watch the waves roar in to dash themselves in mountainous sheets of spray. 'Y'coming?' asked Harry, reaching for the door.

'You mad?'

Harry laughed and opened the door. He needed both hands to do so. I sat tight and watched.

He did not go far, holding hard to a post to stare into the wind. It was a scene to remember. He was wearing a long cloak from neck to his knees, one of those dark green waterproofs, and looking seawards, his hair and beard were forced horizontal by the force of the gale. From time to time an extra large sheet of spray made a brief background to a rugged face. I had no idea precisely what was going through his head and yet from the rigid way he faced the elements I sensed he was not feeling the weather but replaying events and trying to make up his mind.

After a few minutes he returned to the car and wiped his face on a towel I'd put on the back seat.

'Breezy.' He said. But the way his shoulders had straightened announced that he'd taken a decision, but whether to tell or keep silent was unclear.

He sat back. The car shook from time to time as a gust of wind hit it. He said, 'So you want to hear about Maggie, I suppose.'

'When you feel the time is right.'

'You're dying to hear, I'm not a total idiot. I've thought about it and if I can't talk to my brother, who can I talk to?'

'Shall we drive on?'

No. Let's stay here: after, we can go and eat. It's a wild day and a pretty wild story and this is a pretty wild spot. But the story doesn't start with Maggie, it starts with a Japanese lady called Lily.'

'Well it would, wouldn't it?' I said, letting go the car key.

'In my experience, Japanese women are the most demanding of all,' he said, tossing the towel back over the seat. 'And Lily was something special. She was the wife of a car manufacturer so perhaps she had reason.'

'Young?'

'Youngish, hard to tell, but not stupid. She had a degree in Arabic Studies.'

The memory seemed to make my brother silent.

'So, Lily…' I prompted.

Impatiently and with something like bitterness he snapped, 'Believe it or not, Robert, I'd wanted to stop for some time – I'm getting too old for all this malarkey. But I wanted to buy a cottage and install a retired nurse to look after our little community at Loch Eliaze, and I needed a few more months, say until the end of the deer shooting season.'

'So, for that reason you took on this Japanese lady called Lily.'

'Aye, but with some misgivings because the two or three Japanese I've had before have been very demanding. Anyway, car down at the garage, we were in the cottage by the burn – you must bear in mind it has only one room and a bathroom – and there she had me marching up and down, up and down the room playing the pipes. I can tell you I was heartily sick of 'Scotland the Brave,' which is the only tune I can play perfectly.'

'While she sat and admired,' I suggested.

'Inscrutable is the word. It was as though she was amazed or perhaps filled with awe, I couldn'a tell.'

'She just sat and watched?'

'Cross legged on the bed. Said nothing until I paused for breath and then she kept insisting on more, shrieking in her thin, squeaky voice, ''Again, again, again!'' until I had to plead for mercy.'

My brother gave an ironic chuckle at the memory.

'Then she said it was her turn. She had to pretend to be a Geisha, dress up for it and hold the tea ceremony. We sat in the middle of the room and it went on for hours. All I wanted by now was a few pieces of toast and a decent brew but the chat continued, and the gestures continued, and my murmurs of appreciation had to continue until suddenly, by mistake or not I'll never know, she fondled my whiskers. It was like a fuse blowing in her mind: she immediately went berserk and attacked me. Robert, I tell you: it was like a Kamikaze pilot diving at an aircraft carrier.'

'All this happened on Kipper night?' It was a guess on my part.

'Of course. She and I didn't stop until late, by which time I was a spent man.'

Some might have grinned at hearing my brother's tale but I recalled seeing salmon drifting down the river exhausted. 'So you both drove back to the garage where she collected her car and you went on to the pub?'

'I had to sit in my car for a while trying to recover so by the time I got to the pub it had closed. A few stood outside, talking – it was a fine night...'

'And Maggie always kept some for you...'

'So I went inside. Her assistants were somewhere at the back, doing the clearing-up, so she was on her own, picking up chairs and sweeping. 'I said, "my apologies for being so late, Maggie..."'

'I'm glad you're late and on your own,' she said, producing my usual bag. But instead of just handing them over as usual with a joke or two, she came within inches of my face to whisper, 'Tonight, would you rather have me or would you rather be having the kippers, Harry Monroe? Because you canna' be having both.'

Our car at that moment seemed very quiet. I knew what I would have done if I'd been there and felt my blood rise. And Harry had stopped talking, too. It was a moment in his story when I had not the slightest idea what to say: nothing seemed appropriate. He could only look ahead at the grey sea and the high-flung spray.

Eventually he said, 'Her words keep coming back to haunt me, Robert. They wake me in the night. "Which would you rather have: me or the kippers?"'

'And you replied...' The question needed no answer.

With a sudden shrug of petulance he growled, 'I was exhausted, Robert, think of it. Women? I couldn't have cared less. Not even for Maggie. I wanted to sleep, that's all. There's a limit for any man. I couldn'a raise a finger, let alone anything else. And I've always been honest. So when she said, "Would you rather have me or the kippers?" I said, 'Tonight, I'll just take the kippers, if you don't mind.'

'So... she lost her temper.'

'No Robert, she seemed to go quite insane and hit me in the chest so that I fell back, off balance, and then she pursued me shrieking and throwing things… I never did get my balance until I went backwards, clean through the door.'

Harry stopped and scowled at the memory as he tapped his fingers on the dashboard.

'I see, and then you fell out into the waiting crowd.' It was easy to visualise the scene and I finished the memory for him, adding: 'Good God,' for nothing else seemed appropriate.

'Exactly,' muttered my brother.

Fearing that the silence between us might be broken and lead to hearing something worse, I started the car and reversed from the cliff top. 'Let's go and eat,' I said.

In any other situation, I would never have had the nerve to tackle a woman who had been treated like Maggie. However, she had always seemed a kindly woman to me and besides, I have met few women who have attracted me so much. The excuse was there for me to follow up and I took it.

Nobody had the address for Maggie but she was not hard to find. There are only a few agents who specialises in selling pubs and from one, I got Maggie's address and left my phone number and a request for her to contact me. Thus it was that one late afternoon we met at the entrance to Glasgow station before going on to a café-bar I had selected as being a suitable place to talk.

She was dressed in dark blue almost black coat over a lighter blue, two piece suit. She had a single string pearl necklace and wore only a little make-up. To me she looked… pretty damned good.

But the atmosphere was not exactly congenial. 'What have we got to talk about?' She asked, pointedly.

Well, she knew perfectly well what we had to talk about. But protocol said that the formalities of talking about the people of Lock Eliaze had to be disposed of first.

There is a general understanding that women speak about personal matters much more freely than men. So, having dealt with Stef and Mrs Ferguson and one or two others, I only had to say that the community had broken up, once she had left, for Maggie to start unburdening herself.

'I am sorry to hear it but I could n'a stay. There's nowhere in a place like Loch Eliaze to hide, least of all when running a pub.'

To this, I nodded understandingly. 'But you must appreciate my difficulty, Maggie. I don't know the background to all that happened, all I know is that I've been asked to see if there's anything to be done to put things right. To do that, I need to know how it all started.'

It was too early in the evening to be drinking so I had a well-stewed cup of coffee before me while Maggie sucked at a fruit juice on ice through a straw.

'Everything comes back to personalities: some things you grow out of and some things you don't.'

'Such as?'

'My height, there's nothing I can do about it. Now, I don't think about it but when I was younger it was a...bother. Shyness was something else I've cured.'

That left a lot of other characteristics unanswered. 'How about temper,' I asked, smiling to make the question easier.

She did not smile back. 'My temper is as good as most people's.'

'I can believe you. So could all Loch Eliaze as far as I know – you have a wonderful reputation.'

'Nobody has seen me lose my temper. I get angry sometimes, but that's all.

'Perhaps my brother might find that hard to believe.'

'He deserved every bit he got.'

Sometimes a nod or shrug of understanding is better than words. I drank my coffee. It was pretty disgusting. 'I dare say he did deserve it, although I'm not sure if the bike he landed on felt it deserved to be flattened.'

'I did like Loch Eliaze so much,' she said with a trace of wistfulness. 'It was hard work but fun.'

I let a few moments pass while her memory dwelt on the good times. 'Why not tell me how it all began?' I suggested.

Sipping at her drink, she looked around as if to see if she could be overheard. 'Look, Robert, I'm letting you know all this when perhaps I shouldn't but you must understand I married very young. My husband, Kenneth, was a kindly, steady soul and hard working; some might have called him a plodder but I respected him and we were loyal to each other – we worked well together running the pub.'

'And the fish smoking?'

'That was his idea. Some weeks we'd send off fifty boxes but it was hard work – perhaps that was what killed him.'

Whatever the situation, words like 'killed' and 'death' need space. We sat for a while. Does hard work kill people? I wondered. She and her husband must have had a lifestyle of long hours. 'Heart attacks are indiscriminate things,' I said, after watching her sip her drink, 'and I understand he was older than you.'

'Much older – but does that matter?'

I shrugged acceptance. 'So you worked together well... How does Harry fit in to all this?'

'Oh, yes, that...'

Her hands had taken to playing with her bag and she showed a flush of embarrassment. Suddenly she looked at me straight, her blue eyes wide with urgent appeal. 'I have to rely on your understanding.'

A turning point has been reached; she could say anything and I'd believe her. More, I felt myself sliding towards making a fool of myself. 'Maggie, I'm here to be of help,' I said, 'nothing more and certainly nothing less.'

'Very well, you're a good man, Robert, but then' – smiling girlishly, almost giggling – 'You must accept that while a young woman wants to be, and is, totally loyal and faithful to her husband, there can be another man in her dreams. A man who has been there much longer.'

It was the most gentle of brush-offs. I drank more coffee and nodded like a toy idiot at a fair ground.

'The moment your brother came through the door – the very first time – I knew him to be the man I wanted. He was my Gillie Dubh, the spirit I'd searched for. When a woman feels that way, there's nothing else that matters.'

At least she did not bother to touch me in sympathy.

'Sorry, Robert, but there it is.'

Decent of her, I thought, but that was that. I waited until some people behind us settled into their seats. 'But, of course, you were married, I said, sounding like defending Counsel at a trial.

'Yes, that's right. So I could do and say nothing.'

'And Harry?'

'From time to time I had a feeling – a woman's intuition if you like – but nothing was ever said or hinted at.'

Things had become clear. Years of waiting, and then? I looked at her glass. 'Another drink?'

She shook her head and began talking about her job, that of an estate agent's runner. I listened and made the appropriate remarks until a fresh opportunity arose.

'Maggie, I've got an inkling now of what happened between you and Harry that night, some sort of rejection, perhaps?'

Anger at the recollection flared instantly. 'Rejection!' she growled through tightened lips. 'Insult, you mean! I made my feelings plain, too plain; I let myself be vulnerable and your brother insulted me in the way you wouldn't insult an animal. I felt it here, a hurt to terrible to describe,' and she placed a hand on her heart. Recalling the moment also brought tears to her eyes.

I waited for her to blow her nose. 'I understand... but did he mean it?' I pursued.

'How the Hell should I know? If you don't know what an insult is, you shouldn't say it.'

'He was ill that night. Exhausted. Low sugar level in the blood. It happens from time to time and it upsets his judgment.'

'How ill?''

'By all reports, and from the symptoms he described to me, he has never been or felt worse.'

Now a person's body language can tell you a lot. Maggie was coming to doubt herself. And she was coming to doubt herself because, beneath it all, she wanted to.

'He's full of remorse,' I said, leaning across the table and speaking urgently but low voiced. 'He regrets bitterly what happened.'

A sudden crowd surge in the café pushed us together. 'Are you sure?' she whispered back.

'Totally convinced. Believe me.'

'I would like to…'

'You have my word.'

She stared for a moment. We were only inches apart but her voice was so low I could scarcely catch the words. 'Thank you, Robert.' There was nothing more for me to add but as she turned I just heard her say. 'I know I can trust you.'

So, all that was all over. I sat back, suddenly feeling tired. But there remained another hurdle to be negotiated and it might as well be dealt with immediately. I said, 'If he had a past he regretted, and if he was made to take his health more seriously, would you meet him again and talk?'

'If you mean all that gossip about what went on up at the big house, that doesn't matter to me as long as he stops going there. I want him for what he is and will be, not his past.'

I'd heard enough to push away my cup and saucer. 'I'll see what I can do,' I said.

All that took place some while ago.

Now, I am pleased to say, after a considerable effort on my part and lots of to-and-fro on theirs, my brother and Maggie run the pub together. The village has again become a lively place – full of intimacy, neighbourliness and, let's be honest, gossip, argument and intrigue.

As for me, well, the job of running the garage and taxi service fell vacant so I thought I might as well fill the breach. Not only that, but I can assure anyone that the Lady Ann remains an exceptional lady.

Stefan gave up on War and Peace and I put him on to thrillers instead. And there are not one but three trawlers using our little port: in fact the sign over the garage Stefan has amended to, 'Marine and General Engineering'.

As I said at the beginning: leaving the sea was the best thing I ever did.

The Teddy Bear

In understanding people, one thing you will have observed is that work wears down a person's physique and sometimes character. Sometimes both things happen at the same time.

It depends on the job but a publican – as insurances companies will confirm – rarely stays the long course; his work is too demanding both on body and mind. Bus drivers, miners, marketing executives, front line nurses… all are frequently quoted as examples of wearing occupations.

On that late December morning, Gordon Johnson could provide an example of another, if smaller group of stressed out individuals – editors of struggling regional newspapers with struggling staff and struggling finances. Indeed on that day even the weather struggled, finally surrendering to the first truly hard frost of winter. People who had talked sagely of changing seasons and earth warming now complained of the bitter cold. And the forecast predicted that temperatures would fall further, warning of fog inland.

And the temperature had not been overlooked by Johnson's staff despite occupying heated offices in the block overlooking the crowded National Car Park. They might have appeared intent on their individual contribution to producing a good newspaper but privately they were more intent on getting the job done and getting home before the roads became difficult. It was all heads down at desks. All heads, that is, except Johnson's.

His editor's office was at the end of the corridor and there, alone, cut off from interruptions, he worked long hours. Today he was slumped so far back in his swivel chair as to be almost horizontal. A mobile phone rested on one shoulder while he made notes on a pad on his knee.

As the steady outpouring of faint sounds and advice continued, he felt compelled to raise his hand, as though trying to slow down a car. 'That's a very exciting idea, Sir,' he said.

If the person at the other end of the phone detected complete insincerity, the tone and flow of words did not stop. Phone to his ear, Johnson had to listen. 'I'll put one of the best of the team on to it,' he agreed finally. Yes, right away.'

But by now, his stubby fingers had begun to tap impatiently on the arm of his chair: he'd had about enough. 'I fully understand the situation, Sir, and I'll look after it myself.' He scanned the wall of his office looking for help until his eyes rested on the clock. 'Of course, Sir. Yes, yes, at once. There's time to get one of the staff there. I see it's eleven o'clock and at the moment...'

Again he was stopped.

At that moment Johnson might well have said that time is a vast and mysterious thing, not always accountable by the simple movements of a clock but the chance never arose with instructions and advice continuing in an endless flow. Fortunately nothing lasts forever and another break enabled him to cut in – 'As I say, no trouble at all, Sir. We'll make a good story of it, you can be sure.' This appeared to be a satisfactory reply for, with one final few words of deference to his invisible master, Johnson took the phone from his shoulder and flipped it off.

He looked at the offending instrument for some while, pudgy face flat and without expression, blue eyes half closed, fat lips pursed in reflection. In the silence of his office there was no need for inhibitions. 'Bastard,' he said dispassionately. The simple word at least gave him some pleasure. He repeated it: 'A right Bastard.' He tilted his head back to study the ceiling and to consider how to handle this new problem.

A general office and reporter's room, known as the Squat, was only a step down a green and white tiled corridor. Unlike Johnson's office, the Squat sparkled with Christmas decorations. Mistletoe hung over the door and a tree twinkled self-consciously in one corner. The office wit, beneath a large poster shouting 'Save the Planet: No Plastic', had added with marker ink, 'So only cheques this year, please, Santa' and attached a Christmas stocking. Away from the desks, the window had grubby curtains now glinting with stuck-on gold stars. The seasonal note continued with several unstable paper chains stuck to the wall with Sellotape.

At the despatch end of the office it was more like business as usual. Two tables stood covered with stacked newspapers, wall charts of jobs and a typed list of holiday schedules covered the walls. A rubber plant, having just been prevented from committing suicide, drooped disconsolately by the window. Behind the double-doors stood a bright green drinking water dispenser and a rack of plastic cups. In between the two areas of office activity, three reporters temporary work desks were occupied: one by a trainee and two by women half-hidden behind computers.

Johnson lumbered down the corridor and pushed open the main swing door. He was a big man and fleshy. His grey complexion and paunch advertised years of long office hours. However standing in the doorway of the Squat gave him a slight buzz of power: it was his empire and his staff. It was one of those small pleasures that provided a small recompense for all the concerns he carried. Aware that everyone waited expectantly, he allowed a kindly smile as he searched for his target. 'Angela?'

Angela Moore's' screen had a sprig of holly attached at one corner. She only had to raise her eyes to look back at Johnson. 'Yes, Gordon?'

In the exchange of looks, Johnson's mood changed. It was the way she said it: 'Yes Gordon...' Nobody else seemed to say it that way. She was never less than polite and yet never... he found it hard to define what annoyed him. Yes there was always politeness, but politeness with a built in edge of challenge – not a sign of deference, just that whiff of defiance, an independence he could manage without. A year of it and, as far as he was concerned, she hadn't changed or softened since the day she started.

He'd never seen anyone rattle Angela. She had self-confidence because she was attractive and no fear for her job because she was very good at it. And he didn't deny the fact she was good. It was there in black and white as proof in newsprint each week. She turned the stuff out on time and of good quality but he always found her difficult: too bloody self-sufficient, that was it

– someone you couldn't order, only reason with. Trouble was, there was never the time to stand around reasoning. This was a news room, not a debating chamber. State your case and get on with it. And, anyway, reasoning wasn't his style.

Not for the first time he asked himself as he stared at her: why she was on his staff and acting almost like an enemy? For God's sake, everyone else called him The Boss and moved on so why should she be so different?

But now was not the time for a row. 'A story's just come in,' he said, affecting casualness. 'Up in the Fens – Cambridgeshire – north of that and well beyond Ely, somewhere in the Wash area and it's urgent.' Not getting any reaction, he threw in, 'Sorry about it, but there it is. It has to be done today.'

'Sorry…' Insincerity hung in the air about as obviously as the Christmas paper chains.

Aware that everyone was listening even while apparently working, Angela sat back. She carefully and deliberately moved a strand of fair hair from her face with a finger. Her eyes never left Johnson. She accepted he was brilliant on lay-out and recognised his brain was a walking thesaurus but as a man…? She said, carefully, 'I see. Me again?'

Despite feeling she had a nerve to be judging him, Johnson controlled himself. 'As I say, I'm sorry, the job's just come up.'

'It is Friday,' Angela kept her voice very even, 'I probably can't go that far and get back tonight. It's Christmas next week and that'll be the second weekend in a row that's been wrecked for me.'

Yeah, Gordon,' a hidden voice from behind the sports desk clipped in, 'An' it's not very nice – there's thick fog forecast for the Eastern Region.'

'Shut up, Peggy darling,' said Johnson, amiably enough. He could handle Peggy; it was Angela's enigmatic stares that got to him. 'This job has come down to us from the big White Chief himself.'

One hand still on the keyboard, Angela showed disbelief. 'You're saying he's all of a sudden interested in the Fens?'

'Not he himself, he has a friend in high places. It was golf course request: Mammon to Magnate, men-talk, you might say.' God, he thought, this is just like a wrestling match. Why can't she just say 'yes', pick up the brief and get on with it?

'Men-talk on a golf course?' Angela sniffed, 'Tell us something new.' With Johnson silently waiting she produced a brilliant smile. 'Anyway I've got this piece on hair styles to finish – your last order, remember? Very important, you told me. Must be done, you told me. ... and done today.'

'Leave that... and I said I'm sorry – and you'll get the by-line for this new job.' Out-manoeuvred, Johnson took a fruit pastille from a packet in his shirt, put it in his mouth and began chewing with elaborate and slow jaw movements. 'Look,' he said, already conscious he was trying to achieve the impossible by sounding dignified, authoritative, reasonable and at ease all at the same time, 'our Chairman has an important banker he plays golf with -'

'Remember I'm not sports,' she cut in, briskly, 'and especially not golf. I'm arts, fashion and travel.' It gave her pleasure to note that his habit of eating sweets would make him fatter than he was already.

'No, it's not a golf story.'

'Oh, I see... then why me?'

'Why?' Johnson took his time, working his mouth on the pastille and exchanging stares. In no way was he going to be fazed by this bitch in front of staff. 'Because this involves travel in a way, that's why. The guts of it go like this: the banker's wife had some ancient relative who was a highly decorated pilot in the Second World War. He went missing in 1943, why and how we don't seem to know. He flew from some airfield or another up in the Fens, I don't know where, that's for you to look up. It was a temporary airfield, there's no map of the place. It's disused, obviously – may be nothing there now. You can get all the details from the briefing desk and archives. You'd better get on with it while there's plenty of light.'

'Uh-huh.'

From behind the sports desk the hidden but helpful voice chipped in: 'Missing men? You don't need to go as far as the Fens, Gordon. I could name a lot of men round here who go missing when you want them.'

'Do shut up, Peggy and mind your own business...The point is,' said Johnson, wishing this was all over, 'it's the exact anniversary of his disappearance and it all ties in. The Chief thinks we ought to make something big of it, you know: colour, history, poignancy, atmosphere...'

'And lots and lots of nice fog,' said the hidden voice.

'The anniversary date's important. I need the piece tonight. Next week won't do.'

'Yes, I can see that,' she said.

'And it's for the Chairman.'

For a moment longer Angela and Johnson stared at each other. Triumphantly she thought, he's not only fat, he's losing his hair.

'Well?' He asked with edge.

'I'll need to do some homework on it before I go,' she said abruptly and turned back to her screen to begin saving.

Having secured her agreement, there was still something about the neat, hunched back that accelerated Johnson's irritation. If he could, he'd get rid of her tomorrow. The catch was that she was the only top-class writer on the staff and they all knew it: her latest series was up for an award. He stared meanly at the neck with its frieze of golden curls. 'Get the full briefing and if it's too dark when you get there we'll make up some pics from the library.'

'Think about it, Angie and be careful,' warned the hidden Peggy as if Johnson didn't exist. 'It won't just be dark, it'll be black and you'll be on your own...'

'She already has thought about it,' snapped Johnson with brutal intuition. 'She knows that a good piece will endear her to our Lord and Master. To hell with the weather and to hell with the darkness. She's already calculated that if the article is good enough she might soon be moving on to a job in London.' Provoked further by Angela's obvious indifference to his words, he minced, 'Oh, yes, Onwards and Upwards. Oh dear, oh dear, oh dear, I do believe she sees a ticket to fame and fortune.'

'Bugger off, Gordon darling,' said Angela calmly. 'Go back to your mother.' She cleared from her desk both the recorder and her notebook. 'I'll draft it in my car and phone the story in.'

'Wow! Just listen to that!' Peggy giggled her support and, behind her desk, waved a plump arm in triumph. 'Hurrah for the Proletariat!'

'Thank you Angela,' said Johnson with bitter politeness. He chewed and watched before adding flatly: 'I knew we could count on you... for everything... and a bit more.' But as Angela left the room he looked hard at her thinking, 'Just give me one bad article or make one false move... Just one – and you're going to get the boot. You may be good but you're a permanent pain.'

When the door closed behind Angela, Peggy was there to receive his vengeance, 'I want the Xmas schedules in before you go tonight.'

'Yes, Gordon,' said Peggy, dutiful again.

Minutes later, Angela was in the cloakroom when from behind came the recognisable tap-tap-tap of high heels. Peggy's high heeled shoes on her fat legs did not suit her, but then neither did the coarse knitted cover-all which coated her in purple from her knuckles to her waist. Peggy was addicted to large, round, designer reading glasses in bright colours. Such glasses had the unfortunate effect of emphasising her mouth – open at all times as if awaiting information that might excuse a dramatic, 'No!' or 'Really!' Or the truly excited combination of, 'No… Ree-ally!' In fact, Peggy's character and lifestyle were as different from Angela's unfussiness and self-possession as one could imagine.

And again, in work, Peggy's was mostly pedestrian with an occasional flash of quality, whereas Angela invariably set – and achieved – a high standard.

From this one might imagine there could be jealousy but there was none: love flowed from Peggy in a torrent, splashing recklessly in all directions and encompassing dogs, cats, plants, children, men – lots of men – and even inanimate objects like her broken-spouted brown teapot.

'Angie!'

'Yes, Peg?'

'You will think again as to whether to take this job, won't you? I mean, don't go. Make some excuse, have a burglary at your flat or something…'

'Why?' Angela adjusted her hat and tucked her curls away.

'Because it's…well, think of it – it's almost dangerous.' Peggy wondered how far to go, 'You won't get back until nearly midnight and that's dangerous.'

'It won't be dangerous. I'll be in my car and on roads all the time.' At the sight of Peggy's anxious face in the mirror, Angela smiled kindly. 'You really mustn't worry over me.'

'But I dooo!'

Although Angela was nearly thirty, Peggy regarded her like a mother regards a brilliant but heedless child. 'Gordon is a pig!' she blurted out, angrily. 'He's so unreasonable.'

In the act of tightening the belt of her coat, Angela stopped. 'He's got the Chairman riding on his back so he takes it out on me, that's all. So please don't think of him because I really don't give a damn.' She swung herself each way to check her collar was straight. 'Do you like my coat?'

'Beautiful.' Said Peggy. 'How much?'

'Got it cheap. Second hand from one of the models. A hundred pounds. Cash.'

'You were lucky, you gotta bargain.' Peggy fondled the big chain of wooden beads around her neck while she watched: she recognised stubbornness and saw from the tilt of Angela's chin that nothing would change. 'Just promise me, promise me now… promise you won't give anyone a lift in the dark.'

'I promise, but I'll be fine.'

'Haven't you a boy friend who might go along with you?' For Peggy, a man could always fix things or provide a solution, even if it meant bed first.

'I don't have a current boy friend. I've got Chatsworth, my Siamese cat and he's enough trouble.

'Why not a boy friend? Oh Ange! Don't tell me you go to that club, what's it called – The Lilac Tree?'

Angela laughed and turned away. ' Peggy, I'm old fashioned, not a les! I've told you before that I like sensible older men and they're mostly married – the good ones, anyway. Now, do stop worrying – you worry far too much but what I will do is to call you on my mobile when things get sorted.'

'I'm going up straight away to complain to Gordon. I think it's disgusting!'

'You do that – it'll give him something else to think about.' And with that, Angela blew a kiss with her finger tips and walked out of the building.

The research took her longer than she'd expected. Still, with luck she might have been through Cambridge by three, but the Christmas traffic had been horrendous. It was four and getting dark before she drove away from the city towards Ely. A competent driver who loved her small coupe, Angela was unperturbed by the weather, even when the first trails of mist curled across the road, suggesting worse to come. Besides, the story of the missing aircrew, fleshed out by a discussion with Brenda who ran archives, intrigued her.

The pilot had been Mike Foster, one of the few pilots by then remaining who had survived three tours of wartime bombing sorties over Germany. He had been highly decorated, skilled and experienced. However he had taken off with his crew on December 22nd, 1943 and simply disappeared. This was not an exceptional case but generally some other aircrew were witnesses to such a loss or a radio message gave some clue. Experienced or not, this time there had been nothing.

She sensed a story must be there if it could be unearthed after all these years.

At Ely she stopped for fuel. Did they know, or had they ever heard of an old airfield called Warnford Hall? There was a shake of a head. The A10, then? 'Straight on, then right at the roundabout... where you be goin' Miss?'

Angela consulted her notes. 'Somewhere north-east of Littleport.'

'Are you now?' The petrol attendant thought hard. In his slow country voice he churred. 'Wouldn't advise it on a night like this. No, that I would not.'

But she had already the feeling of excitement she got when on the trail of a good story and nothing could put her off. 'Well, thanks anyway.' She paid on a card and drove on regretting, but not being alarmed, when the City lights ended and the mist began to draw down. After all: this was the A10 and if you took care you were perfectly safe.

At Littleport she almost missed the turning off the A10 for Upwell but recovered and took the new road. There had to be some old sign soon for the airfield, surely? But it was difficult to see. The mist had turned to fog and was getting worse. She

70

tried headlights but decided that it was better dipped, wishing she had noted the milometer when at Littleport – it was extraordinary how hard it was to judge distance under these conditions.

More time passed by, there no traffic whatsoever, and with no horizon a feeling of disorientation began. She stared ahead, refusing to be distracted by the car instruments. The fog was so wet it needed windscreen wipers. Cautiously she reached and put on a disk, not choosing which but glad it was the Debussy – it eased the feeling of isolation. It did not matter what the weather was like: just drive slowly she told herself.

A few minutes later – ten, twenty, who could judge? – and out of the murk a glimmer of light began to appear. Finding it came from the window of a cottage, in fact from one of a pair of cottages, she pulled off the road and stopped. This was as good as anywhere to ask the way to the airfield.

A straggle-haired and suspicious woman answered her knock. She had support in the shape of a stocky and partly bald husband who appeared at her shoulder. Only after Angela had explained her purpose and need for information was the door opened fully. At that point the man, open-shirted to display dark chest hair, stepped forward and cleared his throat, 'Yes, of course, young lady we can help…' Becoming aware at such presumption in front of his wife, his voice faded and he tugged nervously on his braces. He turned for guidance. 'Clara?'

'I don't know of any airfield,' grumbled the woman, looking beyond Angela into the fog as if in search of something threatening. 'No airfield out there as I knows of.'

For a moment there was silence through which came the sound of a distant television. At the sound the man jerked out as if embarrassed: 'See, we were only watching the news…'

'I'm very sorry to disturb you…'

'It was over, Miss, just someone reporting on the Christmas shopping – as if we cared out here.'

'We don't know about the airfield,' snapped the woman and made to close the door.

'Yes you do, Clara,' corrected her husband, bravely, putting a restraining hand on the door. Course you do.' He moved closer to his wife to murmur. 'She means that funny ancient wartime place that Jim Baynes uses.'

'I knows nothing about it.' But at this treacherous exposure the woman raised her voice by way of justification. 'An if there is an' I did, nobody goes there anyhow – 'fact it ain't no use to anyone except Baynes an' he ain't no use to anyone either.'

However the husband had taken an immediate liking for the girl with the pretty scarf covering curly blond hair and especially for the bright, honest look, 'You got to invite the lady in, Clara. Ain't hospitable to leave her out there in the cold. Come in, Miss.' He stood aside to make more room.

'Thank you.' But Angela only moved inches and stood inside with her back to the door. Clearly the woman was reluctant for her to enter and so, for that matter was she. If asked to sit down and offered kindly refreshment she knew how hard it would be to return to the car and plunge again into the night.

'I don't have anything to say about the Baynes's. They're a shabby lot an' always have been. You come from Cambridge first 'all? Best you turn round this very minute and find your way back as far as Ely before the fog gets worse,' said the woman decisively.

'I've a job to do.'

Seeing the face in front of her, bitter from work, grow tighter, Angela reacted with some belligerence of her own. 'And I don't give up easily.'

'Huh,' said the woman, not in the mood to give an inch. 'That's up to you.'

The man filled the silence with a weak, 'If we can be of help…'

His wife spun on him to snap, 'In this fog? Don't be daft, George'

'Well, no… but if I could explain,' began the man, taking to rubbing the stubble on his chin as he put some thoughts together.

'I'd be grateful for any information…'

'- Huh,' repeated the woman, scowling, 'waste of time talking to some people.' Nudging her husband to agree she demanded: 'Tell her, George: ain't it ridiculous, out on a night like this?'

Uncomfortable about the turn of conversation, the man went back to tugging at his braces and saying, helplessly, 'Well, if you say so, Clara, it do seem a bit mad…'

'Not a bit: completely mad, I'd say. At this time o'night?'

'But I've come all this way and it must be so very close,' said Angela gently. 'My paper's got a time deadline. Besides, I don't want to have to come back tomorrow or I've lost the weekend.'

'You're too close for comfort, that I can tell you!' The woman laughed unpleasantly. 'Well, if you must, George can explain – if he wants to.' And with this the woman turned and pushed past a curtain to some inner part of the house, breaking her stride only to throw away waspishly: 'Only best you get somethin' straight: just don't say I didn't warn you, that's all.'

Angela was left to smile at the man and give a shrug of apology. 'I seem to have upset your wife, I'm sorry.'

The man moved a step closer and lowered his voice. 'Don't let it worry you, Miss. Clara's a bit psychic: her mother was a Wise Woman but she fell out with one of the Baynes family. In these parts it all gets passed on. Clara suffered. And grudges...' He shrugged apologetically. 'Our doctor once told me that people came to see her grandmother with problems you'd never believe. Y'see, Miss, Knowing runs in the family, it even scares me, sometimes.'

'But why should it worry her?'

'See here...' Bending forward, the man put a finger to his lips to indicate an intimate silence. He whispered, 'In all, they say six hundred and twenty young men took off from that airfield over the last three years of the war and never returned. Some got identified but over two hundred got lost, killed, blown to pieces, who knows? They just went. Vanished. Like throwing stones into the sea. Gravestones and monuments? Don't make me laugh. How can you have a gravestone for someone who isn't there? Clara says that she feels the land tells her of a great emptiness. She says there's a coldness there that ain't natural and she tries to forget it. She won't go there.' He stopped to consider whether he should say more but only added, 'T'were only a temporary place even then: all there is now is the old building they once called a control tower where Baynes keeps his fertiliser. Rest is all dug up.'

'Surely there must be somebody else who knows the story?'

'Baynes will know, they do say his mother had something to do with the flying. Bit of a scandal I shouldn't wonder: airmen, women, you can guess.' George stood back, showed his authority by flicking his braces importantly and said with sudden loudness. 'Now then: all you've got to do to find Baynes is to drive on about two mile and you'll see a five barred steel gate. Go through that and you'll come across Baynes and his daughter: it's called Greenfield Farm.'

Angela smiled. 'I understand... and thank you very much... two miles, you say?'

'May be less. Say, mile'n half. My dad's old pair a' horses, Star and Garter, knew every step: Dad would have called it sixteen furlongs.'

No sooner had the door closed behind her than Angela began to doubt her decision to go further: it was very dark and her torch could only show a few feet beyond her shoes. Yet to go back would take hours and then there was Gordon... The other option – to ask to stay at the cottage she had just left – was distinctly unattractive, given the attitude of the woman, Clara. 'Thank God I had the sense to leave on the sidelights of the car,' she thought, finding that the glow in the darkness allowed her last few steps to quicken.

By now the fog was not just dense, but wet and cold. She could taste it on her lips and it was the taste of smoke or something else, Fen earth, perhaps – or worse. 'Pollution from one of the cottages,' she thought, sliding gratefully into her seat and switching on the engine. She waited a moment to allow the heater to warm the car then peered through the space cleared by the wipers, 'Now, Angela, think of Peggy and drive carefully.'

And she did drive carefully. And, one by one, the furlongs did pass by. But her breath condensed on the windscreen and what with that, and the fog, the visibility became almost zero. It was almost inevitable that a mistake would occur and occur it did so where the road unexpectedly swings right. She never saw the bend at all and drove straight on.

Again, it was a mistake which at the speed she was driving would have had little consequence except that, as frequently happens in this area, there was a big drainage ditch, carved out of black, rich, Fenland earth. The drop was ten feet. At the slow speed she was travelling, the car fell almost vertically down, finding, as if selected by fate, an ancient, pollarded willow.

Angela had a momentary vision of a tree stump illuminated in front of her and then one enormous bang followed by the sound of shattered glass.

76

Lights gone and in total darkness she panicked: snatching at her straps, fearing a fire, falling out of the car and then, from raw instinct, clawing her way up and out of the ditch. When the feel of hard tarmac was under her feet, she gulped for air and calmed down sufficiently to walk in a circle crying, more for her car than herself. Slowly, she began to apply reason to her situation. She stopped crying and searched for her mobile, then remembered it was last on the passenger's seat and undoubtedly now lost in the smashed car and darkness.

The earlier moment of panic had passed and she lectured herself firmly: 'I am here on a road, a small road admittedly, but it must lead somewhere. I cannot be far from Bayne's Farm. And anyone passing by would surely give me some help.' All the same it took some moments of dithering, and a conscious mental effort of discipline, to leave the wrecked car and start walking.

The problem was that it was so very wet and dark. And it came to her eventually that, after the warmth of the car, it was cold, very cold. Cold enough to know the air had come from the North Sea, cold enough to chill her wet face, to condense and then add from time to time with tears of self-pity.

Trying to keep warm she walked briskly but there was something in the utter silence of the night to unnerve anybody. Her footsteps sounded curiously unreal and not her footsteps at all, yet they always stopped when she stopped. So they had to be hers – didn't they? 'Please speak if you're there,' she called out. 'Please…'

But there were no sounds and no lights, only silence, wetness and cold – a bitter cold.

She trudged on, feeling she was getting nowhere and with only the white marking in the centre of the road to offer some help and to give faint confidence. Time passed, discomfort turned to misery, with tiredness added. Also, she became aware that her shoes had started to leak. Doubts circled her like hungry wolves, she felt herself shrinking with cold. With those doubts came more self pity. Why had this happened to her and was there to be no end to this road? 'Please, please don't say I've missed a turning.'

A foreboding wrapped itself around her shoulders like a weighty cloak: she was lost.

The sound, when it reached her, was at first far away and very strange. Some kind of motor but unlike any motor on the road she could recall. The sound had a whining, grating quality, as if the gears were worn and the driver was unable to change gear. 'Rerr, err, err' the sound ground on, rising and lowering but she had to wait an appreciable time before lights appeared.

Then again, the lights were of a kind she'd never seen before – hooded and slatted so that only a narrow shaft of light splayed back and forth across the wet tarmac as the vehicle progressed like a drunk with two torches. The vehicle travelled so slowly that there was no need to stand in the middle of the road to make it stop. When it did so, engine throbbing loudly, it resembled a mysterious and panting animal, happy to be halted. And it was big and metallic and painted in dark colours – a huge and mysterious blob of metal that only at the last moment could she recognised to be some sort of ancient bus, dimly lit inside.

Her teeth were chattering with cold yet she did not make a move. She felt a paralysis come over her, a great reluctance to do anything. She was powerless to make a decision, quite unable to step forward or to step back, or to call out, to wait, to wave or to retreat.

Suddenly the door slammed open with the tinny sound of poor metal operating on even poorer brackets. Someone with a North Country accent shouted out loudly, 'Aye, it's her – an about time, too.' A figure, barely distinguishable as a man in the poor light, beckoned quickly, 'Come on board quick, Miss, we're late already.'

She hesitated.

'Do hurry up,' the man repeated, 'Come on, Miss.'

Just visible were more faces at the windows but, in the end, it was the very ordinariness and cheerfulness of the man's voice that seemed to propel her forward. She was aware of a smile of welcome and of more grinning faces looking at her as a strong hand grabbed her shoulder and helped her to climb the two steep steps into the bus.

In the immediate burst of talking, someone with an affected accent said, 'Why hell-lo!' And a hard, practical voice growled out, 'Well, at least you're an improvement on the last bloody reporter that turned up.' Swamped by greetings, Angela was only aware of the dozen or so men scattered over the seats, most wearing yellow waistcoats with huge collars, some in leather jackets and caps and one so buried in kit and clothing that it was difficult to make out a face at all.

The door was slammed. 'If you can find where the engine is, let's go, Jane!'

The driver, a girl, young and in uniform, looked about to see if everyone was all right. 'You can always walk if you want,' she said to him before calling out to the whole bus: 'I don't need any more advice, just hold tight.' She turned to stare at the windscreen and into the darkness beyond, her left hand feeling for the knob on the gear lever.

'Who do we hold tight to, Sweetpea?' A voice called out above the laughter. But by now the girl had begun working the gears in a way suggesting the whole business of changing gears with a crash box was beyond her capabilities. The engine howled resentment, the bus jerked forward, everyone swayed and rocked. With gears screaming, laughter and cheers filled the bus. A face leaned over to the driver to say with deep seriousness: 'Have a care, darlin' – you want me to give you a hand to help feel your way around?'

The girl kept staring ahead and did not bother to look to see who it was. 'You'll feel my hand around your clock soon, you cocky bugger.'

'But, Darlin!' And I always thought you loved me...'

For Angela, just seeing the girl at work gave her more assurance. As the bus swayed, she grabbed a bar supporting a seat and hung on. 'Where are we going?'

'Why, Miss – to the airfield of course! Skipper and Spanners are already there checking the engines.'

'I don't understand…'

'You're the reporter aren't you, the one sent to go with us?'

'I'm a reporter and someone was to meet me but I'm here to write an article and – '

'Look,' interrupted a firm voice by her side. 'In this old Bedford it's difficult to stand. I know that for a fact. Come and sit down, we haven't far to go.' A hand reached up and pulled her down. The seats were of hard, shapeless and unforgiving leather.

'My word but you're looking cold. Tell you what, take my jacket.' The man half stood and slid out of his leather jacket to drape it over her shoulders. The wool lining was warm and incredibly comforting: she immediately felt better.

'My name's Nicholas but my mates call me Nick. I'm the navigator.'

Angela looked into the man's face for the first time. His brown eyes held friendliness and wryness, understanding and somewhere, behind it all, a worldly tolerance. A shaft of instant realisation came and went, leaving her breathless. The bus and all the others went from her mind. She knew. Nothing needed to be said, nothing else need happen: she knew! And by the flick of his eyes, she recognised he knew too. 'Oh, my God,' the thought made her tremble, 'this is my man! I know it and he knows it and of all places for it to happen: I'm sitting next to him in this awful bus!'

He said, hurriedly, 'You should never be out on a night like this, Miss.'

'Angela, please call me Angela.'

Angela!' picked up someone in the seat behind and shouted, 'Heh, fellers, we've got an Angel with us tonight, can't go wrong this trip!'

'Don't take any notice of Charlie, he's our tail gunner: he's never had either nerves or brains.'

But she didn't care about Charlie, or the Skipper, or the rest, or what was happening. She snuggled deeper into his jacket and, knowing it didn't matter a thing to her anymore, murmured up to him, 'Where are you taking me?

'Out to our Kite. But you're not dressed for a flight, err, Miss.'

'Please! I don't want you to call me Miss. Call me what you want, but not Miss.'

'It's dangerous for everybody if we get distracted when we're on a mission. Agreed, Charlie?' In a lowered voice he said confidentially to her ear, 'You're... if you don't mind me saying so, so beautiful you would distract anybody.'

In an extraordinary way, his presence seemed to fill the bus. 'Call me what you want, it's all the same to me.'

Men were talking but their words were indistinguishable above the din of the engine.

'Our rules are that I should keep calling you Miss,' he said. 'And Miss –'

'Yes, Nick?'

'Clothes. Dressed like that you're going to bloody freeze. We'll have to club together to kit you out once we're on board.'

'This it?' shouted the girl driving above the noise of the engine.

'This'll do us –M for Mike. If it isn't our kite we may as well go on to a pub.'

'Stop!' Someone shouted and stood up. The bus abruptly obeyed and, in the dim light, six men struggled out of the narrow door laden with kit. All the time the pungent smell of hot oil came smoking out of the oval-shaped gear box cover.

'Ours next,' murmured Nick. 'See you all for breakfast,' he shouted after the men leaving. No one, in the effort to get their kit out, had time to reply.

The bus lurched forward again. Condensation ran down windows, the smell of cigarettes was oppressive. 'We're next – this is the Lancs line.'

He had said it with significance. She felt obliged to ask, 'Lancs line?'

'We're on Lancs, Miss. On the north side it's all Halibags. Make a note for your report: they're due to be re-equipped next month with Lancasters like ours.'

The bus stopped. He smiled at her in encouragement, 'There she is – Old Teddy Bear.' And this time everyone tumbled out, saying little. She felt his hands lower her down the stairs and she stood looking up at a huge black shape. What was happening to her? Was this real or a dream? Did she care? No, she didn't care: she had him. And he joined her, 'Come on, this way. Hurry, we're late.'

Torches were waved. Orders were shouted. Figures scurried in the gloom. A short ladder appeared. Something told her not to move but he was there. If he was there she had no fear. He said, 'I'll climb up and then give you a hand.'

An engine coughed, whined, coughed again before starting. The aircraft started to vibrate. Cold air tugged at her skirt. 'Whatever you want, Nick, but what -'

'There's no time to talk, we're late already. Come,' he said, bending down from the aircraft and beckoning. 'You're safe with me –'

'Contact port inner!' And any doubts or questions were swept away as a second engine started. Rather than consciously having to climb, she felt herself whisked up the ladder until she was inside the shaking aircraft. A few lights lit the cramped space. She was thrust past a man working radio dials and through a bulkhead doorway to stare at a fire extinguisher and an axe surrounded by coloured wiring, sockets and plastic signs saying in red, emergency. Nick was already unloading his bag of maps and equipment on to a small table attached to the side of the aircraft. 'Sit on the jump seat, Miss. Put on these overalls and then these socks over your shoes. Welcome to my empire: this is my chart table, see? A few instruments... two hot flasks of coffee, a pen, notebook and what brains I have to get us there.'

All the engines were running now and the shaking had reduced to a steady vibration. She watched him put on a tight leather helmet and plug in a lead. 'Hello, Skipper. All aboard and OK.' There must have been a reply because she saw his eyes look at her, change and crinkle with humour. 'She's here with me. Her name's Angela, and don't try and get your hands on her: navigator's perks.' More words must have been spoken for Nick took her by the arm. 'Go forward and say hello to the Skipper.'

On the other side of the bulkhead she found the captain already at the controls, his face partly lit by the ultraviolet lighting and luminous instruments. A quick glance was all she received. 'My name's Mike. Sorry to be in a hurry, glad to have you on board, but we have to get into line.' His hand pushed the throttles. The aircraft began to move. 'Look to your right: there's a fold-down seat.' His hands were never still: moving levers, adjusting knobs, clicking switches. He glanced at her again. 'The fog has held everybody up and we have to get airborne in turn.'

'Where are we going?'

'Hamburg.'

Hamburg...? Was she in some warp of time? But this pilot beside her was very real – she could even see he'd cut his top lip shaving. He looked at her and half-shouted, 'There's a spare helmet above you. Put it on.'

With the helmet on, suddenly the noise of engines almost disappeared and words were clear. The captain had a quiet, precise voice. 'If you want to speak you turn the switch on your mask but remember: only when you want to speak, otherwise it has to be switched off. That's very important – take it as an order.'

Looking ahead, she could make out in the darkness the tail of an aircraft in front of them: they were in a crocodile line of similar aircraft. Through the earphones she heard, 'Check in everyone.' She heard names but recognised only one, Nick's, who said: 'Diversions for us are Driffield and Manston, Skipper. 'We're not expected back here with this fog.'

'I'll take Driffield every time, Nick: at least they have a good Mess and a decent bed: Manston is the pits.'

She stared ahead, trying to make sense of what she'd been told: the reality was that she tasted the rubber of a mask over her face and that a Lancaster bomber was only twenty feet in front of them. Both aircraft rolled forward in the fog at the same slow walking pace as in a dream.

'At the end of the runway there's a wooden hut on wheels, we call it the caravan. We have to wait there until we get a green to move onto the runway.'

Someone appeared alongside the captain and lifted the edge of her helmet to explain in her ear, 'The girls wait at the caravan to wave us off.'

'Even on a night like this?'

'Sure, it's an early sortie.'

'Kipper,' said the captain, 'dig out the Aldis: I want to see if Sylvia is there.'

'OK, Skipper.'

Someone identified as Kipper produced a large round torch affair on an electric lead. 'Here, Miss, you can press this and direct the light at the caravan. I have to get back to my radios.'

Following a waved direction from the captain, Angela aimed the light and pressed the switch. A shaft of brilliant light cut through the darkness to light up four or five women in uniforms. 'Go left a bit.' She moved the light left. Suddenly revealed was a solitary woman, her pale face ghostly in the fog. The woman half raised an arm in a tentative wave, then, as if suddenly recognising the aircraft, waved a handkerchief vigorously.

'That's Sylvia,' said the captain, quietly. He raised a hand in acknowledgement to the pale face with its open mouth. 'I doubt if she can see me but she will know.'

Angela was only inches away from him, guiding the light. 'Is she your girl?'

'I'd say she's not just a girl, more my life.'

From the doorway of the caravan a green light shone.' That's us.' The captain's hands eased open two throttles and the aircraft moved forward again. 'Best you sit on that seat, Miss. Use the straps. Mind you, we're carrying fourteen thousand pounds of high explosives: straps won't make much difference if this crate doesn't make it into the air. ' He looked at her briefly. 'Scared?'

'Yes I am.'

'So's everyone. Here.' He reached up, drew down from behind the front turret hydraulic pipe a teddy bear and passed it to her. 'Billy the bear. It's our mascot, my crew and I have flown with Billy for the last fifty three sorties. Hang on to this and don't let it go – it'll bring you luck.' He switched on his mike, 'Everyone. OK? Spanners: OK with you?'

'All clear to go, Skip.'

'Let's go.' The Lancaster lurched forward with a roar of engine power. 'Hold tight, everyone…. Hamburg here we come… again.'

Staring ahead, hardly conscious of what was happening from fright, she barely noticed guttering gooseneck runway lights start to pass by at an ever-increasing rate. The lights inside the cockpit shook, instruments blurred, something fell over – a flask, it rolled by her and she put a foot on it.

'Revs OK,' called out the engineer. 'Going through the gate. Eighty, ninety…'

'Roger Dodger.' It was a voice that made it sound blasé. 'Tail up.'

She could see straight ahead, the white centre line of the runway, a few more lights and then nothing: they were entering a world of total blackness and destruction. The speed got faster and faster, she squeezed the teddy bear tighter with one hand, hung on to a strap with the other and held back a scream.

'Airborne.' All the vibration abruptly stopped. 'Wheels.'

'A thousand feet....'

'Nineteen twenty six.' It was Nick's voice. First course: one-o-five.'

'One-o-five, Roger. Flaps going up. Good-oh! Relax. Sort yourselves out, everyone. Back to climbing revs Spanner and thanks.'

At that moment the world changed: the blackness ended and they were in bright moonlight, light made brighter still by the contrast with before, and by the reflected light from a vast sea of whiteness.

Even to someone used to the experience, such a natural sight causes a silence of respect.

'Blimey, that bloody fog was thin,' said someone, eventually.

'Worst of all worlds,' said a gloomy voice. 'Fog below and we'll get picked up by Jerry fighters from miles away.'

'Don't start a flap – we've got an angel with us remember.'

For Angela it was as if waking from a dream. The cockpit was as clear as if they were in daylight. But the put-off desire to escape could not be resisted any longer. 'I'd like to be with the navigator, if you don't mind.'

'Sure, unplug yourself and go aft. Nick will look after you and you can write your notes easier.'

In the cramped navigator's cabin, Nick looked up from his chart. 'Having fun?' He stabbed a finger at a spot on a line. 'Look, this is where we are right now.' She let him explain. He was talking about things called Gee and Oboe but all she watched was the way his lips tweaked in concentration as he manipulated a dial and made notes.

Suddenly she felt tired. 'I'll just sit and watch.' Nick had his helmet loose and could talk. He stopped to look sideways at her. 'Was Sylvia at the caravan?'

The question carried an unspoken seriousness. 'Yes, at least that's who the captain said it was.'

'Bad news. It's the first time the skipper's been knocked out by any girl and it causes concern.'

'Why should it?'

'Remember what I said, Miss? We have stayed alive by the whole team being one hundred per cent on the ball. No diversions while you're on the job. Suddenly the skipper's losing concentration, that's what worries us.'

'Six thousand feet. Time to go over to oxygen. Check in and confirm, everyone.'

'Roger, Skip.'

Nick got up to help her with her mask and to plug it in to the reserve oxygen point. 'We will be on oxygen all the way, now. No more chatting except on the radio.'

She did not care. All she wanted to do was to watch him at work. His face, part lit by ultraviolet lights, looked as sharp in outline as a painting by Edward Hopper, yet the mysterious background of pipes and colours reminded her of some of Munch's work. She felt the teddy bear she gripped so tightly and raised it to her lips, 'Nicholas,' she whispered, 'I shall call you Nicholas from now on.'

The radio in her ear startled her. 'Make sure you take us well south of Borkum Island, Nick. That's a nest of vipers – flack and night fighters.'

'OK, Skip. Come right five degrees.' Above the chart desk, she watched Nick clicked a stop watch and take a note.

Time passed. After the gunners woke her testing their guns it was hard to pretend keeping awake. It became monotonous. The steady tone of the engines mingled with endless technical chatter over the radio blurred her mind. Dreamily she murmured to herself,' Nick can navigate us through life while I do my writing.' She fell asleep.

If the lurch didn't wake her, the violent rush of icy air certainly did. Someone shouted, 'Christ, Skip! That's another Lanc!'

Immediately the radio became confused with shouting

'We've lost part of our starboard wing!'

'Give me more power on the starboard outer.'

'Did you see who we collided with?'

'Outer tank's punctured.'

'Fuel's igniting…'

'I'm using the fire extinguishers…

'Jeezus, just look at that flame!'

In seconds the aircraft was slowly tilting, Angela could feel it and had to hold on. Nick stood and braced himself. 'Here, clip on this parachute.'

'Sorry chaps,' it was again the captain's voice, calm but trembling with effort. 'I don't think I can hold her – something seems jammed and we're going over. …Good luck everyone. Quick now, don't hang about – Out, Out, Out!'

She felt herself dragged and man-handled to an opening where the wind howled past, icy cold. 'Jump!' ordered Nick, 'No time to wait.'

But she could not do it: her arms were rigid with resistance. He grabbed her shoulder and wrenched off his mask to shout, 'Hold my hand, we'll go together.'

She looked at him in the eyes.

'Now!'

And they jumped as one.

There was not the slightest chance of holding the meeting at the offices – everybody wanted to be there, from taxi drivers to part-time reporters to those who only rated as friends. This was not just news, this was their own news – one of them had died, and not just died but died tragically. Johnson had arranged the back room of the Golden Goose and even that was packed. He led Peggy Frobisher to the makeshift platform.

'This is the definitive news you've been waiting for, no more guesses or rumours please. And no more gossip either – you're about to hear the official answer. Miss Frobisher has just returned from the Coroner's Court and she will tell you what happened as briefly as possible.

Peggy said hesitantly, 'There's not a lot that you don't know or guessed already –'

'Speak up, Pegs, we can't hear you.'

She gulped down her nerves and misery. 'The Coroner said Angie died of a combination of shock and hyperthermia, that's all.'

'Now note all that everyone: that was all – shock and hyperthermia. So you see, it wasn't drugs and it wasn't alcohol. It was a simple car accident.' Johnson took the opportunity to make the point and he made it loudly: 'The sort of thing that could happen to anybody.'

'Not a bad accident, there wasn't a mark on her,' continued Peggy Frobisher, 'Not a mark. She was...' Peggy's voice stopped for a moment. '...She was beautiful, she was always beautiful. But it was really the cold. The pathologist said he couldn't judge whether it was the shock of the accident or the cold but that it was more likely to have been the cold. She'd walked about two miles and wasn't found for thirty hours because of the fog.'

In a burst of murmurs, a girl sobbed aloud. 'Poor thing, all alone in the cold. She shouldn't have gone.'

'Yes,' agreed a man, 'Poor kid. And why? She shouldn't have happened at all, she shouldn't have been out on a night like that...'

Peering into the room, Johnson tried to see who said it but failed. 'Angela was a serious reporter,' he said. 'She knew the risk but she went ahead because that was her job.' He turned to Peggy. 'Anything more to add?

'Well, the Court was all quiet an' then another woman came in and immediately a woman from –' Peggy consulted her notes, 'No.2 Fen Dyke Cottages, got to her feet and accused this new woman, saying: 'None of this would have happened if your mother hadn't been a loose-minded good-for-nothing bitch.' That was when the row started with these two women having a slanging match.'

Encouraged by hearing some laughter, Johnson smiled benignly. 'It happens.' He nudged Peggy's arm. 'When you're writing the report, be careful how you phrase that bit, Peggy.' He changed his voice again. 'So what happened then?'

'The Coroner had the two women removed. He said he would not tolerate a personal vendetta in his Court of Law.'

Nodding his approval, Johnson summed up, 'I think it was an unfortunate set of circumstances, that's all. Now, I'm sure that Angela would approve if I say, "let's go and have a drink to her memory at the firm's expense".'

As everyone began heading for the bar, Johnson caught Peggy Frobisher by the arm. 'We need to talk about the obit. What was that you said about a teddy bear earlier?

'Only that the ambulance man told me that Angie was holding a teddy bear so tightly that they could only release it by cutting its leg off.'

He frowned. 'Let's go to my office.'

Inside his office he sat back in his swivel-chair, leaving Peggy standing but clutching her huge knitted handbag defensively. He said, 'It does not sound like her. She wasn't superstitious was she?'

'Not as far as I know.'

'Never seen her with a teddy bear?'

Peggy's mouth sagged further. 'None of us have.'

God! Peggy looks awful, Johnson thought. She looks as if she been black-eyed by someone. He tried a brief smile to encourage her. 'Best forget the teddy bear,' he said, judgementally. 'Wouldn't do to give the public the wrong impression.'

'But that's the human angle! Can't leave that detail out!'

He balanced ideas and took his time. 'No, I don't want it put in. Just say we all loved her.'

She felt exhausted and sat down heavily. 'Well, we all know you bloody didn't!'

He scowled at Peggy's honesty. 'Perhaps we had our differences – but I respected her as a professional. She had a great future to look forward to with us.'

'Damned liar,' she thought and took a deep breath. 'Gordon, if the bear meant so much to Angie that she held it when she died, then it deserves a mention in the obit. It was her life, not the bloody newspaper's.'

The weariness coming from having to make so many delicate decisions made him drop further in his seat until replaced by more irritation at being challenged. For Crissakes, again! Didn't he have enough problems?

Peggy watched his change. He was working himself up into a rage. She knew her Gordon – hadn't she worked for him for five years? Indifferently she listened without looking and waited for it to happen. 'Listen,' he snarled, 'and get this straight: a successful newspaper supplies honest news but it never goes directly against the prejudices of its reading public. What do the public think? They think all reporters are scum and hard as nails. You want tell them that ours are beautiful women going around trailing teddy bears? Don't be bloody stupid! First they doubt you honesty, secondly they take us for a bunch of wets. Clear off and write the obit. Say what a star we've lost: literate, intelligent, brilliant future... lay it on with a trowel. Above all: forget the teddy bear.'

He paused, he could only see the top of her bowed head so added brusquely, 'Got that?' to make sure there were no mistakes.

It wasn't the order, it was the man. The lump that had been in Peggy's throat all day finally overwhelmed her. She began to shake so that words flew from her mouth uncontrolled. 'Gordon, don't you understand anything about life at all? You don't, do you?' Recalling Angela, she began to weep, 'you don't... you don't understand because you can't. Haven't you realised yet that everyone in life needs their own teddy bear?'

'Own teddy bear? What the hell are you talking about?'

The incomprehension in his tone did it: she couldn't help herself. She knew, now, that Gordon had no feelings at all. She blurted out while still sobbing, 'Of course. You fool!'

At the sight of his complete astonishment, and at the depth of her emotions, Peggy ran from the room with huge wet tears mixed with mascara running down her face.

Slumped in his chair, Johnson gazed after her and shook his head in total amazement. 'Bonkers,' he said. 'Completely Bonkers.'

Searching for Mathilde

Out of the tunnel and into the sunshine came the Bordeaux express. At Pont Neuf the driver had eased the main drive to idle so that the train's approach into the Mediterranean station of Narbonne was almost silent. On Quay 4, hearing the warning horn, people stood up; the arrival had been announced five minutes earlier and the platform was full of waiting people and anticipation.

One lady, small, perhaps in her mid-fifties but with dyed hair, remained seated. Dressed in a grey dress but with a defiant, multicoloured neckerchief, her hands twined and untwined as if in apprehension. Around her the noise of humanity swirled like eddies of an ocean current around an insignificant rock.

The wheels of the train juddered to final halt. The crowd hurried into action: bags lifted, children hoisted, coats and jackets stuffed under arms. Finally the doors of coaches automatically swung back but she waited until the crowd had surged forward and left some space.

Only now did she make her way along the platform, passing the coupled engines and blanching at their heat while searching for the chef du train. Time was running out. Panic set in. She caught sight of a man holding a young boy by the shoulder and hurried towards him, pushing her way through several women occupied in animated greetings. A moment of uncertainty came as she approached the man holding the boy. 'Please...' She began.

'Is he yours?' snapped the official.

The gruff, threatening way it was put, made her find it a difficult question to answer. Had there been some sort of problem? She took the boy's hand defensively. 'It's Robert. He's mine, he's my grandson.' Her attitude was one of someone already expecting some sort of abuse.

But now he could get rid of the responsibility, the chef du train had better things to worry about and said rudely, 'Yes, well he's yours again now, isn't he?' He released his grip with a slight shove and took a step backwards, touching his cap but more as if to confirm it was in place than as a mark of respect. Having disposed of all the uncertainties of a young boy, he felt he could become distant once more. 'I have to explain that you have to sign for children nowadays, Madame. Here, on this form: there. And I have to see your identity. Hurry, we have only two minutes left.'

The formalities completed, and feeling she was being something of a nuisance, she gave him a five euro note as a tip and said 'thank you' twice and was half way down the platform with the boy at her side before she recovered herself. She stopped and kissed the top of his head. 'Did you have a good journey, dear?'

'Train.' The boy said.

'That's right, it's the T.G.V. Did you enjoy it?'

'Big train. Like house.' said the boy strangely.

'Yes, dear.'

They both stopped to watch as the train slowly and relentlessly moved away. It was a long train – twelve coaches – and took some time to clear the station. After it had gone, the rails sang a relief.

A draft of air followed, dust swirled then settled. To those left behind, the world became sadly empty.

The lady sighed at something or other and touched at her hair. She turned back to the boy, 'How is your mother? Is she well?'

She saw his face and corrected herself, 'Did your mother give you a big kiss when she put you on the train, Robert?'

'Mathilde,' he said.

The incomprehensible answer left her with nothing to say for a moment.

'No Mathilde,' he emphasised pugnaciously.

'No dear?' She said gently, 'But how did your mother say goodbye to you?'

By way of answer he thrust his satchel at her. 'Chocolate,' he said. His curiously ugly face suddenly smiled. 'She had nice smells,' and he made the noise of a pig.

The lady sighed again; the same difficulties. Poor Marie-Therese, it must be very hard for her. She said firmly, 'We shall have to get a taxi; Granny can't drive. It'll be a nice start to your holiday.' She might have explained that Georges, the boy's grandfather, would not let her touch his car and that, anyway, she never liked travelling at all, preferring to stay close to home. In fact he had bought her a second hand car but that resided, and would almost certainly permanently reside, under the lime tree at the bottom of the garden. Some things are better left unexplained.

It was a difficult taxi ride. The grandmother chattering, first to the boy, then, when she realised he was only interested in staring out of the window more to herself with the driver occasionally looking at them in the mirror but saying little. 'That's the river, dear,' she said vaguely as they crossed the Herault.

'Boat,' said the boy, staring.

'Exactly. You'll see lots more soon.'

The boy made a strange mooing shout as if to show excitement. Encouraged, the lady went on, 'We have lots of sailing boats, September is a good time of the year and you'll be able to see them; we'll walk down to the sea and count the number.'

'How old is he?' asked the taxi driver, abruptly.

'He's only ten.' But she'd seen the taxi driver's eyes and the coldness of the question made the lady put her arm around the boy.

There came a non-committal grunt from the driver. Eventually and slowly he said, 'The beach is a good place for the likes of him, I suppose.'

'He's better than you might think,' she said sharply to the back of the driver's head. But the remark unsettled her – it was a silent agreement that she only looked after the boy for a fortnight every year. Georges, meanwhile, went every month to Paris for a weekend to help out their daughter though, at the same time, he took the opportunity to meet old business friends.

'They say that all boys benefit from playing in the sea.'

'Yes,' she agreed, thinking that she could do without any more advice from a taxi driver. After that she said nothing more until they arrived at the cottage, two streets back from the sea front.

When Georges had bought the house for them, there had been few other buildings to be seen. Time had changed all that and now the house – rather more a cottage – was almost hidden, sandwiched between many superior villas used only in the holiday season. They still, however, had the advantage of a big garden and Georges took considerable gloomy pleasure in getting valuations and finding how much the lot would fetch if ever they had to sell.

He was waiting for them at the door when the taxi left, a sprightly sixty year old, still handsome as well as agile, with a moustache startling white in comparison with cheeks tanned from sun and sea air. His eyes, bright but sunken and somewhat mysterious, were like signal lights showing caution at the end of a long, black, tunnel. He moved forward with impatience as they came towards him. 'Hello young Robert, you've grown a bit even since I last saw you a month ago,' he said, pushing out his hand. The boy stared back but made no effort to shake hands. Without waiting, Georges glanced towards his wife. 'See what I said? He's going to be big.'

'And strong,' she replied, making hidden signals with her hands and face.

He nodded agreement. 'I know. You don't need to say it. We must be careful.' With one more hard look, he led the way to the house saying loudly; 'Well, it's not much after Paris but you'll just have to make the best of it, like us. We've plenty of things here you can do, and there's always the sand and the beach.'

'Boats,' said the boy loudly and made awkward movements with his arms, 'Find Mathilde.'

'Come on dear,' said his grandmother with sudden briskness, 'I'll find you something nice to eat. You like cake, don't you?'

But Robert only picked up an old sea-shell and looked at it on both sides in wonder as if he'd never seen anything like it before. His grandmother waited, uncertain. Sand blown from the dunes lay in swirls about his feet. Even the air smelt of salt and sand. Still without replying, Robert pushed the shell into his pocket. Then, thrusting his big chin forward, he followed his grandfather into the house.

It was a few days before they had developed a routine of what to do. In the mornings Robert was washed and, after breakfast, looked after by his grandfather if he wasn't working, sometimes playing without co-ordination with a ball, sometimes just in the garden. He particularly liked gardening but tried his grandfather with his clumsiness, often crushing plants happily growing where they were. In the afternoons his grandmother took him for a walk. Once, they went shopping.

It was difficult to get Robert to talk; it was as though a few words interspersed by sounds were all he could manage. The name, 'Mathilde,' came up several times but, because it was never connected to anything or anybody, his grandmother could make nothing of it and Georges only scowled and muttered or shrugged indifference.

On one occasion, alarmed by something on the television, the boy said several words, almost a whole sentence. 'You see,' said his grandmother, excitedly, 'listen to that! One day he'll work out an idea and say a whole sentence and then he'll move forward – you see if I'm not right. He needs lots of encouragement, that's all.'

His grandfather was more pessimistic. 'A boy like him will never speak properly,' he pronounced with finality one night. 'He can't get it together.' It was a statement immediately hotly challenged by his wife, after which the question of Robert's deficiency – or his recovery – was never mentioned again.

Of one thing both were certain: the fish in his grandfather's aquarium fascinated the boy. He would squat for hours, arms around his legs, chewing his lips, watching the fish. He took a delight in feeding them, under instruction, trembling with excitement and tension when measuring the fish food on to a spoon. Again his grandmother felt he was on the point of saying something significant, and she fretted about what more she could do. With some diffidence she approached her husband with an idea.

'I think Robert needs something he could nurse and talk to,' she said. 'He can't talk to the fish, and he knows instinctively we're too old. The gap's too big. We don't interest him enough.'

Georges grunted doubts, but after considering the suggestion said, 'I'll give it some thought, only it can't be a dog because we'll be stuck with it after he's gone.'

'And you're allergic to cats so what can we give him?'

'I'll think about it,' he said again, and went out into the garden. But, dissatisfied with this answer, his wife called again from the doorway, 'You really will think about it, Georges?' Her voice trailed like an old hose pipe all the way past the pine tree.

'I said I would, didn't I?' He shouted back, continuing bad-temperedly down the garden to the old car where he could sit in peace. With the driver's seat pushed back it was an ideal place to put his feet up and smoke a forbidden cigarette.

His wife might have pursued him – she knew all he did was to smoke – but she'd come to terms with the fact that love and a desire to please had long been replaced by dull loyalty and she'd always had that from him if nothing else. He might not have been very successful as a businessman but she'd come to accept, with resignation, that at least she'd got a reliable man.

Two days later he brought home the rabbit.

It was a golden-coloured rabbit, three months old and quite large. Robert adopted it at once with one of his high and peculiar moans of excitement. He stroked it, running his hands over the rabbit's furry back. 'Mathilde,' He said, and to his grandmother's delight, took it into his arms and pressed it against his cheek adding, quite clearly, 'Beautiful like Mathilde.'

106

'You see!' She turned on her husband. 'I was right!'

'Perhaps.' Georges raised his eyebrows to show he was baffled by the whole affair. 'Seems like it, I agree but, anyway, if he insists on giving it a woman's name it's a damned good job I found a doe.' With a quick nervous swipe of his moustache he backed away, watched for a few moments and then, with a final grunt of indifference, left them to it. Perhaps he could now expect some peace.

Most children, after a while, might have tired of having a rabbit, but Robert was different; he wouldn't leave it alone, nursing his rabbit, stroking its ears, crooning – even kissing it with wet lips. 'Love-ly,' and 'beauty,' he would murmur, over and over again, as he cuddled it in his arms.

For a few days his grandmother was delighted but then she realised the rabbit showed signs of distress at such human attention. It was unused to such continual fondling and became listless, hiding in the corner of its hutch whenever left alone. The trouble was Robert wouldn't leave it alone if he happened to be home. He would drag it out to stroke and play with it, giving the creature no peace at all. Eventually, with Robert in bed and the night falling, she discussed the problem with her husband, choosing the moment carefully as she washed carrots and beetroot and he sat on the three-legged stool, stringing onions he'd grown and harvested. 'We've got to think of something we can do to stop him killing the poor thing,' she said.

'Oh... Yes'? George's head stayed bowed to his task, signifying doubt. He took his time to think about the problem. 'I agree. It's true what you say.' He finished whipping a string of ripened onions and looked at his wife, 'You can see it happening as you watch.' And he shrugged helplessness at her. 'Can't stop the boy,' he said positively as he cut a fresh length of twine with his knife. 'We gave it to him; it's his pet, he seems to love the thing.' And he hung up the finished truss with care on a hook before adding irritably, 'But why the devil must he call it Mathilde? I don't like it. It's almost embarrassing; a rabbit with a woman's name. It's not right.'

'He didn't get it from me. There's nobody I know called Mathilde.'

'Ridiculous. It must have come from you.'

'Then perhaps he's invented it.'

'Perhaps he picked it up from Marie-Therese...'

'Yes, he must have heard it somewhere or other. He needs to have his mind moved to something else. He's suffocating that rabbit by fussing over it.'

'There's always television.'

'He can't concentrate on that for more than a few minutes at a time.'

'Well, he can play on his own in the garden.'

But his wife was not to be deflected from her own line of thought. 'I think I'm going to let him go on his own to the beach to play – the weather's fine and almost all the visitors have gone home.' Anticipating her husband's reaction, she added quickly, 'He'll be safe enough – he's frightened of rough waves.'

'It's not just the rough waves, is it? What happens if he drowns himself anyhow? They'll say it was our fault.'

Neither of them spoke any more about it that night. If she said nothing it was because she was shrewd enough to know her husband was mostly concerned about the reaction of their daughter if Robert came to harm. Georges adored Marie-Therese; he always looked forward to his visits to Paris. She'd observed that her husband always returned from Paris in a jolly mood and she encouraged him to go on his trips, glad to avoid his sometimes gloomy moods.

And, privately, Georges had already made his own decision: he quietly left the rabbit's hutch door open before he went to bed, telling himself that no animal should have to suffer unnecessarily.

Next morning, Robert found out that the rabbit was missing as soon as he had finished his breakfast. His noise as he blundered around in the garden searching for the rabbit brought both his grandparents hurrying to find the cause.

His Grandfather took the blame immediately. 'I'm very sorry, Robert, must be my fault. I thought I'd closed the cage door but my sight ain't so good, or I forgot, I'm getting more and more stupid'. But when he saw the boy sitting on the ground in tears he grew angry. Why should he find himself caught between two problems not of his own making? The boy was becoming a dangerous nuisance. 'Oh, let him go off to the beach if you want, for God's sake,' he growled before going back in to the house.

The boy's tears brought a different reaction from his grandmother. 'Let's look for it together,' she said, taking his hand. And as luck would have it they did find it, too exhausted to have gone far and hiding beneath the corner of a sack.

The idea of Robert going to the beach on his own had, however taken root. It was the start of what appeared to be a spell of settled fine weather and there were few visitors left, so the beach and sand dunes were almost deserted. In the afternoon, and with his name and address tagged to the back of his trousers, Robert was taken to the sand-strewn beach road and left there. He was given a satchel with a bottle of water and an apple. 'Explorers always have to carry their rations', his grandmother explained as she gave a final brush to his shirt. Wisely, she had not confused him with too many instructions, confining herself to pointing the way to the path along the dunes and emphasising to come back soon. 'Soon, Robert. Soon. You understand soon, don't you?' Even so, and despite the boy's obvious eagerness, she watched him until he was out of sight.

Released, the boy's heart was filled with indefinable wild joy. He ran for some minutes in his ungainly way; up the first ridge, down the first hollow, and up the other side. That was as far as he'd ever been allowed before. Previously he'd not been allowed out of sight. Now he felt the excitement of entering into a totally new land.

The Mediterranean coast was sandy and undulating; the dunes low and scrub-filled, affording shelter from the wind and unlimited hiding places for summer visitors to picnic, or for lovers to disappear.

As the minutes passed by, Robert's enthusiasm slowly ebbed away, drained from his legs by the hot, soft sand and the seemingly endlessness of it all, hillock after hillock of sand and scrub. He slowed to a walk. Once he sat down before meandering on. He wondered at everything he saw, listened to the distant surge of waves, and pulled at sea-grass. The world had become vast and incomprehensible in its size and emptiness; it was nice but in some way dissatisfying. Without knowing why, or how, the meaninglessness of what he was doing, of why he was there at all, made him feel suddenly afraid; he wanted to go home.

It was then he came on the girls.

They were in the bottom of a hollow in the dunes with a rug, picnic things and bottles of Coke. There were two girls who looked like twins and a slightly older girl with long blonde hair. They were roughly his age, about eight or nine.

'Hello,' said one of the twins seeing him above them on top of the dune.

He gave one of his grunts in return but his eyes did not leave the blonde girl. Her beauty immediately transfixed him. The late summer sun had tanned her face golden and her blue dress matched and emphasised the colour of her eyes.

'Who is he?' asked one of the twins of the other but the blonde girl who was lying down on the rug, just frowned up at him. 'What's your name?' She demanded.

'R-Robert,' he managed, and then just gaped, for this was his Mathilde, he knew it; his own Mathilde, the only one in the world. His ears and mind became closed to anything more that was said, Mathilde...the most beautiful girl in the world. And she was here, in the sand dunes with him.

'We don't want a boy,' said one of the twins to the older girl. 'We don't want a boy,' echoed the other twin. 'And he looks funny,' added the first, shrewdly, 'with that face.'

But the blonde girl felt some of her authority was being taken from her by all this and pushed hard at the nearest twin with her foot. 'We can't play at families alone,' she said. 'We need someone else; any boy will do.' She looked up at Robert, who hadn't moved but simply gaped. 'What can you do? Can you make a fire?'

Such a question was beyond him. 'Mathilde,' he said, and would have tried to talk and explain but the words stuck in his throat.

She waited a moment, and then gave up. 'Anyway, we don't need a fire,' she said impatiently, and turned to one of the twins; 'He can be a postman and bring the letters. Come on.'

It was arranged quickly; Robert was given an empty plastic bottle and told this was an important parcel, one he had to deliver to the post office, which was the beach flagpole. After that he had to come back as fast as he could.

Away he went, climbing the slippery sands of the dunes and running down the other side. All the time his heart sang with happiness; he was working for Mathilde! By the time he'd reached the waste bin by the flagpole he was panting and hot; hot enough to be enticed by the lazy sea swirling back and forth only a few feet away, but he had to return to the girls. All that they said and imagined about their camp in the dunes confused him, but Mathilde had said he was going to be their postman and that was enough. A postman! And Mathilde had touched his hand! He began to run again and would have skipped but he was too awkward for that.

In the camp, one of the twins watched Robert returning. 'What shall we do with him next?'

'Tell him to go away,' grumbled her sister, but the older, blonde girl stopped her, 'I said he was the postman didn't I, silly? We send him back to look for another parcel while we get the food ready for the hunters to arrive.'

'That doesn't make sense!' The twin protested. 'He's just taken it to the post office.'

'Well tell him to go and get a letter then. Tell him we are waiting for a very important message.'

Robert was sent off again; this happened twice more before the girls decided to leave the beach and go home.

'Can... Come with you?' Robert managed to ask, his desperation forcing out the words.

'No.'

'No,' repeated the other twin, the one who'd always disliked him most. 'You've got to go to your own home. Go on.'

But the misery on his face was so obvious the blonde girl relented.

'Look, we shall be here again tomorrow, so if you do come you can be something else.'

'He can't do anything,' said the twin, brutally.

It was a challenge to her authority and the blonde girl snapped, 'Oh yes he can!' without thinking.

'What then? He can't do anything.'

'No,' joined in the quieter twin, 'He can't do anything; he's stupid.'

Robert looked from one to the other, realising there was some kind of crisis but not knowing what he should say or do.

'If he comes tomorrow,' the blonde girl searched her imagination, 'If he comes tomorrow he can be the rubbish man.'

This was such a good idea – there was rubbish from the summer lying everywhere – that to emphasise her cleverness to the twins she turned to Robert with a smile, 'You will come, won't you?'

'Yes,' he said, his mind overwhelmed.

And then the girls left him.

That evening his grandmother tried to find out where he'd been – she'd worried at his time away – but he couldn't explain. How could he? His grandmother realised he was happy and excited but every question came back to 'postman', which didn't make sense at all so she gave up, still puzzled, but content to imagine it must have been a successful afternoon.

The sun shone brightly the next morning, taking away the early haze, revealing some, far-distant coastline, and promising another fine day.

'Looking settled, Mother,' said Georges with satisfaction as he came back from the store with a loaf. 'Robert can help me to sack up potatoes.'

'After that he can go again down to the beach, can't you, Robert? You'd like that, wouldn't you?' And the old lady smiled when she saw Robert jump up and down in that awkward way which she knew meant he was excited by the thought. 'Mathilde,' he said.

'That's right, dear,' she said, blinking away the uncertainty of what he meant.

Watching the problem, the grandfather's irritation returned. 'Why on Earth can't he think of another damned name – or even put a simple sentence together?'

'It's just that, well, he can't. One day I know he'll manage to get it all together and then we will be able to understand what exactly he's thinking. In fact I'm certain of it.'

'I can't wait for that day.'

'No, neither can I.'

To show his frustration, Georges slammed the bread down on the table. 'Well, just tell him to keep away from the sea, that's all.' He tried to rationalise his thoughts. 'I know the sea's calm but Robert's Robert and the sea is… well, you know what I mean. I don't need to spell it out.' To his wife's frown of displeasure he gave a final threatening look and stumped out into the garden to collect his spade.

Later that day, and after lunch of soup and boiled eggs served in homemade wooden egg cups, there came the time when it was the moment to let Robert go. Again his grandmother carefully took him to the start of the beach path and pointed the way. 'And don't be away so long this time.' These were her parting words and she watched him galloping up the slope, satchel banging on his back, so obviously enjoying himself, any qualms she may have felt simply disappeared.

But Robert had a horrible feeling the girls would not be coming, so when he came to the spot and discovered them already down in the hollow he gave a bellow of relief. Not that the girls seemed equally excited and one of the twins said, 'Oh it's you again,' and carried on building the sand farmyard as if he wasn't there.

'Now you're here, you're to clean up the beach because you're to be the man who empties the poubelle,' said the blonde girl with blue eyes. She thrust their empty picnic basket at him. 'Go on, take this.'

Suddenly he was apprehensive. It was so important; he didn't want to make a mistake and upset Mathilde. Panicking, his badly formed larynx forced out his thoughts. 'Which rubbish?'

And then, 'Where...take it?' Only this ended in more of a mooing sound than words.

The blonde girl then looked at him harder. He looked so silly; his shorts were too small for his big fat legs and his queer, flat face carried such a worried expression that, suddenly seeing him, she couldn't help laughing. When she finally stopped, her tone changed and sharpened, 'Listen; you pick up rubbish, you understand? Get all the plastic stuff first and take it down to the flagpole where the bin with all the rest of the rubbish is. Go on. Hurry.' But after he'd disappeared again over the crest of the dune with the basket, she sat down with the others and had a giggling fit.

And so the afternoon passed like yesterday, with Robert toiling back and forwards but happy to be doing work for Mathilde and especially happy when she spoke or laughed at him. But at the end of the afternoon he had a shock. 'We shan't be coming anymore to the beach,' she said. 'All the others are going home to Paris and I'm not coming down here on my own; it's boring.'

'You not coming again?' he asked, and in his bewilderment repeated, 'You not coming again?'

'No. Never. Not until next year.' She contrived a grown up shrug and flicked her long blonde hair with indifference. 'So we shan't see you again.'

He stood looking from one to the other, not able to comprehend what this meant. Did it mean they would be gone for good? It wasn't possible!

'Yes, goodbye', echoed the twins, and they began stuffing sandy feet into worn-out shoes.

He stood, not knowing what to do. 'Tomorrow,' he began helplessly, beginning to feel the onset of fear as he watched the twins, now beginning to pack.

'I'm fed up with the beach everyday and, anyway, I'm not supposed to come down here on my own,' said the girl. She shook sand from her clothes and didn't pay any more attention to him. 'You can carry the rug between you,' she ordered the twins.

A desperate idea came to him and he moved forwards, pawing at the air with his hands. 'Tomorrow – a present for Mathilde!'

About to leave, the word made her turn around. 'A present? You mean you'll have a present for me tomorrow?'

He nodded, dumbly, then seeing her face light with anticipation, and realising she might change her mind, he blurted wildly, 'Big present.'

'A big present for me!' She gave a little jump of excitement. 'You hear that!' she called after the twins, 'I'm going to get a big present tomorrow while you're only going home.' And she made a face at them before turning back to Robert. 'Really you're quite nice and I like you,' she said, 'but you've got to come here tomorrow because I don't know where you live.'

He nodded again, twice, and in reward she smiled at him a great big, wide smile. It seemed to him in that instant to be so warm and inviting that he felt himself powerless, lifted up in some vast cloud of happiness. When he recovered it was to see her scrambling up the dune side, hurrying to catch up with the others.

But by the time he had wandered slowly home, his confused mind had become filled by one big, massive worry; how could he find a present for Mathilde? He had thought to take something from the house, but the house only had old people's things. And any present would have to be very special, something very valuable.

In the end he found something. It was something he'd wanted himself and he found it at the back of his grandfather's garden shed: a big nobbly stick made of some heavy wood. Only, when he looked at it, it seemed far too ordinary for Mathilde so he got the garden knife and tried carving into the wood, sitting down cross legged with his tongue hanging out in concentration; it had to be very special, the best present he could possibly give her.

From the kitchen Robert could just be made out between blackcurrant bushes. His grandfather watched through the window, curious. 'What's he doing?' asked his grandmother. Georges scratched at his moustache and frowned. 'Carving something. A bit of wood, I suppose.'

'He seems so much happier, have you noticed?'

Georges grunted. 'Wish he'd just read a book sometimes.'

'He can't read, you know that. He starts at that special school next year, perhaps they can teach him there.'

'P'raps they will and p'raps they won't. Anyway we've only got him for another ten days before he goes back to Paris – I'll take him myself. In fact I'm already looking forward to it.'

'Georges!' His wife was shocked. 'You can't count the days like that; he's your own flesh and blood!'

'You're right, mother; you're right.' But to make sure he didn't have to continue the conversation, Georges abruptly left the kitchen, took his usual seat against the wall and pointedly switched on the television.

It was almost dark before Robert came in, blubbering. This had never happened before and the old lady couldn't understand it. 'What on earth's the matter?'

'Stick... no work.'

She shushed him, gave him ice-cream and let him watch the television until he stopped crying. However, when he was in bed all his worries returned. The stick was no good – it had been too old and hard to carve – and he must have the best present for Mathilde.

Then he thought about the rabbit.

But... Perhaps they would stop him? Perhaps, if they knew, they would even stop him from going to the beach!

He would have to be very cunning. Finally he went to sleep: fists scrunched up with determination.

The fine weather held. They said it might continue for several days yet but that meant nothing to Robert, whose mind remained fixed on seeing Mathilde again. His morning's job, that of weeding the old onion bed ready for the autumn, was done with even less success than usual and left his grandfather grumbling and muttering about having to do it himself.

His grandmother was more concerned by Robert's lack of appetite. She took away his half eaten bowl of lunchtime soup and carried it in front of her like an alter offering, tut-tutting to herself all the way to the kitchen. Furthermore, Robert did not eat much of his favourite pudding but rocked back and forwards on his chair in silent excitement.

'I can't think what's come over the boy,' she confided to her husband, but as he was already half way into an afternoon's nap, she only received a grunt in reply, and soon his slow and heavy breathing signalled it was time to send off Robert to play on the beach. She didn't notice that Robert's picnic satchel seemed bulkier than usual and the fact that he avoided walking close to her she put down to his familiarity with the route.

The first hundred metres of beach had duck boarding and Robert could run along this stretch easily, his feet pounding on the wood. At the start of the dunes, however, the duck boarding stopped at a convenient place by the now closed-up ice-cream kiosk with its gaudy painting. This was as far as his grandmother had ever gone. From here the path up the dunes ran steep at first, then confused, going this way and that between tufts of scrub and grass until, eventually, no discernible path any longer existed.

But he had now travelled this way several times and had no difficulty finding his way. Unconsciously, he knew the sea always had to be on his right side. To his joy she was already waiting, at first not in the hollow but on the crest, her long fair hair blowing to the sea breeze. As soon as she saw him she dropped out of sight, not that it mattered because he held her present hidden behind his back.

'Mathilde!' he said happily when he reached the lip of the dune and found her sitting on the sand at the bottom of the hollow.

'I almost didn't come; I'm not supposed to be here,' she said, flicking her hair and barely glancing at him, 'but it's such a nice day and I thought I'd better. Well I didn't want to let you down, did I? Now, have you brought the present?'

He slid down through the sand of the dune to join her. 'Present. Mathilde.' But he still kept it hidden because he wanted her to smile.

'Yes.' She stared at him. 'You have got it haven't you – I know you have, you're hiding it, aren't you?'

Robert remembered what happened whenever his mother had given him presents. 'Guess games.' He managed to say.

'Oh come on, I can't guess!' But this was a tease she understood and was delighted at the thought. When Robert only looked baffled she smiled encouragement, 'All right, I'll try to guess... It's a cake. No! Not a cake, umm... a book? I know – it's something to wear!'

All these words said so quickly confused Robert and suddenly he knew he didn't understand what it all meant and so he just opened his satchel, dragged the creature out, dumped it on the sand and sat back contentedly.

Hauled abruptly into the light, the rabbit just crouched, apparently dead; a bedraggled brown blob of hair. As they watched it slowly raised an ear.

In horror she squealed and jumped back. 'It's alive!'

'Mathilde!' he said proudly.

Uncomprehending she looked first at the rabbit and then at Robert. 'It's a rabbit, isn't it?'

'Present,' he explained earnestly.

'But it's only a rotten rabbit!'

He smiled at her. 'Present. Mathilde.'

'Look at it – it looks sick – ugh!' She shuddered. 'I'm not touching it. It's... awful!' The rabbit made a tentative move towards her and she backed hastily away. I don't want that.'

Something had gone wrong; he could only look at her.

Suddenly realisation dawned on her, this was Robert's idea of a present – and she'd come all this way just for this! Tears of disappointment pricked her eyes, 'You got me to come here just for this nasty animal?'

Robert sat on the sand and began rocking back and forth in agitation.

Seeing his moon face made her temper snap, 'This is just a stupid rabbit and you're just a stupid boy! How do you think I could ever take it home? I can't, can I? I should have known better; you're stupid, stupid, stupid!'

She spoke so quickly and threateningly his head began to spin. What had happened? What was going on? He began moaning to himself. Nothing seemed right. It was like the many times when people shouted at him. 'Mathilde.' he said, trying to find words to ask what she meant.

But she had moved on to feeling self-righteous as well as angry. Hadn't she allowed him to play with them? The twins had never liked him. It was she who'd defended him; she who'd had all the ideas, and now, when she could have gone shopping with her aunt who'd promised her new shoes, she'd come here... It was all a waste of time because of him.

In sudden rage she leapt to her feet and kicked sand at the rabbit. The boy gaped at her, shocked and not understanding.

'I don't want to see you again!' Her voice rose and grew shrill, 'You're horrid, you're not right, you're stupid'

'Mathilde. So-rry, so-rry.'

'And stop calling me that silly name,' she raged on, stamping her foot. 'I'm not Mathilde, my names Louise, everyone knows it's Louise. You knew that, everyone else calls me by my proper name. Mathilde's a stupid name – stupid like you!'

124

In his confused mind only one thing registered: she was not Mathilde; she was some other girl. Now he looked at her he could see she wasn't Mathilde, for Mathilde had a sweet face full of love and gave him sweets, while the face in front of him showed only mean anger and fierce aggression. She was hateful; a thing of rags and teeth; a wild animal.

He moved towards her, desperate to clutch her throat and do anything to stop her noise.

But Louise had seen enough. She was not wasting her time with this idiot boy and was off; running lightly, her thin legs taking her over the top of the dune and away in a trice.

He was not quick and could not keep up with her. By the time he'd reached the top of the dune she was already one dune away, long hair flying, skirt swirling. He scrambled after her in a mad flurry of sand, but after one more distant glimpse of her, she was gone.

Alone, he wandered about, finally remembering his rabbit. Where was the rabbit? He searched but either the rabbit had gone or he couldn't find the right hollow. His energy became exhaustion, and exhaustion became silence.

He sat on the sand and looked in all directions but on that late September day there was nothing to be seen, only a lazy sea glinting silver, and tufts of coarse grasses in the dunes moving this way and that to the wind. There was no Mathilde: no beautiful girl, no smile, no sound, no other person and no rabbit. Wherever he looked there was nothing.

The awful silence became a weight. Down his malformed face began watery globs of desolation. Mathilde was lost; she was somewhere else; the fairy creature had vanished. Words began to escape noisily through his broken larynx; jerked out in slow, squirting pulses. 'Mathilde! Come to me – Mathilde...Where have you gone...' On and on, animal sounds that dissolved in the air.

He stopped and listened. So far it was the longest thing he'd ever said, but nothing happened, nothing answered and nothing changed; the sea moved gently back and forth, the few clouds hung motionless, the grass continued its indifferent sway.

As the minutes passed and nothing happened, the sounds of the waves slowly dulled his mind, exorcised pain, dried his eyes. He sat down and clawed at sand.

Back and forth, back and forth went the surf with long, slow, tumbling swishes of water and seaweed; the sun inched slowly down, the events of the past hour might have started to slip from his mind until a sudden knife-stab of kaleidoscopic recollection jerked him back to his feet. Bewildered by an outburst of anger he could not define and could scarcely control, he struggled up to the top of the nearest dune to shout at the empty sky in desperation.

It was the shout, the final shout that was almost a scream that alerted the search party.

Much later one of the gendarmes who found him returned Robert to his grandparents. The strangely silent boy had to be lifted into the cottage and taken straight to bed leaving the gendarme to give many laboured warnings about the care and custody of children, and about certain children more than others.

After the conversation had finally moved on and with a conciliatory cup of coffee in his hand the gendarme asked, reflectively, 'Now tell me, you two wise people, just who is the Mathilde the boy was on about all the time?'

'Why?' Some indefinable fear made the grandmother sound hoarse.

'Why? Because, when I found the boy he was shouting – or, I don't want to be rude but, well, I must say it was more like howling to me: 'My Mathilde, my Mathilde! Must I spend my whole life searching for you?'

The gendarme's voice had prepared her for some kind of shock but, even so, she spilt some of her coffee exclaiming. 'Oh, Mon Dieu! He said all that – but he's never said that much before!' She turned to look at her husband, 'Robert must have been terrified!'

'Terrified of what, for God's sake?' Georges, furious at involving the police, furious with himself at allowing Robert to be taken and left on the beach and furious at all the fuss, could only just contain his anger. 'Anyway, the boy's asleep now, isn't he?'

But the Law cannot be side-tracked. 'I must repeat the question,' said the gendarme, 'who is this Mathilde, Madame?'

The old lady stared at her husband who scowled back. 'Mathilde... We don't know anything about a Mathilde, do we, Georges?'

Georges scowled even more but thought hard. 'No.' He lifted his shoulders in a dismissive shrug.

'But you must know something,' pursued the gendarme, gently.

'No we do not,' repeated the woman.

'Are you quite sure?' The gendarme's voice took on a more formal tone. 'Listen, I must get to the bottom of the name – there may be other girls at risk from... well you understand what I mean.'

'I know nobody – do you Georges? Think hard, the police must know if we do.'

The room grew silent.

After a few moments and with a face of someone having to search his deepest memory for something only hazily remembered, Georges turned to the gendarme and answered with extreme casualness: 'Mathilde...? Mathilde? Oh, now I wonder if it could be *that* Mathilde... But she's far away in Paris. One forgets things, you understand; a name here or there...'

'Would the boy have thought her pretty and attractive?'

'I can't say. Some would, no doubt.'

'Did she give him sweets?'

'I've no idea. Perhaps. Probably, I suppose.'

'Well, did she have long blonde hair?'

'Not that long; it only comes down to her shoulders.'

'Well there you are then!' The gendarme stood up. 'As so often happens, a boy gets a fixation on some young woman and, voila, the hormones kick in. Even at a young age, it's only natural.' He turned to the grandmother and smiled. 'That tidies up the incident for me; just remember to keep the boy, or any boy, under better control in future.' Always polite, the Gendarme handed his empty cup to the grandmother. 'Don't forget, now.'

'Control?' She appeared to have to think twice before remembering the gendarme was there. 'Oh, control... Oh, yes, Sir, believe me, I certainly will...'

'But Sir,' interrupted Georges quickly, 'you said it was only natural and given unusual circumstances...'

'Not all that unusual,' said his wife.

'Unusual,' said Georges more firmly. 'Allowances have to be made.'

'Allowances for what?' The woman stepped sideways to look at her husband.

'Being alone, just to start with.'

Observing the staring eyes of the stressed man and the woman's thin hands opening and closing fiercely, the gendarme felt a moment of sympathy for the old couple trying to cope with life's difficulties and tried to show understanding. 'It can't be easy. He's, well, we can all agree a very unusual lad.' He nodded upwards towards the bedroom, 'But one must take more care.'

'You may rest assured,' said Georges, 'that a lot more care will be taken.'

'Very good, Sir,' said the gendarme with a polite salute, so I leave it in your hands to deal with things.' And with a few more pleasantries and after receiving from the grandmother a generous pat of thanks and a quiet, almost whispered, 'And thank you for being so understanding,' he left the house with the couple standing at the door.

As he stowed away his notebook and started the car, the gendarme noticed the moon starting to rise. It should be a very fine night and might be improved further by a beer at the Café Des Sport in Town. He waved a final polite farewell but there was no wave back, just the woman folding her arms and the man still staring as if amazed by it all. They gave the impression of being very individual and almost lonely.

A couple of odd ones, he thought as he drove off down the beach road past the empty café, still flying a faded flag above full rubbish bins.

He turned on the radio, searched for the local station and forgot them; he was going home; the incident had been successfully concluded and no harm done.

The Photograph.

I was asked to visit an elderly friend in France. It was early summer; roses filled our garden, the cherry orchards were laden and the cycling season had started. By the time news of my friend's illness reached me, he had already been admitted to a small hospice in the South West. My friend was dying. 'Why? What's the matter?' The reply was simple, polite, and to the point: 'Why, Monsieur? Because you always die when you stop eating.'

Bereft of answer, I was left to wither on the unspoken, 'Les Anglais…'

The hospice turned out to be a small modern clinic on a hill, adjacent to a village; one of those stone villages that have grown out of the land and are seemingly timeless. My first impression of the clinic was that it was little more than an extended bungalow with a stunning view to the south and the Pyrenees.

I paid four visits to see the old lad, the last as he slept lying on his back, gaunt face staring sightlessly at the ceiling. After that you could not say he died, but rather that he had stopped bothering to stay alive. It was as though he deliberately tip-toed away through a door left open and we were left to ponder on his departure.

And that's how it all might have ended when Fleet, the clinic's odd-jobber, a handsome, muscular, but blank-faced man whom I had already identified as being one card short of a Full House, came carrying the request for me to visit the clinic's Matron, one Professeur Colbert.

Of course I'd already heard of her name and always with respect or even with fear, but I'd never met, or even seen, the lady. She was in charge of the hospice – that I knew but nothing more. Her office, shuttered and approached through an arch of roses, was set apart from the main clinic. Fleet and I dodged though sprays of thorns to arrive at her door where, having looked at me vacantly, he knocked before letting me in.

There are times when you go into a strange office and realise, in a second, that you're entering an entirely different world. Far from the modern clinical environment elsewhere, confronting me was a huge antique pedestal desk loaded with papers and, almost hidden behind it, a mature lady was sitting bolt upright. She had a strong head of white hair, pinned on top with what looked suspiciously like a knitting needle. This, when taken with a black dress with white collar, large glasses and fleshy lips, gave the impression of a rather proud and haughty penguin.

Behind her chair, a very large gilt mirror on the wall reflected both the back of her head and my apologetic face. To be honest, I found it rather disconcerting.

Worse, with eyebrows merely angry gashes of make-up, Professeur Colbert simply stared at me. And it was a severe stare – challenging, even – especially when you do not know quite what you are supposed to say. I waited for her to speak, vaguely aware of carpets and of paintings hanging on the walls describing scenes of a past age. The desk carried a green table lamp, a small side table had a vase of mixed flowers, there were

132

musty scents… At this point my awareness stopped, for with a sharp movement of both hand and head, she indicated I should occupy one of two ancient oak chairs with carved armrests.

Still rigid in attitude she began formally, 'Thank you for coming…' but had to stop with a half-cough. I was left to wonder if she suffered from asthma and had time to observe that her face was as lacking in wrinkles as a sheet of stretched cowhide but unfortunately had much the same texture.

She began again; 'My apologies… I am sorry about your friend.' She made one of those minute gestures of hand and fingers that indicate, better than any words, the inevitability of events.

For that gesture, I gave her credit for showing tact.

'I think he was a friend to everyone,' she elaborated. Some of the haughty severity fell away – but only temporarily, or so it seemed to me. Anyhow, it was the appropriate moment to thank her and the staff. I did so, feeling that she expected nothing less and yet was impatient for me to get it said so that we could move on.

'Thank you, Monsieur,' she said finally, taking time to start tapping a pencil: first one end and then the other, on her desk while all the while watching me. 'Do you live locally?'

'About an hour's drive away.'

'And do you live alone?'

'Alone?' A shrug of indifference can hide a lot of irritation. 'As it happens, we have a lot of animals so usually one of us has to be at home. I came here on my own.'

She nodded. 'Good,' she said, as if it mattered. 'We have another Englishman here. It is unusual but that is how it is. French, English, Spanish, what does it matter when this is the last place they will know?' She placed the pencil used for tapping back into a tray as though it had done its job. 'He is a very fine man. His name is Walton, prenom Jim, and you will like him: he is a cheerful man, still handsome and with lots of stories to tell.'

'You mean: you'd like me to see and talk to him?'

'Of course; the English only like talking to the English.' Seeing my doubt, she added, 'He has no relatives and he is lonely. I try a look after him – well, not personally, of course, but…' Her hand again made vague signs.

'What's wrong with him?'

'His heart. It is very weak indeed.'

There was no point in being soft. 'Months or days?'

The slightest of frowns passed over her almost impassive face at such brutality. 'He may leave us at any time. He knows it but doesn't seem to care. He is not,' she repeated it, '*not* depressing. You will find him interesting, I assure you.'

'It's not that,' I said. 'Your nurses only had to mention it and I would have gone and talked to him anyway.'

'I know,' she said tautly, sitting very upright and regal in her chair, 'But I wanted to be certain that you were the right man to allow. He is… how do you say? Valuable to me.'

The oddness of this remark only came to me much later.

After Professeur Colbert almost anyone would have come easier, but Jim Walton was a breath of fresh air. He was sitting up in bed, broad shouldered and grey bearded. His spiky eyebrows arched into cheerfulness the moment I introduced myself. He had a long English face, made to look almost comical by the child-like quiff of remaining hair, with a chin resembling a warship going into battle and yet it was his eyes that captured you: gleaming chestnuts of good humour.

He was an irresistible character, handsome still, one who challenged you to be gloomy – if you dared.

During that first visit we rattled like an express train through all the places in life he'd visited, appropriately hooting with laughter at stories of jobs he'd done in Europe, Canada and Australia: mining –he'd driven huge bulldozers – taxi-work, farm labourer, warehouse manager… The list never ended.

He dismissed as irrelevant all the disasters he'd suffered. 'I learned early on that you must always assume everything that happens is for the best.'

Seeing my doubt, he carried on. 'You want an example? Well, here's one. I was driving through Canada when my car, a black Chevy – they don't make them anymore, do they? – packed up.

'It was a wet day, in the middle of the Rockies and pissing down when the old banger stopped. Soon after I heard another car coming so I rushed out to flag it down only it didn't even slow down! Middle of nowhere and it didn't slow down for someone in trouble! No, instead it just threw a bloody great sheet of water over me. Insult to injury, eh? I was soaked.

'Anyway, there I was, standing there, wet through and with the blighter having disappeared round the bend in the mountain. Then I heard shooting. You know what? That car was full of drugs and the police were waiting for it! You could say I was unlucky to break down but I say I was lucky I didn't get a lift with druggies and finish in jail. Get that – like I say, it was for the best!'

We enjoyed the thought together. Encouraged, he pulled out another story from his memory with the enthusiasm of a boy scout unpacking his food bag.

'Did anyone tell you I was once a dog stuffer in South Australia? I had twenty dogs to stuff in a car, three in the engine compartment, four in the boot and the rest inside: under seats or wherever. Me and Bonzo Butler ran the show. Everyday we'd do a dog obedience demo for paying onlookers. One by one a hidden dog would leap out of some nook or cranny of the car and do a turn. Twenty of 'em, and damned good they were; in London we would have made a fortune. Only problem was: Bonzo drank. One day I went into Hawker – that was the local town – and when I got back he'd shot a couple of the dogs, then shot up our house and then shot himself as a grand finale. Y'see? Lost all me money at the time but it didn't matter in the bloody end, did it? Might have all died some miserable death in wup-wup land while here I am in a comfortable bed!'

At the remembrance, Jim lifted his head and laughed until the bed shook and some medical equipment fell off the shelf. After I'd picked up the bits, I asked; 'What happened to the other dogs, Jim?'

'Took off into the bush. Well they would, wouldn't they? Dogs aren't daft. No point in hanging around to get shot!'

Eventually – and Lord knows how long we were talking in that small room – I had to slow him down, 'But, Jim, you never married? Never had time to, I suppose?'

A sudden weariness came into his manner but against such weariness he thrust out his chin defiantly. 'Married, no – but almost. I suppose you could say I married a memory...' He tried to carry on. 'Might have, a girl...'

Like a switch being thrown, his face sagged into contemplation. Remembering his heart condition, I was alarmed. He had been talking almost non-stop for an hour and now I noticed his face was as grey as the hair over his ears. Abruptly, he raised a tired hand. In a lower tone of voice he said, 'Tell you all about my girl next time.' And to my extreme concern, I recognised sweat on his forehead – I'd kept him talking for too long.

I moved. 'Time I was going, anyway,' I said looking at my watch.

'Bring us an English newspaper, next time, matey,' he said, with an effort to return to normality and apparently unaware that sweat, or was it tears? – running down his face. 'Please.'

'Of course.' I said. 'Look forward to seeing you again,' I said – and meant it.

On my way home, it was easy to compare in my mind the two people I'd met: the straightforward Jim, a volcano of high spirits who knew he had but a short time to live, and Matron in charge, about as lifeless and immovable as an Eastern-Island monolith. *Incroyable*, as they say in these parts.

When I next visited Jim he was out of bed and in shorts, sitting at the window. He did not look up but pointed to the two men he was watching. 'See old Claude, our head nurse?'

'With Fleet, the odd-job man?'

'Yeah. He's trying to show him how to start the mower.' Jim chuckled. 'Thing is – Claude has to show him the same thing every week.' Jim turned away from the window. 'Still, Fleet might be simple but he makes a good odd-job man 'cos he's as strong as you want when it comes to lifting.'

So we sat alongside his small table and I showed him a few things I'd brought him including, of course, a two-day old copy of an English newspaper. When I pointed out that Professeur Colbert spoke good English, he agreed and explained that she visited him from time to time and just sat there, looking and: 'passing cold comfort, a French magazine and bloody advice I can do without.'

We had been talking for a while when, as if taking a decision, Jim said. 'I want you to pass me my wallet from on top o' that cabinet.'

That done, and wallet in hand, he began the tale of his girl, sometimes tapping or pointing at the wallet with a finger as though a secret lay within it.

'I had a small yacht, a thirty-footer, and was moored in a place called Agde. It's on the Med, not far from Sète. The engine was a sod, always giving me trouble, and I had my head down working on it, sweating my guts out because it was as hot as hell, when I heard a woman call out in a hesitant sweet young voice. I looked up and there she was: six feet away, standing up, looking straight at me and the most beautiful thing imaginable. Can you visualise that moment – me, hot and filthy, looking up and seeing before me a Greek Goddess?'

This deserved a smile: how many times have men said that? But Jim had stopped talking, his eyes were wide and I saw he was back and onboard his boat once more. The girl, *his* girl, stood before him. My mind jumped ahead, guessing that he'd repeated that single memory over and over again.

He began again, slowly and to himself, in a tone almost of awe: 'She was in the pulpit of this other yacht, holding a rope looped in her hand. All she had on was a one piece bathing costume and she was perfect. Can you imagine? In front of me, smiling, standing straight, the most gorgeous thing ever.' He repeated more slowly and tapping his wallet. 'You'll have to excuse a man on his way out like me, when I get romantic and tell you that in that second I lost my heart as well as my wits.'

Not about to disagree with him but to help him move on, I said: 'A coiled rope is the universal request for help to moor up alongside, right?'

'Exactly. Moorings were in short supply and she was asking for permission to come alongside my boat. Meanwhile, in the stern of her boat, some wild looking young guy steered and revved the engine against the flow of the river.'

'I get the picture. A perfect woman in a bathing costume, asking for your help and only six feet away. Naturally you told her to bugger off?'

'I couldn't speak; at least I don't remember saying anything. I just took the rope and tied it to a cleat.'

May be it was because I was still smiling, but Jim seemed to think I needed convincing because he suddenly scrabbled in his wallet and brought out a photograph and handed it to me, almost diffidently. 'Look,' he said. 'See for yourself.'

Now it's a dangerous thing to do, looking at something you've been assured is a photo of the most beautiful girl in the world and I took my time.

The photo must have been taken on one of those ancient instant cameras. It showed all the signs of being much handled and one corner was torn. It was of a smiling girl, dressed in a red, one piece swim suit on a quayside. She did have perfect proportions, and dark hair, and a wide smile, but her features in the photo were not too clear: it had faded as instant photos sometimes do.

'This was taken from your boat?'

'No, on the quayside in Corsica and not by me. I'll explain later.'

'I see... Her hair comes almost down to her waist.'

'Isn't she beautiful?'

'Oh, absolutely.'

As soon as politeness allowed, I handed the photo back but Jim did not put it back in his wallet. 'I believe it's the most valuable thing I have,' he said, looking at it.

But wistfulness in a man is not easy to accept. I said, 'You'd better finish the story. You obviously didn't marry her, so what happened next?'

He smiled. Carefully replacing the photo in his wallet, he looked at me. 'Our two boats were alongside each other and all that morning I was conscious of her cleaning the boat – and it needed it because I've never seen a boat in a worse state; it was a shambles with nothing in place at all. At the same time, I saw she had to return from time to time to attend to a very young baby. Meanwhile the man had disappeared below deck and stayed there. A feeling that this was outrageous grew – she working hard while clearly he'd taken to his bunk and had left her to it. Disgraceful, I thought.

'You didn't speak?'

'Didn't like to. It was hard work keeping from gawping at her all the time. I did ask if they were they all right for food and she said, 'We can manage, thank you Monsieur,' in a low Frenchy voice that was wonderful on the ear. And that's how it went on all day until suddenly she leans over into my boat and says, 'Please, may I ask a very big, 'ow you say: present. I need to get to the railway with my baby. Could you 'elp me?'

'Could I help her? Blimey there was nothing I'd like better! So I got my old Fiat and ran her to the station: her, the baby which she kept in her arm, and one big bag she slung on her back.'

'So, at least you had a chance to talk…'

'Unfortunately, the distance from the boatyard in the town and Agde station is very short. Five minutes, that's all. I discovered her name was Julie Moreau, they'd sailed from Corsica, and that she was catching a train to Perpignan. That was about it – Oh! And that she called her baby Chips.'

'What about the husband or boyfriend?'

Jim smiled secretively and looked at the window as if it held the answer. 'Not a word said at the time –but in the end I found out.'

The sounds of the hospital – the rattle of trolleys, the clink of instruments – came to us as we sat, saying nothing: me waiting, he remembering. It was as if we both recognised that good stories always take time. Only eventually did Jim continue his tale.

'It was almost two days later. I heard the guy on the boat moving about so, for the hell of it, I shouted if he was all right now. I was being sarcastic but all he said was, 'Come aboard and have a beer.' And that's when it started. I told you he was a wild looking character and by now he looked even wilder – unshaven, hair a mess, filthy tee shirt, bare footed...'

'Still?'

'Yeah,' Jim said, 'but he was very cheerful, happy, even. I said what's up? And he told me. It wasn't as I'd imagined it at all. The girl was someone that had begged a lift from Corsica because she was broke – robbed, according to her – and needed to get back to France and to her uncle, a baker, for money. However, the moment they sailed they got hit by a storm and for six days he'd been on watch all the time, not able to get sleep, struggling to keep the boat from going under. When they arrived alongside me, he'd simply collapsed with exhaustion.'

A knock on the door of his hospital room stopped Jim. 'Time for your treatment, Monsieur Walton,' said the nurse.

By now more aware of his heart condition I picked up my bag to leave.

'You'll come again?' Jim asked urgently.

'Of course.'

Grinning, he grabbed hold of the nurse's arm. 'Mi-mi and I will be waiting for you! And... don't mention Mi-Mi to my wife, eh?'

Uncertain, the nurse giggled dutifully.

Jim tapped the photo in his wallet and winked, but as I reached the door he half-lifted himself to shout: 'The most beautiful woman – you saw her for yourself, didn't you?'

You'll kill yourself, acting like that, I thought, and closed the door behind me.

In the courtyard as I emerged, a large Renault saloon waited. Seeing me, the driver leapt out and opened the rear door. Professeur Colbert leant out, presenting a harrowed face made worse in daylight. 'May we drive you to the main road? You see the clouds? I think there could be a shower.'

It was curious that she should know I caught the Agen to Cahors bus on the main road, but she was right: it was a day of showers and it would have been silly, if not downright churlish to have refused. I eased my way in to sit beside her – and her world of perfume.

She coughed her asthmatic cough. 'You don't have a car?' It was a throw-away question asked without looking and in a manner suggesting she was quite indifferent as to whether I had a car or not.

I said, 'My wife has the car. It's as easy for me to catch the bus.'

'Ah, yes, of course.'

The road from the clinic ran through the narrow streets of the village; the driver drove with circumspection. After a while Madam Colbert, with further haughty casualness asked, 'How do you find Monsieur Walton?'

'Very lively and very entertaining…'

'A lovely man. But do not be, how shall I say… Deceived? He has a lot of imagination.'

'Really?' I was genuinely surprised.

'And he is a very sick man. When they are close to death, people's minds stray.' She prodded the driver with a finger. 'You're not close to death, Laurence, so keep your mind on the road and don't drive too fast.'

'Yes, Patronne.'

'Then do it.' In a change of tone she said to me, 'Monsieur Walton has so much charm; it is tempting to believe all he says.'

It suddenly came to me that she had been waiting in the car especially to give me this warning. 'I have to say that I like him,' I told her, shortly. 'I like him – and his stories.'

'We all do.' She sighed. 'I am glad none of my nurses speaks English.' As if it were an afterthought she added: 'If he gives you any concern, please come to me.'

From the village, the road descends steeply to the main road and the bus shelter. A splatter of rain briefly covered the windscreen. The significance was inescapable. With a lift of her hands she said, 'We are going to Cahors, would you like to come with us?'

But I detected the offer lacked true warmth and turned it down. 'Thank you, but no. I have an appointment in Agen. The bus is due soon.'

She did not sound surprised. 'Until next time then...'

And that was how Professeur Colbert left me.

A few days later I found a message had come from the clinic to say could I come as Monsieur Walton had been asking for me. I was there next morning.

I found Jim on his bed, a sheet half covering his wasted legs. He was wearing a long sleeved shirt, unbuttoned, with a brilliant red scarf of defiance around his neck. For the first time his eyes, circled by shadows, had a feverish look as if he could be under some inner strain yet his greeting was as warm as ever as we embraced.

'Problems?' I asked, pushing aside his trolley of untouched breakfast.

He screwed his face into a wince, tightening his lips. 'Bit of an attack yesterday.'

'I'm sorry...'

'It's normal.' He cut me short. 'When you're on your way out, it's normal.' Seeing me about to resist he hurried on: 'Got to be practical and that's why I wanted to see you. Don't want worries when I'm sleeping; don't want to leave any loose ends to my life.'

'You mean a will…?'

'Nothing to leave, chum, and no family except a sick sister in England. No, I wanted to finish my story about Julie.'

He looked at me as if expecting a challenge. And it was true that I was more interested in his tales of adventure rather than in any girl. 'We can talk about her later,' I suggested.

A rare scowl passed briefly over his face. 'I see you're not convinced. Julie has never left my thoughts and I'm trying to share her with you: I need to. I think you're a sympathetic bloke; I've nobody else to talk to and by telling you about her, somehow I don't feel so responsible for her: maybe she might even go away. Or maybe she might come closer, that'd be the best. I care – but I don't care, or rather, I wouldn't care anymore. Does that make sense? I suppose you think I'm bloody mad?'

To me there was something comical about a man so concerned about some girl in his past but clearly it meant a lot to Jim and he was a man on death's row. What could I say to him – forget your memories? Memories were all he had left.

'I don't think you are the slightest bit mad,' I assured him. 'People would say you are trying to exorcise a ghost.'

He grabbed my hand and held it fiercely. 'You're so right,' he said tensely. 'Ghost is the word. She haunts me and has always haunted me. If only I'd said something to her at the time. If only…' His hand flapped his helplessness.

There was nothing for it but to give him and this girl all my attention. 'Go on with your story, then.'

'You remember I was drinking beer with this sailor? He was called Jerome, I found out. Nice guy in the end, but a bit dim. Anyhow, he'd agreed to take Julie back to France thinking that not only was she beautiful, but he was certain to score at some point. It was his bad luck that this storm hit them. Day and night he had to fight to survive: they nearly foundered.'

'From him you picked up a lot about, err, the girl?'

'Not much. He said she wouldn't tell him any details at all about her life; only that she wanted to get back to Perpignan where her uncle was a baker. He reckoned she wasn't on drugs but just a bit fou, as he put it.'

'Did,' I asked the obvious question, 'Did he learn how old she was?'

'Nineteen, he reckoned, but she didn't tell him. I think he was about right.'

'And the baby?'

'Hers, but he was certain she wasn't married.'

On his bed throughout all this time, Jim had been leaning on one shoulder, holding my hand, watching my face as he explained everything. Now he let go my hand and turned onto his back, obviously tired. He stared up at the ceiling for a while as I waited. When he began again he spoke more calmly, almost distantly. 'We drank a lot of beer. Jerome wasn't really interested in the girl. She was very beautiful – we agreed that, especially after drinking a few – but he reckoned if he'd kept her she'd have cost him too much because – according to him – she was flighty. He gave me the photo; by then he was quite drunk. He said that girls like that were dangerous to men and that there were plenty of girls who might not look much but who were less trouble.'

'Uh-huh, but you did not agree with him.'

'No. But I said the right things, didn't I? It would have been daft to have argued with a drunk with a bottle in his hand.'

'And inside a small boat when he held the only bottle opener.'

'Yeah.'

The joke had missed Jim completely. He rolled back to face me again, clawing at his sheet as he raised his voice. 'I was certain that, if I could find her, she was the one for me. I didn't care what Jerome said, I just knew that she and I could have made a go of it. You see, I'd looked into her eyes and she'd looked into mine: *I knew*. I knew it then and I know it now – believe me.'

His stare carried conviction. 'So you thought more and then went looking for her?'

Abruptly, he laughed and relaxed. 'Oh, yes, I thought about it a lot. I thought about her a lot. Then I thought about her and me... a lot more than a lot. I came to the conclusion that if I didn't search for her, I'd never sleep again so I padlocked the cabin door, threw a bag into my old banger and drove to Perpignan. It was only an hour away.'

Down the corridor in the clinic, I could hear attendants talking as they pushed a trolley. Hoping to finish Jim's story, I guessed: 'However, you didn't find her...'

'It was only a long shot. I visited all the bakers in the city and showed them the photo. After two days I came across her uncle and aunt in a small baker's on the outskirts of the town on the main road going towards Montpelier. Yes, she was his niece and yes they'd seen her recently. They invited me in. They were curious, I suppose, and gave me coffee and bread – straight from the oven – and butter. I told them the whole story: the boat, the storm, everything and they heard me out.

When I'd finished, the uncle folded his arms and said that she'd left the day after they had given her a loan and he didn't know where she'd gone because she wouldn't say.

I asked him to think again. 'You've no idea at all?'

'No.' Then the old beggar looked at his wife in a way suggesting that they'd talked a lot about the girl and didn't altogether agree. He said, 'My advice is to forget you ever met her. She's wilful, our niece. I'm sorry to have to tell you, but she's reckless and irresponsible. It's her age. She'll grow out of it but that's how it is right now.'

Entirely silent previously, the aunt now chose to really wade in. 'Good for nothing young vixen, going around as if she was on

150

heat; Monsieur, attention if ever you catch up with her because she's wicked.'

'No, Stephanie, not wicked.'

'I say she is.'

Detecting that Jim's voice was getting slower and slower as he recounted the events I cut in: 'And you never ever caught up with the girl?'

'No – but she's out there somewhere. I've had my eyes out looking for her ever since. And she wasn't a bad girl: all she needed was me to take care of her. That's all any girl wants – the right man to take care of her. That's the way it is in life: find the right one, the one in a million. Only I've let her down by not finding her.'

By now Jim had slumped back on his pillow, tiredness showing in every feature, a bead of sweat on his brow and his arms slack. It was high time to leave him in peace. I do not think he heard me as I made my apologies for leaving.

I never saw him alive again.

My arrival at the crematorium – a modern building whose design rested somewhere between a car show room and a large bungalow – increased the attendance by all of twenty five percent, for the only others present were Professeur Colbert and two recognisable staff from the clinic. The Prof wore a midnight blue light-weight coat with gold buttons, a black scarf, and a wide brimmed black hat. To my irreverent mind it suggested that, despite not having an eye patch, she could be passed off easily as a pirate.

So we listened to the funeral director. Readings were made, recorded music played, the coffin disappeared behind curtains and that was that. The ceremony was perfunctory, a matter of meeting the minimum legal and social necessities. As an observer, I felt that a lot was unsaid or missing but I don't think that Jim would have cared a jot one way or the other; in fact he would have thought it a huge joke. 'Everything happens for the best.'

The necessary business completed, we emerged into fresh but cool air and shook ourselves free of gloomy thoughts. There had been a storm during the night; the summer heat had finally gone. Professeur Colbert asked me if I could accompany them back to the clinic as she had some things to deal with in her office. Naturally this was agreed and, as I had my own car, I followed behind them at their stately pace, a pace unusual to anyone accustomed to driving in France.

It had occurred to me, as we chugged along, that perhaps I might be offered a drink in her office; a large glass of Armagnac would have suited me very well at that moment, but that was not to be. Instead, taking off her hat, she immediately took me to a small table covered with the few oddments remaining in Jim's bedside chest. 'Monsieur Walton told me some time ago that you were to have everything he left in the clinic.' She made a dismissive gesture towards the table. 'Well, everything he had is there.'

We looked down at the table together. There were two books on Buddhism, a copper arm band, a wallet, a diary or notebook – I wasn't sure which – several coins, a concertina of files and numerous bits and pieces of little consequence.

'I don't think he was a true Christian,' she said disapprovingly. 'We have disposed of all the magazines and papers as well as his clothes, I hope you don't object.'

'Not at all.' I opened the wallet. It contained quite a lot of cash in notes. 'And this money can all go to a good cause.' Probing deeper, my fingers came across the photograph I'd been looking for. 'For old time's sake I'll keep this.'

The Professeur took it from me quickly. 'No. I'm sorry but I think that I have a prior claim on the photograph.'

She said this so decisively that I looked at her with no little astonishment, particularly when she only stared back with what one can only call defiance.

'Sorry? How do you mean: what claim?'

As I may have said before, Professeur Colbert had a blank face with a rough, coarse skin and yet anyone would have sworn at that moment, a blush appeared and she had to turn away.

That wasn't going to stop me and I pursued, 'I understood you to say Mr Walton's effects were given to me...?'

She made a snuffling sound. 'Surely you must have guessed by now,' she said with a kind of arch coyness, 'that the photograph is one taken of me when I was young?'

It takes something to make a man speechless, but this woman in front of me managed to do so totally. Perhaps the forty or so years explained the figure, but the face? The most beautiful girl supposedly captivating Jim for a lifetime and now standing here looking like... I couldn't put it into words. And why hadn't he recognised her, for God's sake?

'He was my man: it was, how you say, ordained?' As I said nothing she added with a flare of anger, 'It was cruel luck we never met properly. But he was my man.'

She walked over to the window and looked out.

Overcoming my amazement with the greatest difficulty, I managed to ask, 'Then why didn't you tell him when he arrived here?'

She turned. A laugh filled the room, jarring my ears with its bitterness. 'I'm not what I was; do you think I don't know that? He held the photograph of a dream and it gave meaning to his life; the unattainable desire for perfection... was I to destroy the dream of a dying man? And perhaps I loved him; I could not bear to see pain in his eyes as well as in his body.'

Perhaps seeing my look of astonishment at all this news, she put up her hands to the bun of white hair on top of her head in a young girl's gesture of shyness. 'You see, when I was young I was very, very beautiful.'

It was so out of character I was appalled by it.

I did the only thing I could do under the circumstances – made excuses and escaped as soon as I could.

As you might have expected, I told the whole story to my wife, not once but several times. We discussed it at length. My wife did not believe that Professeur Colbert could be as bad as I made her to be, while I was troubled by the notion of a man with a vision that sustained him, and the caricature of his dream hiding the truth for the love of him. We were never able to agree as to what should, or could, have happened and the consequences that would follow.

It happened that some six months later my wife and I had to drive to Cahors, passing close to the where the village stood. My wife wanted to see the situation for herself so, despite my serious misgivings, we drove up the hill to the clinic.

When we found that Professeur Colbert was not there, for me the news came as a relief. 'She might or might not be back in half an hour, would we wait?' After thinking and talking, I went back to the car, ready to give up immediately, but my wife went wandering off on a tour of inspection.

Ten minutes passed before my wife returned, leading a rather pretty lady by the hand. 'Meet Madame Duran; she needs to get to Cahors to catch a train. I said we were going that way and could take her there.' Such acts of thoughtfulness are my wife's stock in trade so I was not altogether surprised. We made our introductions.

Madame Duran was a tall, willowy woman while my wife is short, so my wife insisted on giving her the front passenger's seat and we drove off. It rapidly became apparent that Madame

Duran, besides being attractive, was also a chatterbox. I had to explain my connections with the clinic.

'Such a depressing place,' said our passenger with a sniff. 'I cannot simply hate the place: all those people dying, how my sister puts up with it I'll never know.'

My wife leant over the back seat. 'Then... is your sister Professeur Colbert by any chance?'

'Ah, yes!' Madam Duran nodded vigorously. 'Of course she is – but she's the older one. She's the sensible, caring one while I am just the opposite – I don't care at all: for anything or anybody, that's how I am. And, of course she has been successful while I just enjoy life.'

As we drove along, we then had to listen to stories of failed marriages and life changes. I rapidly came to the conclusion that she was just a silly and rather reckless woman.

A thought struck me. 'Were you ever in Corsica?'

'Of course, my...let me think... she giggled, 'my second husband was a Corsican. Besides, my sister lived there at the time.'

Wanting to get an idea straight, I pursued the point. 'But did you ever sail back to France in a storm?'

Giving the impression she was trying very hard to remember, she put a finger to her lips. 'Did I? Oh, dear, perhaps I did, there are so many storms in that part of the world. I expect I did. You have to excuse my memory, please understand that I never look back at the past: too, too, sad, don't you think? Men, love, pain...'

Impatient with such silliness, my wife said sharply, 'Can't you even remember if you came back in a storm with a man in a small yacht?'

'My dear, I have had so many men in my life that unless it was a serious affair, they are all best forgotten: one man is much the same as another, you know.'

We were drawing up at Cahors railway station and I had to have one last try. 'I just wonder, Madam Duran... Did you have a son, by any chance at around that time?'

'Of course, that's why I was at the clinic; my sister brought him up and has always looked after him.' She giggled yet again: 'I would have been such a terrible mother.'

Trying to park the car while struggling with the implications of what I'd heard I persisted, 'I don't suppose... Would that be Fleet, the odd job man?'

We stopped and she opened her door to leave. 'Not Fleet, Monsieur, *Frites*. It may sound the same to you but it means chips in English. I call him *Frites* because that was my main diet when he was conceived.' As she left the car she paused and peered in through my window for one last giggle, 'You understand: in those days I had no money.'

We watched her skirt around some luggage and enter the railway station: a slim, elegant, attractive woman without a single bloody brain in her head. I let in the clutch and we moved forward.

'Well?' Asked my wife.

'In the words of Jim: things usually work out for the best,' I said as we waited for the lights to change.

'I think,' said my wife very slowly, 'To put his mind at rest he should have been told and, good or bad, learnt the truth before he died.'

Knowing my wife, I didn't argue. I changed the subject and drove us home.

Red Socks

Sometimes, the old man felt as though waking up was like a pearl diver rising from a deep reef: a pause at various levels to get rid of toxins from the bloodstream – car insurance, arthritis, cramps, cleaning the pond, holiday bookings, the roof...

Not for the first time, the General tried to sleep it all away.

However, slowly within the uncoiling of subconscious thoughts a more serious problem began to emerge in a bubble of worry, something to do with breathing, a curious breathlessness to signal that something was wrong; something to worry about, something like... Starting hesitantly, it snapped the barriers of his consciousness – the smell of smoke!

The abrupt awareness jerked his eyes open only to find a conventional bedroom ceiling above his head. What? Burning, where? Under the sheets there was nothing to feel; no warm body, no scratchy toes, no snuffling snore, the bed was empty. This was not right, nothing was right: 'Mary! Mary – where are you?'

Below, in the kitchen of their country cottage, his wife loaded the toaster for the second time as she waited for the kettle to boil. A small, cosy woman cuddled inside a Japanese style house-coat in gold and white that echoed her reading glasses and white hair.

It was a pretty kitchen, dark beamed, lace-curtained, decorated with willow patterned plates and hung with many examples her hobby: photography. Some said she was talented in this way but she resisted all such compliments saying that, after all these years, to have a talent was quite impossible.

'Ma-ry! There's something burning.'

She urged the kettle with a shake. Such a penetrating voice, such a demanding …

'Mary!'

'Coming.' Be warned, she thought, today will be difficult. She raised her voice. 'I forgot the toast again. Won't be a minute.'

'That's twice this week,' came authority through the floorboards. 'I've told you countless times to use a proper timer.'

'Yes, you did but I forgot.' The issue of the toast did not worry her, what did worry her was that the General had looked forward to today with such keenness that it almost demanded fate to spoil it in some way.

The steam rising from the kettle had caused her mind to be distracted. It was as though steam resembled her own life: featureless, essential, yet soon to disappear. The thought of death did not worry her; what was the value of a person's life nowadays when the world was so overpopulated, according to the General? Anyway she'd served him faithfully for fifty years and a golden wedding must count for something in the afterlife, surely?

160

Of course, once upon a time it would have been Briggs, his batman, who would have bounded up the stairs carrying the breakfast tray. And Briggs, as the General had frequently pointed out, never burnt toast.

There were wives who would have resented the interference of a batman but he had always earned her admiration by the way he carried the tray shoulder high with the pride of an Olympic torch-bearer on his way to light the military fires. And memories of those past times softened her face as she stirred the teapot. All that ended, of course, when the General retired and she had taken over Briggs' role. It hadn't been a conscious decision: these things just happened.

'Mary!' The General's voice carried through floorboards as though they were made of paper. 'It's Friday the eighth. Have you forgotten?'

'No, dear.'

How could she forget? His invitation to be Guest of Honour and to Take the Salute had occupied both of them for the past week: he preparing his speech and rehearsing it; she finding and pressing his uniform and making all the resulting arrangements, seeing to his hair, cancelling appointments and dealing with visitors. His excitement over the invitation was only matched by her resignation at fate dropping yet another wreath of dead flowers round her neck – and just when it seemed that at last she was rid of all that sort of thing for good.

Even Livingstone, the cat, seemed to have sensed something was up. He'd stayed out all night which was unsettling; he wasn't like that. All the same, she opened a tin for him and put the saucer on the window sill and hoped.

In bed, the General sat erect in his red-striped pyjamas and listened for the stairs to creak. He was still formidable though at eighty five his face lay in folds and his hair rippled in waves as grey as the North Sea in winter.

When his wife entered the bedroom he was ready for her. 'Don't hang about burning toast, old girl, got to get on with it today.' As she walked around the bed, his eyes followed her like a hungry tiger following a straying deer. What's the weather like? Mustn't dawdle, eh? This passing out parade could be my final time on a parade square; nobody lasts forever, y'know.'

'At least it's not raining.'

'Good. Imagine all those men getting ready at this very minute: polishing buckles, shining boots... Ha! Been there, done that... all old hat to me.'

It's dull, no rain forecast.'

'That'll please the C.O. All C.Os hate rain on parade day and for a good reason. No, don't put the tray down there: put it over here. I may have long arms but nobody other than a gorilla could reach it there. Do come on Mary: chop, chop, there's a good girl.'

She put the tray on his lap, wondering why he talked so much just when she wanted peace and to listen to the BBC on her own in the kitchen. 'There's an anticyclone or something.' She

162

plumped up his pillow. 'Oh, and they think there are still more casualties in that nasty air crash in the Andes.'

He only grunted as he moved the tray to a more comfortable position. 'So they say. It's always exaggerated. Think of today: a hundred men passing out in one go.'

'Not a hundred. I heard it was a hundred and fifty at least.'

'No, Mary, ninety eight if you must know. High fliers, all of 'em. Or so I am told.'

'I remember distinctly it was over one hundred and fifty. I know that because I thought it meant three bus loads.'

'Three bus loads? What the devil are you rambling on about? Oh I see what you mean, the Andes, you shouldn't confuse me like that. And all dead, eh? Poor blighters. Still, South America... plenty more where they came from.' He pointed at the tray with his knife. 'Dammit, Mary, where's my chunky marmalade?

'Safeways were out of it.'

'Out of it! How?'

'They didn't have any, Charles.'

'What the devil's the World coming to? None of my marmalade? Told you before you should shop around a bit more.'

'I know, I know, but you can see I bought Old English instead.'

'Mary, Old English is not my Special Chunky. Come, come, you should know that by now.'

'Yes, and some of us have noticed that you're getting more and more fussy in your old age.'

'I'm not fussy at all. Far from it. Just drawing a clear distinction. If I'd demanded tank support and they sent a company of mortars; I wouldn't call that being fussy if I complained, would you?'

She said sadly, 'No dear, I wouldn't,' and drew the curtains aside. 'Charles, I'm worried. I can't find Livingstone anywhere and he wasn't in last night.

'Cats are cats,' said the General, buttering his toast and scowling, 'Find cats anywhere but no chunky marmalade's a failure of the Quartermaster. Remember, old dear, reconnaissance, that's the thing that's missing. The High Street's a supermarket battlefield nowadays; read that in the F.T. and they are always spot on.'

'Yes, I'm sure you're right.' She opened the mullioned window to peer down the garden. 'There's still no sign of Livingstone.'

'You worry too much about that cat; he'll come back. They always do. Forget Livingstone for a moment and concentrate on today.' After eating a mouthful, the General added, moodily, 'And marmalade's more useful than a cat, ask any chef.'

'I'm terrified he's been run over, that's all.'

'Run over? I feel sorry for any wretched damned driver who ran over Livingstone with you around. Dammit, the driver'd be lucky to be given the chance to commit suicide.'

'Oh, do eat your breakfast, Charles, and shut up saying such awful things, you know it upsets me. Livingstone's got such a character... Ugh, I just can't think of it.'

'Well, think about this passing out parade instead. They march on as snivelling cadets and march off as soldiers of the Queen: youth to manhood in one salute. Yes, and as it happens, I'll be the one taking the salute today.'

Mary gave up looking for Livingstone with a sigh and turned back into the room. 'I wonder why they chose you for the occasion? Not to make too much of it but, well dear, you are rather old.'

'I am old. No need to beat about the bush. Eighty five this year.' With a derisory grunt and a deluge of crumbs, the General pointed his knife at his wife. 'Hardly needs explaining why they chose me: I represent tradition and past history. The army gets it esprit de corps from tradition, not from any damned book. Today's a show piece; pure theatre, but it'll stick in their memories. It's like a confirmation service.'

Growing tetchy at his wife's silence: 'You've seen a hundred parades like this in the past: the band plays, there's the march on and then the inspection, after that the supporting companies march and counter march, slow time, quick time ...'

'Yes, but I repeat: why you? It must be twenty five years since you were last on any parade ...'

'All the while the band play, rum te tum, rum te tum. They said it would be The Marines' band. I hope they play Colonel Bogey. I might have to shed a tear if they do; they played it when we trooped the colours – at my request, of course.'

'I know all that as well as you do by now. What I am asking is why you?'

It occurred to the General that his wife, whom he normally regarded as pecking about his feet like a pigeon in the park, could sometimes hang on to his trouser leg like a terrier. 'Because some would say I still have a reputation.' He let that rest a moment for her to take note. 'And I earned it, Mary, I earned it the hard way even, if I have to say so myself. Remember Malaya and then the Mau-Mau?'

'My dear Charles,' she allowed herself to smile, 'that was over fifty years ago.'

For once he forgot his breakfast and stared at her. She was a good wife but she could be unbelievably stupid. He pointed a shaking finger at her like an agitated service revolver. 'An army runs on three things: training, equipment and discipline. The army supplies the first two and officers like me supply the discipline.'

But even just explaining that made him reminisce. 'By God the men feared me! Feared me more that any Commie or African. They were only too glad to rush into lion territory or sink into a swamp just to get out of my sight. One order from me and they shot into the Bush like rabbits with a dog after 'em. Mad King Charles was my nickname and I suppose, looking

166

back, I was a bit mad, but we laid out dead enemy by the side of the road like so many dead cats.'

'You say that just to worry me, you know that.' All the same, dead cats... her eyes close in pain as she saw Livingsone with his chin pressed against the tarmac and the rest of him squeezed into a three foot long strip of multi coloured toothpaste. Horror on horror, her imagination sped onwards to the twelve-wheeled giant lorry that had stopped down the road. And the driver, looking uncannily like her husband in his youth, grinning an offhand apology; 'Never mind, Ma'am, there's plenty more like him – I squash half a dozen a week.'

It was hard not to cry, but then she looked up and saw her husband solemnly chewing toast while watching her. For a moment she hated him. 'Hurry up and get dressed,' she snapped.

An hour later and he stood magnificently attired in full General's uniform in the centre of the room. 'Not bad, eh Mary? Still fits like a glove. Haven't put on weight like poor Mike Peddler.'

He looked into the mirror, no longer quite six foot three but still impressive. 'Yes, I think I'll do for the new lot of squaddies.'

Padding round him like a squaw around a totem pole, Mary refrained from saying his legs were now as thin as sticks. The truth was that, for her when he dressed in uniform, he still awoke the feelings of awe and apprehension that had swept her off her feet all those years ago.

'I wish you wouldn't wear those socks,' she said.

He pushed out his chest at the mirror and grimaced fierceness at the reflection. 'What's wrong with 'em?' He turned to see himself sideways and nodded approval. 'Red socks are my symbol of rebellion. Like Monty's beret, shouldn't be worn, what? I started wearing red socks when I became Colonel and got known for them. Bit like a woman wearing red knickers: cheeky.'

'I now all that but all the same ...'

'Well I'm not changing now to suit anybody. Bought them when we were in Hong Kong, remember? Socks and shoes together at that cocky outfitters near the Harbour opposite Kowloon.'

'Of course I remember them. Tarty I called them then and still do. A man should look, well, nice.'

'Rubbish, old girl. Red's a man's colour. Spice of danger; show 'em you don't give a damn.'

The General put his cap on and turned around twice. 'Have you got your camera all set-up?'

'I thought I'd use the camcorder for the inspection and my camera for the Salute.'

'Don't want any cock-ups; this could be the last opportunity. It's for the kids. Don't forget the lens or something stupid like a dud battery.'

'Charles! Give me credit for something! I do know a thing or two about photography.'

'Uh-huh.' He looked at his watch again. 'Suppose we've got to give you that, old girl, you do take a good picture. He raised his arms and was satisfied but rising on his toes, he winced. 'I say... the old shoes are a bit stiff. Did you rub plenty of polish into them?'

'Of course I did.'

'Don't feel quite right.'

'Hardly surprising. They've been lying in the wardrobe for thirty years or so – ever since you were last in uniform. Naturally they're stiff.'

'Wouldn't fancy a twenty mile march in 'em.'

'They'll probably soften up as you start walking.'

'Dare say you're right. You usually are. Anyway it's only for a few hours. I can take a stroll around the garden while you're putting on your things. Don't be too long: time's getting on.'

'Do, please keep any eye out for Livingstone for me. He may be somewhere in the garden.'

'Of course.' The General had his mind already on the Parade Square. 'You don't need to bang on about the little beggar. I'll roust him out, never fear.' He wandered, stiffly, into the garden and instantly forgot.

Time passed. The Adjutant arrived with a staff car to take them. They were saluted and fussed over then briefed on names as they drove to the camp. More salutes at the guardroom, acknowledged with a curt flick of the swagger stick, the barrier swung up and thence to the Officers Mess. More salutes, handshakes, introductions, coffee, a few jokes about the past...

Mary was taken off by the Commandant's wife and he was whisked away in the car again. Salutes and more introductions. His sense of belonging increased, he sniffed tension in the air, men waiting for orders, protocol, precision, military pageantry: why, dammit, it felt just like the old days! A short tour and the on to the parade square, arriving exactly on time.

Attention! The band, to one side, instantly struck up. The crowd of spectators on the specially erected temporary seating stopped talking. The General could see his wife sitting and already filming his arrival. Splendid! He held himself a little more erect.

Stamping his way across the Parade Square, the Captain of the Guard marched up and gave a quivering salute with a sword glinting in the sunlight. 'Parade ready for inspection, Sah!

The General gravely saluted back. 'Thank you, Captain.' And off they went: first the Commandant, then the General, the Captain, the Course Commander, the Sergeant-Major and the Company Sergeant, one after the other in a dignified amble of military authority; each inspecting cadets with eyes that ran up and down from caps to toes as carefully and impartially as a team of doctors at a sex clinic.

It was going so well.

Sadly, in every man-made thing lies a weakness. It may be so hidden that it never comes to light, or it may be revealed only under exceptional circumstances. For a pair of shoes, thirty years of disuse, while forced to lie next to a radiator, could be considered exceptional circumstances. On the Parade Square, that kindly morning, the very first strand of Chinese thread decided it had had enough and demonstrated its resentment at outrageous treatment by parting company with its companions for ever.

The band tootled gently in slow time.

But the Chinese are noted for following obediently. Alerted to the change of pressure, more strands of thread realised they felt the same way; an exodus of stitching began.

The General stopped to ask a man his name and where he came from. 'Bristol, Sir.' The Company Sergeant cleared his throat to rasp 'Wiggins,' and to glare straight into the man's eyes.

The General smiled benignly, 'Bristol, eh? Good, good. Great City: know it well.'

The inspection party moved on, swaying to the military rhythm, a giant undulating centipede in motion: left, pause, right: left, pause, right.

Somewhere towards the end of the first rank of men, a strange sensation came over the General. Not quite a feeling, more of a presentment: an unease, a disquiet. For the first time his feet felt quite relaxed. It was as though he'd unbuttoned his tunic and flopped in a chair. All was, um, not quite right.

The band was well into a medley from Gilbert and Sullivan and woofing well. It had to be his imagination.

'Been abroad yet, soldier?'

'Yes Sir, to Norway, skiing.'

'Lucky fellah. Stick with the Army and you'll see every part of the World.'

The crowd watched patiently as the line of inspection stopped, chatted to a man, began again.

At the end of the first line of men, the General had the chance to look down at his foot. It took a moment for old eyes to focus properly, rather more recognise a large red toe protruding from a gaping shoe. Several slow automatic steps passed while frantic signals of recognition and confirmation passed between foot and brain. Damned impossible!

Oh no it's not! A shiver worse than the awareness of approaching death passed over him.

'Tak,' another Chinese thread joined the others; his shoes were fast disintegrating.

Panic de-coupled his mind such that he couldn't think. What to do? Nothing. Life carried the inevitability of a body tied across a railway track with an express approaching. Time became immeasurable. Men's faces became a meaningless blur. The Parade Captain stopped politely to allow the General to stare into a soldier's eyes where the unfortunate man's eyeball seemed to dissolve into one huge red toe.

The sight jerked from the General an incoherent string of unanswerable questions about the Falklands, all snapped out from a distance of three feet while the Cadet's mouth slowly fell open.

In the following silence, the Sergeant Major reacted swiftly. 'What's your name, lad,' he hissed in the Cadet's ear.

'Watson, Sir.'

'It's Watson, Sir,' barked the Sergeant Major proudly, managing to condense the significance of the entire army list into one word.

'Ah, yes. Good.' The vision of the red toe seemed to disappear and with it the Falklands War. Somehow they moved on. 'My God,' muttered the General into one face, but it wasn't the man's acne but the impossible calculation of which was worse – to walk quickly and take a risk or to move slowly in a kind of shuffle.

At the end of the second line he braced himself and looked at his shoes again. It took but a glance this time, indeed he could only afford a glance; the entire top of one shoe had parted from the sole while the other shoe now sprouted a bright red sock.

Unnerved, he laughed into the face of the next man until the man's face ran with sweat.

The Commandant glared at the Company Commander, the Sergeant Major's face took on the inscrutable look of iron discipline, the Company Sergeant's fingers twitched to rising irritation until the General moved forward again.

As the band moved on to war music, the fact that his shoes were starting to flop reminded the General that it was only a matter of time before he was walking in bare feet. My God! What to do? What could he do? Like a drunken sailor chucking stones randomly at windows, he began tossing rambling comments about aspects of army life at every man he passed.

Not a face changed, not an eye blinked. Parade Square discipline had concentrated all human awareness into an abstract concept. 'You don't need to think, Lad. You listen for an order and above all, you don't move a muscle.'

'Get up early,' advised the General wildly.

The Captain of the Guard, while keeping step with the shuffling General, frowned. Certain signs gave him some unease. Signals began to trickle almost imperceptibly down through his brain like drips of water down a stalactite, accumulating, calcifying, solidifying…

'Today,' appealed the General, stopping before the thinnest man on parade and grabbing at his tie, 'We must have an army, you understand?'

The Captain of the Guard shifted his upright sword from one hand to the other and looked at the Sergeant Major. Neither blinked, neither showed emotion, but the decision passed from one to the other.

'Never mind aircraft carriers, the Chancellor of the Exchequer, says your pay's secure.'

The soldier stared ahead but his lips said, 'Secure, Sir?'

'Yes, locked up.'

'Locked up and secure, Sir?'

'Don't borrow anything,' shouted the General, 'above all: don't trust banks.'

Together, in perfect time and in perfect step the Captain of the Guard and the Sergeant Major closed in. It was done so smoothly as to be unnoticeable. Hand under each of the General's elbows they half lifted, half propelled him past the last line of the guard and back to the saluting base.

The General's wife looking through the viewfinder of the cam recorder, and knowing as much as anyone there about parades, lowered, then raised again the camera in fright: what should she do?

'Guard of Honour,' roared the Captain of the Guard from the steps of the saluting base, 'Slo-ope arms!'

The parade rolled on, relentless as a flow of larva.

The band raised the tempo of the music. 'Parade will march past…'

Shoulders moved, guns were slapped, orders blared from one side of the Square to the other, the mass of synchronised men kept everyone's attention.

Up on the dais, under the flags, the scene stretching before him was so impressive that even his shoes became irrelevant. The army was mightier than any one thing or man. In his mind, the General was at one with all past parades, in all barracks, in all countries, in all situations.

'Eyes Right!' Roared the Parade Captain, saluting with his sword. Gravely, the General took the salute with a precision honed from years of repetition.

The stamping, the shouts, the orders, the combined rhythm of movement and sound, brought back all his forgotten colleagues and file on file of ageless faces: men in camouflage, men wounded, men long retired, men now dead.

And he was there at the bugle call, old mad King Charles; it was his parade, he was in charge, they were all his children. The parade was in Penang, in Oldenburg, in Aden, in Hong Kong. His back appreciably straightened, haughtiness replaced bewilderment, memories overcame age and the thin arm held the salute as rigidly as at any time in the past.

Behind him his wife had seen everything through the view-finder of the cam-recorder. Finally she put it down to focus on her camera.

176

The band played on, troop after troop marched past until all that was left was the band following the last of the men with trombones pah-pahing with relief and encouraged by visions of beer.

The General was the last of all to move, his mind reluctant to leave dreams and return to reality. As the sounds moved off the Square and down the road past the M.T. section, his wife came to touch him on the arm. He turned slowly and looked down at her and the camera.

'Mary? I suppose you got all that?'

'Most,' she lied. The truth would have to be hidden, for the telephoto lens showed everything, including the ignominious departure from the parade. Once more she would have to face ridicule for bad batteries and blank the film. But she had lived with him for so long and knew no man to whom humiliation would matter more. She dabbed away a tear; she had so wanted him to have a last success.

'I think the cam-recorder may have failed but I am sure I got a good still photo of you taking the salute.

'No movie? Bloody fool, I might have guessed.'

'Oh Charles, I'm so sorry...'

He relaxed his shoulders and only grunted. Suddenly the uniform seemed to hang on his shoulders as if on a coat hanger that was too small. 'Perhaps it was just as well; they weren't a patch on my old Brigade.' The visitors were streaming away to get to their cars. With a flare of indignation, he said, 'When it all comes down to it; they were just a parade of smartened up boys yet to prove themselves.'

'Exactly, dear, that's what I thought: so young and just a little bit scruffy.'

'Wouldn't have happened like that in my day. But of course one mustn't say that: shows your age. You still sure you don't want to come to the reception?'

'I'd rather not. Small talk with a lot of people I don't know and will never see again. I don't see the point. Besides, there's an Aide already waiting for me with a car.'

'Quite right too. Well, leave the rest to me, I've been told there's some spare shoes on their way to replace those damned Chinese things. What a situation! I honestly believe a lesser man wouldn't have known what to do.'

His wife straightened his tie and looked up into his face. 'Not you, Charles; not you – never; you're not one to panic.'

'Panic? Don't be ridiculous: I was perfectly calm. I thought I handled the situation very well.'

'Exactly, dear, we all rely on you.'

She was rewarded with a grunt of acknowledgement and, after a pause, a wry chuckle. 'All the same, I could do with a decent drink right now.'

The cottage was silent when she arrived but in the garden, on the kitchen window sill, Livingstone greeted her with a stretch, a quiver of the tail and a plaintive 'Meow!'

She swept him up into her arms, 'Oh, Livingstone! Where were you all that time?'

The relief was mutual: there would be no necessity for hopeless searches. Livingstone began to purr with happiness.

She knew what pleased him and gently rubbed his ears, feeling him wriggle with pleasure and purr even louder. In fact, nursing the cat she forgot entirely the happenings of the day and began to wonder what to do about dinner that night.

The Pump

I stopped the car at the crest of the hill, remembering that it was here, or hereabouts, that poor old weak-in-the-head Father Christmas – or so we called him – had been killed some fifty years ago. It was a quiet spot with not a sound other than tall, dry hedge grass answering to a light wind. The lane, with a ditch on either side, was narrow.

In our village, Charlie Steadman, thumping about in his muck boots, had hastened the news to me with rustic glee, shouting through my cottage doorway, 'Silly fool 'bin wandering all over the track waving his arms in the dark when this yer car came speedin' along and, whoosh, up 'e went clean over the roof!' After that, Charlie, a farmer and no newcomer to pain, had hurried on, spreading the message as fast as he could, at each cottage repeating his laughter at the thought of the old man dying abruptly in such a bizarre fashion.

But recalling memories of Father Christmas was not enough reason to stay for long and soon I returned to my car for a last look around the horizon; there was nobody about: no walkers, no bicycles, nothing – nothing but clean Dorset air and a circling late skylark.

More thoughtfully, and with a sense that disappointment might lie ahead, I released the brakes and continued down into the valley, rather dreading unexpected changes and wondering what might have been lost in the cause of progress.

Drawing on memory's faulty store, in those days it had been an average Dorset village: a straggle of cottages and buildings on either side of a stream, yet with an endearing beauty stemming from the lush growth of uncontrolled flowers, fruit, vegetables and above all, weeds of the wilderness.

Even before I had parked the car, and certainly before I began my search along the stream, those feelings of apprehension began to be justified. The affluent, retired, middle class had taken over. Porches had been added to flint cottages. The thatched-roofs, previously raggle-taggled and riddled with holes and homes for hundreds of sparrows, were now in pristine condition and almost completely bird-less. Looking along the lane, bright, blue or white doors, shiny brass knockers and twee name plates replaced old planks, stained whitewash and worn stone steps. The casual wild beauty of memory had been replaced by careful gardening and precise tidiness. Scarcely a head of wild parsley could be seen while the rough grass and sedges of the stream bank had been trimmed to lawn standard by some mechanical strimmer. Even the old bridge, then a simple oak plank of vast thickness coated with water weed, had been replaced by a self-consciously splendid teak creation, no doubt there to be photographed by every village visitor.

It seemed impossible that I should find what I had come for, so much had changed. Gravelled roads replaced dirt tracks; an empty space was now three small houses; the old turning area in front of the church had been resurfaced to justify it as a pay-and-park and the pub had children's swings and a plastic play castle outside it – imagine that! A plastic castle where the stone horse's trough had stood for centuries!

I'd about given up, concluding that it had been a serious mistake ever having returned to the damned village, when, behind a flint wall and almost totally hidden by scrub, I caught a glimpse of the dull gleam of something metallic. It was enough to raise my hopes and to have me clawing away at the brambles and blackthorn. Finally I'd cleared enough to reveal the object of my search: the long swooping handle of an ancient water pump sitting on top of an old well.

Naturally, the first thing to do was to give it a heave. It didn't budge. Even bronze bearings will solidify, given enough time. I gave it all my strength but it still wouldn't budge, however I was not surprised or disappointed – it hadn't the last time, and that was in an emergency and more than fifty years ago when I was young and strong.

But I run ahead of my story and must start somewhere near the beginning: a hot summer not long after the end of the Second World War.

We had married as soon after University as we could. Clara, my wife, had a job working as a teacher in Dorchester. I had followed on from Uni with a design job with the Navy base in Portland. Not having much money, we rented in the village from Charlie Steadman; it was an empty cottage next to his farmhouse. This worked out well for I could often work from there while my wife went to work in our car, an old Morris Eight.

Clara did not like the village, or village life. She suggested we moved. I prevaricated: wasn't it summer, the village beautiful and could we ever rent as cheaply again? All very correct but truth to tell I liked the feeling of being a big fish in a small pond. In the remote world it was then, all the villagers had lives revolving around the land and I, a novelty, was known in the pub as the young naval boffin.

Charlie Steadman, my farmer landlord, had two daughters. The youngest, Rachel, was almost eighteen and as beautiful as they come, with exceptionally deep blue eyes and natural tight curly blonde hair. She was also, on first acquaintance, deceptively demure. She obviously got her looks from her mother, who had the same almond-shaped eyes and, at the same time, the same demure – almost sly and calculating – manner.

Rachel had long ago left school. I suspect this having served little purpose other than to sharpen her rejection of control, and now she was supposed to help around the farm. However, Rachel had a mind of her own and it was apparent that she was a handful. On one occasion I heard her say straightforwardly, to her father, 'Shan't,' when asked to feed pigs and I watched her flounce away with total indifference to his request.

In fact she drove poor Charlie mad. In some desperation he said to me 'She jus' won't be bidden, that girl o'mine. ''No I won't,'' she says. Whatever I tells her to do, she finds a bloody good reason not to do it. Fetch in the cows – they're too big for her; come baling, cuts her hands; drive the tractor, she can't work the clutch; help in milking, she's got sewing that's more important…'

In return, I muttered something like probably she'd grow out of it but my private hunch was that she took great pleasure in showing her total independence.

Mary, Rachel's sister was about three years older and totally different. She worked quietly and spoke little. Nobody needed to ask her to do anything; she knew what was wanted and simply got on with it. The difficulty for her was that she was not particularly attractive. She had brown eyes and brown hair and no faults or ugly features but somehow, when put together, she lacked what her sister had in over-abundance: physical appeal.

It was full summer. Some said they'd never known a season like it: every day hot and the evenings mellow with the scent of jasmine and flowering tobacco and late honeysuckle. I worked mostly in my so-called office at home, seated before my drawing board and stopping only when my wife returned in the evening.

My office overlooked the small strip of grass separating our cottage from the Steadman's farmhouse. It had a few hollyhocks but, like most farmers, Charlie was not one to waste his time on gardening.

Rachel took to sun-bathing every afternoon on the grass in full view of my window. I was sure she had worked out precisely where I was and did it deliberately, wearing as little as possible. You can say what you like but I don't believe there's a man who could resist glancing at such a desirable figure for she was of the time in life when a young woman can look close on perfection. Of course, from a glance comes desire and with desire comes imagination and with imagination comes... well, it was damned hard to get back to work.

I did my best but I was still a young man and she a daily distraction – as I am sure she calculated. I resented serving her as amusement but rather more for being unable to stop myself.

One day we met by chance – or perhaps not – I have always wondered, at the village post office. She wore a simple flowery dress, drawn in tight at the waist and with short sleeves and a little lace collar. 'Get's mighty hot in the afternoon, don' it?' She said, looking straight at me from those amazing eyes and with an elaborate coyness of manner.

'It's the time of the year,' I said, trying to sound impersonal. 'It will probably end in a storm.'

To which she said nothing but gave a throaty chuckle of knowingness and deliberately brushed against me on her way out.

Now you may be sure that all the local young men knew all about her and they came by in droves every evening. They would be on one side of the farm gate and she on the other. 'You comin' to the dance', they'd ask; that's after they'd stopped fooling around, smoking awkwardly and trying to sound big. 'Don't know,' she would reply, swinging on the gate. 'Don't know if I want to, or who to go with.' She openly laughed at all of them and they never got a complete answer.

Frankly, I don't know how they stood it: she had the entire youth of the neighbourhood by the nose. I seemed to hear it again and again: the same game of words, the same creak of the gate, the same inane laugh of young men caught up in a fundamental urge over which they had little control, and I could smell, or imagined I could smell, her cheap perfume above all the farmyard muck smells.

I got to wondering how it would end as my ears tuned in, unbidden, to the low murmuring every evening.

'Let's leave here,' said my wife for the third or fourth time as she did her face before coming to bed. But I could not agree.

Late one morning, Mary knocked on my door. Could I come and help? A delivery of fertilizer had arrived and Charlie was away at the market. Naturally, I said yes and followed her to the yard in front of the farmhouse.

A lorry had forty sacks of fertilizer on board. The waiting driver, leaning against the lorry and smoking a cigarette, said he suffered from a bad back and couldn't do a thing to help. If they wanted the stuff, he said, somebody else would have to shift the buggers or he'd take the lot back for some other time.

It was a man's challenge and I was young enough to be up for it. I set to at once.

But if you have ever lifted a hundred-weight sack, you'll know that while the first few can seem heavy but manageable, by the time you've shifted twenty or thirty every new one seems to have grown to a ton. I came to feeling near exhaustion but by this time the watching Mary had been joined by both Rachel and her mother. In front of them, sheer bravado made me finish the job with some sort of panache. As the lorry, having squelched through slurry spilt over from the cow shed rumbled away, Mary's mother – Betsy – practically ordered me to come to lunch by way of reward. 'Lay the table,' Betsy said to her daughters and threw me a towel to clean myself up.

Betsy I liked, she was a mature, comforting version of Rachel, retaining most of her beauty but more deliberate and steady and certainly less vain.

I stripped to the waist and washed in the outside sink they used for cleaning dead pigs and chickens while Betsy, in an off-handed way, thanked me for my work and watched me at the sink.

The farm kitchen was in the shape of an 'L' with the table to eat at squeezed into one part of it. I found myself sitting opposite Rachel and her mother Betsy, with Mary at the end where she did the fetch and carry. We ate a bowl of soup in near silence and then Mary served some kind of chicken stew with potatoes and summer greens. All the while, I grew more and more conscious of the two women opposite me. Never mind how the conversation shifted, their blue almond-shaped eyes seemed to be staring at me every time I looked up. It's hard to explain why but I felt uneasy. 'Eerie' was the word that came to my mind, almost 'spooky'. In fact I was sufficiently uncomfortable to resolve to leave the table at the first polite opportunity.

Rachel was talking to Mary about a dance at the next village when her mother cut across her to speak to me in a slow, deliberate, word by word voice. 'You ever bin a ridin' man, Mr Alan? I don' mean now but afors?'

Innocuous words in themselves yet with an implication to the question I could not grasp. 'Only once or twice…' I began.

'Wonderful creatures, 'orses,' she said, as if I'd never opened my mouth. 'Powerful things with a mind of their own.' She was watching me with that curious stare. 'Need taming. Now I like a good 'orse underneath me. 'Ad one once. Big brute of a stallion called Jo. Never forgot that one. No I did not. Could ride him forever an' he never let me down.'

'My family live in Manchester, we were never in to horses.'

'...Orses need a firm 'and,' said Rachel, in the same low, sly voice of her mother. 'Don't do to let them get on top of yer or they'll ride you to Kingdom Come. Stands to reason. Show them who's boss, that's the secret.'

'Yor.' Her mother did not move her head. 'A firm 'and... But a gentle one. Gentle, I always say. They know when they're loved right. A good horse responds to love an' stroking like nothin' else I knows.'

'...Horses need a lot of exercising',' said Rachel, now as still as her mother. Can't let them be doing nothing but eat all day. Need space ter play around in.'

'You'm right there, daughter. A good run from time to time get's rid of energy like nothin' else does. In the fields, in the evening when it gets cool.'

'And then a rub down when they sweats, or a stiff brush on them great thigh muscles an' a long drink to settle 'em for the night.'

For me, trapped behind the table and only four feet away, the two women's eyes were hypnotic. I felt unable to move and

188

worse, couldn't think of what I should say or do. Should I just continue, grinning like a fool? I had no slick answer and, anyway, knew instinctively that banter – or anything I said – would be ignored. There was a strange relentlessness to their words. It was banter and yet it was not banter. As crazy thoughts scrambled my brains, I could imagine a hunt being conducted and a wild horse, lassoed, helpless, being drawn in to be branded.

'...Yor.' Betsy was agreeing slowly but taking her time as she watched me. 'Sweats a bit... can't let them get cold. A good run and then a rub over their muscles, that's what they likes.'

'Ard muscles,' repeated Rachel, nodding. 'Ard'n strong...'

'There ain't no woman who can't like a strong 'orse between her legs.'

Suddenly, Mary, who up until now had only watched and been silent, rose to her feet. Loudly, she said, 'How is your wife, Alan? We haven't seen much of her lately.'

It was too abrupt, too spell shattering: it was like a tray of glasses being dropped. After a moment of shocked silence, Betsy laughed, stopped, and then took to chuckling. She pushed her plate away and didn't look at any of us as she stood up. 'I got work to do an' all. Can't stop 'n' gossip when there's work to be done.' She stopped as she left the table to look straight at me. There be a time an' a place for everythin' – ain't that right?' And she laughed again as she went.

And that was all there was to it. But as for me, I felt a massive sense of relief it was over and I hadn't made a fool of myself in some way.

Now, you will say, after such a warning, you should have moved out of the village. But I didn't; it was as though I had to know the ending; that something bigger was to come and that I had a part to play.

Well, the summer continued as before, right up to the time of the last wheat harvest. Then I helped loading stooks of wheat on to Charlie's carts until late into the night and the first dew stopped the harvesting. With the moon coming over the hill, we trundled the lot back to the farm ricks while singing and making a hullabaloo. Charlie driving the tractor, and me and one or two others on top of the wagon, sometimes with Mary as well... I still think of those times as being the very essence of summer, a moment of experience, almost magical, and always to be treasured.

It came to the first frost of winter. It was some time after midnight and I was hard asleep in bed. All of a sudden there came to me that there was one hell-of-lot-of-noise going on somewhere outside. It woke me up just as my wife punched me in the ribs, 'See what it's all about. Go on, don't just lie there. Hurry.'

I went to our low little window under the thatch and peered out. The glow told me even before I could make sense of the shouting. 'The big barn's on fire,' I called back. 'They'll need me to help.' And I stopped only long enough to shove on some shoes and grab my dressing gown before running out of the cottage.

The big barn, made of flint with a thatched roof, was next to Charlie's farmhouse. It contained special calves being fed for veal, his stud bull called Jason and his ancient tractor, a Fordson. More to the point it held a huge mezzanine stuffed with hay that gave home to dozens of stray chickens. When I arrived the yard was bedlam with flames leaping out from the upper loading door. In smoke and in the light of the flames, Betsy was pulling out panicking cattle; Charlie had his tractor out and was standing up on the seat shouting instructions to his daughters – and to anyone else who cared to listen – while two or three neighbours were already throwing buckets of water in a pathetic attempt to stop the blaze.

I ran for a pitchfork to start moving hay but was stopped by Mary grabbing my arm. 'The old well pump!' She shouted, 'Yer'll have to help me – it be our only chance!'

She was right: I saw that immediately. The tap from the house merely piddled water while a good pump could shift gallons. Besides, there was a metal trough that sometimes I'd seen carrying water to the cattle nearby. It might be too late but it was the only possible way of defeating the fire – or even just containing it. I sprinted to the far side of the yard where the well stood.

The pump was true Victoriana: God knows when it was made, the long curved handle made to give leverage for one person to work was now so little used that it had grown encrusted. I grabbed it and tried to pull it down. It wouldn't move. I tried with both hands and all my strength and it began to budge, slowly and very, very, grudgingly: Ahrr, the metal screeched as if in pain. I pulled it up, inch by inch: Eehh! It creaked. After several more goes I looked for water to be flowing but nothing came. I continued. Ahrr-Eehh, Ahrr-Eehh! Still nothing: dry as ever and by the shouting, the fire accelerating.

Suddenly Mary was at my side. 'Ere, my dur, you'm needs water ter prime a pump!' And she began to pour water from the bucket she carried into the barrel of the pump. Things began to happen: the pump eased a little and you could feel some gurgling noise.

We took up a place on either side of the pump and set to work. Ahrr-Eehh, the pump shrieked as the water started to fly out, splashing our feet when it hit the metal runway. In the ruddy light of the fire, I looked at Mary who, despite all the panic going on behind us, managed a smile back. She wore a raincoat over her nightdress and her hair swayed and shook as we worked in unison, Ahrr-Eehh, Arhh-Eehh!

Out of the smoke and flame, Charlie appeared, waving his arms and shouting almost incoherently, 'More, more! More water – go faster!' He disappeared again into the smoke, wellington boots flapping.

So we did the best we could. Each time the pump handle went down, our cheeks touched, each time the handle went up, our bellies met. 'Ahrr-Eehh, Ahrr-Eehh!' The sound is with me now. And so is the memory of the heat, for the fire was at my back and it lit Mary's face. I could see her raincoat had fallen open and her breasts shook to each thrust of the pump. Ahrr-Eehh, Ahrr-Eehh!

'Keep goin', keep goin'! Someone shrieked. Who, I don't know but supposed it meant us. And we did keep going, but sweating now and hardly thinking of anything but the effort of keeping the pump working while, in some corner of my brain, I wondered how it must end.

Again, I looked at Mary: her face was tilted back; there were beads of sweat visible above her lips in the red glow. As if she felt me looking at her, she opened her eyes. I must have surprised her for her eyes widened and it was as though I could see into her soul for it revealed unmistakeably, that secretive thing called lust; lust as nakedly exposed as by the sudden flash of a camera at night on some wild creature

We sweated on and she licked her lips as if to speak. But at that moment – and perhaps fortuitously – a huge whoosh of heat hit me in the back and I stopped – I had to, I was burning hot.

'It's gone! Oh, it's gone!' Mary let go of the pump handle. Turning, I could see the roof of the barn had collapsed inwards accompanied by rising sheets of scarlet flames and with black smoke rolling along the ground towards us.

People were running as if for their lives and then we ran too, it was all we could do: like everyone else we ran into the night.

An hour later and I was back in my bedroom, looking through the window at firemen dousing the remains of the barn and causing great guttering masses of steam and smoke. I said to my wife, 'You know… This place will stink of burning for weeks to come.'

'Well, then what are we waiting for…' The question hung in the air; there was no doubt as to what she wanted.

'You are right, of course you are right. We should go as soon as we can.'

'I'll get on to it tomorrow,' said my wife.

And that was that.

Some four months or so later, I paid a visit to my old friend Bumper. We were now living in Weymouth, our departure from the village so soon after the fire had attracted little comment: people were still dealing with the aftermath of an event which would be talked about for years to come.

Bumper had a business down by the quay; he was one of those people who could turn his hand to anything and we went fishing together. He was rough but genuine. He seemed to know something about everything that went on in our part of the world. A bit older than me and something of a cunning old fox. You could say he was as near to being my confidant as anyone I could imagine.

'Fancy a trip into the country?' I asked him.

He took the pipe out of his mouth and tapped it against the wall. 'What's up?'

'It's Valentine day next week. I want somebody reliable to deliver a present.'

'So...' He said cautiously, inspecting the suggestion from every angle.

'I'll pay for you to rent a car. It won't be a problem'

'A present? What kind of present? Is it that big?'

I smiled at his suspicion. 'Just a very big box of chocolates.'

'Huh.' He sniffed and said disparagingly, 'Bloody chocolates...' as if, somehow, I had fallen in his estimation.

'For a woman I know.'

'Well it wouldn't be for a fuckin' camel, would it?' He began the laborious job of refilling his pipe. 'And I suppose, knowing you, it has to have one of them literary inscriptions.'

'I don't know about that. It's simply: 'To the loveliest lady in the village.''

He nodded, thoughtfully. 'An' that depends who you mean, don' it? Can't be that many in a piddlin' place like that.'

It was the moment when I had to make sure he got it right. I tapped him on the knee in emphasis. 'It has to be given to Mary on Steadman's farm. Remember that – give it to Mary.

'You be sure of the name? Bumper's face, eyebrows raised, showed surprise. 'Thought you always said it was the other sister, Rachel, who turned heads, bein' so beautiful an' all.'

195

'Rachel will say it's meant for her, that's why I want to be sure you give it to Mary.'

He chuckled, stopped and chuckled again. 'You old bugger,' he said, 'Putting the two against each other like that.' But after a moment's more thought he said, 'But didn't you once tell me that it was the mother who was the sexiest woman you'd ever come across?'

'I can't remember but you may well be right. She certainly could be, that's if she wanted.'

'I sees, uh-huh.'

A silence followed but it was not necessary to say anything: Bumper always took his time before saying yes, after that he could be relied on completely.

'S'pose there's no reason why I shouldn't,' he said.

But then and as I watched, he stopped filling his pipe so that he could look at me direct. He calculated, nodded to himself then slowly smiled a wicked understanding, 'What you really want is for them to fight it out between themselves, ain't it?'

I wondered if I was doing the right thing but felt I'd already committed myself. 'Something like that,' I agreed.

He pointed his pipe at me aggressively. 'Now that's what I like to hear: the truth at last. An' I always thought you was a bloody fool: you should have taken your pick whilst yer had the chance. 'Fact is from what you say you could have had anyone of 'em.'

Sometimes Bumper doesn't seem to understand life at all. In fact I began to wish I'd never asked him to help. 'Of course I could have done,' I said, 'I'm not daft. I always knew what they wanted but, as I saw it: what was the point?'

Beyond Frank

It was just another day and just another town in southern Morocco. Carswell was in no hurry; he'd posted his mail.

It was already getting hot and even the dogs had given up scrounging to lie sprawled carelessly in the dusty street.

He picked his way between rubbish, stared without interest at stalls of fruit and vegetables spilling across the pavement and pondered on the likelihood of seeing her once again. The question that bothered him came down to one fundamental thing: was chance separated from the inevitable only by time? Surely her arrival could not be explained by coincidence? And yet the very idea that it was inevitable troubled him. It carried implications he'd rather not face. It had to be by sheer luck, there could be no other reason.

He failed to resolve the problem so went into a cafe to forget.

It was an untidy and struggling little town, not much more than a street supported by a small port used by sardine fishers. There were half a dozen like it in that part of Morocco, all scattered along the desert coast and none of them having the slightest obvious attraction. He ordered a coffee , fifty-fifty – the black he found undrinkable– and waited.

If she appeared again, he sensed it would be in her own time.

To any Moroccan, Carswell was merely passing through; a tanned ginger-haired older man with a rounded beard that was attached to his face like golden fog tinged with grey. Carswell's wife said that he would look both shrewd and distinguished if he only wore a shirt and tie and shaved. He did not wear a shirt and tie and did not shave. In fact he did not give a toot as to whether he looked distinguished or not. It was not that he was too old; he'd never been one for suits and had forgotten the world's preoccupation with appearance; all his life he'd been a field geologist where the only thing that mattered was expertise.

So much for the past: now waiting for another assignment, but more or less retired, his interests were reduced to escaping the Northern winters and trying to catch the elusive Corbine which he considered to be a very fine fish to eat. It barbecued well and only seemed to exist in the waters off Southern Morocco.

He sat at one of the tables in the street outside the café. Inside, a huge television screen portrayed a European football match: a repeat. Few bothered to watch. The waiter – to belittle a respectable profession – grudgingly left his group of friends and brought Carswell's order. This service Carswell acknowledged with a lift of the hand and a faint smile, regarding the grubby glass of coffee and cracked sugar bowl with the resignation of one who'd expected nothing better and who'd experienced far worse.

The morning continued. The heat rose. The dogs did not move. Dust, whipped high by the wind, gusted down the road.

The first time he'd seen the woman she'd been shopping at one of the stalls and he'd only caught sight of her as she left: a graceful figure with a covered head, apparently sufficiently attractive for the stall-owner to stare after her even while serving someone else.

The second time he was in a taxi and she in a small bus with open windows. She wore a large straw hat, something almost unknown in the South of Morocco and their eyes had met. But what had stayed most forcibly in his mind was the radiant appearance of happiness that flowed from her, indeed so strong was the impression he envied her; certainly his curiosity was aroused; there had to be a story behind it; a new love, sudden good fortune, some new event. It was a passing situation and he'd concluded that he'd never know the answer.

And then came last night.

She had arrived and sat on the next table at dinner, one of four people, two men and another woman. Now he had the chance to observe her more closely and found himself again approving what he saw: a woman darker than a white woman could ever hope to achieve by suntan, yet lighter than any black woman could dream of becoming by nature.

She'd worn an off-white dress with short sleeves and half a dozen gold bracelets on her left arm. Dark hair, swirled high into a contrived bun, brown eyes, a very fine skin, long fingers that found it necessary to draw her shawl closer against the chill of the desert night. He'd thought hard about her but finally judged, in between his main course and desert, she was not beautiful – her face was one of intelligence rather than beauty. Again he'd approved of that, aware that beauty can only retreat but intelligence advances with age.

200

Their eyes had met once or twice before she'd turned quickly away, smiling. Carswell had recognised in that instant that the smile was meant for him and felt a surge of life in response but that was the end of the matter – the four at the table were joined together in conversation.

The curious thing was that she reminded him of someone long forgotten. He could not place having seen someone like her before and that added to the puzzle.

So now he sat at the café, watched two urchins with a punctured beach-ball and enjoyed the pleasant mystery of events until his mind drifted back to geology and his surroundings; the land hereabouts being littered with the historical fragments of the time when much of Southern Morocco lay under the sea. This led him to recalling his time in Southern Spain studying the old R.T.Z copper workings near Almeria; worked out caves still showing green traces of copper and going back to early 20th Century.

And in thinking of Spain, the convoluted trail of memory suddenly threw up a picture of Frank: Frank under the flapping iron sign painted in red and rust, 'Frank's Bar'. Frank hauling crates of empties, Frank leaning over the counter of his bar, winding up his shirtsleeves to reveal powerful arms, Frank adjusting the glasses forever falling over his nose, Frank in his leather working apron, Frank's big backside as he worked at the back of the bar and above all, Frank's heavy Glaswegian Scottish voice, uncompromising, challenging – often belligerent even to his best customers. Ah yes, Frank, now long gone so let him rest in peace.

'Hello,' she said.

Carswell was startled to find the woman had arrived unnoticed and stood next to his table. Struggling to rise to his feet, she waved him down. 'I'll join you if I may,' adding, 'Of course, I shouldn't be here.'

The 'shouldn't be here' was not said in a way suggesting that Carswell carried any responsibility but was said flatly, as if she surprised herself.

What could he do but to offer hospitality to the woman of the night before? And with some eagerness while, at the same time, wondering what his wife might say if she saw him with an attractive woman half his age.

She sat but declined his offer of coffee. 'I would prefer to talk, if you don't mind. I think we have some things in common.'

'You do?'

'Spain. Nana Norman. And Frank, of course.'

'Frank?'

'Frank. That's why I'm …'

'You *knew* Frank?'

'You should not be so surprised. Many knew Frank.'

'Possibly so, but how did you know he was in my mind?'

'One thing leads to another, does it not?' She waved a dismissive hand. 'The point is that we both knew Frank.'

'Really? You knew...' Carswell stared back at her, uncertain. 'I still don't...'

'Come, let's not waste time, we have to talk about Frank, don't we?'

He laughed at that, not being a man to be hustled. With the advantage of age, he smiled a little condescendingly at her. 'My dear young lady, I don't even know your name.'

'My name doesn't matter – we looked at each other last night and already have some understanding; isn't that correct?'

'Possibly.' He paused, not sure of how honest he should be. 'In a way, yes. By the way my name is Brin Carswell... and yours is...?'

'Call me what you like: let us only agree that we know each other.'

He moved the cup around in its saucer while debating with himself how he should react. To deny everything would be a lie and that was not in his nature. He decided there was nothing to be lost in playing along with this provocative woman, besides she excited him, was highly attractive and he had nothing better to do.

'If you won't tell me your name,' he said, 'I shall call you simply "Lady".'

'As you wish. Now talk about Frank.'

He laughed again but more gently this time. 'But you already have said you know all about Frank.'

'I know what I know. I want to know your story of events. And please start at the very beginning.'

For a few moments he hesitated; what on Earth had it to do with her what had happened those many years ago. And how had she guessed about Spain being in his mind? In fact, this whole encounter was too weird for words. And yet he felt so comfortable already in her company so why should he not explain what had happened – he had nothing to hide, and besides, it was true he'd often thought about Frank and his tragedy. He fished about as to how to start the story.

'My dear Lady I came to know of Frank years ago when my wife and I had a place in the south of Spain. It was so long ago that my memory may sometimes be at fault.'

'Very good,' said the Lady, holding up both hands as if receiving something valuable 'That's a start and we can always fill in the gaps between us.'

Carswell frowned at being interrupted but began the piece of history more firmly. 'At that distant time there were no high rise buildings, no motorways and, to tell the truth, very few cars. Spain was like that then. Most of the women were permanently in black as a sign of mourning for some family member or other, we drew our water from a spring at the bottom of the mountain, and the most used means of travel was the donkey. Life was primitive.

Our village, and it was then a real village, dated back to Moorish times and overlooked the sea. Hot in summer, sometimes viciously cold in winter when the wind swept down from the Sierra Nevada, it was not an easy place to live. We had a dozen or so permanent northern Europeans or Americans living amongst us. Most were characters in their own right; a few were drop-outs or 'resting' actors passing through. To our resident community one had to add seasonal visitors, including Spaniards escaping from Madrid.

But of the people there at the time, only Frank, our failed Scot, remains strong in my memory.'

Carswell paused to look hesitantly and to judge her reaction so far

'Keep filling in the details,' said the Lady, touching his hand by way of encouragement, 'I must hear all the details.'

He decided, in that moment, that she could express more with her eyebrows lifting and falling and by the blinking of an eye than some lecturers could cover in an hour.

'Very well, I'll do my best,' Carswell said and rocked back in his chair, thinking as he recounted.

'Now Frank ran a bar in the highest part of the village called, simply: Franks. In my experience – which is derived from having once, when at University, worked as a salesman calling on pubs – it was the best run bar you might ever hope to come across. It was small and intimate, with snug and cushioned tucked-away permanent seats made of plaster, and a horseshoe shaped bar made of wood more lovingly polished than the

Queen's dressing table. Most of all, the bar had a character that sprang from simple necessity. Lamp shades made from old pots, ludicrous and sometimes frightening paintings cunningly lit on the walls, low ceilings, a den-like feel, old tiles, whitewash, local bric-a-brac, hanging mugs, an old cow bell rattled to say thank you for tips; it had it all the makings of frugal originality.

'But, if you recall, dear Lady, it was more than just a drinking den. At the back, beyond fridges and beer crates was a plancha and here Frank did his cooking. The menu was simple: spare ribs "with fifty two spices" or hamburgers made by Frank to his own formula. Chips were mandatory. You didn't argue about the fifty two spices title or the fact that the hamburgers – he insisted upon calling them Frankburgers – were made from grated pork: either were delicious.

'In between holding Court at the bar and serving customers, Frank had to do the cooking, for he was mostly on his own. Perhaps the activity kept him fit for he was a tallish, broad shouldered man of about forty, moustached, and with glasses which kept drooping on to his nose and which had to be pushed back with one finger. An articulate, knowledgeable, highly opinionated Glaswegian, self-taught and fluent in Spanish, there was no room for doubt as to who controlled his audience.

'Whenever asked as to where we should go in the evening for a bite to eat, we always plumped for Franks, not only for the food but because his outrageousness held a fascination. You might say he lived on the edge, for his effrontery even with strangers could be breathtaking. Or perhaps he was just very good at weighing customers up. On almost our first acquaintance he walked over and said to me as if he'd been thinking hard; "You know, lad, with your money and my brains we could go somewhere." To which I grinned up at him, ignoring the contemptuous finger tweaking at his moustache and the casual, almost sneering provocation. And yet, in a sense he was right, for he was a natural leader of men, a commander without an army, an explosion with nowhere to go – except to fall out with all and sundry over what, some might call his insolence, and some might call his arrogance. Few of the local expats could tolerate him but I could, perhaps because I was only there in the winter when I caught up on the local news

'Once, I asked him what he'd done before coming to Spain. He said he'd run a sales team in Scotland, "We had the best results of anyone." Why did he leave? "The Management was useless." By which I assumed he'd had a row and left in a huff.

'By this time we had become almost friends, or as close to friends as the sharp tongue of Frank would allow. Once I asked him his surname but was made to regret such a presumption, "I tell no man my name except the police, you just call me Frank and there will be no misunderstandings."

'However, sooner or later it had to come into the open: he had a problem. Until then, when there was a sign hanging on the door saying, "Closed. Sickness." we had assumed this to be the case but it was not quite that simple. Normally he only drank water and if you offered him a drink he'd accept the money "for the end of the night." His abstemiousness ended about once a month in an almighty solitary binge which could last for a much as a week. After that, everything returned to normal until the next time.

'One day I arrived to find his isolation was ended: he had a girl living with him in his one-room home above the bar. The startling thing, for Frank could not be called a man of great handsomeness, was that she was half his age and very, very lovely in a soft and fulsome Spanish way. For a few months she decorated the bar, moving things around, finding bottles and collecting glasses without giving any sense of urgency. Like a butterfly in a sunny garden, she drifted around from table to table, saying little, just smiling and being beautiful.

'We watched this happening with something like disbelief. Could it be that old Frank had achieved a miracle? Could it be that this smiling and gentle thing of grace, hewn out of another world than our village, was happy with her choice of man? Then, to our equal astonishment, one day she was no longer there; she had moved on as abruptly and mysteriously as she had arrived. And rough, tongue happy old Frank was openly heartbroken in a way only Celts can fully demonstrate. Many heads wagged but whatever had happened, you had to feel some sympathy for him.

'The sickness sign went up several times that holiday.

'Some eight months later when we arrived back in the village, Frank had a young boy to help him called Pepe. A stocky, cheerful lad who listened in awe to Frank's advice and instructions. Indeed, there arrived a time when Pepe ran the bar on his own when business grew quiet. We thought that Pepe would become permanent until, next year, he too was gone and instead, another Spanish lady had taken his place: Anna.

208

'But the devastating news this time was that Frank had married her.

'Now, Anna was very different. Older, perhaps approaching thirty, she suffered, poor lady, from being a cripple. One leg was in irons and she walked with some difficulty. Not that this problem prevented her from having fun. 'Jolly', sprang immediately to mind when we went for a drink and found her at what, for a while, was her bar stool at one end of the bar. And things did seem jolly and fine, for she and Frank would gabble at each other like a couple of excited geese. In fact we were only mildly surprised when we heard when we were back in France that she had produced a child: a boy they named Frankie.

'On our return to Spain we were quite anxious to find how things were at the bar. Frank was to be found on his own again. Yes the child was quite amazing; pride came into Frank's voice as he described how advanced the child was for his age, and yes Anna was fine too, 'only she feeds me too much: I only have to sit down for a second and she's pushing food into me.' That sounded all right to us and when we left at the end of our stay, Frank was holding Court at the bar as in times past.

'Next year when we arrived it was to find Franks bar closed. It took some time to find out what had happened and then we were told that Anna had left Frank and taken the child with her. Where was Frank? Nobody knew. Two years later, we discovered that Frank had been taken into a Spanish Mental Hospital as a permanent patient.'

Carswell stopped recounting the story of Frank and smiled at the Lady. It was the end of what he knew. He'd reached this

209

same moment in his memory many times and always with the same uneasy feeling. The life of Frank must have continued but to what end and to what purpose he could only guess and speculate.

'So then what happened?' asked the Lady, gently.

'I never found out.'

'But you tried?'

'Well, I asked around but nobody seemed to know. Frank never invited friends and nobody seemed to care.'

'So you did nothing? You never tried to discover where he was?'

'You must remember that he never told me his full name.'

'There can't be many Spanish Mental Hospitals with Scotsmen in them.'

Carswell shrugged. 'It really wasn't any of my business.'

'But if you'd found where he was and visited him it might have made all the difference.'

Carswell shrugged again but said nothing. The lady smiled. 'And then there was Nana Norman…'

'She died. You must know that.'

'Yes, she did die; she died of starvation.'

'Nobody guessed the state she was in!' Carswell scowled indignation.

'Nobody guessed, that's right. And nobody knew. All the same, she died of starvation. With all of you around the village and she died of starvation. Alone.'

'Put like that it looks bad but...'

'And Jonathan...'

'Jonathan simply would not take advice or help. We did our best.'

'Of course you did your best. And did he die of the cold?'

At that moment, the background buzz of the television sports commentators was abruptly overcome by the sound of a cheap metallic chair being knocked over by someone getting up to leave the café. The waiter was obliged to come over to help, a glass was fortuitously caught, words were exchanged and Carswell was distracted. When he finally turned to continue the conversation with the Lady, she was nowhere to be seen.

Nowhere to be seen but completely vanished? Was it possible? She had been so close to him. Carswell peered down the almost deserted street. No woman was to be seen, only two men in deep conversation. She had gone, disappeared.

He felt a great emptiness. It was not a lost chance of a passionate love, more like feeling the loss of a partner or even of mother-love.

He paid the waiter and went on, through the dust and town debris, past the newest camp site entrance, reconciling himself to a return from memory to reality. The surf, bursting over distant reefs of mussels, rumbled massively. It might be an evening for fishing.

And yet, as he stopped to indulge in the smell of the sea and to judge the tide, he knew that there must be an acceptance of more Nana Normas and Franks as time passed, there could be no escaping the regrets of life. By the same reasoning he knew that he would see his Lady again, in one guise or another, more and more as he grew old.

And he sensed that he, and she, would grow closer and closer as they covered and recovered the passing of years until the day would come when they would be so bonded that they could not be parted. Yes, and when that moment came, all the talking and remembering, the laughing and loving, the successes and the failures, all would end in a small, thin, column of smoke. One day, one day... but not quite yet.

When the Walloo Blows

I am of an age when a daily walk is a necessity. My life depends on it. But it is curious how often your feet take charge and take you somewhere without any conscious decision.

Sometimes it is a walk without the slightest awareness of time or surroundings. If I asked later one would have to say that it was impossible to recall where or what one was doing – a condition well known to the police from questioning witnesses. And of course, if this aimless and unconsidered stroll leads to some unlikely encounter, you blame fate.

Perhaps I am alone in this. Perhaps you have never had the experience of loss of awareness, perhaps I am just getting confused; I've lived so much of my working life struggling to understand other people's minds I admit I sometimes grope for reality myself. It is like losing one's place in a book and then trying to find where you were again.

Let's leave it there; my story is real, even if I have to search for the right words.

It happens that I leave my room each afternoon, winter or summer, with no thought in mind and no particular task to achieve unless it is to remind myself of at least one accomplishment in a career which, like all careers in psychiatry, rarely produced anything that could be called a clear-cut success.

And success is the opiate of old men in the same way that grandchildren are the opiate for old women. Do I have need of this age-sustaining drug? For that, you must be the judge but on this particular autumn day, nothing about personal success, or its absence, was on my mind.

Dressed in my heaviest overcoat and with my necessary stick, I turned left at my white-painted gate, avoiding the playground to the right and headed for… where? I did not know, and did not particularly care. Worse than that, neither knowing nor caring mattered much any longer for in my late condition of health, all directions must lead to the same destination.

Already I digress, a lifetime's fault of mine. We are back to the academic consideration of imminent death. Already? Or should I say again? Let's dismiss that gloomy thought and be factual: on the afternoon in question I was in a good mood as I strolled along: no pains, no limp and my eyes for once as bright and searching as any birds.

The day reflected my mood. The rain of the weekend had long cleared the hills we like to call our local mountains, leaving the air as sharp and crisp as fresh Chablis. Our park by the river was at its finest; trees clutching at the sky in dark ranks, their golden leaves reduced to huge drifts on the ground that crunched at every step. Red rose hips sprayed wands of blood over hedge and fence and blackbirds scuttled angrily in and out of cotoneaster bushes. The passing moment had wrenched from nature a memorable autumn day.

Some of this I noticed and more I did not as I continued steadily onwards, my feet scarcely stumbling as the way ahead curved invitingly past lake and willows. The smell of the last cut of grass before winter hung thick and rich, filling me with nostalgia and leading my mind to wander into times past and only occasionally returning to the present.

Suddenly, in front of me, towering above my head I found the big brass entry gates of our Municipal Art Museum.

To be there comes as a surprise. It always comes as a surprise; I can't help it for it is a pretentious building built to impress and I hate pretentiousness, but there is something about it that directs my feet; the Museum is like a second home.

Yes, it is a home and yet it is not a home; it holds friends who are not my friends; the staff know me but they do not know me; I talk to them but you could say I do not talk to them for I am not particularly interested in them or in art; I am not an artist and I am certainly not a museum devotee, yet each week – sometimes more often than that – you will find me there, shuffling through the galleries, unconsciously moving at a faster pace as I approach my destination.

'Mornin' Doctor Curtis,' says Johnson, the security man, putting down his newspaper and rising from his stool, mechanically straightening his tie.

'Good day to you Johnson,' I reply. 'Are the galleries busy today?' Johnson is disgustingly heavy: his shirt buttons strain at their misfortune, there are stains under each armpit and beads of sweat sprinkle his forehead. Like many fat men, his medical and physical problems find refuge behind the broadest of grins and the most vacuous of eyes.

I wait. Johnson stoops, fists on desk and studies his monitor screen with a show of authority. 'Heh, heh! Passing busy in the Classics rooms... Yep, just I thought: there's a class from Northern High going through. I see you're late today, Doctor. A bit of oversleeping? No trouble, I hope?'

'I stayed and watched some men in the Park.'

But I felt this move towards familiarity needed checking. I said, maliciously, 'Do you know that the reaction caused by the sound effect of ball against wood or pad has never been psychologically understood? Some say that men respond to it because, subconsciously, it reminds them of their mother's heartbeat in the womb: do you agree?'

I had the satisfaction of seeing Johnson's smile become fixed and his assistant move slightly to one side as if to avoid getting in the line of fire.

'Err, yes. Just as you say, Doctor.' Johnson made a thing of being busy. 'The Post-Impressionist Room is quiet.' He frowned a reproach at his assistant and thrust a file at him.

'Good,' I said.

I moved on: I had made my point.

It is quite a walk across the foyer, through the open oak doors and then you turn left, past the bust of Hadrian – a replica, of course – but a good one, and thirty strides more (I've counted them) before I get to my destination; the first gallery of the Post-Impressionists, sometimes described as the Mad Moderns by irreverent staff.

216

It is a high room and lit by natural light coming from the glass ceiling. The collection is a good and a representative one – or so I'm told for I know little about such things. I am interested in only one painting, *the* painting and it hangs in pride of place, dominating one side of the gallery.

Almost in front of it, but a little to one side is a viewing bench. It is not being used and I take my seat with some relief. In fact it is there that you will find me at least once a week, the same seat, the same room, hands on cane, slightly hunched, thin grey hair, heavy old-fashioned glasses, an old man apparently nodding off but in fact peering intently; not looking at a paintings, not walking the corridors, just sitting discreetly to the right of the painting that everyone comes to inspect and ponder over.

I have no need to travel further for I am there for one purpose only: to watch people's reactions to the painting.

Once or twice, men on the staff have asked me to explain my purpose – a not unreasonable question. When this happens I usually make a hoarse noise, say I am interested in people and blow my nose. Silly old fool, they think and move away to avoid my cold, wondering if in reality I am really in the gallery to keep warm.

But it is true: I *am* only interested in people. My Doctorate in Psychiatric Medicine was earned fifty years ago although my interests, later, were devoted to psychoanalysis. The study of people has been my life and will remain so even now that I'm long retired and with little left to give and nothing at all to take. And if that is not a sufficient explanation for sitting on that precise spot, just look at that viewer studying her notes!

Already three times she has looked first at the painting and then at her notes, now her finger goes to her lips, she steps back, then to one side and looks again. She is an older woman with a composed character, her glasses come off and then go on again, her lips tighten, she is not easily disturbed but, look! See the way she turns her head this way and that, trying to make sense of what she sees.

I feel like shouting to her that you can't make sense, don't even try to make sense, lady! That's a painting without sense: you can only *understand with instinct,* lady, remember that, instinct and *feelings – gut feelings.* Now she turns away, her head so full that she passes the next three paintings without even noticing them! It is clear she's more than puzzled; it has her worried; she's been disturbed by the imagery.

Distraction comes when the swing doors opening and the woman I know as Gloria ushers in a small group of visitors doing the tour. This is the last gallery she brings them to and, of course, it is the picture they all want to see. They form a dutiful half circle as she unclips the restraining cord to stand slightly aggressively, proprietorially, alongside the painting. I cannot quite hear her but I can watch and guess as she lectures them on the style. What she cannot know, but what I do know, is the reason behind the painting. And I know the reason because I know the painter.

Eventually the group begins to dissolve; the tour is over, some will linger, some will hasten away for an overdue cup of coffee. One young thing, looking like a hairy tube in an exaggerated and rough knitted coat which comes down past her knees, wanders about the gallery apparently aimlessly, almost as if dazed.

218

Seeing space on my bench, she comes over, heaves up her coat like a mariner hauling up an anchor, sits herself down and ignores me.

I wait. I do not move. This has happened before and time is on my side.

She looks at her gallery brochure, then at her notes. From her dishevelled appearance I take her to be an arts student, she has huge white cubes as earrings and hands seemingly covered with chunky jewellery. Meanwhile, her knitted tube has collapsed in concentric rings so that, finally, she looks just a small face on top of a shrunken hairy pyramid.

No doubt that she's trying to analyse her impressions prior to making more notes. There are some who have minds like a drawer of files and need to drop impressions into their rightful place. Catching sight of me looking at her, she is reassured by my age that I have no covert physical interest in her. I nod and make an understanding face.

'That's one helluva painting,' she says, picking off her words as though it was a relief to say anything.

'I'd say,' I agreed and as bait added, 'Perhaps a bit weird, you think?'

There was no need to ask which painting she meant but I wondered from what background she drew the authority to make a judgment. Fortunately she instantly provides it. 'I'm studying industrial design; all this is recommended for my course.'

'I see... art in general or just modern art from which you might take designs?' I put the question wisely. 'Here or anywhere?'

She looked shocked, as if I had just flashed a police badge at her. 'We're taught that design springs from both practicality and art; I'm in my second year and this is the art bit.'

I nod again as though I'd guessed that already. Then all the old tricks of the psychoanalyst inevitably return; my voice drops from gruff to gentle: sympathy and understanding exude like treacle from a cut pudding. I'm inviting confidences: she's on the couch: what the Hell?

'I'm sure you're doing the right thing in studying art,' I agreed. 'So, in the end, what do you make of that one?' To avoid doubt, I incline my head almost imperceptibly.

'Gerhardt's painting? Terrifies me! But it has nothing to do with design.' Perhaps seeing doubt on my ancient face she dragged out, slowly and doubtfully, 'Surely not....Sir?'

'My dear, you already know more about these things than I do.' My stick taps the floor of its own accord in irritation. 'But all paintings contain a design both mentally and physically.'

'Oh, sure,' she blinks, 'but...' She turns away to look at the painting from the distance of our seat.

You would not call her a pretty girl, attractive but not pretty. Short dark hair, not well kept, streaked in the modern way. Able to study her for a moment I note a tilted chin, suggesting a combative nature. Also, that she wears black nail varnish and that it's chipped. I do so dislike black nail varnish but the job of

220

the analyst is not to let personal feelings intrude. She's young and modern, that's all. I see her clipboard is full of notes written in a large hand suggesting an outgoing personality.

After allowing her time, I reflected aloud, 'I would say... that the artist achieved whatever he set out to achieve, don't you think?'

'Frighten kids so that they have nightmares? Sure. But is this design? Mrs Toner – our guide – said Gerhardt's present popularity is just a fad.'

'Heh-heh!' I cannot restrain a wheezy subsiding snicker. This ends in me dabbing awkwardly at my mouth with a tissue to stop damned dribbling. Stuffing the tissue back in my pocket, I explained myself, 'Gloria hates the painting, that's why she says that! She'd rip it from the wall if she could. I'd take a bet she referred you to the Florentine School as setting a standard.'

'How did you guess that? Say... someone said her name's Ann, not Gloria. Ann Toner.'

'Ann? With that hair? A golden mess of curls? Good grief, child, she has to be called Gloria and that's what I always call her: she knows that and I call her that even to her face. And she doesn't resent it because she can recognise the truth!'

It is a joke and she has the sense to recognise it. We smile at each other: my mistake: I can see that I'm now being evaluated. I have allowed myself to become somebody with views and that is not good at all, a psychoanalyst should be an unidentifiable but wise presence, not a living person.

It is necessary for an analyst to sound non-judgemental so down goes the voice to a confidential whisper, 'But... you say... the painting terrifies? Why would you say that was – is it the colour that is disturbing or is there something else?'

Uncertainty. Tongue touching lips. It's watching an actress testing her lines and gauging each word for meaning. There's a sudden shrug as if indifferent, an impatient heave at the woollen coat and then, not wanting to be overheard, she glances about before saying in a positive tone, 'With Gerhardt's painting you find yourself looking first at the face and saying, Wow! That face grabs you and won't let go. But then that sort-of hurts so that you find yourself having to look away at something else in the painting. Suddenly you're looking at the legs and find yourself worrying that they are almost human – perhaps they are human; even a woman's, and hairy, and that's awful – sickening, almost – and then you look back at the face and those eyes are just, well, just *evil* and they are smiling at you, ugh, as if they, and the whole damned painting understood your problem of understanding!'

'I think that's a very good description of a common reaction and that's what someone like Gloria hates about it.'

'Being understood?'

'Induced insecurity. A latent fear in all of us but you must not let that affect *you*.

'Oh, I won't!'

The emphasis amuses both of us – but for different reasons.

Abruptly, she stopped smiling. 'I'm Isabel, Isabel Mordella de Puncta, what's your name?'

'Curtis,' I say with a vague flap of the hand to show it's not important. 'One day,' I say with professional speed to keep the conversation from becoming personal, 'Gerhardt's painting will be seen as a masterpiece. Perhaps that won't happen until he's dead but I am certain of it.'

'You mean he's a genius?'

The word "genius" is like sensational or unique: always overworked and usually misunderstood. I answered her shortly, 'A man becomes a genius only when enough of his peers say he is. That's why it's easier to become a genius after you're dead – there's no chance of someone betraying the title.'

Perhaps this is a bit too rich for it produces a scowl and the earrings sway about in irritation.

'Curtis, I don't get it. You're confusing me. Are you saying you think Gerhardt's a genius or are you saying he's not?'

There are moments when someone plays into your strengths and I defy anyone to resist responding earnestly if not enthusiastically.

'Look,' I said, leaning towards the girl, 'Almost all great works of art are produced by people so screwed up they are under intense strain to achieve a goal. Often we shall never know what screws the artist up, but I say that most masterpieces are born of some inward pressure bordering on a desperation of expression.'

'And not,' she smacked her lips again in relish, 'from simply being a *genius*?'

Precise answers are a trap; there is no such thing as precision in human behaviour. 'I'm of the opinion that Gerhardt's painting you see up there will be recognised as a masterpiece one day: that is not the same as saying that the man's a genius.' I was tempted to add that I could personally vouch for the fact that Gerhardt was no genius, but that might reveal that I knew too much so I sunk my chin on to the head of my stick and waited.

'Mrs Toner described the Canaletto, here, as being the work of a genius.'

'You don't surprise me.'

'But more people wanted to see the Gerhardt, which don't make sense.'

'It would to Gerhardt.'

Repeating what she'd heard, the girl chanted as if it were Litany, 'What Gerhardt does, is to first surprise and then shock the viewer.'

'That's Gloria talking. Don't apologise; I recognise the opinion – heard it all before and it's baloney.' Something more was missing and I stopped growling over my knuckles and stabbed my stick in the direction of the painting. 'Well, let me tell you something, young lady: that *Gloria* would be surprised and then shocked if she was fired. Gerhardt's painting draws ten

224

percent of the visitors here and she'd be out of a job if it went. The Canaletto illustrates a style: it only impresses by its cash value.'

'Is that so? Really?' Clearly I was not in the Gloria league of persuasion because, from the girl's indifference, I might have been commenting about someone having just missed a train. Next, I received a low monologue based on scrawled notes, sometimes interrupted by a quick glance around the gallery to be sure she was not overheard. She came strong on modern artists that could be considered to be the present day geniuses. More advice from our Gloria!

So I sat and listened politely. At last Isabel Mordella de Puncta (how I loved that indiscretion!) set off through her own land of opinions instead of trotting out ill-perceived wisdom. This was more interesting. Isabel now reminded me of a cat prowling through long grass, glancing about sometimes, fearful of an ambush of embarrassment or gaff, but always on the look-out for some new thing on which she could pounce and bring away in triumph.

'You see?' She ended with a self-satisfied purr, a brief scratch at the collar of her coat and a drag at her skirt to make herself comfortable, 'Art should satisfy by design, colour or form; it does not need to shock.'

'True,' I said.

More was expected and finally I obliged her. 'It just so happens that Gerhardt does shock, doesn't he?'

'Oh, sure,' she said as if that were something that anyone could do.

'And he does more than shock,' I said in pursuit. 'Gerhardt tells you of his problem.'

'What problem?' She said, frowning as if I was keeping some secret from her when all the time it was obvious, or at least obvious to me.

'Look,' I said. 'Have you seen any of Robert Capa's photographs? You must have done – the famous war photographer.

She only paused a second before nodding vigorously.

'You remember the dramatic one where he photographs the soldier in the moment of being shot in the Spanish Civil War?'

'Someone said it was a fake.'

'Perhaps it was, perhaps it wasn't. I'm only using it as an illustration.' Damn the girl, there's nothing like youth to be pedantic. I felt forced to wheeze for a moment. It became an effort to say; 'My point is that it makes a factual statement, no more than that: the unfortunate man in the picture has just been shot.' I wheezed again.

'Say, are you all right?'

'I'm, uh, OK,' I said, forcing myself to sit upright as much from anger as pride. Consideration is one thing but consideration from youngsters clearly incapable of telling a heart attack from a cold is another. 'I have a... something of a condition, that's all.'

Despite the stab of pain that had smacked me in the chest, the situation had its grotesquely funny side: a girl's huge embarrassment at suddenly being stuck with a corpse was being prevented by a three-inch stretch of rotten artery holding together. And would it hold? I did not care. At that moment, the temptation was there to pull the damned plug just to see her eyes widen and her face go white. Despite a clear brain and a desire to laugh, all I could offer was a wrenched grin at my lousy physical state.

'You wanna coffee or something?'

'No. All right. Maybe in a minute. I must try and make you understand, first.'

A hesitant hand withdrew from my arm. 'Understand what? You were talking about a man being shot.'

'I said that the picture by Robert Capa of a man being shot was factual and dramatic but no more than that; the thing is that Picasso, of the same war, drew a mural depicting the bombing of Guernica. It was not factual and some, well I'd say most, might say it was not immediately dramatic, but it's now agreed by all that it carried an unmistakeable meaning and message to humanity.'

'Meaning, huh! It's all about meaning?'

'Gerhardt's painting has *meaning*,' I gritted out.

'Oh, yeah?' This in a polite tone which hung about until she added, suddenly, 'Oh, now I get you: Canaletto doesn't have meaning, that's what you're saying.'

'Precisely, my dear Isabel; it's a factual picture, that's all. It's a Robert Capa of the seventeenth century.'

She was not really interested in what I had to say, that was obvious to me, what had caught her imagination was that she was on a trail of conversation that might be more diverting than sitting and discussing art. I took her arm. 'Come, young lady. I will buy you a coffee and explain what lies behind that painting; about the man, I mean.'

We rose together. 'Did you know him – Gerhardt, I mean?'

'My dear, we effectively lived together for more than a year. I can tell you much more about him than he could tell you himself. Much more. I know every minute detail about him and what happened and what produced that painting; of that I can assure you totally.'

We took our seats at a quiet end of the coffee lounge, well away from the book stall. I put down my stick and relaxed my coat without taking it off.

'But I want the whole story,' she said, as if afraid I'd short-change her.

'You have the time?'

'The whole morning.'

'Then I'll start at the very beginning; just how Gerhardt told it to me,' I said. 'And I won't miss out a single thing.'

Gerhardt's story began when he returned to work too soon after a nervous breakdown. He knew it was risky but, being a highly intelligent man, thought he could monitor his health sufficiently. The office was short of a creative art director, clients were pressing and with phone calls for his return daily, the pressure to get back to his studio became unendurable.

But, this time it was the small, everyday problems that cracked him. To start with, it was late autumn and the weather appalling. Getting to work became a task of its own. In the endless stop-start traffic the windscreen wipers took on a life of their own. They'd slammed happily back and forth – bam-bam, bam-bam – until the rain turned to sleet. After that he'd watched them slow, become erratic, finally stop altogether.

Alone and trapped behind the wheel of his car, he came to the conclusion that the windscreen wipers represented life. Peering through what was still left of the windscreen he began muttering to himself, 'Grey, white, grey white, it's all I am, just like the snow. Come to that, it's nothing more for anyone else; we're all just grey and white.' Then, incredibly and in front of his eyes, the wipers started again, flinging aside wet slush in a sudden mad frenzy: bam-bam-bam! But a few goes more and they stopped with a final and desperate quiver. Well, nothing surprised him any longer; fish died the same way; he'd seen them flapping and shaking at his feet in the bottom of his fishing boat.

Red lights, gear-shift, brakes and forward again. It was only an old Chevy and the traffic was getting worse. Fortunately a supply of the clinic's special downers was in the glove compartment if the trembling got out of control.

The whole week had been the same; the city a dismal pall of grey and white, a world built of snow and slush: roofs white, walls grey; sidewalk white, people grey. He hated grey, and the sky was the greyest of all. Why couldn't the sky be blue or green or maybe yellow? That's what it should be: yellow sky, green fields – or red fields, or any colour you happen to like: anything but grey.

He preferred yellow. Yellow spoke of life; shouted energy. He'd paint the whole town in Van Gogh yellow, that's what he'd do. Drop out and paint it yellow.

He played with the idea. It wasn't so stupid: just say goodbye to the lot of them and pull out. (Gears, brakes, gears. What on earth were they doing in front?). He had some cash... could raise a bit more. Really there was nothing to stop slinging it in – he wasn't on the permanent staff. Painting was what he'd started out doing. He only wasted his time here doing poster-painting for cash. He'd get out of the city and take his paints with him.

Why not!

When the right decision comes along, it feels as easy and comfortable as pulling on an old pair of gloves. As Slingsby Drive came up on the right, Gerhardt took it with relief; banging over lumps of ice, plunging through wet slush and not giving a damn any more.

The streetlights were still on. Hunched and miserable in the bitter cold, night workers were already leaving the city for the long struggle home. By the look of it some cars had already been abandoned. Sensing worse difficulties ahead, Gerhardt dumped his Ford in the frozen muck behind Walters Store. Nobody, on a day of such mean, winter weather, took any notice of him; he was just a lanky, wild-looking man, grinding car keys in his right hand. A man with shoes that squelched in the slush and who hadn't bothered to do up his coat.

And the shakes were coming on.

At the entrance to the Eastern Estate Office, Gerhardt rehearsed what he had to say, took a breath, and wrenched the door open with the determination of a man opening the hatch of a sinking ship. Immediately he was hit by a waft of brilliant neon light; stopping him dead and making him blink. Recovering with a self-conscious laugh, he aimed himself at the man behind the long counter. 'Say...! I've worked it out and taken a decision. I'm on the move. I need a small place in the country; a ranch with land; a hundred, two hundred acres.' He stopped to gulp for air.

Behind the door and already waiting, two women stared, curious and amused at this strange man.

In the sudden silence Gerhardt hurried on. 'It'll have to be some kinda busted down place, I guess. But not too bad. I don't care where. Peaceful. In fact not just peaceful: remote. Get that? And cheap, it's got to be cheap.'

With all that said, his tension fell away in a great sigh and he found he wasn't going to start shaking after all.

It seemed minutes before the agent behind the counter looked up. 'Yes, mister?' They looked at each other as though through prison bars. 'Remote and kinda cheap, or cheap and kinda remote? I need your priorities if I'm to give you help.'

Gerhardt saw before him a frog-eyed man with thin, suspicious lips, occupying a strewn desk, set well back behind the high counter. The man wore a jazzy waistcoat, flaunted a bow tie on a scrawny neck, and appeared to have been distracted from some massive deal. From his stony, blank expression, Gerhardt thought it must involve the whole of City Hall.

In the old days he could have dumped this one on his head, now such an abrupt face-to-face confrontation started his stammer again. 'R-remote means r-r-remote and it's two-fifty thousand dollars top. That's got to include a ranch house you can live in. M-my wife even grabbed the contents of the freezer when she left.'

The man frowned, nodded, looked Gerhardt over. He sat back with a roll of plans between his hands and thought. 'You buys land when you buys a farm,' he murmured vaguely, taking in Gerhardt's appearance and pale face. He waved the plans in front of him like a flag of surrender. 'Don't matter where; invest in good land. My advice is take land on the flat, never mind the godamned house. Live in a tent if necessary.' He didn't move in his chair: this buyer was a nutter.

Gerhardt clenched his fists. 'N-no. I want somewhere in the mountains. A bit north if you like. A cabin, shack, plenty of space. Must have space. Anywhere, as long as it's quiet.'

'North of here? That's a no-good place for land,' said the agent, turning peevish. He began peering into a computer and scrolling down. 'At least not unless you're a squirrel and want trees.' He'd come across academic ravers before: this one was tall and thin and looked strained, you don't get that pale unless you've been ill; it was clear that within a year he'd come back complaining and want to sell it again.

'Remote,' repeated Gerhardt harshly.

'Oh, sure. Remote. I got that. Three fifty with a river?'

'Too expensive, I told you.'

'You could try 'em with two-fifty?' The suggestion was made without conviction but he had a big Adam's apple and it made the bow tie jump up and down on his throat like a butterfly dancing. He looked again. 'Yeah. Well now, there's a place near Purdo.'

'How near to Purdo?'

233

'Mmm. An hour, it says here.' He sat back. 'Hey! Would you believe it? It says it's got a view!' The snicker was sarcastic, so was the shake of the head. 'A farm with a view! Anyhow, you wouldn't like it: it's grade three-minus for land according to the local agent.'

Gerhardt felt the shakes coming fast. 'I-I don't give a f-fuck, about the land! I'm going to keep g-g-goats and paint.'

At the change of tone the agent looked up quickly and took in the desperation, the dark shadows under the eyes. Maybe the sooner he got this one out of the door the better. 'It's in Chance Valley, fifteen miles west of Purdo.' He rubbed at his chin and looked thoughtful. 'Goats you say? That's sure interestin'. Ain't heard anyone keeping goats afore. Funny that; been here twelve years come Halloween an' never heard of anyone wanting to keep goats afore.'

'And paint.'

'Oh, sure. And paint.'

'Listen,' said Gerhardt, fighting down a scream, 'I'll t-t-take a look. Give me the details.'

'Had a nasty suicide in Purdo, last week,' said the agent, searching his desk but turning perversely difficult. 'Some farmer took a combine out and jumped in the blades.'

'In this weather? Take a combine out? You're kidding!'

'You'd be surprised at what some guys will do when they're going for the big thrill.'

234

Gerhardt shoved out a hand for the papers but didn't look up. 'Suicide don't bother me, I've been there and come out the other side.'

The agent chuckled as if he'd been told a huge joke. 'That so? Well... Don't say I didn't warn you,' he said.

At this point in telling the story of Gerhardt, I stopped. The girl, Isabel's face told me a question lurked and only waited for the moment to interrupt me. 'It's very interesting,' she said, 'but how come you know all this? Not that I don't believe you,' she added hastily, 'But...'

'Simple,' I said. 'I heard this story repeated a hundred times over the period of the year he was with me. I made it my job to check for discrepancies. I took tapes – over a hundred hours of tapes. Naturally, there were a lot of differences as you'd expect. But by analysing the discrepancies, mathematically, I was able to put together a precise and detailed description more accurate than even Gerhardt could ever hope to recall.'

I waited for any further question. There were none.

'Well, go on then,' she said impatiently.

I smiled and continued...

It took two months to get the deal completed and then another three before Gerhardt was in his farm and had time to take stock of his position. It seemed he hadn't stammered for weeks, in fact he was ninety five per cent sure his stammering had stopped for good. There were times when he just sat down and dreamed.

And he liked the place. It was peaceful, calm and stunningly beautiful. In fact it was almost too close to being perfect; reminding him of a tray of delicate bone china waiting to be broken. The view from his porch was awesome; paddocks, trees and rocks jumbling greens and browns as far as the eye could see; natural, casual, yet so balanced as to be delicately but deliberately planned; the whole being surrounded by mountains, some jagged, others with massive shoulders reminding him of the shoulders of giant men hunched and peering over the valley below.

Sometimes it was too calm, as though something brooded, but he told himself that was only when the mist hung on the trees with the air still. Or perhaps it was the overhanging mountains, which gave the feeling he was being watched. Normally the air was crisp and he felt invigorated – he was already fitter, stronger, and too busy to notice or be worried by any sense of eeriness. He could look down the valley and only see one ruined and empty cottage, that was all there was between him and Purdo, fifteen miles away on the river. Above him, on a crag half way to the bluff at the head of the valley were the Wilsons, his nearest neighbours, in fact his only neighbours. He could just make out a roof and figured it was perhaps a half-hour's walk away. It would have to be a walk because the track in between them hadn't yet been repaired. He had that work now out with a contractor.

In Purdo, he'd asked about the Wilsons. 'Nice people,' everyone had said. Which was enough to reassure and yet not enough to make a visit essential until he felt he was ready for it

– which was always next week. Now, suddenly, he'd run out of excuses and recognised the walk would have to be made: you couldn't be strangers forever.

But the business of paying a visit bothered him, he felt that it meant another twist in life, just when he knew he was making good. It was a whole new area of uncertainty when, for the first time in three years, he felt completely free of any fear of people.

He bolstered his spirits by washing his sandy mop of hair as he showered, and by taking time over selecting what to wear, settling for a woollen check shirt and clean jeans. Nothing too classy, probably they'd be suspicious of anything too classy.

The mirror gave no help when he took a last squint. 'You don't look a day over thirty,' he told himself fiercely, 'Not a day.'

But you seem so damned ordinary, said the mirror, just who the Hell do you think you are?

'Every man's an individual,' he said, trying out a frown to see if it made any improvement. 'Unique unto God, whoever He is.'

The mirror shook with laughter.

Of course he should have visited them when he first moved in; common courtesy, friendliness, mutual help – he should have visited them; but he'd been far too busy with the small herd of goats he'd bought in.

He rehearsed the excuse to himself.

It wasn't the real reason, but it would have to do.

Yet conscience is a deep-rooted vine, and guilt weighed heavily as he trudged up the slope and through the buckthorn and cottonwoods. It weighed so heavily it turned to petulant irritation after he'd passed over the small stream that showed the property boundary. Hell, why should he be the one to feel under some sort of obligation? They could just as easily have called on him.

He climbed further and his irritation moved back to unease, he would have preferred not to have to meet anybody. Since the time of the crisis he'd avoided human confrontation. Chance Valley was a lonely valley – that's why he'd been happy from the moment he'd first seen it.

Short of breath, for the last few yards had been steep over the granite ridge, he stopped at the Wilson's gateway to observe their farm in close-up for the first time.

It was simple and built of stone. Besides two added wooden barns, there was an open barn still nearly full of hay. The yard was too tidy and he guessed they still had their cows under cover. A few chickens roamed and he could see a grain bin. It had every appearance – windows freshly painted, healthy vegetable patch – of being reasonably successful but he was left with the suspicion that, like other farms in the district, most of the money would be tied up in the farm with little left for luxuries.

238

A voice interrupted his thoughts. 'Why stand there, why not come in?'

He turned to find a woman in blue dungarees with big brass buttons, leaning against a doorway, arms folded. She wore tinted glasses and held herself motionless, as still as a heron fishing in a pond. For a moment Gerhardt had the impression she must always stand there, watching for someone to arrive.

'Hi! Didn't see you. I was only catching my breath after the climb.' It was a hard wrench to overcome the rusty lever on the yard gate but it then flew open with sudden force, which then took him with it. 'Hup!' He stumbled awkwardly. 'Sorry, that's a tough gate you've got. I was on my way to call on you. Name's Gerhardt, by the way. Digby Gerhardt. I'm your new neighbour.'

Still wary, she rationed out a smile. 'You actually walked?'

'Had to, my Chevy won't take the muddy crap near the stream. I'm going to get it fixed.'

For the first time, she moved and shook his hand, giving him a straight look. 'I'm Jane Wilson, good to meet you.' She stuffed her hand quickly back into the top of her dungarees as if relieved to get it back.

'So... you are Digby Gerhardt – the one who's taken the Morgan place.' She nodded as if unsurprised. 'Jake, the seed-man told us about you but said you wanted to be quiet so we didn't call.'

'That's me. The old man – did you know he was seventy-five? – sold it to me and retired.'

The small, neat, face, showed disapproval. 'Huh, him! He was only sixty but he's been practising retiring for years. See the bottles and junk in the yard? He became a hop-head. You'd better come in.'

He followed her retreating back, continuing to explain. 'I'm sorry I didn't call before. Soon as I took over I had a delivery of animals and haven't gotten my head above water since.'

'Don't worry, we're busy too.'

They passed through an entrance hall and along a corridor before entering a big living room. A waft of warmth greeted them from the wood stove. There was the smell of cooking coming though the door.

'I brought a bottle to say "Hi" with. It's a Syrah, Christian Brothers. In the liquor store they said it's quite good.'

He looked around while she took the bottle, hardly noticed what she said as he admired an old carved wooden platter from some European country, a man sitting alone on a stone. Timeless. He heard her saying '...Michael will be pleased; Michael drinks wine – he learned all about it in the Marines – but I don't much, I find it gives me headaches.'

'I'm sorry...'

She stopped and faced him, 'Do you always keep on saying you're sorry?' It was a question softened by a long flat smile that slowly loped across her face.

Gerhardt looked into those glasses again and tried to make out her eyes. 'Sorry – er, no.' Out of his control, he grinned nervously; the way someone in the Agency had unkindly complained made him look like a ginger cat caught stealing the fish. He was absorbed with the thought that she did not seem like a farmer's wife; her face, and neat sharpness, made her look more like a young school mistress or a librarian.

Awkwardly Gerhardt shuffled his feet and put his hands in his pockets, 'I'll bring something else next time – now I know.'

'There's no need, but thanks, this'll come in handy anyhow.' With a half-gesture, she indicated a chair. 'Take the weight off your feet. Michael's gone to a meeting and to pick up a load of seed, he reckons to sow as soon as we get a forecast of rain.'

'I'm...' He was about to say sorry again but managed to change his words, 'Only here to introduce myself.'

'Well you're doing that fine. I'm Jane, in case you haven't guessed. Sturt's somewhere about.'

'Sturt?'

'Sturt. Well, Stewart's his name, but he's always Sturt. He's my brother-in-law – Michael's younger brother. Sturt's in the cottage at the end of the track.'

'I see,' he said, not being sure if he did or not.

'I was about to make some coffee.'

The percolator suddenly seemed pointed at him like a pistol; demanding a decision. 'Th-that would be something I'd sure appreciate.' Gerhardt cursed himself for not simply saying, 'thanks'. 'Be natural,' he told himself, 'That's all you've got to be, just be natural. Unwind. Forget the past. Relax.' But the little knot inside tightened again and made it difficult to speak without a stammer.

She busied herself with cups and saucers while he watched. He began to ease again at the familiarity of it all, the sounds of cutlery, the creak of a loose floorboard under her foot, the brief struggle with a bad drawer – he approved the way she worked and the kitchen, if primitive, was bright and cheerful. She had sun-bleached brown hair drawn back and held with a snatch of red ribbon. The light way she used her hands and the quickness of her movements still suggested she would look more in place in front of a class of young children. She wasn't much to look at but he found himself liking her. Perhaps it was because she didn't seem to be so threatening now

'You're not much of a talker, are you? Tell me about yourself.'

'I'm sorry,' he said automatically, and curled his toes in embarrassment once more, even as the words left his mouth. 'I'm on my own; you get out of the habit of talking except to the animals.'

The spoon went back and forward between the blue tin and the coffee pot several times. Without looking at him, she said,

242

'We've got animals here, too. You should try talking to *them*.'

He wondered about this, but as she concentrated on pouring the boiling water and apparently had no intention of saying more, he tried again. 'Personally, I'm into goats; Angoras, going to breed them for selling on. I'm working with the help of the University on a breeding programme. It's good country for Angoras.'

'On your own, you say?'

'Yes.' He hesitated then thought; hell, why not tell her everything and get it over with? 'I'm trying my hand again as a free-lance painter,' adding, to her back, 'Couldn't do it before, not until my divorce came through.'

She didn't seem particularly interested. 'Divorced? Uh-huh. Is that a good thing or bad?'

Cautiously he said, 'I guess it's good but I suppose only time will tell.'

In the act of putting down the kettle, she stopped to look at him; he fancied he detected some kind of weird humour behind the glasses. 'Time generally only tells you you've made a fool of yourself, and the longer the time interval, the bigger the fool you look.'

The remark left him flat. He babbled on, 'I manage, but it's pretty difficult at times – the animals always need something just when you're about to eat – I've written to the Ag people for an assistant.'

'Wish you luck. We tried one and it was a disaster. Black or white?'

'As it comes, I don't mind and one spoonful, please.' He watched her hands moving. They weren't the stubby, powerful hands of a straight manual worker. It was enough for him to take a chance, 'Are you new to farming too?'

'Dropped into it seven years ago. Dropped into it by mistake, I guess.'

This carried a tone of indifference and as he took his mug of coffee he probed again. 'And you like it? It suits you?'

Her expression didn't change. 'You make it what you make it.' An afterthought of a smile enabled her to add, 'And time passes pretty quickly in Chance Valley, hardly notice the years go by.'

'Sure,' he said. He frowned, uncertain. Somewhere outside, a fridge came to a stop with an epileptic shake but the generator still kept going.

'Michael does the general agriculture and runs the office while Sturt and I run the herd.' The same wispy smile came and went. 'Yep, we've got sixty at the moment, that's enough.' She took a sip of her own coffee and sat back on her chair. 'So who does your washing and cooking? Don't tell me you do it all yourself.'

Gerhardt recognized it was only fair for him to come under scrutiny, in the country it was usual to get to know your neighbour's business; you didn't know when you might be called on to help in an emergency. 'I can cope,' he said. 'But nobody should look too closely, there's never enough time. I'm always chasing my tail.' He realised he'd allowed his to voice trail away which led him to panic at the thought he might come across to her as pathetic. Hastily he threw in, 'I really don't care, I'm not fussy, and I'm a pretty hardy character under the surface.'

She looked at him carefully over her cup, neither smiling nor showing feelings. 'Good; you'll need to be if you're to be a long-time farmer.'

'I will be.' (Bravado? No, I must be positive). But there it was again: an underlying and unanswered thought, which bothered him. 'But I sense you don't really enjoy it: am I right?'

She placed the cup on its saucer with great care. He thought he saw her face tighten. 'Enjoyment is a relative term, Mr Gerhardt. I am not an Epicurean. You can enjoy a beautiful sunset and be depressed a few hours later with a wet sunrise. Nobody has any right to enjoyment per se and you can't buy it. Sometimes I think enjoyment is as irrelevant as feeling full after a meal. Come to that, we eat well and we're healthy, so why hope for anything on top? Have you ever read Berkeley on the things we perceive?'

'Err, no. I was always on the Arts side. I paint. Philosophy kinda left me at the same time as I left the school yard.' But this was certainly more than he expected. Gerhardt took the safer route and changed the subject. 'Well, then, how much land have you got up here, about five-fifty?'

'And another fifty we rent from the forestry. We've everything between the forest and the crags. It's mostly cattle but some grains – a good mix but not good for profits. Your place is a bit bigger as I recall.'

'Yeah, but most of it is only grade three mountain land. "Scrub", the agent called it, and he was right.'

They looked at each other cautiously. Gerhardt decided she was a very self-sufficient person. He admired anyone who seemed self-sufficient. He wondered if his own present feelings of contentment for his farm and solitude came down to mere self-delusion and a willingness to settle for second-best.

He tried to put this thought into words but failed while she appeared content to swill the coffee around in her mug and wait for him to say something. But before the silence became oppressive there came a brief noise in the corridor and the door opened to allow the entry of a big, powerful man, with a Yankee's cap slapped on the back of his head like some kid home from school. His wide-smiling face turned blank when he saw Gerhardt.

'Sturt, this is Digby Gerhardt who's taken the Morgan place. Meet my brother-in-law, Stewart. He won't eat you.' Jane Wilson rose abruptly to leave, picking up her cup as she did so, 'There's more coffee in the pot if anyone wants it.'

The powerful man, his belly gaping through a torn shirt, moved hesitatingly forward. He took Gerhardt's hand, wrapping his own over it – a hand which felt solid and rough enough to have been made of oak-roots. 'Good to see you, Mr Gerhardt.' His voice came over as curiously high and doubtful, like the worried man at the far end of the queue for tickets. It did not match his body.

'Call me Digby.' Gerhardt knew it was an unrealistic request; familiarity did not come easily to the lips of farmers in this part. He looked into a brown and puckered face, teetering on the brink of a smile but restrained by blue, apprehensive eyes. He tried to be cheerful. 'Didn't I see you ploughing next to my top strip last week?'

The apprehension seemed to ease a fraction, 'Probably tha-at's so, I can't remember.' He stood there pulling his knuckles: a chunkily handsome lump of a man. Despite his unlined face, Gerhardt put his age closer to thirty than twenty.

'Good ploughing weather.'

'Yup.' Having fully answered that, Sturt allowed a weak grin to break through, he moved apprehensively, looking at Gerhardt to say something more.

'I'm trying Angoras myself,' ventured Gerhardt

'Uh, huh?'

'You reckon that's a good idea?'

Under Gerhardt's stare, the blue eyes began looking for a way of escape again. 'Can't say I knows much about Angoras. They goats or sheep? You want to speak to Michael about such things as Angoras.' Suddenly, as though a secret switch had been pulled, a huge smile of pride filled his face. 'Yeah, but ask if you want to know anything about raisin' cattle, you jes' ask Jane'n me.'

Gerhardt felt he was on stronger ground with Sturt; he'd met others almost as bad at the auctions, usually they were casual hired men and were safe. 'I'm looking forward to seeing 'em. Are you keeping 'em still inside?'

'Jane don't reckon to let 'em out of the barn to grass yet, it's still too cold. I'll be glad when the weather changes.' The big man thought hard, his brow furrowed with unhappiness at such complications. Then, as if he'd just remembered a phrase everybody else used, he jerked out, 'Let us know if you needs a hand.'

It was too good an opportunity to miss and Gerhardt could feel himself getting more positive by the minute. 'I could do with borrowing a low-loader if you've got one spare. I've got sacks of feed to shift.'

'The low-loader?' The big face went blank again. He poured himself out some coffee slowly, and offered more to Gerhardt, his big hands dwarfing the pot, 'Reckon we can,' he said vaguely. 'If you've sacks to shift... what you needs is a low loader.'

As Gerhardt wondered, Jane Wilson returned carrying a plate of cookies. 'Apologies for disappearing, but I just remembered I'd a casserole in the oven.'

'Smells good from here and...'

'He reckons to borrow the low loader,' interrupted Sturt. 'Can I take it, Jane?'

'Sure, honey, want a cookie?'

'We eat marvellous well in this house,' said Sturt, clumsily pawing away traces of spilt coffee with his red neckerchief while, at the same time reaching for a cake. 'No better cook anywhere than Jane. Isn't that right, Jane?'

The praise and the smile appeared genuine. But the woman frowned at some hidden doubt. 'Depends on your standards. I'm no Fannie Farmer but I've a couple' dozen recipes I can trot out. As fer you; you'd eat raw turnips and say they were good.'

'Aw Jane... Well you must come for a spot to eat and try it for yourself, Mister.' Sturt's face lit up with a massive, nothing grin, 'Come with a good appetite, an' all.' At a sudden thought he became anxious and apologetic. 'Be all right, won't it, Jane? I mean – won't it?'

She only nodded, eyeing Gerhardt calculatingly as though working out how to say something. He noticed for the first time that, behind her tinted glasses, her eyes were slightly uneven, or maybe it was something else, but there was something there.

'An' Jane!' the big man interrupted. 'There was that high cloud today!'

She stopped to put a hand on his shoulder as if to quieten him. 'It was only a bit of Cirrus – no problem.' As Gerhardt sat watching, she stared back defiantly. 'We get a warning from the clouds before a Walloo hits us, but Sturt has nightmares. He's frightened of nothing in this World except that cloud.'

'I don't mind the rest, the wind an' everythin', but it's the big cloud, Jane, the big cloud over the bluff, the one that turns brown and looks like the Devil's tongue sticking out. I wakes up sweatin'.'

'Sure, honey; we understand and I tell you there's no problem, it's just a down-wave of air. Anyhow we ain't going to get a Walloo, least not today.'

'It gets bad, real bad; the devil waits behind the hill and one day he'll take us all, I can feel it, out there and nothing but space! It's as if...'

'No he won't. The Good Lord will take care of him, never you fear.' Now her face was full of apology. 'Sturt has a vivid imagination but that wind sure can blow.'

Gerhardt cleared his throat, 'Nature can be pretty rough...'

She cut him short. 'Pretty rough? It's helluva rough here, I'll tell you, when a Walloo sweeps down the valley. It's a freak of nature; when the air comes from just the right angle, the shape of the mountains funnels the wind – or that's what they say down in Purdo. Sometimes you have to wonder... Anyhow, we haven't had one for nearly a year; you could say one's overdue.

'Been thinking: if you would care to, Mr Gerhardt, come next Sunday, say about one? Michael will be with us, you may find him more interesting company that Sturt and me.'

Gerhardt found her short and formal way of talking easy to listen to; she seemed well educated. He glanced at Sturt Wilson for confirmation and found him agreeing and nodding indulgently, his worries apparently over as though it had been a rumble of a storm, which had blown past. 'Sure I'd like to come,' Gerhardt surprised himself by saying, 'That is, if it's not too much trouble.'

'Michael will be here,' echoed Sturt, automatically, 'You'll sure like Michael – he's my brother, he's more interesting to talk to, he's going to be a pol-i-tician.' There was the pride of reflected glory mixed with admiration in his voice.

Gerhardt felt this was a signal to go and anyway, he'd already committed himself more than he wanted. 'Sunday then.' He was glad it was over. 'I'll shake aroun' at my place and look forward to Sunday.' He turned back suddenly at the doorway in a farewell gesture, shoving his cap on his head at the same time. They were both staring at him, the woman standing behind the man's chair. The woman acknowledged with a quick, instant smile, but it wasn't done in time to prevent Gerhardt from seeing she had been massaging Sturt's neck. Not that the big man seemed concerned, he had both hands on the table and was looking vacant and faintly puzzled, as though he still couldn't quite make out who Gerhardt was.

The walk home seemed quicker than Gerhardt remembered with his mind filled with speculation. He was glad the woman was plain; he'd had some horror that she might turn out to be like one of the prickle-haired blondes at the Agency, all bright and smiling and sharp as razors. Perhaps she hadn't liked him? But he hadn't made any bad mistakes – perhaps she didn't like

251

anybody? She had strong features... too much angularity... Toughness. Probably from all the manual labour. In the end he came to the conclusion the visit had gone much as he might have expected.

He wondered if the new Angoras had settled in or if they would start fighting

Somewhat to his surprise, Sturt arrived early the following morning towing a low-loader. Gerhardt saw him from the upstairs window as he finished washing. He watched him lift easily with one hand, the heavy steel bar connecting the low-loader to the tractor. Beneath the flapping check shirt and baggy jeans, Sturt was a powerful man.

Gerhardt hurried to meet him in the yard. 'Great. Exactly what I need; I've got a load to shift before we get rain – had a delivery two days ago, need it for stock.'

'Michael could have sold you hay – you should have asked Jane, I'd have brought it round – it's what I do.'

Gerhardt scratched at a cut in his arm and studied his man. 'Waddyer know? An' I didn't think.' He slid comfortably into the local vernacular – and told a lie – but only a small one.

They walked round the low-loader, discussing it together, admiring the dents of hard use. 'There was one here,' Gerhardt explained, 'it came with the place but when I went to use it, the axle was bent.'

'Uh?' Sturt scowled and cracked his knuckles, 'That so? Mighty handy things, come harvest. One of the best investments we made.'

Gerhardt detected Sturt was repeating something he'd heard. He took another turn round the loader and calculated. 'How many tons can you shift at a time? Five?'

There was a silence while the question hung. The big man's face had moved to an already familiar worried look. 'Reckon I'll need it a lot, myself,' prodded Gerhardt.

The silence continued for too long. Embarrassed, Gerhardt hastily let Sturt off the hook. 'Well, anyhow, it's sure useful for me. The way the weather's building up suggests rain – did you get the forecast?'

But Sturt was worrying away at his own speed on Gerhardt's question about tonnage. 'I should think,' he said slowly, 'A heap more'n five.' His face suddenly altered from being scrunched up in a frown to an engaging grin. 'Y'see it's Michael who does all the figurin'. Me, I'm just a load of muscle – everybody says so. Michael was born with two lots of brains and I was born with two lots of muscle.' With some satisfaction he added, 'Ma told me that.'

'I'm looking forward to meeting your brother.'

'He keeps awful busy with his talking 'bout politics an' things – but he has medals too, from all foreign places.'

'Mrs Wilson, don't she get involved?'

'Jane just laughs at him,' said Sturt wisely, 'She's got even more brains'n he has.' He stared at Gerhardt. 'Jane's beautiful an' all.'

Gerhardt smiled at the serious and deliberate way it was said. Later, he reflected to himself that that was the way brains often went in a family. Life was pretty haphazard in its favours.

'Right, that was good.' Michael Wilson shoved aside his empty plate with such a decisive gesture he had to catch his glass before it was knocked over, 'Now tell us, Gerhardt, how come you came to settle in this God-forsaken place?'

They were coming to the end of the Sunday meal.

Gerhardt looked at the three expectant faces and felt his smile confident. 'Where would you like me to begin?'

Sturt, the slowest eater of them all, watched intently like a schoolboy watching a particularly difficult party trick. Neck thrust forward, he continued chewing in silence.

Wilson smiled encouragement, 'Begin where you damn well like, the parade ground's all yours.'

'I think,' said Jane Wilson, 'You could begin with what you were doing before you came here.' She held her head tilted on one side from interest, the light from the window gleaming on her glasses and her nose, reminding Gerhardt of a wary bird.

There seemed no point in beating about the bush. 'We-ll...' he admitted, 'This is my first time in farming.'

'There, I sure guessed that!' Satisfied with herself, Jane Wilson turned to her husband. 'Didn't I tell you? He's not hard enough to be a farming man.'

'You're a helluva brave man, that's all I can say.' Michael, a rugged aggressive man with a red face contrasting with black eyebrows, now added a knowing frown and judgemental nod. 'Farming's tough enough as it is – even when you know what you're doing. I've known some of the best farmers fail if they hit a bad year. Damn me, starting from nothing and on your own, too!'

'On your own, too,' echoed Sturt sorrowfully. 'That'll make it extra tough.' He shook his head then, after a long look, took another helping of meat with a slow, deliberate stab of a fork, making the act a piece of swordsmanship.

Gerhardt, abstracted by watching Sturt, picked up the conversation again. 'You have to remember I don't have many personal expenses. I'm taking it slowly, only fifty goats so far.' He wondered how much he ought to explain in order to try and defend himself. 'Top stock. Fortunately I own what I have, and animals grow naturally.'

'Yeah, and they eat naturally an' get bugs naturally.' Gloomily, Michael Wilson shook his head. 'After that they die naturally. You see it all in the accounts.'

But Jane Wilson had been watching and thinking. 'You still haven't said what you did before coming here.'

'I was in advertising.' Seeing blank faces, he explained, 'I was responsible for all the art work on Drift.' Gerhardt turned to Jane Wilson, 'You've used Drift, haven't you?'

'Sure, it's good stuff. But are you telling me you were behind it?'

'Kind of. I started with general poster design – I was always an artist – but it went on from there. In the end, for a while I became the advertising brand manager. My job was to tie up the ads, co-ordinate with the client, sketch ideas, design promotional material, things like that.'

It took them some moments to take in this alien idea. The outside world, brash, clever, modern, had suddenly appeared inside their stonewalled farmhouse. A strange creature sat at the table with them. Sturt paused in eating and stared in amazement, a forkful stationary in mid-air.

'Hum.' Thoughtfully, Michael glanced at the others before saying, 'that must have been quite a tough job, an all. Marketing's a jungle, they tell me.'

'You can say that again.'

Jane Wilson's head straightened and then tilted forwards inquisitorially, making her earrings swing. 'So what made you give up that for... this?' They waited; it was up to him now.

'I was ill. Then my divorce came along. It seemed time to make a change.' Gerhardt had already decided that was as far as he would go, he would not tell them what had started it or what had happened since. People got the wrong idea and anyway it was over now.

'But here?'

Gerhardt shrugged, 'Why not? It's quiet.'

Sturt seemed to find the thought funny. 'Y'hear that, Jane? He came because it's quiet!'

Indifferent to the others, Michael homed in. He had completed his assessment and changed his approach. 'Let me tell you this, Gerhardt,' his voice had become serious, 'You've backed yourself into a one-way street. I'm sorry to tell you but this is a dead end. You'll be trapped here like I am. Once you've bought you can't sell; nobody with kids wants to be here, nobody older would be damn fool enough to buy. A blocked valley miles from anywhere? You must be out of your mind! There's your place – and there's ours. And that's all there is now. De Groot's old farm has gone wild since he died and, anyway, he never made it pay. Yeah, and the weather can run against you, it's difficult land in these parts. Autumn and spring, that's the time you gets a downdraught from the Walloo wind. Jeez how that wind can blow! Flatten an entire crop. Seen it happen in minutes. A Walloo is something scary – I tell you the saying in these parts is that it can blow a man's brains clear into the next County. Worse, it can go on for days – gets everyone on edge. When it's like that it could drive anyone crazy. If I had my chances again, you wouldn't catch me here, no Sir. Never.'

'Cool it, Michael.'

Wilson looked at his wife, then at Sturt's hanging mouth. 'He's got to face nature in the raw like ev'ryone else.'

'It's different fer him.'

'He's a man, ain't he?'

Jane Wilson stared tightly at her husband, put her hand lightly on to Sturt's great paw as if to comfort. 'We've all got our hang-ups...'

Wilson ignored her, turned back to Gerhardt. 'My advice to you is to get a good woman and go in fer tourism, make a camp or somethin'. Me, I can't; we're too high up in the valley, people ain't goin' ter come this far.'

It seemed odd to Gerhardt that Michael should say this in front of his wife, but having made a show of protest and squeezed her mouth in irritation, she now appeared indifferent. Maybe she was used to such an outburst. 'So far I've been too busy to notice any problems,' he said mildly.

'T'aint all that bad bein' here!' Said Sturt in his weak voice, hurt by what his elder brother had said. 'The Walloo don't come offen. Devil's too busy somewheres else. Gen'lly Jane an' me get along with it pretty well.'

'And of course, you'd all know,' muttered Jane Wilson mysteriously to herself as she began clearing the debris of the main course. She stopped to look at Gerhardt, 'You've heard about a pecking order? Well we reckon the pecking don't matter as long as there's enough feathers left and enough seed on the table.'

258

Michael leaned back in his Captain's chair and teased at a piece of meat stuck in a tooth with his tongue. He managed to continue talking as though nobody else mattered or even spoke.

'If you can, get out now before you're too committed, Mister, that's my advice. Otherwise you'll rot here – I'm telling you that.'

Handing his plate over, Sturt looked up into Jane's face to say, contentedly, 'That sure was the best pie ever... Could have gone on eatin' an' eatin' till I burst. Wasn't I right about the food, Gerhardt?'

Gerhardt agreed, glad to be able to sound genuinely enthusiastic. 'Reminds me of what I'm missing.'

'*Missing?*'

He noted Jane's ears were sharp enough, despite apparently not listening. 'I mean all those working lunches with clients in the big city.'

'Is that all you're missing?'

He looked at her, wondering if she meant what he thought she meant. 'Sure,' he said. 'When you're painting you forget where you are – or who you're with.'

She smiled to herself and turned away.

'Personally,' said Michael heavily, overriding everybody with a voice laden with the rich self-satisfaction of a fleshy man following a heavy meal, 'I'm determined to get out of here and into politics. It's the only way I see of escaping the slog of farming. Besides, you can't tell me of a more worthwhile job. Politics is the art of leading the advance of humanity and civilisation against natural resistance to change.' He pondered the thought and added hastily, 'Of course having a proper and sensible regard for economics at the same time.' He ran his fingers through glossy black hair, which curled attractively at his collar and smiled with pleasure at what he'd said, adding, 'Now that sort of challenge calls for real leadership.'

'You won't leave us Michael!' There was alarm in Sturt's voice. 'You ain't goin' anyplace?'

'Course he won't, honey, your brother's just dreaming aloud.'

'That's all right then.' Sturt looked happily up at Jane.

Michael grinned at them both complacently.

At least he already had a politician's smile, thought Gerhardt, and the slogan he would have read somewhere. He felt he was beginning to know his man. 'You sound like a country Liberal,' he said, with some of his old cunning as he began helping the woman stack plates. But his irony would be lost; he knew that even as he said it.

Michael Wilson shoved his thumbs in his armpits. 'I don't hold with any particular party, I listens to them all. I'm the sort of man who has to hear both sides of the argument and then likes to make up his own mind.'

'You!' Jane threw the word with a tacky laugh, as though she could not allow her husband's boast pass by default, 'You're as

260

flexible as willow, look at what you said when Byrde refused to support the farm bill.'

'An' I say he was right to do so – only he hurt us. And anyone who hurts me won't never get my vote even if I agree with him. Stands to reason, woman, can't blame me for that.'

But as she left the room laden with plates, Jane Wilson looked sideways and sniffed, 'You're a man who blows whichever way the wind takes you; you're like wild cotton seed.'

Michael looked after her as if amazed, then winked chauvinistically at Gerhardt. 'Guess I does whatever I wants,' he agreed, and smiled, contentedly, at the thought.

'Michael does what he wants,' Sturt repeated to Gerhardt seriously, as though it was something new and important he felt Gerhardt should know.

To emphasize his independence, Michael abruptly pushed back his chair and went over to the window. 'You see, Gerhardt' – he moved aside the net curtain with a stubby finger, squinted down the track, and spoke to the glass – 'it's no good worrying too much about others if you want to get anywhere. I mean, sure you've got responsibilities for food and such like, but you mustn't let others hold you back. Jane an' Sturt know how I feel; when the moment comes for me to step into politics they won't stand in my way. Ain't that right Sturt?'

'Me and Jane can run the place, Michael, you knows that – only don't leave us, it wouldn't be right. Things are good now.'

Michael sighed and stopped squinting down the track to frown at Sturt. 'That's the trouble; I *don't* know you can run the damned place. I reckon you can't run the place without me. This place needs more'n two people, there's too much sharp figurin' to do, too many forms and organisin'.'

'And too much work,' said Jane without a trace of humour as she came back bearing a plate of mixed cakes and cookies. She dumped them on the table before turning back to the kitchen. 'I'm making coffee now – and don't eat too many brownies, Sturt,' she said as the big man's hand immediately stretched out. 'Go on like that and you'll start putting on weight.' She gave him a friendly nudge with her stomach as she left the room.

Gerhardt wondered at that nudge, in fact he thought most men wouldn't mind being nudged like that. He looked at his watch; he ought to get back soon.

'I still don't see how anyone can run a farm without someone else,' said Michael, eyeing Gerhardt narrowly as if trying to decipher in Gerhardt's face a secret he would like to know for himself.

A shout came from the kitchen, 'He already told you, hasn't he? He's a man who don't need anybody. Not like you.'

'I mean,' continued Michael calmly, 'There's too much to do with animals. Corn maybe you can manage: animals, no.'

'What I've done,' said Gerhardt, 'Is to put all my Angoras on computer. They are all tagged electronically. I have them weighed automatically each day; their food is individually calculated and as far as dried food is concerned, dispensed

262

automatically. I run a check over each animal every day. All I have to do is to clean 'em out and even that's not too bad if I switch 'em around.'

'Sure, and what happens if things go wrong? What happens if there's a Walloo; what happens if we get snow, if you want to go away? What happens if you're ill?'

Jane Wilson had returned with a tray of cups and the coffee pot. 'A farm is a dangerous place, Mr Gerhardt, accidents happen and then who'd be there to give you help?'

It was the word "help" that did it. His confidence began to be undermined. 'I'm looking for an assistant,' he repeated.

'Assistants come,' Michael grunted sarcastically, 'And assistants go.'

'All right, a worker then.'

'Cost a fortune in taxes an' anyway they generally rob you blind.'

'I know – but what other answer is there?'

Michael yawned and grinned simultaneously. 'Marry some girl or other – there's plenty in Purdo.'

'Plenty in Purdo,' echoed Sturt in his high, thin voice.

'Plenty in Purdo,' said Jane Wilson, flatly.

Gerhardt wondered.

Jane, could I have another brownie?' asked Sturt.

'Just one more then.' Jane Wilson leaned over to pass the plate. It seemed to Gerhardt the smile she gave Sturt softened her face to what could be described as tender.

'I wish to hell you'd stop him eating those damned things,' said Michael. 'Why do you have to keep baking them for him?'

'Because he likes 'em – why else?'

'He's addicted, that's what. It's like a drug.'

Gerhardt looked at his watch for a second time and got up. 'I have to go,' he said. 'I've got six that are on compo and the machine isn't set-up properly yet.'

'You'll come over another weekend and join us for a meal?' Michael asked. 'Sure enjoyed talking to someone real – at last.'

'Yeah, we enjoyed talking to yer,' echoed Sturt, without moving or looking.

Gerhardt turned to the woman for final confirmation. She was reaching over the table to pour Sturt some more coffee. 'Why not?' she said, and didn't stop pouring. Gerhardt noticed that she hadn't shaved under her armpits. It was an ordinary enough sight but for some reason it made him go hot as if a match had been tossed casually into a mass of dead emotions. He heard himself say, 'Sure I'll come.' as though it was not his voice at all. Then alarmed by what he had said and still fascinated by the tuft of brown hair under her armpit, he added, 'I'll give you a call when,' and wondered why he should feel guilty about it.

264

'You've got a deal,' said Michael.

Usually Gerhardt finished off his day with a few minutes watching television on satellite, drinking a beer, sometimes going to the trouble of making a whisky sour. Tonight the channels seemed lousy, or else he was too disturbed in his mind. Anyway he felt tired and went to bed early, only to go over his thoughts again. It was something Michael had said which had resurrected some buried concern. How, in the name of all that's holy, had he arrived at this point in his life? Was he really doing the right thing?

The Vice-President had been remarkably kind when he'd visited Gerhardt at the rehab Centre. 'Give yourself a break, Digby, try something else... come back to us when you like, but come back only when you feel like it – not for any other reason or you'll screw up again and finish back in the bin.'

Gerhardt vaguely remembered apologising profusely for letting them down and being surprised by the agreeable reaction. He remembered, more clearly, the shock of finding a man he'd always thought of as a bastard, in fact being considerate.

'Forget it. You put yourself under too much pressure, that's all, and I reckon you're one of those that can't take the stress. Anyone ten percent under budget gets squeezed, we all do; you were just unlucky when the competition launched their new brand. Guess it was my fault as much as yours – I kick butts, it's my job, and maybe yours got kicked more'n you deserved.'

265

It was not what Gerhardt had expected, nor was the generous cheque. He'd set his mind to hating them all: these human touches confused him. Later he wondered if it was conscience money but decided it was meant as recognition of all he'd put into the job. It made him feel better.

Sleep finally came, but only after he'd dropped back to an old habit and spent some time doodling. This time doodling ad strips for selling glasses, using Jane Wilson's face as a way of showing how not to do it. Even then it was only a troubled sleep.

He dreamed he was by the sea, on a long sandy Caribbean beach on a hot day. The sea came and went. A gentle, summer sea, coming right up to his knees with each wave as he lay there, waiting. The waves came higher and higher. And then he was somewhere else, a woman by his side. But she was covered with some voluminous nightdress he couldn't remove. He struggled to take it off but it wrapped itself round him and his struggles got weaker and weaker and yet he felt so comfortable. The nightdress was warm and soft, he fell into it... such comfort... he finally slept again. He made a mess in the bed; it was the first time for years.

A week went by and much of what was said fell away from Gerhardt as he worked long days, putting together his run-down farm and creating his studio for painting. Only the faces of the people somewhere above him in the valley came back to him and led him to wonder what they were doing. On the Monday it rained and he worked in his kitchen, listening to the radio. The following day the sun shone and he went to the edge of the larch and spruce forest to complete putting up shelters for the goats in bad weather. It took several hours but as the numbers increased, he'd have to pen them further from the ranch house.

It was when he returned he found the plastic pot alongside the door. There was no note, but when he took off the lid he found an apple tart nestling in foil and some fresh baked biscuits in a bag.

It was such a shock he sat down and looked at his findings again, feeling a flush of embarrassment that anyone should go to this trouble. He could imagine her putting things together and then walking all the way down the valley to deliver them. So she had been here and looked about the place...

But as he thought, a second feeling came, that of outrage that his silent world should be threatened by visitors; this was his secret retreat, here nobody came; this was a refuge, a home of peace and security. All this was gone, somebody had been and the place would never be the same again, it was just somewhere where people might drop in at any time.

This feeling of outrage ran its course to return to one of embarrassment, finally to be overtaken by a nibbling curiosity about the woman. He hadn't imagined her as being anything but a cool abstract person, uninterested in anything outside her own world high in the valley. He muddled away at all these ideas and was left to feel more disturbed than embarrassed.

Eventually he went indoors and was on the point of picking up the phone when a thought struck him and he backed off; there was a better way, and he knew what to do. Already he had half a dozen small paintings, oils on hardboard, of the valley. They were intended as a run of pictures along the corridor from the door to the kitchen. He selected the best, wrapped it up, and put it on one side.

The routine each day was always the same: first the animals, then breakfast, and then the computer analysis. The day after finding the tart, he set off up the valley as soon as he could, the painting in his hand. It wasn't until he was over the stream and half way up their part of the valley that he had second thoughts: what might she say to one of his paintings? What if she didn't like it? Hadn't room for it? Didn't want it? Could he stand the humiliation of knowing it was put aside only to be produced if she knew he was coming over?

As he stood, he heard the sound of shouting and the revving of a motorbike. Scrambling up the bank, he saw in the distance all three of them moving on a herd of stock, Jane Wilson riding a motor-bike and wearing some sort of dark green slicker. As he watched, she stood up, holding the bike with one hand, waving at a cow with the other, the wind pulling the slicker behind her like a cloak. The image of the woman riding her bike like some modern-day witch on a pepped-up broomstick impressed himself on his mind; the wild clouds in the sky, the woman pointing, and the cloak. He saw all things first in visual terms; that was how he saw everybody that was how he saw her. He grinned at such an idea and with the grin came a strange elation; as though something had happened to lift his mind above the narrow confines he'd allowed it to follow over the last few months. The witch of Chance Valley. He vowed he'd paint the image that night while it was fresh in his mind.

268

The sight of the three of them with the animals also answered his doubts over the wisdom of the painting as a thank you. It would be absurd to bother them while they were out there, and he couldn't go back without being seen, he had to continue and leave the painting in the same way she'd left the tart.

He continued up the valley and left the painting on the boards under the porch: stepping back afterwards and looking about; guilty of being there on his own, but wanting to know more. He noticed the signs of economising: the patched slippers at the door, the worn tools. He peered into the barn where they kept house gear and disturbed some chicken. When it came to the personal washing on the line he knew he had gone too far and walked back to his own ranch curiously embarrassed. He wished he'd just dropped the damned thing and left.

The following day it began raining. It started with fine drizzle at 2.30 in the afternoon, just as he'd been on the point of starting on a new fence, but by four it was coming down heavy. There was no wind, just solid rain, and it grew worse. By supper it was a downpour. Before going to bed he checked around – the animals, the sheds, each room – everything. There were no leaks except over the porch; things were wet but normal, it was just that some feeling of premonition hung in the air. It was the total blackness: the blackness and the way the rain appeared relentless, as though it were determined to wash the world away. He wasn't scared but he could have been. 'Some rain,' he kept repeating to himself, 'Some rain.' It was a night when anything might happen, and he made sure his flashlight was to hand before climbing into his bunk to sleep uneasily.

When he woke it was in the middle of the night. At first he couldn't make it out, and then he recognised the sounds of creaking. Odd, he couldn't place where; it wasn't close... Then the roaring registered, but listening more closely it wasn't a vague roaring, it was the sound of water; running water, a stream, but there shouldn't be a stream, the stream was way above – or was. Or was? He shoved on boots, a coat, gloves, and stumbled from the ranch, looking for trouble.

And he found it.

Above, and to one side of the house, stood the reservoir. A small lake with a dam. Fed from the mountain by a small stream and with large, concrete pipe as an overflow, it supplied water; good clear water to the ranch and to the stock. A pretty and comforting sight, but not any longer. His powerful flashlight showed the water being lashed by rain, the outlet spouting water as never before, but it was the stream entering which transfixed him; it had become a plunging torrent, a waterfall, far beyond the capacity of the exit pipe to deal with as excess water.

The dam now overflowed along its entire length. It took a moment for him to comprehend the full significance; how long before it gave somewhere, causing thousands of tons of water to sweep down on his ranch, he could only guess. Running back to his tool shed, he grabbed a shovel and charged up the hill to where the stream boiled over the rocks.

Three, four, five times he attacked with the shovel before throwing the thing away as useless; wading dangerously into the darkness, fumbling and groping in the stream, then hurling the rocks into place in an increasingly hopeless effort to divert the flow. He sobbed with the effort, the pain in his fingers and the soaking coldness of the water that slowly numbed him towards careless oblivion.

Suddenly the night surrounding him was split with a beam of light and he felt his shoulder grabbed from behind. 'Waste of time, here, fellah; c'mon, follow me.' The glistening wet face of Michael Wilson appeared, and then disappeared. Gerhardt hauled himself out of the water, wondering and swaying before staggering after the bobbing light.

Wilson led the way uphill, seemingly knowing where he was going and what he was doing. Gerhardt could only follow and try to keep up. They went over some knoll and plunged down a steep incline to join the stream again. Wilson shouted at him to lend a hand, and then ducked under an overhang. There, lit by Wilson's torch, Gerhardt could see a massive wooden arrangement diverting the stream from some much older waterway.

Wilson tugged at a plank and motioned Gerhardt to help. Together they shifted one, two, finally three planks. Water flew in all directions. Gerhardt was soaked before; he was doubly soaked now. But the rush of the stream had diminished. 'Reckon that'll just about do,' shouted Wilson above the din, 'If not....' he drew from his pocket a pad of some explosive and showed his teeth in a grin, 'I'll give it the Marine's fuckin' hello...'

'Great! But we'd better go back and see,' shouted Gerhardt in return.

Wilson looked, nodded, stuffed the explosive back in his pocket and grinned again.

They returned to the dam and found the stream quieter, steadier, no longer flying in madness: the water leaving the overflow seemingly just about winning the battle. 'We'd better watch it for ten minutes, then we can check again against the level,' said Wilson, 'Jeez I'm cold. Could do with a drink – you got some whisky somewhere?'

'Sure.' Gerhardt crossed the stockyard and brought back a bottle and two glasses from the house. Wilson was sitting down on the edge of the dam. 'Here. You taking yours neat or with water?' He pointed across the lake by way of a joke.

Wilson grunted appreciatively, scooped up some water and held out his glass for whisky. As Gerhardt poured whisky he said; 'I was up at my place lying there, listening to this lot coming down, when I thought to myself; 'I bet that son-of-a-bitch Gerhardt's never heard about storm floods, an' no sooner had I thought that, I thought I'd better come down and see for myself. Didn't Morgan tell you about the old stream bed when he sold you your place?'

'No,' said Gerhardt, 'And I'm mighty glad you did turn up.' A nagging question came to his mind. 'But how the Hell did you get here?'

'Got my horse, Sally, she's somewheres over there in your paddock. In these conditions, a horse is one helluva sight more useful than a wagon.'

Gerhardt thought about the rain, the journey, and the effort Wilson must have made. This was a real debt. Gerhardt said so and tried to express his thanks.

Wilson cut him short. 'Just being neighbours. 'Sides, you and me are the only real men 'round here; we've got to stick together – ain't that so?'

'I suppose... Yes, that about says it all,' said Gerhardt, finding the words painful.

'Nature's all around us here, trying all the time to wipe us out,' continued Wilson, happily; 'You, me, all of us, we got a fight on our hands.' He chuckled into the night. 'Remember, there's something out there: something without a name. Sometimes it tries to catch you unawares, like jus' now. Or sometimes it creeps up on you – like when our well water went bad – but always it's there: waiting, watching, and always trying to get you. Some jus' call it Nature but I reckon it's more'n that. You got to fight it, Gerhardt, fight it all the way 'cos it's a killer. This is some place; it's you versus... It.'

'Godamn it,' said Gerhardt with sudden realization, 'I believe you're enjoying all this!'

'You bet your fuck I am! There's nothing I enjoy more than a good fight. This is a bastard of a place, Gerhardt. In the end you'll hate it. I hate it; I hate all of it – the silence, the mountain, the work – but it does give you a good fight now and again.'

Gerhardt took a mouthful of neat whisky. It arrived at his cold, empty stomach with such a bellow of warmth he winced. 'I'm getting the message,' he croaked out, hesitating, 'Only... You seem better at it than I do.'

'You'll learn,' said Wilson. 'Notice anything?'

Gerhardt listened, puzzled, and then realised something else: it had stopped raining.

'We can go back to bed,' said Wilson. 'It knows it's bin beat.' He finished his glass at a gulp, gave a deep sigh of pleasure. 'That's it for tonight. Battle over. Chalk it up as a win.' He whistled for his horse.

There seemed nothing more to say. 'See you, Michael,' said Gerhardt. 'And thanks again.'

'See you,' said Wilson, and groped, as if with second vision, into the dark for the reins. He pulled himself into the saddle. 'Remember what I said Gerhardt, if you stay here, it's you – against it.' There was a flash of teeth as he chuckled, and then he was lost in the night.

Gerhardt sat hunched, hardly aware of the clack-clack of hooves slowly disappearing. He sat on: cold, wet, and incredibly weary, too weary to get up and walk back to his house. He drank more whisky – much more than he normally drank, enjoying but hating its liquid warmth. Wilson's words worried him, he couldn't say why. He'd wanted to be here on his own, to live a solitary life and paint. Surely it wasn't much to ask? Just to escape from the lot of them. Instead he seemed destined to have neighbours who intruded and worse, much worse, he saw, now, he needed them.

He finished his glass. The night hung around his shoulders, but after Wilson's words, it could be imagined as a something... It was black and hairy, no, it was dark blue and rubbery, or grey and misty: it was murmuring, or whispering, but it was alive, always alive, and it was *there*. He knew he was getting drunk but drank again from the bottle and waved it in defiance. 'I don't give a damn for you or what you are, I've been here before; you're an immense black beetle, I've got sprays for things like you. Black beetle, black beetle...' It was all so funny he chuckled, waved the bottle again and shouted, 'You can't beat me Mister It!' Appalled at the noise and his audacity, he stopped and listened, was there a sound besides that of the stream?

For a moment he sat totally still but there was nothing to be heard but murmuring waters and suddenly his own voice sounded hollow, as if he stood at the end of a long black tunnel. When there came no reply to his next and hesitant shout, he drank again and laughed; only now it was a harsh, ugly sound and the echo mocked him. He shook his head, swearing at his own stupidity. He rose and stood, swaying and muttering, then blundered down the slope to his house.

The darkness crept in to circle the house, only pausing at where the light spilled out from the left-open door. It listened to the banging as Gerhardt crashed his way back to bed. Then it settled down and waited.

Purdo County isn't a tourist attraction and isn't on the main highway. It has no history apart from the bank robbery in 1976, and no interests in anything other than itself. Purdo people are the same; most of them like the place and now there is a golf course say there's plenty to do. They'll accept outsiders – slowly – but not foreigners. And they know the difference, only *that* you have to find out for yourself. Sunday mornings are a time warp of silence before cars begin to arrive and the church congregation starts to gather under the oaks.

Gerhardt watched people drift by through the window of the drug store. He did not feel part of them and did not wish to be part of them; he was a farmer from Chance Valley drifting in for supplies; an outsider, an observer – and a disinterested one at that – with no desire to know anybody in Purdo, no interest in their names, nothing. It was better that way. They were like moving pictures on a screen and of no relevance to him; his life was in two distinct parts: his working past ending in the Agency, and his farm now. There was nothing in between and nothing outside.

Somebody sat up at the counter next to him but he continued munching a cheese toasty which did for breakfast, watching through the window, marvelling at people's apparent happiness.

'Good morning, Mr. Gerhardt. I hope you're not going to ignore me for ever.'

He turned to find her sitting on the stool next to him: Jane Wilson.

'Oh...Hi!'

'Coffee, flat.' She ordered it from the Sunday stand-in behind the counter and turned back to Gerhardt, 'I'm here for church, what's your excuse?'

She wore a blue jacket with a creamy-white skirt, a smart combo if slightly out-dated, but it was her hat which drew his attention; it was years since he'd sat beside a woman wearing a hat, it made him feel he'd arrived at a wedding.

Gerhardt overcame his surprise and laughed. 'My excuse? Very earthy. I needed supplies. I ran out of bread amongst other things and knew the Two-Bye store would be open.'

'So you stopped in here for a snack. What's that piece of scrummy you're eating?'

'Cheese toasty, a late breakfast. Like one?'

He looked up the counter and made to order for her but she shook her head. 'You said you would call us and come over again. That was three weeks ago, ain't you hungry for something real yet?'

Somewhere a bell began tolling. Gerhardt hesitated over replying to the invitation while he noticed that, under the oak trees, nobody seemed in any hurry to move. 'It's been in the back of my mind, I didn't... well I didn't want to intrude.'

The hat, a straw thing brightened by flowers, tilted in disbelief. 'Uh-huh. Anyway, can I thank you for your painting without you getting' all tongue tied and embarrassed?'

'I think I got the bargain, that tart of yours...'

'It was a run-on from what I was baking, no problem, but your painting – it was lovely. No, more than that, it was beautiful. And I have just the spot for it – in place of an old mirror. I suppose, well, would I be right in guessing you must be a very sensitive man?'

Gerhardt made a deprecating face, 'I ask you: could anyone ever admit to not being very sensitive?'

'We all know some who aren't, don't we?'

They shared a mutual smile. With some show of indifference she said, 'I jus' figure you don't like coming out of that place of yours: you've got to make more effort.'

'I've got a lot to do,' Gerhardt parried. 'The old place was run down, nothing works.'

'Oh, sure.' Disbelief made her smile again. Gerhardt could just make out her eyes moving behind the smoked glasses and wondered if behind the apparent certainty there lurked nervousness. He thought about it, couldn't be sure, finally gave up and took another mouthful of toasty.

The counter-hand poured coffee and milk from flasks on the Cona set-up and Jane Wilson paid him from her handbag before Gerhardt could offer. She lifted her cup, 'Well, here's to dear old Purdo County,' she said, looking at him.

The movement of eyes behind the glasses fascinated him again. You saw them only enough to know they watched you keenly. Why did she wear them? He worked out she narrowed her eyes when she peered at him. He raised his own cup. 'And here's to Chance Valley, cows an' goats.' It was only a joint sardonic gesture, but looking across the brim of his cup, and her so close,

278

produced a kind of intimacy. The thought ran through his head that she was more attractive than he had remembered.

'Yet you like it here?'

He said, firmly, 'I like it here – and I know I'm going to like it more.'

'Even on your own?'

'Especially on my own, well, for now anyhow.'

She looked him straight, smiled, and said nothing.

Suddenly, despite the slam-bang going on behind the counter, the silence between them seemed to sound louder than anything else.

Something changed in her mind; she finished her coffee quickly and put down her cup. She said, quietly, 'You haven't answered my question. When are you coming over to see us?'

For her it was some kind of turning point, of that, he felt sure. There were no obvious signals, no overt gestures, yet the very ordinariness of the question suggested more. Perhaps it was nothing but a subtle change of tone and yet... He still hesitated before throwing it to fate. 'Can I give you a call on Wednesday?'

The church bell tolled again. People began drifting in through the gateway, a huge concrete arch supporting a cross.

'Call when you like – but don't feel you have to.' She groped for her bag without looking down.

'Oh, I want to come!' His own words surprised him.

'I don't believe you; I think you want to escape from our world and this world for some reason only you know.'

He gaped at this abrupt ripping away of his privacy.

'I think that there is some dark secret in your life, and there's nothing so intrigues a woman than thinking a man has dark secrets; you should know that.' She didn't look at him but slipped off her stool and straightened her skirt, brushing out the pleats at the back and pulling a face at what she saw.

The indifferent way the comment had been thrown off jerked from him a chuckle of admiration. 'One person's secrets can be blindingly obvious to someone else – perhaps!'

'I must go,' she said.

He tried backtracking. 'Mrs Wilson, unravelling other people's problems can be an exhausting occupation...'

'I was two years into studies of mental illness before I married. I don't think I'd have made much of it but...' She shrugged.

'Then you should know all about these things.'

'About men? Me? Surely not!' The head was tilted coquettishly. He didn't notice her glasses.

The words appeared from nowhere. 'Damn right!' He said.

Suddenly she laughed. He'd never seen her give a pure laugh before and for a second he saw neat white teeth. 'You should come to church more often, Mr Gerhardt.' But before he could think up a snappy answer, she left the store and joined the last of the congregation moving under the gate.

Gerhardt had spent a few years struggling to make it as a freelance artist – London, Paris and New York – before he'd thrown in the towel and gone into advertising for the cash. But one theme had run throughout his eighteen years of working life: lovely women had always surrounded him. Some were lovely and intelligent, some lovely and sexy, at the time he'd thought his wife all three, but lovely was the common theme. In some way he couldn't fathom, he seemed to attract lovely women. He put it down to some deeply mysterious thing to do with being an artist being seen as desirable, he was sure it had nothing to do with his appearance and after years of wondering left it at that.

Since his illness and the period in the care-institute, he'd had no close contact with women; the shock over his wife had erected a barrier of avoidance and fear he'd thought quite impregnable. The meeting with Jane Wilson unsettled him, first because he felt unusually interested in her as a person and second because she broke all the obvious rules of being attractive. Her glasses were a turn-off for any man, she didn't present herself well, and she didn't seem to care if she caught the attention of men or not. Yet strangely she was attractive; you added up all the negatives and it came out positive. It was bizarre and unsettling.

The thought ran through his mind driving back from Purdo, and it remained in his mind while he binned up the concentrates for the goats in kid. Perhaps the answer lay in mannerisms; perhaps in the way she could appear so mysterious. In the end he persuaded himself to the view that probably it was just that he hadn't been with a woman for so long that anything might seem attractive. He didn't entirely believe it, but it had to do, and it was sufficiently persuasive to enable him to get back to his monthly stats analysis and put the matter to one side. Anyhow, he'd take care and try and evaluate his reactions better next time when he went up to visit them

Wilson joined Gerhardt looking at the blunt end of an enormous bull tethered inside the barn. Wilson chuckled aloud. 'If he farts while you're standing there at that end, Gerhardt, he'll blow your head off!'

Delighted with his joke, Wilson rocked on his feet.

Preoccupied with the animal size, Gerhardt only smiled. Wilson misunderstood this lack of enthusiasm and frowned in self-defence. 'That sort of joke of mine goes down well in politics here. They like plain-speaking folk who'll keep it simple. They've been fooled by too many pansy-talking smart-asses in the past.'

'Uh-huh.'

They walked round the bull. Wilson watched Gerhardt's face. 'Like him?'

'He's so big.' Gerhardt picked his words. 'I'm only used to goats.'

'Yeah, but why keep goats for Crissakes, nobody keeps goats.'

'Exactly. I'm not competing with experts. And with the latest genetics, goats are going to get important again. Much of the world is growing drier and hotter, goats will survive in the worst places; goats are the animals of the future.'

'Oh sure.' Wilson showed his disbelief by slapping the bull on the rump. 'But do you like him?'

'He's what I call impressive. So are the rest. All that power on four feet!'

'Yeah, they're a good breed. Sturt an' my wife look after them. I used to, but I got kinda bored.'

Gerhardt continued on his conducted tour of the Wilson's farm. 'It's an experience being here... such a mass of flesh in such a confined space and so clean... I can see how someone could get enthusiastic'

'Sure. Guess it's how it takes you.'

The tone in Michael Wilson's voice begged a question and Gerhardt accepted the opportunity. 'You don't sound like a dedicated farmer, how did it happen?'

Wilson took his time. Gerhardt could see he wrestled with the complexity of the question. 'Wa-al, y'see it was like this – at the time it seemed a gift: Uncle Jo died and I inherited. I thought, "this is it, Michael: your big chance to make it on your own!"' So I bought. Then I found I had to put down what dollars I had from the Marines to modernise the place. After that, I found I'd driven myself into a box-canyon; I'd trapped myself. Spent my money and couldn't git out. Yes, Sir, trapped myself in with nobody else to blame.'

Gerhardt thought about what he'd observed so far, it seemed reasonable. 'And Sturt? How does he fit in?'

'It's a long story but I've always kept an eye on him and most of the time he's been with me.' Michael Wilson paused to look at Gerhardt. 'As you will have noticed, he's a nickel short at the counter but he's devoted and hard working. I guess that counts a lot nowadays. 'Sides, he's blood o' mine. Don't know why my kid brother should be a Klutz – there's no history of it in my family. He's seen a dozen specialists and it just comes down to the fact he's not right.'

'He's a helluva physical specimen,' grunted Gerhardt. 'Looks good too. That comes from my Mother's side.'

Wilson led the way through the barn. The smell of cattle was strong. Eventually he explained, 'Sturt gave a bit of trouble a few years back – fought the police. They gave him a few days inside to cool off. Now he hates jails. Terrified of them. The worse he did was to borrow a car but you know what cops are. Get a reputation and... anyhow he seems to have settled down now.' Wilson was disinterested. 'No girl wants him, you can see why – he's only got to open his mouth, poor guy, and they fall about laughing.'

They passed under a long steel pipe. He patted it. 'Takes the chaff from the blower.' Here, let me show you the grain drier.' They walked through the door in the side of the stables, passing balks of timber leaning against the wall. Gerhardt looked up at the tall, galvanised tank, humming from the drier. 'I feel more comfortable with grain, it doesn't walk – or fart.' Wilson chuckled again at his own joke. 'Should have been a simple dirt farmer, I guess.'

'I'd say you've got a fascinating mixture. I admire...'

'Listen,' Michael Wilson suddenly grasped Gerhardt by the arm and spoke with suppressed tension, 'I keep telling you; this place is a trap. You can't leave it because of the animals; you can't make a dollar without them. Cereals only pay their way – the price is on the bottom. Corn, you can't compete with the market. There's plenty who can grow corn cheaper than here. Y'know the most time I've had off the place on my own at one go? Three days to go to the Party Convention – and that's in the last two years.'

The outburst startled Gerhardt. 'If that's the way you feel, then that's not good...'

'You're damn right it's not good! I'm thirty-nine, Gerhardt, and I ask myself if this is all I'm going to get in life? It's not enough, I tell you!'

'What will you do?'

'What can a man do? Financially, I'm trapped, and with a wife and an idiot brother as well. If I were on my own I'd walk out. You're lucky, Gerhardt, bein' divorced I mean.'

They looked at each other, feeling their way into a deeper relationship. A bell clanged; the sound abrupt and clear.

'That'll be for chow.' Wilson wiped beads of sweat from his forehead using his large neckerchief. 'Come on Gerhardt, seen enough?'

Gerhardt was feeling hot himself; the grain store was not insulated and the sun unusually strong for the time of year. 'Enough f'now – and I still say I'm impressed.'

Wilson gave a snort which might have meant embarrassed appreciation or might have meant disparagement. They walked over the yard to the house in a friendly way.

Gerhardt looked up at the sky and thought it very clean, the clouds bright white against the blue. He shrugged at the weather and followed Wilson through the oak doorway.

'Now nobody's to leave a single thing!' Jane Wilson dumped the pot on the table alongside the dishes of string beans and potatoes before wiping her hands on a cloth. A wisp of hair hung over her face to be pushed away by her arm. 'You guys get started; I'm just fetching more sauce.' She looked flushed from cooking.

'Shan't leave a drop,' said Sturt, taking off the lid. Steam and an aroma of rich meat filled the room.

Gerhardt sat back and watched for a moment.

'Juice, Sturt?' Michael Wilson busied himself with bottles, pouring pitcher-wine for himself and Gerhardt.

Sturt was not able to reply, open-mouthed, he frowned hard at stirring the pot. It took all his concentration. Wilson poured him juice anyway.

'Gerhardt said he admired our set-up in the barn.' Wilson raised his voice loud enough for Jane to hear in the kitchen.

'Why not? It's a good enough for most people.' She came back into the room, removing her apron at the same time.

'Maybe 'tis and maybe it ain't but nobody with any sense would want to know.'

'You've made your bed, now lie on it.' Jane Wilson spoke brusquely, turned to Sturt, and changed her face into a smile. 'How'd y'like y'beans today?'

'They're good.' Sturt jabbed a fork in the direction of Gerhardt. Through a mouthful of food, he said, 'But he ain't eating his share.'

Gerhardt, caught dreaming, sparked with anger and hurried to help himself. I'm slow, that's all.'

'Or not quite with us yet?'

'Lay off,' Michael grumbled. 'Don't let her hassle you, Gerhardt. Given a chance she'd chase a prairie dog down its hole.'

'Oh sure, sure – and you'd make a good Majorette at the next Convention.'

Sturt stopped eating in surprise. 'How could he make a Majorette, Jane?'

'Joke time, honey.' She patted Sturt's arm. 'There's baked Alaska to follow.'

'Looks like being a close run election this time,' suggested Gerhardt, more as a way of diverting attention than from interest.

It was enough to start Michael Wilson off on his principal concern and he talked with the length and fluency of a veteran politician. It went on and on. Jane looked at Gerhardt with an expression of disgust, he grinned back at her, for once enjoying himself. He ate with simple enthusiasm until he realised he was being observed in between her eating her own meal and passing round dishes.

'...So in a nutshell, that's why we reckon we're gonna wipe them arseholes out, come next spring,' concluded Michael, and he dabbed, roughly, at his mouth with a cloth. He looked about him as though on the platform of a meeting and smiled, benignly, at the unheard applause, the barely visible audience.

'What sort of food do you cook for yourself, Mr Gerhardt?'

'Mixes. I use a wok, it's quicker.'

Michael glowered at his wife. 'What the Hell's cooking got to do with the Convention?'

'Nothing-what-so-ever-at-all.'

288

'Well, then?'

She said carelessly, 'Food is more interesting, that's what. It's more fundamental. Right, Mr Gerhardt?'

Gerhardt smiled noncommittally.

'Huh. Without the right political decisions you don't get the choice of food, tell me if that ain't correct.' The words were growled out but Michael sensed this could be controversial and hastened on – 'There are rumours I could come up for election myself.'

Mercilessly, Jane Wilson pursued the point: 'These rumours came up last year as well – and the year before that.'

'Sure,' said Michael Wilson, equally grimly, 'And one day they'll come true and then we shall see...'

'We shall see you'll have to forget it: you can't afford to walk away from the farm.'

'I keep telling you: we shall see.'

Sturt had watched the exchange with alarm but Jane smiled brightly at him and said quickly, 'An' don't you mind Michael, honey, he only says these things.'

Wilson's face had taken a deeper shade of red and his lips were tight. Gerhardt felt sorry for him, a politician without even a press secretary. 'Who knows the future?' he said, trying for neutral ground.

'There's no future in this kind of mixed farming, that's fer sure.' Michael commenced another political diatribe, this time aimed at Europe and Australia.

Jane Wilson now ate more thoughtfully. Gerhardt thought she now deliberately avoided looking at him.

'Can we go to Europe one day?' asked Sturt, making it sound as though it was in New York State.

'One day, maybe,' said Jane.

'Don't start that again,' grunted Michael. 'If he asks for the moon, tell him straight he can't have it.'

'You can tell him.'

'I can! Why the Hell can't you?'

Gerhardt watched, waiting to see how she'd respond. 'Listen!' she said quickly. 'What I want to know is why a man like Mr Gerhardt came to turn to farming – it's not like him.'

'Neat,' he thought.

'No, woman; it's not like him because he's a man with brains.'

'Life is made up from fragments of chance tied together by time,' Gerhardt suggested, forcing a grin but only to ease the situation. 'I could right now be sitting at a farm table somewhere in New Zealand.'

She leaned across the table and stared hard at him, her chin only a few inches off her plate. 'But you're not. You're here, and that must be for some reason.' She sat back again and waited.

'Don't ask such damn-fool questions,' snapped Michael, still smarting from the casual dismissal of all his skilful political analysis. 'He's here, ain't he? Question is: does he know what he's doing?'

'I spent a year studying Angoras and marketing wool with Ben Talker over in the Rockies. He's one of the few experts in North America.' Gerhardt carefully avoided saying the Ben Talker worked as part of the hospital rehab treatment set-up.

It was enough to make her smile widely. Her lips still tweaking with amusement. She said, 'Why! A whole year with goats! There was Billy goat an' Nanny goat and Kiddie, the teeny weenie baby goat…'

Michael thrust his neck forward aggressively. 'That's what he said. A year with his damned goats. Don't seem strange to me, woman, if you want to be a fuckin' goat-farmer.'

'No? Perhaps not.'

Gerhardt thought bleakly, he calls her a woman and yet he doesn't see her as a woman at all. Gerhardt was aware of her as a woman – she had on a silk blouse and her breasts swelled against it when she moved forward – but there was an aura, an intensity, which disturbed him more. He turned his eyes away and tried to think it through. They've gone their own ways and Sturt doesn't rate, so Michael sees he's only got me. I'm going to have to be his buddy. For no particular reason he found himself saying, 'Goats have characters, I've one big goat I call

King Billy. He always seems to smile at me and he's got golden eyes with that black iris goats have. Can't say I like his eyes – they're kind of watchful 'n calculating. You could have nasty dreams thinking about his eyes.' Gerhardt stopped; Jane was smiling at him again in open amusement and said, 'The Devil comes dressed as a goat.'

'Animals can talk,' announced Sturt, loudly, startling all of them.

'Tell you what that goat would say if he could talk,' Michael began shaking with laughter, 'Know what he'd say? He'd say, "Hey there!" Get it, "Hay!"' The cutlery rattled with his belly laugh.

Sturt didn't even smile, didn't even seem to hear his brother, 'And I saw a great grey owl today,' he said.

'Where?' Jane hadn't laughed either.

'In the Aspens. Stood out against the white bark like it was soot. I see all sorts goin' on out there. All sorts. Out there is where it happens. The world moves out there. Nothing happens in here.'

Michael stopped laughing. There was an awkward silence while everyone thought of different things.

'When I'm out there, it's as though the sky tells me things, tells me where people are, what's goin' on.'

'You been at them magic beans agin,' said Michael, brusquely.

Jane Wilson seemed to wake from a dream. 'Do you ever go to Church, Mr Gerhardt?'

'I did, but somehow it's got lost along with a lot of other things.'

'We have a good church in Purdo with a wonderful Dean.'

'Don't you let her sweet talk you into something you don't want to do,' warned Michael. 'She's damned good at it.'

Gerhardt managed to put on a smile. 'That sort of thing needs a lot of thinking about,' he said. He didn't have church in mind.

'Perhaps it does,' she agreed, and began clearing plates. 'Perhaps it does.'

It was as though he were back at High and there was to be an exam at the end of the week; no matter what he did, the matter surfaced in his consciousness, a mixture of depression and excitement frothy with elements of danger.

He tried to ignore it at first. Then he rationalised his thoughts, and took himself sternly in hand: some things were to be avoided; he wasn't some screwball teenager any more. Think of the past and try and learn your lesson.

It did no good; he was continuously coming back to the thought of Purdo on Sunday. Clearly he must not go, to do so would be to invite trouble.

But deep down, the drag of fate, carrying its own momentum with the irresistible force of a slowly sinking ship, took him down with it – as he knew it would; for he could say or reason what he liked; it was certain he would go. He would find his way to Purdo even if he had to walk on his knees.

And of course when he arrived she was there, drinking a squash at the drug-store counter, feet on the steel bar under her stool, the same jacket now loosely over her shoulders, apparently indifferent, but watching keenly in the mirror above the fresh-fruit machine.

'I won't bother to say I'm surprised to see you,' he said and slid his newspaper on the counter as he took the next stool.

'Good, but you're later than I expected.'

'Probably my nerves.' He made a laugh at his own joke but felt an uncommon tightness in his throat.

'Nerves? With me? Why?'

'Because,' he lied, 'You're going to interrogate me.'

It was her turn to laugh and to study her shoes as if suddenly finding that perhaps they needed replacing. 'Interrogation is the wrong word. So's curiosity. Obligation's closer but too hard...' She didn't look his way but frowned as if studying a puzzle.

The waitress, neatly packaged and labelled as Alice, arrived with her pad open. Gerhardt ordered coffee and a bagel Jane Wilson shook her head and waited till the girl had left. 'I think, Digby, perhaps I can be of help if only you'd open up.'

She could help? Was that what it all meant? 'You reckon I need help?' He laughed. 'Goddammit it, have I come all this way to get help?' Lost in a sea of dishonesty he threw in: 'look, would that make sense?'

She shook her head. 'The world is a big place; people sometimes, well... just kinda lose their way.' Her voice turned cold and flat. 'There must be a lot of folk in Purdo who could do with a hand, you ain't so special that way.'

Conversation like this Gerhardt did not want. His nerves wouldn't stand it. It was all or nothing and it had to be nothing. No way was he going to speak about the past; it was too painful. Out of his unease grew anger; damn them all, he was finished with all that. He looked at her but she was sitting as if unconcerned. Seeing her calm, made him calm – but cold too. He said, 'Why don't we just talk about the here and now? Aren't there enough problems in the immediate future? Why not talk about something simple?'

'This bar? The weather? The airline strike? Michael's ambitions?' Her face worked its way to open amusement. 'What do you want to talk about, Mr Gerhardt? You can pick any lousy subject you like.'

The tone hurt. 'Listen, Jane,' he took a deep breath and started again. 'Listen, you want to know more about me and I want to know more about you. Right? Be honest. Why don't we start there – keep it simple, no entrails of oxen, no dissection of motives....'

'And no risk to you? I get it. Receiving you fine, Houston. Very well, I'm thirty, give or take. Yeah, I'm married, I can't tell you my weight because I never bother to weigh myself, I'm five-six in height, and take fives in shoes. Start with that.'

All right, so perhaps he should use her rules. He snapped, 'Why do you wear those glasses?'

'Doctor's orders.'

He thought she said that too quickly but he let it pass. 'OK. And you're married to a farmer; handsome, well set up, ambitious – could go far...'

'Will – if he gets his way.'

'Let me be frank: from all the vibes and from the way you were both talking, I can't make out if you're married to the farm or to him. If you're his wife...'

'Even today, marriages can be marriages of convenience. When a girl of twenty thinks she's pregnant.'

'Ah... And yet you haven't...?'

'I had a miss, seems as though I've got a short womb, but by that time I was at the marital launch-pad with all engines running. Believe me, Mr Big Advertising man, when all that's going, you've got to be one hell-of-a-sure with yourself to call a halt.'

There was genuine anger in her voice and it silenced him.

The church bell tolled for the first time, neither of them noticed it. Alice had taken up her position at the far end of the bar and listened to the radio as she polished glasses. Most people had left; some were on their way into church.

He apologized, uneasily – if he'd touched a raw spot he was sorry – but already she'd recovered. 'There's nothing to be sorry about, as I told you, the past only shows you made a fool of yourself.'

'Maybe.' He wondered at such rationality.

'Anyway, Michael was a major in the Marines then, and far too handsome to be left alone.' She shook herself free from memories. 'Now it's your turn – only I'll ask the questions to the point, it's a lady's privilege.'

Gerhardt sipped his coffee, watching her cautiously. 'Go ahead, Counsellor.'

'Did you choose Purdo because you thought you could get lost here?'

He took another sip to give himself time to think. 'Partly. I had been ill, a lot of overwork, I needed a break.'

'Physically ill or mentally ill?'

He scowled. 'Plaintiff asks if he has to answer, your Honour.'

Jane Wilson chuckled. 'The Court must make up its own mind. You wanted to escape from everyone, was that it?'

'Perhaps, it is difficult to see these things in the abstract.'

297

'This *is* the abstract but, anyhow, let's get down to specifics. I want you to say precisely why you wanted to move away from people.'

Gerhardt wanted to talk about how it had happened but could not imagine himself telling her; it was too horrific. He said sharply, 'I thought we had agreed not to go in for dissection!'

'Objection overruled, you must answer the question.'

'I wanted peace and not to be pursued by crazy questions of no relevance!'

Jane Wilson inclined her head and allowed herself a small, tight smile. She was moving her empty glass around on the counter in circles and watching beads of moisture roll along the surface. 'Prevaricating as usual. Well let's put it differently. Why don't you like meeting people, Digby?'

She had dropped her voice and had asked the question gently enough to unsettle him. 'I don't know,' he said uncertainly.

'But I think you do know. You know but you don't want to look at your problem squarely.'

The second church bell began ringing and people began moving into church. Jane Wilson continued moving her glass in small circles. 'Can't you let go and tell me?'

He felt closed in and panicked. 'Another coffee down here!' He called out loudly to the waitress.

Smiling, Jane pursued him steadily, soft-footed, as if from the shower with a towel round her, 'Sooner or later you'll tell me and feel a lot better for it.'

The old nervousness dug into him and wouldn't let go. Some things must not be opened. It was like having a locked door behind which lay a deep well, so dark and profound that it had to be concealed from everyone. He managed a smile, 'I don't see why the past should be allowed to dominate everything.'

'Oh but it does; the past has an effect on everything, in fact the past often controls people entirely – unless you spread it out so fine it can't be felt.'

With a sudden roughness he said, 'I want to bury all that, I don't want to dig up old memories and continually inspect them. Jesus Christ, Jane, can't we let it alone and talk of us?'

She looked outside at the empty street. 'Us? The dangerous double? Uh-huh. Listen, I must go.'

Now he panicked because she seemed about to leave. 'You might as well stay here, your too late for church – it's started. They've gone in.'

'Better to be late in Heaven than early in the other place. I must go. But I want you to promise to come over on Wednesday morning, say around eleven. Promise?'

'Why?'

'I want to show you where the bees keep the honey. Meet me by the top barn.'

Gerhardt watched her every inch of the way across the road and into the church. She didn't bother to look back.

He slowly finished his bagel and a second coffee without noticing it. Every conversation with her had ended up with feeling more interested and he still didn't understand why. 'It's those damned glasses,' he told himself. 'If I could only see her clearly I could follow her mind.' But the worry of where it was leading and what she wanted remained – and so did the tingle of pleasure at it all.

He had no recollection of driving back to Chance Valley at all.

Monday, Tuesday, the time to Wednesday dragged. If he'd had the choice he'd have spent all his time observing the Wilsons' place, but as it was he was more than occupied dealing with the problems of his first crop of kids. And he found he couldn't enter the results into the IBM. And he couldn't sort out the weights, and there were the supplementary feeds to adjust, and there were men to see working on the road... After spending much of his time thinking of the meeting, he only just had time to shower before racing across the valley to make his way up to the Wilsons' farm.

He found Jane Wilson sorting out equipment in a store at the back of the barn and in some sort of hurry. With only the briefest 'Hi!' she showed him a pile of gear. 'Grab a net for yourself in case you need it. Bee-gloves are over there; pick a pair your size. Come on, I've a dozen hives at the base of the

Bluff and I want to be up at there when the sun is still on that side – it's for your benefit.'

The track led away from the house and on, through patches of aspen and spruce, up towards the dominating Bluff at the head of the valley. The sun slanted through branches, lighting patches of yellow in clearings, illuminating spider-webs, early butterflies and hover-flies. Gerhardt marched behind, at first marvelling at the figure in front but finally only concentrating on keeping up. Always she was ten yards in front of him, walking with the easy lope of the agile and fit.

It did not stop for half an hour, until they reached the base of the Bluff and were under its shadow. She waited for him to join her and pointed out the row of hives. 'Here, they're protected from the Walloo when it sweeps down the valley.' He nodded, saving his breath. 'Work first,' she said, and put on her head-net and gloves. 'You can do the same and follow me, or you can just sit there and enjoy the scenery, I don't mind.'

She took each hive in turn, checking on the frames, if necessary adding syrup from containers in her small rucksack, taking notes. It took a while. He watched her as much as the scenery and all the time she explained as she worked. Finally she straightened her back. 'There, that's it; they should be OK until it's time to collect more honey.'

He was on a knoll a few yards back. She joined him, taking off the netting from her head. 'Like the view?'

From where he stood he could look down the entire valley and see his distant farm as well as the Wilsons'. The valley was in the shape of a vast horseshoe, encircled by the low ridge of crags, green and lush although he knew for a fact much of it was rough blueberry.

'Take a *real* look, Digby, take it all in, the fields, the trees, animals... the view; take it all in.'

'It's great. Fantastic view. Takes your breath away.'

'See the way it turns to blue haze at the end of the valley?'

'Yes.' They contemplated, together, the long vista speckled by passing cloud shadows.

Hands on hips, she said slowly 'I suck it all in, every bit of it. Every time I come here I think of Christ in the wilderness being tempted by the Devil. Remember how it goes when He was taken to a high place and shown the World?'

'Wasn't that where he was offered it all if he acknowledged the Devil to be the master?'

'That approximates – but he didn't accept, he stood firm. Now do things make more sense to you? I say to myself, this is your valley, girl; this is your world and, click, suddenly I feel better. I could live up here in a tent.'

'Are you a God-clutcher, Jane? Sorry to put it that way, but are you?'

'I think there's something out there that's better'n you or me or any of us, looking down this valley from here, I reckon sometimes I can just about get a glimpse.'

'From here, it's a beautiful valley.'

'Just as God made it.' She laughed briefly. 'I reckon the Devil must be jealous, that's why he sends the Walloo.'

He thought about this. 'Does Michael ever come up here?'

'No. He's a people's man. He needs humans to touch and other people, fresh faces: to speak, listen. Argument and ideas, facts and figures: that's him. I'm with concepts and feelings... Say! Is all this boring you?'

'No,' he said, truthfully, thinking she was remarkably trusting.

'Because when you understand this place, you understand how I feel, and when you understand how I feel, we can talk together. Until then you won't understand the place or me. Indians must have come here and felt the same – hundreds of times over the years. Sometimes I almost reckon I can sense them strolling about but perhaps that's being a mite fanciful.' She swung around and almost danced. 'Feel it? It's called being primitive!'

Gerhardt wondered, said nothing.

She sat down on the flap of her rucksack and patted the ground by her side. 'Park your butt, Digby, but use your hat – the ground's pretty wet.'

He eased his lanky frame down. 'You said you were into concepts. I don't quite follow.'

'Farming's a life and death cycle. I can live with that, I guess you can too. As a concept it's clean and simple. Living in a city blurs the edges – you hardly live and you're not even allowed to be seen to die. When I was in New York as a student, I'd spend my spare time in places like the Morgan imagining over pieces of ancient junk. I guess I must have been a bit of a weirdo at the time. Here, the problem is you work like a dog, I never worked so hard in my life, but when I come up here, click again and it's all right. Get me?'

'Just about. So what you're really saying is that you wouldn't much want to be advertising Drift – am I right?' He was rewarded by a chuckle and encouraged to expand. 'Does this mean you've cut yourself off from human contact?'

'Only that I can live with less. Look!' she pointed with a finger, 'Over there – by the maples, there's Max, our bull. A great big chunk of unthinking sex. Getting on for a ton on four legs. I admire him; I say again, it's being primitive.'

'Where are Michael and Sturt?'

'Michael took Sturt into Purdo. Sturt has an appointment with the dental hygienist – I insisted.'

'Does Michael always have to take him?'

'No-o... But Sturt's always terrified of ending up in jail again on some old grudge charge by the cops, so generally Michael sees him around. Michael's a great one for seeing people around, other people, I mean and, oh boy! Do I mean it!'

Gerhardt pondered this, tried to read the body language, felt he was still far away from closing the mental gap between them.

'But I still want to know why you came here, Digs. You're all wrong for this place.'

He'd been expecting this, waiting for it; now he could say, calmly, 'Some things are better left unsaid. Only dogs want to go back to their vomit, I sure don't. Leave the past alone. Forget it.'

She thought for a while, pulling at a piece of grass nervously, then began again only this time in a different tone, lower, husky, intimate. Her fingers touched his hand. 'Digs... I want to hear from you. I don't want excuses; I want to feel I understand you. I can't understand if you don't tell me.'

It was like suddenly having a purring cat against him, very physical and full of sensuality. 'I want to know all about you: know what you think, know what you want. I need to know all about your past.'

'Please, don't ask.'

'But I have to know! You're on the edge of telling me; it's there, in your face. I see it, I feel it.'

Gerhardt looked at her, for once she'd taken off her glasses but her eyes were closed. She spoke as if from memory or from some inner certainty that made looking at him for confirmation unnecessary. And for him, feeling her so close became an invitation to reach out and touch her.

He struggled against any such commitment. It would be too final, too dangerous and against all his own rules. He had an impulse to jump up and run away and yet he didn't, couldn't. All he wanted to do was please her. That was it, just to please. And yet, and yet...

In the silence of the valley, the minutes passed as Gerhardt sat and waited, hoping for some solution to arrive that made no demands on him to take the decision.

She spoke again, softly, almost as though they were husband and wife in bed together, 'Yes, tell me the whole story now, when we're here alone under this warm sun and with the whole world at our feet. It will be between us, a secret. It's the right time for saying outrageous things where nobody else can hear and only the sky can see. This is bee-land: just you, the bees, and me. You can say what you like and I shan't be shocked.' She added, insinuatingly, 'I won't scream.'

Hot and cold, he knew he was losing the battle. 'But why must you ask like this?'

Suddenly she became practical. Sensing he was hers, she lost any previous nervousness. 'I told you; I'm someone who is curious about people. I like people. I'd help anybody. I'd like to help you, in any way I can. Something about you fascinates me... and I can help you, Digby, I know it. I shall put you right again.'

Somewhere he detected a lie but he was too confused to care. He began closing down mental defence switches. It was like

306

struggling through a foetid jungle and sensing the edge to freedom was only a few feet away. It was too much. Let go, and he would be in some beautiful world of gentle comfort beyond imagination.

'What difference will it make?'

'Everything. Your world will not be the same again. You, me, we can deal with it together.'

He could no longer cope. Without being conscious of the how, the words slid inside his skull; wrapping a coil around his thoughts, putting a moist tongue into his ear, stroking, easing and moving him into some supine position where he would disintegrate. Could he resist? Why did he have to? He made one last, choked, effort. 'No,' he said, 'it's not possible.'

'Oh, Yes! I must hear you, Digby, you must, you must!'

'I... I...' His words collapsed and he began to stammer like six months ago.

'Go on, go on!'

'B-b-because...' Gerhardt's chest pained with trying to hold back words he'd vowed never to say. 'Because...' Abruptly his voice changed, it had to be done, had to happen. It was fate and nothing to do with him. He dug the fingers of his hands into the turf and let go his mind. 'See, Jane, it was so stupid at the start, I came home exhausted after a funky conference on subliminal advertising and almost at once my wife and I got to arguing.' But now at the abyss, his courage failed again. 'I admit it; I was already on edge. Work was in a crisis and they needed a

307

scapegoat. They were all at me, everyone, everyone, everyone! Then she started…' He stopped; he couldn't say more.

'So? Then?'

Gerhardt shook his head, unable to speak.

'You can't leave me there, you've got to go on, you've got to do it. I'm waiting. Go on!'

'And then...'

'And then?' Jane Wilson swayed close to Gerhardt, clutching his arm, leaning in to him, staring into his eyes, ignoring his pain, 'Let's hear it at last.. Then what happened?'

'Spat in my face.' He ejaculated the words. 'Spat at me – it hit me in the eye.'

Jane Wilson swayed away from him while she thought. 'Uh-huh… So she spat in your face.' There was a long pause. 'That wasn't nice. But that wasn't all, was it? It couldn't have been. So what did you do about it?'

'I hit her.' Inexplicable tears came to Gerhardt and he had to wipe them away. 'It may sound nothing to you but then I cracked up. I hit her and I kept on hitting her. I had to, don't you understand? I didn't want to, but it was something inside me driving me on. I couldn't stop. It was though half of me watched, and was ashamed, while the other half punched again and again and took pleasure in her pain. It was revolting. She deserved it but I disgusted myself, I was less than human.'

He was there again with the kitchen walls whirling round and his wife half over the table, her upturned face screaming at him. 'I hit her, I hit her and I kept on hitting her. I didn't want to; I was ashamed at what I was doing. Worse, I knew what I was doing and still didn't stop. I was going to murder her.'

'But you didn't?'

'No – but I carried on. It was revolting. Then she fell down and I stopped.'

Breaking the silence which followed he said 'disgusted' several times and shuddered.

'Digby,' she breathed the words so gently they hardly hurt, 'You may think you're a fucking arsehole; the world may think you're a fucking arsehole, but it's over, all over. And when it's over, it's finished; don't you understand? It's finished: move away.' She touched his brow, and then moved away a fraction to peer hard at him. 'Time goes on and on and you're looking back at a ghost that only exists in your head. Maybe it happened that way, and maybe it didn't happen that way, but it's far back. Wounds heal, trees mend, grass grows, you were a man and you're still a man. You, she, and the world, have all got other things to do. Other places to go...'

It was like a dog licking a cut. He felt that whatever she said, her words would soothe.

Abruptly, she asked, 'What happened after that?'

'After?'

'Yes, after. Something happened after that.'

He could not answer at first, then: 'My wife must have left,' he muttered. 'I don't know... Don't know.' Memories kept flickering back. He felt his arm jerked hard, he sensed she was breathing up at him.

'Don't try and escape. You heard her go? The door slammed? You went out yourself? Well, you didn't just stand there like a fuckin' penis, you did something.'

He looked at her, dazed; this woman seemed to vibrate with energy and demands. 'Yes, something, I suppose. Jack Knowland, our neighbour, heard some sort of din and found me in the middle of the night wandering naked... I had a breakdown, didn't know where I was, they threw me into the Westbourne clinic.'

'Found you naked!' There was a yelp of savage humour that echoed around the Bluff. 'That must have got 'em yakking! My, can't eggs fly! Jane Wilson let his arms go and opened her mouth in irresistible triumph. 'So, let's be simple, you beat your wife up and you had a breakdown!'

'Yes, that was it.' Like a bull in the last moments of a bull fight, Gerhardt waited for the final blow. It wasn't simple; the memory was a gaping, open wound, bleeding his psyche. But at least he was done; there was no more of him left. All that remained was to be killed off, released from this torturous process.

Jane Wilson repeated slowly to herself, 'It came to something as little as that – all you did was to beat your wife up and it led to you having a breakdown. And that's driven you ever since? But it was nothing! Digby, honey, you're just a baby in life. A gorgeous great baby.'

'She spat in my face,' repeated Gerhardt dully. 'It was the look when she did it. I can't forget that look; it haunts me and will always haunt me. She hated me and I didn't know it – couldn't believe it, imagine that! All those years of living and loving and perhaps she always hated me.' Now he was back there on that sultry night; heard the shrieking of insults banging on his head, saw again that once beautiful wide mouth drawn back in a snarl... that expression, the spite in her eyes, the lipstick on the teeth. She scratched him across the face and he hit back; one, two, more... until the room went purple and he stood over a motionless whimpering woman, his heart thumping, chest heaving like a maddened horse. Only then came the awful realisation that a black madness existed somewhere inside him and only required the right trigger to be released.

His memories slackened their hold and he felt a hand brush over his brow again. 'Take it easy, take it easy, honey, it's all over. You've gone through it for the last bad time, now it will get less and less.'

Gerhardt came back to reality and the present. He let go the turf and turned to the woman beside him. 'To see pure hatred is to see into the very soul of evil, did you know that? Perhaps they teach you that in Church, but me, I found it out for myself.' He flexed his fingers and tried to relax. 'Yes, I beat up my own wife... I didn't think I could beat up anyone. I never ever hit anyone before... and she hated me; she wasn't frightened at all; she didn't care about being beaten, it was just naked hatred. I

311

think she wanted me to beat her just so's she could hate me more. I saw hatred even when she fell down on the floor. My God!'

'It's your memory: you only recall the worst bits.'

He knew the real Jane Wilson was close to him, leading him along a cliff-face of a memory, but all he could do was to sway from side to side, exhausted of all feelings.

He became aware she was saying, softly, 'I feel I know you now – I've got you worked out at last. You're just a gentle and sensitive man who ran up against the razor-wire.' There came a pause and then; 'It's all there and I have it out of you. It was a poison and now you will be better. What you were was a man trapped inside his own head, it's as simple as that and your recovery starts now get it? Now!'

They sat on the ground together but five years apart, looking, unseeing, down the long valley. He felt like an Olympic runner slowly recovering from a race; the pain of effort slipping away by the minute and being replaced by an increasing feeling of release.

As an eagle circled over them, she moved fractionally closer to touch him with her hips, so close her voice reduced to no more than a murmur in his ear. He wanted to lie down, put his arms round her and fall sleep, but, instead, he continued sitting; waiting stupidly for something to happen. She ran her hand through his hair, he was surprised but didn't resist. She nibbled his ear and he found himself trembling. She rubbed against his body and her hand slid up his leg. 'Come on,' she whispered,

'There's a time for everything and the moment has arrived. I know of an old cave near here where it's always dry. Wipe everything out of your mind, Digs, sweetheart; you're rid of all that mental baggage now; you can enjoy yourself once more. What you need is something good and old fashioned. It's what we all need, what we all want, what we must have, sometimes, somewhere. I know where it is and you know where it is. We do it together. Do you know what it's called?'

'It's called bonding.'

'Almost,' she whispered and pressed against him. Moments passed. She rubbed the inside of his thigh. 'Try again.'

He caught her fingers and moved them upwards. 'Bonding, pair-bonding. We bond together you and me.' The words were difficult to say.

'Digs, you don't understand what I have to give. Feel me properly... There. Let me spell it out, it's called... what's it called now? It begins with "S..."'

It was like standing in summer woodland, warm and full of scents. Such words suffused him with warmth but more than that, a sudden protectiveness towards this woman who seemed unaware of her effect on him. 'No,' he said, 'No, it's not just sex. Jane, I want you properly. I don't just want that, I want us to be one. And it's not called that, then; it's called pair-bonding.'

He felt her become tense. 'No.'

'I need more, much more. I need to give to you all I have, to wipe myself out, to…'

'No! Stop right there! It's called screwing, that's all we do; it's always called screwing.'

He almost said nothing more, his heat was now so great, but an impulse to start off right with her, made him insist. 'No! Bonding – it will last, believe me.'

'Screwing!' she said harshly, twisting in his arms. 'Screwing!'

He couldn't understand her. 'No, Jane,' he said. 'No.'

'It's called screwing because that's all it is – nothing more than that.'

'I'm not going to agree, no!'

'Yes! 'She thrust at him so suddenly he released her and she scrambled away. 'Right feelings but wrong words,' she snapped down at him, astonishing him with her intensity. 'You don't understand a thing – why did you have to say anything? Just screw, that's all you had to do, just screw.' Anger crackled into rage as she snatched her things in one sweep of hand and set off down the hill. 'See you again.'

Bewildered, but still on some new high, he lunged after her, calling her name.

'Better luck when you try next time,' she shouted, breaking into a run down the slope.

He called again but she did not reply.

Slowly he followed her, wondering... all the time wondering, wondering, shaking his head, somehow nothing quite made sense. But under it all he felt better; the relief was massive, he felt good.

He walked down the valley and passed the Wilson farm without looking.

From his porch, Gerhardt squinted into the setting sun and watched the car come up the track leading from the main highway. A Chrysler. He had a hunch he knew who it would be and yet surely she wouldn't have told him? No, that would have been impossible. Gerhardt sipped the drink he held, and waited. He was quite calm.

The car spun round in the parking area ready to leave again, the impatient manoeuvre of an impatient man. Michael Wilson got out and slammed the door.

Gerhardt watched casually as Wilson stumped, determinedly, across the gravel. 'Hi!' Gerhardt said and raised his glass.

'Wanted to see you, Gerhardt. Got something serious to discuss.'

'You time for a drink?'

'Whisky. Maybe with a little water. Thanks.'

Wilson followed him into the kitchen and watched as Gerhardt threw some ice from the machine into a glass. 'You seem to have set yourself up fine and dandy here.'

'More or less. The men have only just left – they were improving the track to your place, it's passable now. Say when.'

'Whoa! I still got work to do. Been at a committee meeting all day.'

Gerhardt added water, handed him the glass. 'You're a pretty busy man, Michael.'

'Got to be, it's all happening. Your health, Gerhardt.'

'Take a seat.' Gerhardt tossed a fresh log onto the cooking fire and sat down. He stretched his legs out, since that time up at the Bluff he felt remarkably relaxed, whatever was coming was not going to disturb him now. Anyhow, Wilson didn't seem to be looking for a row.

With the scene set, Michael Wilson suddenly appeared less certain of himself, twisting the glass in his hand and frowning. Eventually he said, 'Mind if I ask you a personal question, Gerhardt?'

Gerhardt grinned slightly but didn't look directly at Wilson. 'Go ahead, ask what you want.'

'Are you serious about this farming of yours?'

It was not the question Gerhardt had expected and it was his turn to frown. 'Serious as I can be. I've sunk all my money into this.'

'Oh sure, sure, I can see that, but do you want to be a serious farmer?'

'I'm not sure I get what you're driving at.'

Wilson grunted as if accepting the fact and took a drink, setting the glass back into the palm of his hand. Gerhardt thought he looked tired and a mite blousy. He'd lost his usual sharpness.

'See here, Gerhardt, I've got to make a big decision and it could be you're part of that decision. Tonight I've got to demonstrate to the committee just what input I'm prepared to give.' He took a quick mouthful of whisky showing all the awareness and enjoyment of a man taking a pill.

'I'm sorry, but I still don't understand what it's got to do with me.'

Wilson peered at Gerhardt shrewdly. 'This is private and there's a hell of a long way to go, but the committee want to know if I'm prepared to run as mayor of Purdo and then perhaps go on as far as Governor.'

To give himself time to think, Gerhardt stood up. A load of new possibilities came to mind and a few more problems as well. 'It's a compliment to you,' he said, looking into the mirror; wondering how it could be he still looked unchanged by events, how he could still appear honest.

'Maybe yes, maybe no.' Wilson chuckled at some thought or other. 'They want me to run because I look and sound like a true farmer. Can you believe that? A simple, decent farmer – but one who's just smart enough to do the job without being yet another smartass shouting at them from City Hall.'

'Are you complaining?'

'Hell, no – but it gives me problems.'

Gerhardt left the mirror with a shrug, went over to the window and waited. He liked Michael Wilson, didn't admire him but liked him. Behind the bluff was a man doing his best with what he'd got. He might slip through your fingers but he'd be straight, or at least straight in his terms.

Yes, but at the same time there was the question of his wife and the thought gave him pause; it was a situation of treachery – if you wanted to see it that way.

From behind him the voice continued; 'See here, there's a condition to the offer they've made to me; the condition is I've got to devote at least half my time to being Mayor and politics.' There was a pause, 'And that's the minimum, mind.'

At first Gerhardt didn't get the connection. Then he made it – what would happen to the farm? Wilson couldn't be in two places at once. 'I'm beginning to see where you're coming from... So what are you going to do?'

There was silence. Gerhardt turned round to look at Wilson. Wilson stared back from tired, red eyes and took another drink before sighing. 'I'll give it to you straight, Gerhardt; I won't try and bluff you. This is my chance and I'm going for it. You've come at the right moment; you're my way out so I'm going to offer you the best deal of your life.' Wilson nodded to himself and wiped his lips with the back of his hand. 'Now listen, this is it: we'll put the two farms together, the whole lot, land, farms, cattle, machinery, go fifty-fifty, and you can run them. You'll have the whole, damned, valley to yourself. Me, I'll move into Purdo and operate from there. Waddyersay to that?'

Whatever Gerhardt might have expected, it was certainly not this; it was all too abrupt. Stupidly he exclaimed, 'But I haven't a team to take the place over!'

'You'll have Jane and Sturt; they'll stay of course. All you'll need is one hired hand and you've got it made.'

Gerhardt made to sit down again, feeling behind him for the chair arm like an old man, 'Oh for God's sake,' he muttered to himself, his mind fizzing and whirling with all the implications.

'Think of it,' urged Wilson, 'You'll be King of the entire valley, it'll all be yours; the land, the stock, farms... all yours. Don't want to be personal, but my place is worth double yours so you win all the way. Me, I'll take a small salary as consultant and we share the profits fifty-fifty at the end of each year. What's more, with me as the local Mayor, I can fix things for you. If you want permission for a meat plant, consider it done.'

The fatuousness and irrelevance of this last remark crystallised Gerhardt's thoughts and prodded him forward. 'You make it sound good for me, but what about your wife? Hell, in effect she'd be working for me! You said she'd stay but how do you know – have you asked her? Is she really going to stay if you move out?'

'Jane'll do what she likes, always has done, always will. Howe-ver,' and Wilson dragged on the word to emphasize the point, 'In the past, when we've talked about such a possibility as me getting an offer, she's always said she wouldn't budge, come what may. For some reason she's nuts on the place an' anyway she won't leave Sturt; he'd crack up if she left, she's like a mother to him an' Sturt's got nowhere else to go.'

He waited, looking at Gerhardt expectantly.

But Gerhardt was a cautious man and now he tried to look at the deal from every angle for flaws. He couldn't see any that couldn't be overcome and yet it was too smooth to be true, his caution prevailed and he began going over all the possibilities and problems for a second time.

Patience had never been strong in Wilson's make up and he had his whole future at stake. He saw only the sandy-haired, slumped out figure of Gerhardt, still silent and looking blank. It was too much; his mind began that familiar build-up which would lead to an explosion. 'What's wrong fer Crissake? I've offered you the best deal in the world and you just sit there dreaming! Come up to my place an' we'll knock off a bottle of champagne!'

'Hey, slow down, take it easy.' Gerhardt wasn't going to be rushed. 'I'm only just into farming.'

'Listen, how much to sell your Angoras and run some of my cattle in their place?'

'Including electronics, I'd drop fifty thousand dollars. To sell completely now, I could be wiped out.' Gerhardt thought about it. 'Of course, together, we could treble your herd...'

'Yeah! And the money's in the stock so there you are then! You'll be a big man – king of Chance Valley! And I'll still be around fer advice. I ain't going to disappear. Hell, I can't get away from this place even if I tried – I've got too much to lose as well. I'll come back up as often as you want an', anyway, there's always the phone.' Wilson began to perspire and padded away at his forehead. He spoke quickly and urgently. 'See here, Gerhardt, the pressure's on fer me. The election's only three months away and I've got to be down there pressing hands, speaking, meeting the people that count. There's a Hell of a lot to do and for me it's now or never. What more can I do? Come on, tell me; don't make it more difficult than it is.'

Gerhardt took a breath. 'Look, all this sounds great, but we've got to be careful...'

'Of course you're worried about the legal side, we'll get a lawyer to draw up a proper contract. I understand your hesitation; that comes first. Tomorrow. Before midday.'

'There's that too, but...' Gerhardt avoided looking at Wilson, 'I'm still worried about Jane. She's your wife and you haven't even told her. That's not going to go down well.' In his mind he heard a voice saying, 'Please give yourself away, Wilson. Tell me straight you don't care what happens to Jane. Tell me you'd like to get rid of her. Go on, tell me. Don't make me take all the blame for wife-stealing.' Outwardly he knew he looked calm. He smiled to encourage.

Wilson waved an impatient hand. 'No problem. Jane an' me go our separate ways, we're like that, both of us strong characters, I guess; too strong, you might say. 'Sides, we've always agreed I might move over into politics.'

In some way, Gerhardt felt that by arguing against the whole idea he could silence his conscience about Jane. Silence it once and forever. He chose his words with the care of a soldier crossing a minefield. 'What people say about an abstract hope can change when confronted with the reality.'

Wilson looked blank, and then dismissed the suggestion abruptly. 'You're barking at the moon. Jane'll just shrug and say, "Do what you want."' Seeing disbelief pass over Gerhardt's face, he turned angry. 'Jane an' me have been married a long time, sometimes I think too long, but it means we know we can rely on keeping out of each other's way – get me?'

'Rely is sure close to need.'

'Bullshit. Jane's more into farming than I am. She don't need me. Listen, I'll leave it to you, then you'll see – you can speak to her yourself.'

Was it enough? Gerhardt stared at Wilson who stared back. Surely Wilson had gone all the way and committed himself? There seemed nothing more could be squeezed from the situation. Gerhardt finally shrugged and inclined his head. 'OK. You've got a deal; I'll talk it through with her.' He hoped his feelings didn't show too much.

'You're certain? You wouldn't be a son-of-a-bitch and back down now, would yer? I've got to commit myself to the committee.'

'I won't change my mind, won't let you down. You've got what you want; now I've got to make it work.'

Wilson finished his whisky in a gulp and bounced over to shake Gerhardt's hand, pumping it up and down as if he'd just scored a touchdown. 'That's our side rolling; I won't say thanks – but thanks anyway. Now I'm off to Tom Farrow. He's our Secretary... wish me luck.'

Gerhardt watched him drive away. It was going on dark and the tail lights glowed intermittent red as the car sped down through the trees and took the bends; heading fast for the highway.

With Wilson gone, for the first time Gerhardt felt the silence a burden. He looked at his glass and found he hadn't even finished his drink and anyway he didn't want it; he wanted something and it certainly wasn't a drink. He grunted, looked at the sky and could just make out clouds scudding by: a wind was starting. Hell! So what? The young animals were safely bedded down; those in the top paddock had the metal shelter.

Unsettled and full of vague worries, he barged indoors to his office and fiddled about. Still not able to relax, he tried some figures, finally taking to doodling ideas for ads on selling farms. He became aware that outside branches of trees thrashed about, gates slammed back and forth, a tile crashed down and bottles clinked. He got up and peered from the window, but all he

323

could make out were shades of black and grey and the sense of a relentless wind searching its way into every cranny like a snuffling monster sniffing out its prey.

The Walloo had arrived.

Next morning the Walloo was blowing with a full throttle, shaking the roof, rattling gates, bending fencing. Sometimes he wondered if the windows might cave in. Gerhardt hurried over the early morning routine, clawing his way against the wind all the way from the store shed to the security of the main house for his breakfast. He guessed that the routine over at the Wilson's must be much the same and with his second cup of coffee he gave her a call on the Sat.

'How's the patient?' She came back immediately. He thought she sounded cool.

'The patient's fine – how's the nurse?'

'It's blowing sixty up here, I've been up most of the night and I'm feeling pooped. Is that a good enough answer?'

'Any damage?'

'Not that I know of yet, but I saw a garbage can fly by like a cannon-shell.'

Gerhardt tried to send empathy sliding down the phone. 'It's rough here, too. Listen, something important has cropped up, can I see you?'

'Uh-huh. How important?'

He could visualize the small nose tilted suspiciously but more significantly, he read into her tone a backing off, a distancing of herself. 'I had a meeting with Michael last night, didn't he tell you?' he said.

There was a satisfactory silence.

She said shortly, 'He stayed the night in Purdo.'

He understood her unwillingness to be drawn further, sensed also a deeper unease. 'Then we certainly should meet up. Should I come over?'

'No.' A reply which came just a shade too quickly, 'I'll come over to you. About an hour.'

'Fine.' He switched off the phone and sat, thinking. Suddenly he smiled and helped himself to some food: an hour isn't long and he felt so amazingly good. Life had never been better. He wished he could sing.

At the window, he watched to see how she could cope with the wind. It was howling in the chimney, thrashing the maples and snake-barks on the far side of the yard, uprooting some early fire pinks. He watched the car reverse the car almost to the front gate, changed his mind when he saw her struggle with the car door with hair flying; dropped the curtain and hurried to help, shouting against the gale. Together, they fell into the porch and laughed at each other.

She pulled herself away to shake out her hair, then took off her anorak, folded it and dumped it on a chair. 'What a Hell of a day! Saw a dozen trees down. I've no idea what possessed me to drive here, there were broken branches flying across in front of me all the way.'

Embarrassment is always impossible to hide so no direct answer was necessary. 'Come through to the kitchen,' he said, leading the way and thinking how different she had become.

'What a lovely clock!'

'It came to me from my Grandfather. It's called "Old Faithful" in the family.' He opened the door for her to pass under his arm. 'I don't think it's an original name, I seem to have heard it before.' He followed her in and closed the door.

Already peering about, she snickered dutifully. 'Seems fantastic how you've changed the old place... I see you're well organised.'

'More or less.'

'Hey! It's nice!' A wheel-back chair stood by the table and she slipped into it, sitting back and sticking her legs out but avoiding looking at him.

All of a sudden the situation had become unreal; his home had become a place where actors made speeches. Gerhardt felt he was reading from an unrehearsed script; one he wasn't prepared for. He measured his steps to a chair opposite. 'Afraid it lacks personality, there wasn't the time. I had a team come in and put the lot together.'

'The personality will come once it's worn in.'

'Yes.' He paused, 'That's if I stay long enough.'

'If?'

'We have a lot to talk about,' he began, but was instantly interrupted.

'Don't get too heavy about it, Digs, huh? Just tell yourself yesterday was one day; today's another. You're feeling better aren't you? That's the main thing.'

'I can't forget yesterday, Jane.'

'Why not? I have.'

'I don't believe you, you're only pretending to yourself.'

'Listen, Digs, there's a lot more pain out there, someplace, and I wouldn't want to see you get involved. Just leave it. You don't have to say anything.'

Her face was neat, cool, controlled – a schoolmistress before an appointment committee. But inside? Vulnerable? He wondered. An enigma perhaps, but there was a sensuous side he'd seen, a side which could whisper in your ear and arouse your senses in a flash. Somewhere in between the two there had to be the real woman; he determined to try and find her. 'You came here to talk,' he said. 'That means a lot to me.'

She thought, grimaced and pulled nervously at her sleeve. 'I came here now because you said Michael had been here, and I'm pretty damn sure you didn't just talk about chicken shit.'

'He didn't get home to you last night because he went from one political meeting to another, did you know that?'

'Perhaps he did and perhaps he didn't, but you can bet your shirt that whatever he did, he'd finish up at a certain second floor apartment on Third Street.'

It was the calm way she said it that astounded Gerhardt. He took his time over the implications. 'Do I understand you correctly?'

'Understand?' She sniffed, 'A curious word, "understand". Who understands these things? At what level do you stop trying to understand other humans any more and just ride with it? But you're a man aren't you, so you understand – or don't you?'

Gerhardt swallowed. 'And you've known for some time?'

'Four years, give or take.' Her smile did not include Gerhardt or anyone except a memory.

It took a few moments before he pulled himself together and jumped to his feet. 'Look, some coffee? The percolator's on.'

'Just a juice.'

'Orange? Grapefruit?' In strides he was at the icebox, peering.

'Any juice, Digs, any juice.' With a sudden weariness she said, 'The first damned thing that comes to hand.'

He felt the change of mood, poured a juice for her, a coffee for himself, and brought them to the table.

'Strange how life keeps surprising you like some crazy, leaping frog in long grass,' he said to keep it going. 'I watched a frog the other day...'

'We all have our problems...' She watched the liquid swirl in her glass, 'Orange...' She said it as if puzzled, then looked at him. 'So what's up with you?'

There was still something wrong, it wasn't going quite as he'd expected. Uncertain as to how she might react, he held his cup on his lap and looked at her hard. 'Michael's been offered the backing to become Mayor of Purdo.' He took a sip of coffee and waited.

'He'll take it,' she said indifferently.

'Only if I help him.' He made the point slowly, still watching for a reaction.

Apparently not surprised, she merely played with her glass. 'Yes... And will you?'

'In a way, that's for you to decide. You see he's offered me a deal; we put the two farms together and I have a half-share and run the place, while he goes off to be Mayor of Purdo.'

A gust of wind shook the ranch house, giving them the excuse to go silent for a moment while they ran through individual thoughts. The front door rattled.

'I see.' The words were clipped out.

'It was so unexpected, I hardly knew what to say when...'

Suddenly full of menace she growled, 'And-he-didn't-have-the-guts-to-tell-me-himself. Is that right?'

Expecting something strong, Gerhardt could still be startled. He found himself defending her husband. 'You have to remember it only came to a head yesterday. There hasn't been much time...' He moved uneasily in his chair, recognising he'd given a pretty damned inadequate response to somebody whose husband has just quit. Maybe he should put an arm round her?

As emotions crossed her face, lines tightened and her anger turned to black humour. 'The retreat continues,' she said.

'Sorry?'

'I don't see how life can keep going wrong forever. I mean – can it?' Abruptly, she stretched her hands out as if she were on the beach and the sun was shining, leaning back and gazing at the ceiling, feeling the heat of the sun play over her body. Gerhardt saw her moving away to some shut-off mental world and had an uneasy feeling if he didn't find a way of stopping it, she'd be gone.

'Perhaps,' she said to the ceiling. 'As the commentator put it, "that's the way it is." Perhaps you must accept nothing but shit, shit, shit. For a long time he's been going and now he's gone. Finish. End of story. Move along, kid.'

'But it does clear the air, doesn't it?'

'Digs, what you've just seen was only the medicine cupboard door finally being closed. The problem's still there and all that's happened is that one possible cure has gone. This patient has come to the end of the line and can't see a way out.'

'I don't understand. You mean you're not worried by Michael leaving or you are?'

It was a prod too much. She jumped quickly to her feet and began pacing the room, her arms tightly wrapped round herself. 'Michael was part of it, that's all. The rest is up there.' She nodded her head in the direction of the farm as she paced.

'Sturt?'

Jane said nothing.

It was the moment when a terrible thought went through Gerhardt's head. 'Jane, did you take Sturt up to see the bees?'

She still said nothing, just paced up and down, eyes on the floor, not listening.

'You did, didn't you? You took him up to see the bees and then you took him to the cave, didn't you?'

The steps continued, left-pause-right-pause-left.

Gerhardt's mouth felt dry, he wet his lips but could only just get the words out. 'So that's the way it was... Sturt's dumb, he's not all there, he's a child, but you laid him, didn't you?'

'Sturt,' she muttered, 'has the mental age of seven but his zip can go up and down like any other man's.'

It was enough. Gerhardt exploded in rage. 'For Crissakes, you stupid woman, how can you say it like that? You know I want you and all you can do is make a joke about screwing with an idiot child! What the Hell's the world coming to?'

She continued her pacing, shaking her head as if indifferent. 'He was aggressive with everyone, he was a danger; he had a need for a love he'd never experienced... I thought perhaps it might be a cure for him – and it has been.'

But Gerhardt had seen her other side and could imagine the scene. Sturt was a man of muscle, handsome, a raw hulk of a man, He snapped, 'I don't buy that one. It wasn't only medicinal, was it? You wanted him. It wasn't just for his benefit – you wanted him.'

'Wanted him?' The pacing stopped and anger took its place. 'All right, if you want to be a bastard and rub my nose in it – I wanted him then. I wanted him bad 'cos that's the way it was that day. I had a husband screwing some Baby Doll in Town every week and I wanted something real for myself. Not just real, but honest. There, does that make you feel any better? And before you get too mighty about it, ask yourself what else was a woman to do in my situation? There was nowhere else and there was nobody else. It was a way out, that's all. And that's why it's only screwing; you screw or you don't screw, animals screw or don't screw, we're all animals, that's all; I've lost the understanding of what else there is. I don't want to know what else there is.'

There are times, thought Gerhardt, when you just have to continue regardless of pain to get to the bottom of it. He stood up and went over to where she was standing. 'And is this still going on?'

He thought she'd closed her eyes. 'Yes,' she said automatically. 'I don't want to now, but if I turn off the tap, Sturt will revert – he'll crack up.'

Seeing her appear so calm, a fury worse than anything he'd known began to make him shake. T-t-take off those bloody glasses, I c-c-can't see you. I've never ever seen you.'

She just stood there so he wrenched them off for her. She closed her eyes. Tears began to appear on her face. With a fresh suspicion he looked closely at the glasses and peered though them himself.

'Don't leave me naked.' she said. 'Please don't leave me naked.'

He tried the glasses again. 'Why! These d-damned glasses are nothing. What do you wear them for? They're only fancy very strong sun-glasses.'

'Please Digs, put them back.' The tears were now streaming down her face.

'Why?' He demanded. 'Why the f-fuck should I?'

She began crying. He grabbed her by the shoulders. 'Why?' But all she could do was shake her head so he pulled her head back and looked into her eyes. Despite the tears and redness, he could see they were odd, one was green, the other brown, perhaps there was a slight squint as well; he couldn't be sure. 'What's wrong with your eyes?'

'I've always been laughed at, even as a child.' He could barely make out what she was saying through the sudden outpouring of sobs. 'My mother made me wear glasses to hide my eyes. She said she wasn't going to be criticized because of me. I always had to wear them. It became a defensive habit, I guess.'

'I see nothing wrong with your eyes, you stupid woman!'

'Behind my glasses I feel protected. I can look at the world and not be seen. Give them back, I need them.'

'You don't need that sort of protection; I want you for yourself, not your bloody glasses!'

'I can't, I can't... They're my glasses, don't you understand? My glasses are me.'

Through Gerhardt's frustration and rage, it slowly penetrated that she really felt vulnerable without her glasses, he couldn't understand it and probably never would, but she was scared. Now her misery made her smaller, her face pinched, the wetness of her tears spread down to her chin. He took out his handkerchief and wiped her cheeks but she pushed him away angrily. 'Give me them back, I don't want your sympathy.' The tears began again.

He handed back her glasses and walked over to the window to give her time to recover. Eventually, when he turned, she was sitting on her chair, hand supporting her head.

Calm but feeling a numbness in his chest, he said, 'Listen, your eyes are perfectly all right to me, get it? You can chuck them into the river for all I care; your eyes are fine.' This didn't seem to work so he continued feeling worse and worse. 'I'm sorry I took them from you, I'm sorry. I didn't know it mattered so much.'

'I shouldn't be so stupid,' she muttered. 'I rationalise it out but in the end I still always feel naked without them. I know it's stupid but I tell myself there's no harm in it so why should I stop? It was the way they all laughed and called me names. After that I always wore them to new places so's nobody would laugh again and they never did. It's left a mark. It shouldn't. They may look bad, at my age I know I should be over it.'

'I told you I don't care; I just want you to be as you are.'

'I'm sorry,' she continued, as if he hadn't spoken.

'For C-crissake stop saying you're sorry! It doesn't matter to me what your eyes look like.'

'No. No, I understand that.'

When misery between two people becomes total, words are merely uninhabitable islands, floating in a sea of silence.

She muttered, 'I can see it doesn't matter now.'

Frustration took over and he walked round the room raising and lowering his arms. 'What are we to do?'

'There's nothing we can do,' she said, stonily. 'I can't leave Sturt; my conscience wouldn't let me. If I leave, he'll go berserk and they'll put him away for good. He doesn't deserve that; he's done no harm, he's gentle, he works hard; he's only a child.'

'I couldn't stand it... With you... knowing it was going on.'

'No. Nobody's asking you to.' She got up and collected her anorak. 'It's been an eventful day.'

There came to them the sound of a truck and they went to the window. Sturt, crouched over the wheel, his eyes staring, was arriving with the old pick-up. He parked it next to Jane's Toyota, beeped the horn like crazy and gazed, open-mouthed, at Gerhardt's ranch house.

They looked out at him.

'He's here only because he's scared,' she said.

'I can't ask him in, be reasonable.'

'He's got it into his mind that the Walloo is an evil creature and that it's real: it terrifies him. There's nothing I can say to stop it, only try and comfort him like a child.'

Gerhardt said nothing, simply stared. The old feelings were returning: the knot in his stomach, the buzz in his head. He needed time to think, maybe he wanted her, maybe he didn't, she was a different person, he needed time – or no time. He couldn't think. His head grew worse.

'Goodbye, Digs,' she said.

'He didn't move. Time. He must have time. Like an old photo, the room had crinkled and become sepia. 'B-b-bye Jane.'

It wasn't until he heard her steps start down the corridor that he dared to turn round. He saw her gloves left on the table and thought to call out and tell her, then decided against. He played nervously with his pocket knife, an old habit that had immediately returned. The front door opened, he heard the suck, then blast of wind, before the door closed again.

The kitchen window overlooked the yard, but by the time he recovered sufficiently to look, the cars had gone, the yard empty except for flying leaves and a gate that flailed back and forwards erratically, as if jerked by a cord worked by an unseen hand.

After automatically opening and closing his knife a dozen times, he dropped it back into his pocket. The room was exactly the same as an hour ago and yet when he looked at it – his chairs, his paintings – he found it totally alien. He could be anywhere. Nothing he saw seemed familiar or his, everything strange, remote.

His main unfinished canvas now seemed a waste of time. A waste of time, was all his painting just a waste of time? He worried and pulled at his fingers... What to do? Just leave? Impossible. Already he knew that he had to stay: he was tied now to Wilson, while Jane was still up there in the house with Sturt. Anyway he'd lose everything if he sold out. Tomorrow would be the same, they'd all be the same, the next tomorrow and the next, and on, and on. He knew it as if it had been handed down to him as a judgment from some Supreme Court.

For they were tied together, all of them, as certainly as the planets round the sun. And like the planets, they must orbit each other until time finally merged into dust and space.

With the wind howling, he took down his old coat and reached for his boots; he had no spirit, no interest, but the animals could not wait; they must be brought down from the mountain.

High in the top paddock, the goats huddled against the tin wall of the shelter, waiting. All, that is, except King Billy, who stood apart gazing down the track to where the man would appear first. His beard flicked in the wind, gusts shook his body, but he never took his eyes off the far clearing. Eventually the familiar shape emerged and King Billy's golden eyes narrowed with interest, watching the man stumbling and hauling his way upwards through the trees.

But the new arrival seemed to invest the elements with fresh fury. Trees rocked and creaked; twigs, branches, debris, all scudded past. Pinecones flew like shuttlecocks and a curious groan filled the air from wind shredding its way through the leaves of the giant cedars by the water tank.

Unflinching, King Billy watched it all; eyes unblinking, the struggles of the man becoming clearer as he climbed, coat wrenched with each snatch of the gale, face contorted and wet from stinging rain drops, curly hair slicked flat.

And the man was not as usual; he was tired, he frequently stopped, holding his side, bending forward. At the paddock gate, opened only with difficulty, furious words were sucked from his mouth by the wind. 'The whole Godamned, shit-faced lot of you – git down!' came the shout. 'Now, now, now!' And he waved his arm at them in a final and abrupt flourish of anger. 'Git!'

The herd, with something of a panic, hurried through the gate in relief; but King Billy, showing his yellow teeth in a smile, walked easily past, every calculated movement of muscle offering slow insolence towards a man.

'One day,' a desperate Gerhardt thought, as he followed them down the slope, he'd damned well wipe that evil smile off his face. 'One day...'

But between the man and the goat had come a knowing of power.

Daylight was ebbing away in fits and starts. Overhead, the blue-black clouds streamed past like flotsam on a powerful river; coming out of nowhere, journeying into time with a mysterious sense of urgency.

Gerhardt threw more wood on the fire.

It had been a day to forget. Now he was left with wondering how to stop the shafts of air that penetrated every crack, visible or invisible. Without enthusiasm he contemplated a night with emergency food – a tin of soup, packets of dried pasta – before taking to a sleeping bag fully dressed; the noise of the wind and the sounds from the ranch would prevent peaceful sleep, and who knew what emergency might occur?

In the general racket the arrival of a car passed unnoticed and he failed to hear footsteps. The crash of a door came as a surprise. There was a roar of air as Michael Wilson barged his way into the room. In one grinning, stamping movement, he'd removed his coat and tossed his hat on to a chair. Gerhardt felt curiously irrelevant, the small room abruptly full as Wilson clumped about on the wooden floor, throwing comments over his shoulder as if he were in a down-town bar: 'Got room by the fire for a frozen man? Holy Crow it's all going on outside – and could carry on fer a week yet by the looks of things!'

Without any attempt at formalities, Wilson dropped on to the old stick-back chair, shoved his legs out in front of him and stuck his hands in his pockets. It was as if he'd been there for all time and he spoke the same way: 'Hi Digby, it's a crappy life, n't it? Bad one day, good the next. Same fer all of us: either not enough women or jes' too many. I'd like to say I preferred men but y'can't say that sort of thing any more or they'd run you out of town!'

He grinned more widely to suggest a great deal, but then left it there with just a meaningful wink, going on to talk, and then only vaguely, about Chicago beef prices. 'Getting crazier everyday. I tell you it's like they was at the bottom of the escalator shaft with the wires broke.'

Generalities passed. Gerhardt wondered what lay behind the visit. Wilson appeared in no hurry to get to the point and now rambled on about City Hall personalities until Gerhardt decided to give some encouragement by interjecting; 'Still, you found time to get back here... you were worried about the ranch in this weather?'

'Oh sure...' Wilson failed to follow through, instead, with a frown, said, 'I s'pose you're thinking I'm here about the contract between us, but it's still with my lawyer – don't worry; he'll send it in a couple of days.'

It wasn't what demanded a visit and Gerhardt wondered what to say next as Wilson went quiet, slumped inside his clothes, pondering something in his mind. Minutes passed. Clearly something was bothering him but Gerhardt could not see how he could help. Wilson finally stirred himself with a sigh. Having taken some kind of decision, he became confidential; 'Digby, there are some things that only come to you slowly, like as if you ought to have thought of them before only, somehows, you jes' didn't get round to 'em. Truths you ought to have seen but didn't.'

'Uh – huh.' Gerhardt left to give the fire a prod with his boot. Sparks flew as he watched them. 'Michael, if you've got something on your mind you better say what the Hell it is an' stop me guessing. You want a drink?'

'No, thank y' kindly. What I've got to say concerns her up there.' Wilson took the time to indicate, coldly, and with a dip of his head, the direction of his own ranch. 'Only it's kinda difficult for me to put into words, 'cos you know me and you've only seen her.'

Gerhardt would have put it the other way round but let it pass with a shrug of agreement.

For once looking embarrassed, Wilson ploughed on; 'See here now, forget all the romantics; forget chasing ass; forget all the crap; being married is a matter of giving, huh?' He snickered self-consciously. 'I mean... it's instinctive; what a man wants to do is to give – you agree to that? All men are the same; we just want the pleasure of giving.' Wilson looked challengingly at Gerhardt, daring him to regard it as funny.

Gerhardt inclined his head and pursed his lips.

'You give and give until, after a while, it becomes tedious; you get kinda bored with marriage and the whole goddamned thing. After that, the giving starts to turn into taking; you both start taking. You take and take and watch who gets what. Ain't that so?' Wilson waited again.

'Hating comes into it somewhere,' said Gerhardt, after a pause.

'Maybe that's true, but it's never gotten as far as that with Jane an' me. We just started taking and then built fences so's to protect what we got.'

'Not sure I follow...'

'I mean,' – Wilson loosened his collar – 'You get bits of life you hang on to, like she stops me bawling at Sturt when I lose my temper, an' I insist on my poker evenings downtown.'

Nodding, Gerhardt still couldn't see where this was leading. Changing his tone, Wilson said, 'Say, if that offer of a drink is still available, maybe I could handle it now.' He watched Gerhardt walk over to the drinks cupboard. 'Bourbon. You got some Three Feathers there? And go easy on the agua, thanks.'

He took the drink Gerhardt offered, then got up, stuck his backside towards the fire and took a thoughtful sip. He peered at Gerhardt as if calculating the effect he was having before starting again more quietly. 'Reckon I'm like most men... I don't understand women; I only understand men and especially men like me.' He tried again. 'Now listen, amigo, let me be frank. I got someone in Purdo. Nothing special but she's good – and she's got class. Name's Chrissy. We see eye to eye, Chrissy an' me.' He paused, smiling, waiting for Gerhardt to be surprised.

'That's your business, Michael. I don't reckon it's got anything to do with me.'

'Oh, Boy, but it has!' With his smile slowly changing to a frown, Wilson ambled heavily across to Gerhardt and caught hold of his lapel between a thumb and a finger. He leaned towards, meaningfully, staring at Gerhardt as though his eyes could add persuasion. 'Listen,' the words were murmured in an awful confidentiality, 'I got the nomination fixed. After the meeting I had a word with Tom Farrow again and we discussed things – a good man, Tom, an' highly respected – anyhow, he's advised me to get a divorce, pronto.'

Trying to ignore Wilson's closeness and his sour breath, Gerhardt saw a face starting to show a hedonistic life style, but beneath that level, a man trying to be honest according to his

343

own rules. Gerhardt worried away at his words. 'What the hell's Farrow got to do with it?'

'A whole heap and, anyhow, what he said made sense; Purdo's a quiet town and the folks there are all a bit backward. True?' Sensing possible doubt, Wilson moved back and spread open his arms in demand, then, immediately, as if regretting showing weakness, closed them to shake an accusing finger. 'Sure that's true! Gerhardt, c'mmon, now, admit it! But, I tell you somethin': them stupid penguins down there also know what's goin' on around the beach! Don't be fooled – they don't miss a thing. For me to come up for election, when they all know I'm shacked up with Chrissy, it won't go down well. No, Sir. They'll accept a guy getting a divorce, but they won't accept someone two-timing – not after that Washington business.'

Gerhardt grunted and moved away from the finger; he hated anyone pointing fingers, it reminded him of the past and the first signs of an onslaught. He thought he should pin Wilson down. 'So... are you going to break the news to Jane?'

'Yup, right away. Can't say I relish it but probably she guesses something's up. Maybe this drink's what I need.'

Angrily, Gerhardt snapped, 'Reckon it might be.' He felt sick of all he was hearing, he shouldn't be told, shouldn't be involved: couldn't Wilson see how private this was?

As if they were talking about someone he'd never met, he said; 'Michael, your wife could be pretty mad.'

'I doubt it. Funnily enough, reckon it might be Sturt who takes it worst.'

344

This was beyond Gerhardt. Sturt was only the hulking brother who screwed up relationships just by being around. He waited for more.

'Sturt admires me – well that shows he' nuts, eh?' Wilson chuckled expansively. 'He thinks the sun shines out of my asshole. "Famous military man"' – Wilson parodied his brother – '"Gee, Michael, all those medals... you won them all?" – well you can imagine the kid's crap. He might not like to know things have broken up.'

'You needn't tell him that.'

'No point in lying, I'll tell him straight.' But visualizing the scene worried even Wilson, and he muttered elaborately to himself, 'Yes, Sir, the boy-could-be-just-a-mite-difficult.'

'How?'

'I don't know, Gerhardt, but he could. Can't read his thoughts – he's not rational, you know that.'

'But you're going ahead anyhow?'

Michael Wilson banged his glass down on the table and glared. 'Sure! It's my life! Why the Hell not?'

Gerhardt thought that at this hour, for once maybe, just maybe, he might have a drink as well.

King Billy weighed the best part of a hundred kilos. He was a big goat, well-horned and had never been aggressive. All the same, as he started the early morning chores the next day, Gerhardt felt uneasy about him and kept a wary eye. He felt they were antagonists circling each other in an arena, looking for an opening to attack and destroy. There was something eerie about the way those horns moved towards him, then stopped. The goat was only waiting, he was sure of it. And he was big enough to be dangerous. If things got worse, he'd use the electric prodder but for now, in the early morning, and still constrained by the weather, he had King Billy and the main herd, in the home paddock where there was a good barn for shelter and he could feed them without going far.

The bleep on his portable was faint under his clothing and it took a moment to disentangle it from his inner pocket. 'Gerhardt here.'

Jane Wilson's voice came over with urgency. 'Can you come up? Am I interrupting? I've a problem...'

'Sure I'll come up... What's your problem?'

'It's Sturt. I don't know what to do. He's disappeared.'

'Disappeared?'

'Yeah, taken his truck and gone.'

Gerhardt looked through the open barn door to where King Billy stood watching him as if listening in. 'I'll be along right away,' he said.

He took the car and drove carefully; down the first slope, round the hard bend, then up the steep bank on the other side of the gully; taking time to admire the clarity of the rim of mountains, with – above and beyond the rim – the blueness of the sky; bluer than ever he could ever remember, an inhuman blue, sharper than cathedral glass but cold with it.

As the bonnet of the car moved along the horizon, he saw the one cloud hanging over the tall peak like a sign. What had Sturt called it? A tongue, the Devil's tongue, a good description, only it wasn't the colour of a tongue – unless a very anaemic one – for it was pale grey in the centre fringing to white at the edges. A typical standing-wave sign, according to Gerhardt's book, and associated with a jet stream. Perhaps he should show it to Sturt when he turned up again and see if it solved his hang-ups over the Walloo. Stupid having such wild notions in this day and age. A jet stream came between two air masses, it could happen or disappear at any time, and it only needed hot and cold air masses in proximity. Simple. It would be interesting to see what Sturt made of that.

He turned on the car radio but there was nothing except some old Country and Western. Then he arrived at the Wilson's place.

Jane was waiting for him and led him straight into the kitchen, talking as she went. Gerhardt was not worried by Sturt's disappearance. A hulking man like that couldn't come to much harm. He sat and eased his back into the rocker, looked about. The difference between her place and his, he thought, was that hers had a comfortable lived-in look, whereas his varied between being a tip and an office, depending on his meal that day.

'...So Michael said he wanted a quick divorce – can you imagine his face as he said that? Sturt just sat there looking at both of us and not understanding what the Hell was going on.' Jane sounded suspiciously practical as she bustled about the kitchen and slid pots around. 'Michael, as you know, is not the most tactful person you'll ever meet.'

'And you weren't surprised? About the divorce, I mean?'

'The timing, yes. That surprised me, all right. It's not like Michael to act that quickly. He might have been brave in the Marines but he's a coward over moral decisions – he'll talk all around a subject like someone going around in a whirlpool until he's carried down in a sudden rush, still thrashing his arms and talking. But I was already there. It was obvious it had to come to a divorce.'

Jane hid agitation with an elaborate search for the sugar, finally getting satisfaction from slamming the kitchen cupboard hard. 'It couldn't have gone on with me up here and him down in Purdo with her. Wouldn't have made sense. But it made me mad when he had to say it in front of Sturt.'

Gerhardt watched her pour coffee. She wasn't wearing glasses he noticed but perhaps that was because she was too preoccupied to notice. He still found her brisk matter-of-factness amazing, but her face looked peaked and he wondered if she'd spent the night lying awake. Perhaps she was one of those who corrode from the inside where it doesn't show. It was a time for soothing words, but the thought of Sturt standing in the doorway kept intruding in his mind; the image of Sturt was all around, looking at him blankly, like some child who doesn't quite understand, a child who shouldn't be there; a child who is an embarrassment.

He took the cup she offered while nodding, talking, and more or less agreeing with everything she said; 'You're right, I know Sturt's always very proud of his brother... said Michael had won medals... moral decisions never come easy.' He rambled on, saying anything that came into his head, at the same time watching and reading her face.

As though only half-listening she said, 'I'm responsible for Sturt. I can't escape that.'

'Look,' said Gerhardt, taking a decision, 'If you have to, and if you can stand the shock, with human relationships a brutal amputation can be the best solution.' He meant it seriously but felt he sounded like the advice of a shady moral guru, the sort that charges twenty dollars a shot.

Her reply was by way of a grimace.

Now, as they faced each other, the noises in the ranch – the clicking of the freezer, the rattle of dishes – became magnified until eventually she rubbed her eyes as though tired. 'When people leave you, it's like watching the coast slide away behind a boat; it happens so quick an' easy, you wonder why you struggled for all those years keeping things together.'

He drank his coffee and waited for more.

'After Michael had done his worst and gone,' she continued, 'it took me a clear hour tryin' to get it across to Sturt the right way.'

Gerhardt managed calmly, 'I see. And what was the right way?'

'I spun him some kid's yarn about the Government saying it was necessary, something like that.' She sighed. 'To Sturt, the Government is like some great big angry old man who lives on the other side of the mountains. You just say, "Government" and he shuts up.'

'And you told him that Michael had to go away? And that you and he would be up here, together, alone?'

Slowly the colour rose in her face, her odd eyes making her anger very human. 'Oh for Crissakes, Digs, I couldn't cope with that as well! Not last night. All I wanted was to get Michael out of my sight as quickly as possible. Standing there and lying his head off! What the fuck else could I do?'

Gerhardt chewed his tongue and didn't know. He tried looking at his watch. 'When did you notice he'd gone?'

'Not till this morning. He could have gone in the middle of the night, I wouldn't have heard him.'

'Have you tried phoning Michael?'

'Yes. He wasn't concerned, said he'd look out for him in town.'

'Did Sturt take anything with him?'

'Not that I know of. To tell the truth, I didn't like to search his things.'

'Let's take a look at his shack,' said Gerhardt.

Together they walked the fifty yards along the gritty track to the shack where Sturt slept. It was not locked. With a quick look at Gerhardt, who nodded, Jane opened the weather-bleached wooden door.

Gerhardt had some vague expectation of a room decorated much in the way a college graduate might have done, with pennants, sporting gear and a hi-fi; instead he found himself in the room of a wild life enthusiast. The walls were covered in pictures taken from magazines interspersed with animal fragments – bones, skulls, paws, tails; the dried-out wings of birds. In one corner stood a bubbling fish tank, in the other, a stuffed, and rather annoyed looking beaver, crouched on a pedestal made from a tree stump. Everywhere Gerhardt looked there were items from the animal world. It was not easy to see where Sturt actually lived; such was the mass of collected objects, and most of them no more than collected rubbish from the nearby mountains

'Kinda stinks, don't it? But it's what he wanted.' Jane opened a door. 'Nothing seems gone in the way of clothes – but I didn't expect it. That's only the john,' she said, as Gerhardt opened another door.

They combed the place. There were two other rooms, one of which was full of work tools – the whole search didn't take more than ten minutes – but they could find nothing missing for sure.

They looked at each other and worried more. 'Surely you wouldn't go off without taking something?'

Gerhardt grew impatient. 'I guess we'd better get back. Maybe he's just gone off hunting.'

'And taken his truck? He's never done that before.'

'All right then. Maybe the stupid Dodo went for Michael...' Gerhardt didn't finish the thought.

Wide-eyed, she snapped back; 'He might have been in a few fights with strangers who jeered at him, but he's never ever been dangerous, never! Especially not with Michael!'

Gerhardt thought many things as he humped his way into his coat. 'Well... anyhow, if it is Michael, we'd better warn him again.'

Again they walked the path back to the main ranch house; Gerhardt thought the wind was freshening up once more.

It took some time to get hold of Michael. He was not on his mobile and it appeared he was moving between meetings. Eventually he was hauled to a phone and they heard a resentful voice snapping that they were panicking but he'd call up the cops and take a drive around the town. After that he'd give them a call or come back. They heard the phone cut off abruptly.

There was nothing more they could do but wait.

Gerhardt helped shift some feed from the dry barn, after that they drove the herd out into the home paddock for better shelter and left them there. All the time there was a sense of anticipation, of filling in space. 'Let's get back,' said Jane and

Gerhardt didn't disagree. They went back to the ranch to sit in the kitchen again.

'More coffee?'

'Thanks.'

It was now close to ten in the morning.

'I ought to be mending his pants.' Jane, sitting with her hands behind her head, indicated, with a nod of her head, a heap of washed clothes.

'Whose? Michael's?'

'Are you crazy? She can mend his; I'm talking about Sturt's, of course.'

'Shouldn't he mend his own at his age?' Gerhardt grumbled at the thought. 'How old is he? For God's sake, Jane, it's time he coped with the basics. There are plenty of other things to deal with. You can't spoon feed the guy.' His irritation grew. 'If he can't cope with basics he needs a nursemaid.'

'Years ago, once I got used to him, I swore to myself I'd always look after him. He returns it in his own way – by devotion. And he's truly kind.'

'Devotion! Gerhardt scowled. 'You could be talking about your dog!'

She didn't smile. 'You've got to get something clear in your mind, Digs; that man, as you call him, is still a child. He can't do the simplest things without losing concentration at some point. If he's sewing on a patch, he gets distracted and you're left with a half-sewn patch and a needle. Or maybe not a needle, which is worse. I tell you I've tried for years, but it's gotten now I figure it's quicker to do it myself.'

Putting all thoughts of the bees and the mountain behind him, Gerhardt said, 'You're mighty generous with your time, Jane.' It was something he really meant. To him, it was quite clear she had too much work to do. Muttering to himself he added; 'Time is the biggest gift of your life – can't throw away gifts as important as that.' He left it there.

She said, carefully; 'He's so innocent, that's why.'

Gerhardt was shocked. 'Innocent is a mighty strange word to use!'

'Of course it's strange; it's rare, that's why!' She shook her head as if surprising herself and doubting what she found. 'It's like finding a diamond ring in a garbage dump. When you find innocence, first you don't believe it, after that you simply know you have to guard it. It's called responsibility.'

Gerhardt turned away from watching her; she looked so comfortable, so domestic, so right, so, so, *close*... He turned to the window to escape.

There was a particularly good view down the valley in the direction of his own farm, though he couldn't see all the ranch house for the dip in the ground. It seemed to him the trees were not bending so much to the wind, although the herd still gathered for shelter. Peering through the window, he began to relax again; it had all the contours, all the colours; it was a view he might paint one day.

'Seems to me there's no such thing as innocence,' he said. 'Seems to me there's only ignorance. Once we were all innocent but it's all there in the story of Adam; we were given the apple, we learned, we were told. Once children learn, all innocence goes.'

'That's a thought to go along with.' Jane folded her hands and rocked gently in the chair. 'But it's gotten more'n that; true innocence isn't just a trade off against learning, it's not a definable thing; it's a state of mind. Sure, Sturt's stuck at a mental age of seven and can't take in anything, but, I don't know, it's more, much more... he's just... innocent, that's all.'

There was a movement in the distance; it looked like Michael's car. Perhaps it was. His car had the same colour. Gerhardt felt relieved, with Michael back, his own immediate responsibility would end, and he would go back to his own spread and wait for them to sort it out.

Speaking to the window he said, quietly, 'I want to paint you, Jane. I want to paint you like Goya would have done – sprawled out and naked. I want to paint you as sexy as is humanly possible.' He heard a movement behind him but continued, relentlessly, 'I can't live with you while Sturt's with you, I can't share: I'm not a sharing person. If I can't have you to myself, I want to see you as a dream and talk to you in my bedroom.'

'My body's not worth much…'

'It's not just your body, it's your mind; it's what is behind your body; it's everything.'

'Digs, don't be so intense. We're not kids, we've both been through the mincer before. You must know that it can't last for ever.'

'It's the quality, not the time. Time grinds down everything except quality. If it doesn't start with quality, it will never be more than trash.'

She laughed nervously. 'I'm not sure I can handle all this.'

'Yes you can,' he said, watching for Michael's car to appear. A minute passed.

'Before you get out your palette and start on your masterpiece,' she paused. 'Just how many women have you talked to like this before? Ten? Twenty?'

'They're written off to experience. There comes a point where you know what you want.'

She thought more, tried out her lips with her tongue. 'I don't reckon I could strip in front of you. Not cold like that. And, anyway, I'd know where it would lead.'

'When I'm painting, I don't know where I am; I'm a professional. I wouldn't know who it was; you'd be quite safe. At the time you would be just be a technical problem.'

'Gee, thanks!' She laughed a little crazily, 'At least that's sure good to know.'

'Only, afterwards, every brush stroke would be like stroking your nipples with my fingers; my memory would return. Your contours would be as familiar to me as my own, your tufts of hair as soft as a rabbit's tail, and every night I would devour you as though you were made of chocolate.'

Gerhardt peered hard through the window and wiped away the condensation with one finger. Speaking softly, he continued, 'Your fire comes from within, it would be hard to paint. It's a glow, and that's what would warm me at night. Warm me when I was lonely and thinking about you.'

'Wait a minute...'

'In my imagination you would be lying naked with me in bed, not doing anything, just listening, just enticing, just waiting for me to lick you.'

Another self-conscious giggle. 'For Crissakes Digs, you could get the pants off anyone, talking like that!'

Gerhardt turned from the window, smiled at her and for a while his face stayed warm. But seeing her still at ease in her chair, the ache slowly returned. Abruptly he came back to his original grudge. 'Jane, I still can't accept a man like that an' working around the farm being called, "innocent".' Unable to prevent himself lashing out, he added, 'He must know all there is to know about breeding – that's to start with.'

'You can kill things and still be innocent; children kill beetles and spiders all the time.' With only the slightest change of tone she added,' and if you like, you can screw and still be innocent, as well.'

It was what he'd wanted to be said, but now he didn't want it to be said. Now it was out, he didn't know how to deal with it. 'Can you? How can you?' Gerhardt groped for words of the right meaning.

'Didn't you ever live in the "pretend" world? Didn't you "pretend" this and "pretend" that?' Watching, Jane tried to understand Gerhardt's difficulty and to make it easier. 'Digs, if you didn't play at pretending Mothers and Fathers, or nurses and patients, you missed the most fascinating part of your life. I tell you, Sturt can be persuaded to "pretend" anything. At least my books taught me something.'

This, thought Gerhardt, is where I go through the floor. My mind is a hamster on a wheel; the faster I go to try and escape the faster the wheel turns. Pretend sex, who, in the name of Hell, can pretend sex with a seven-year-old-fully-grown man? This one has to stop. I can't cope with the idea. I've nothing to say.

About to reply, he could only shrug bewilderment.

'Sex with Sturt meant nothing, no more than cleaning my teeth. That's the way women can be and how it works. It can be just another job like washing socks – and God knows I do enough of those.'

358

Jane, without any emotion, spoke to the clock on the wall as she rocked slowly on her chair.

'It wasn't a relationship; it was Sturt I was thinking' of – it anchored him. For me it was a stupid game, dangerous too, but for him... He didn't understand what it meant, but any child understands the feel of love.'

In the silence, they heard the slamming of a car door.

Jane looked to the window, lowered her voice to one of urgency. 'It's something you have to understand.'

Gerhardt recognized a new note of pleading. Strangely, it pleased him, but time was running out. He had to find some solution, some way of joining two ends together, but how? His mind floundered.

'I haven't told you,' she added hurriedly, 'but I took the opportunity to try out Sturt with another "pretend".'

'I don't want to know.'

'I said let's pretend we're getting a divorce and won't touch each other again.'

'Never touch each other again?'

'Never.' She sighed. 'I said we'd always pretended to get married and now we'd pretend we'd get a divorce. It was what the Government had said.'

Gerhardt took a moment, trying to follow this new twist. 'How did he react? Did he agree?'

'He said nothing, just looked. I became worried in case I'd gone too far. Then he said he'd seen one of the bears up on Great Peak with a new cub.'

'A new cub? Nothing more'n that?'

'Nothing. Digs I didn't like it, I can't bear the thought of him going off alone, I don't know...'

Whatever she was about to say was halted by the violent arrival of Michael, who burst into the room with the flushed appearance of a man who had run all the way from Purdo.

Although the car was only just outside the door, his face was red and sweat stood on his forehead. Gerhardt and Jane stared at him, while he glared back, mouth open and wet.

Jane half-rose; stopped, 'Michael! We sure need you! Sturt went sometime in the night.'

'Fer Crissakes, don't I know!' Wilson came and stood over her, then bent and snarled to her face. 'Why did you let him go?'

She sank back. His violence was so abrupt she couldn't respond. Gerhardt wondered if he'd been rehearsing and building his anger up on the drive from town.

Wilson stalked across the room to wrench open the drinks cupboard; it was done with the deliberation of someone determined to get a drink at all costs. There was a fury in every movement that couldn't be mistaken.

Gerhardt and Jane Wilson looked at each other. Gerhardt said, 'At least you might tell us what's happened.'

With his back to them, Wilson raised his voice and sawed off the words. 'He-drove-down-to-find-me, that's-what-happened!' Glasses clinked before he spun round, already clutching a whisky bottle to his chest. 'Two o'clock in the morning they tell me now!' As his emotion unlocked, the words fell over themselves and flecks of white spittle appeared unnoticed on his lips. 'Two o'clock in the morning and he got picked up by a couple of cops on Brown-Creek Straight, that gravel bit near the transformer. When they spoke to him, he talked stupid as usual, so they reckoned he must be drugged and tried to take him in. So then the Godamned idiot socked them both! Both of 'em! One's still out with concussion.'

'We can deal with that,' said Gerhardt, putting a restraining hand on Jane's shoulder.

She said, calmly; 'We'd better go-get John Wilmot, he's a good lawyer.'

Michael stared at her strangely, and then gave a mad laugh.

'Oh, sure, go and get a lawyer! That's good, that's very good.' He turned back to rummage in the cabinet, frantic for a glass... 'Stupid bitch,' he muttered shakily. Gerhardt could see his hands were trembling.

Jane's temper began to fray under this assault and she squirmed away from Gerhardt's hand to look at her husband. 'I don't see the need to be such a damned pain in the butt! We've been worried all the while, too.'

Michael faced her to say, icily, 'You'll worry more when you hear the rest. Sturt escaped in his car but got picked up by a posse by now out looking fer him. Four of the toughest cops and they worked the boy over. Macmarran at the Sheriff's office told me all this as a favour. As a favour! Jeez, what a fucking favour.'

'Where is he, Michael?' Jane's voice rose. 'He needs us. Michael you've got to tell me, he can't be left alone! Where is he now?'

He pointed the whisky bottle at her accusingly. 'He's dead, that's where he is, Godamn it! Hung hisself by that old rawhide belt of his, strung it from the bars and stepped off a chair!'

Gerhardt felt the room going in and out. His mouth opened and closed. 'Dead?'

'They took him to the poky, slung him inside and shouted through the bars that they'd never let him loose again. What a stupid thing to say to Sturt of all people. Can you imagine? Y' hear that – never get out of jail again? I said to you, Gerhardt, can you imagine Sturt's mind?'

Wilson, his face contorted as if he'd swallowed something bitter or as if he were about to cry, lifted his shoulders in a massive shrug of hopelessness. He searched their faces for some kind of reassurance or sympathy.

There wasn't any to be had.

Seeing their appalled incomprehension, his look changed and he seemed suddenly both smaller and older. He grunted,

'There, you've got it all now, the whole Godamned lot. When someone went to see how he was this morning, they found him hanging like a dead turkey.'

Wilson began to offer the bottle, but at the sight of their blank faces took it back and without another word strode out through the back to disappear into the living room. They heard the clink of glass and the sound of pouring.

There was silence in the kitchen until Jane shrank back into her chair and began shivering violently. It was clear she no longer had any connection with Gerhardt, the room, her husband or even the present. Jane Wilson was now somewhere else, somewhere downtown in a jail, sitting on the floor nursing in her lap a dead body she'd once loved. What Gerhardt saw was only her image that had been left to crouch, taut and white-knuckled in the old kitchen rocker.

Gerhardt's mind imagined the jailhouse scene: the white, hygienic walls, the steel door with the peephole. He stepped back to begin wandering aimlessly round the room: raising and lowering his arms and shaking his head with incomprehension.

He found himself at the door of the ranch. Happy to escape, he pulled up the catch and blundered outside.

With the Walloo blowing, there were no chickens pecking busily away; instead, the wind swirled viciously about the yard. As he stood there, a miniature dust storm spun into the air like a genie from a bottle, carrying a few leaves and bits of rubbish way up into the air. The sun, high in a sky blurred by dust, gleamed dully to make the world curiously yellow. It was all one: the yellow sun, the yellow ground, yellow dust; everything was yellow. And there followed a sound, at first unidentifiable, coming through the open doorway. It was the low, lonely, miserable whimper of a woman who'd lost her only child.

Gerhardt swayed this way and that. All he wanted was to escape but the sound went on and on, never changing, never stopping. In the end he had to put his hands over his ears to shut it out.

The wind seemed to get stronger, pushing him down the hill and towards his own ranch. In his mind grew an overwhelming thought: people hurt.

It was where he'd come in. People were simply no good; people were bad, evil. Keep away from people. The world out there was a mess of pain that came from people.

Only one escape remained: to be alone; to be alone and to paint.

The wind tugged him along and he began to run. It snatched at his collar, raised his hair. He ran faster, uttering a sound half way between shout and a howl. Escape! People brought nothing but trouble and you had to escape them all. He'd curtain the windows and padlock the gate so nobody could ever get to him again. Nobody.

Escape! He'd just paint life as he found it.

And Gerhardt did just that.

'Jeez...' The girl at my side stirred, 'That's the most horrible story! Is it true? Is that what happened?'

I pointed at the painting with my stick. 'The answer is there, my dear child.'

'I see that, but how come you to know all this?'

The moment had come: the moment to kill your professional self. 'I was his psychoanalyst,' I said.

'But...' She looked at me with doubt, 'But surely a psychoanalyst is sworn not to reveal what his patient tells him!'

'Have you not heard the fable of the King with ass's ears? How, in the end, the boy could not live with such a secret in his head and had to reveal it by whispering it to the reeds by the river's edge?'

She frowned at me her disapproval of my act of betrayal.

'My dear, I am very close to death: I feel I have to tell somebody.'

'Oh!' She said. Then, and very lightly: 'Well, in that case there's no harm done.' She smiled as young people do when they don't know the significance of what they are saying, 'I shan't tell anybody else so you're secret is quite safe.'

I knew she would, eventually, but let the thought go past.

We both looked at the painting for the last time. The title is King Billy and the painting is that of a huge male goat standing on an elaborate throne in the middle of a swirling storm: a king amongst animals, illuminated by lightning and beard twisted sideways. Yet the painting keeps hinting that the goat is in fact part human – or is a human in the form of a goat; you are never sure which. The reality is what shocks. You see the figure, recognise it then, suddenly, realise that the gleaming yellow-and-black eyes are looking at you with malice and possibly derision. In fact you get the distinct and very uneasy feeling that you are being studied – just as much you study it. The goat's head becomes a mask through which some brooding thing stares and evaluates. From some angles it all seems to change and get worse; the eyes follow you to become a startling reminder of the rheumy eyes of an old and evil man.

You turn away from the painting with the uncomfortable feeling that if ever the Devil chose to appear on Earth then this is what he would look like.

The girl sighed and put on her gloves. 'Has Gerhardt painted any other famous paintings I should see?'

'I have to admit to a crime against humanity,' I said, using a finger to tap her knee and to emphasize my point. 'I slowly cured him of his, shall we say madness, but in my doing so his paintings became weaker and weaker: only *that* painting, the first he did, is truly great.'

'Gosh! What a responsibility you carry!' She began pulling at her coat; I could see she wanted to go. I called out, softly, as she went, 'There's a chance you'll see a man in a wheelchair on the way out. If you do, and if it's pushed by a woman in funny green hat, that'll be Gerhardt and his wife: he often comes here.'

'Cool!' She exclaimed. 'In that case, should I, could I...?'

'Sure. Speak to him by all means but try and avoid that wife of his. I warn you: that one is as nutty as they come.'

I watched her until she passed through the swing doors, kind enough to give a final wave. I smiled back; not to my taste but she wasn't a bad girl.

So that was that. To hell with the rules: it was a strange relief to know that at last I was not the only person to know the secret of the painting.

With something of an effort I stooped and picked up my stick; it's quite a long walk back to my room and I hate being late for my nurse.

And now I could die in peace and leave the story with the whispering reeds.